Other Works by Truant Memphis

NOVELS
Littlethumb Sneezed
Post Oh!pocalypto Poppycock
Daffodil

NOVELLA
The Boy Who Fell from the Past

SAVING MARIA

Truant D. Memphis

tdm, ink

Creative consultant: Dustin Booksh
Editor: Sherry Mooney
Fight choreographer: Tae Kwon Doggie
Artwork: Steve
Cover design: Judy Bullard, Robert Lowe, Truant Memphis, & Professor Huff
Book design: Maureen Cutajar

Print ISBN: 979-8-9868939-5-2
E-book ISBN: 979-8-9868939-4-5

Dedicated in loving memory to Kareem Lee Alvarez, aka KMAZING, and Carlton L. Franklin, aka C-Note. True Electric Medicine Men.

We'll see you soon, my friends.
We'll see you soon.

MY DEEPEST, MOST SINCERE, I mean I really, really mean it, gratitude goes out to Dustin Booksh, aka Gusthoff Gusthoffsen, aka Three Chord Monty for your completely biased and unbridled commitment to this story. Thank you for helping me figure it out. Thank you for helping me bring it to life in the real world. Thank you for everything, you know what you've done.

A special thank you to editor Sherry Mooney for reinvigorating my belief in this little fighter.

A super-duper heartfelt thank you to my family and friends for your constant support and engagement with my nonsense. Your encouragement, love, and blah blah blah, yadda yadda, blah blah, yadda, blah blah blah blah…screw you guys. I love you all. I love you all.

Thank you to my fellow indie authors, and all the readers around the world that I've never met, who've read and supported my work. The internet may often be a dystopian hellscape, but it's at least good for a little something…

Last, a belly scratching, ear scratching, ass scratching giant thank you to the best friend a boy could have. I couldn't have done it without you, Roscoe. You're the best, doggie. The Best.

SAVING
MARIA

Traveling backward through the future is an easy trick. The curse of the old, the fate of the young. A spell cast by Mother Nature that insists upon itself. You will stumble and fall and rise and succeed over and again as the circle completes, shuffling toward the grave, satisfied or aggrieved, and eventually bemoan the world as it is for a world that used to be. Life is a merciless port to shore for your soul. Death is freedom into the sea.

Then again, without life there would be no fried chicken.

I

Our story begins in Canada. A friendly eagle provides us with a sweeping view of the early morning bustle in a winsome rural town. We fly over snowcapped woods to an isolated cabin. We descend on the cabin, noting a young coydog curled up on the front porch. In through a fog-covered window we float, act one, scene one.

Inside an intimate sanctuary dressed in warm colors and illuminated by the soft light of candle flame, a man sits quietly, deep in a meditation used to fulfill the requirements of sleep. So deep, in fact, that in this instance he is asleep. An unusual occurrence gaining regularity of late. Gently snoozing through metaphysical lessons on the benefits of active thoughtlessness. Oh well, one way or another, sleep requirements fulfilled.

A hodgepodge of personal effects adorns a small wooden table, organized to serve as an altar for personal reflection. Among the items are a handmade paintbrush, an antique metronome, the tiny portrait of a baby, and a weathered nametag inside a plastic sleeve. The name on the tag? Smith.

To the man's left, three tamarin monkeys wearing kung fu uniforms sit in the lotus position with their eyes closed. Their names are Sir Alister Pickney, Stevie Two Sharks, and Zeus. One final moment of peace and quiet as we zoom in on the monkeys, finishing with a closeup of Zeus's face as an alarm clock sounds. Zeus's eyes flash open. Here we go.

Squirrel-sized monkeys rise to a squad formation. The alarm hasn't shaken their master from his inward state. Stevie Two Sharks lets loose the shriek of battle and the diminutive warriors attack.

Tiny furry poopers jump up and down on the human's shoulders, legs, and head while slapping at his face and pulling his ears. After several minutes with no response, Sir Alister Pickney bites his master's nose. Gently, though, so as not to break the skin.

Littlethumb Brooks's eyes creak open and cross themselves to view the mouth locked onto the tip of his nose. His brain has not yet arrived. Slowly but surely, the serviceable part of his mind returns to the present.

"Did I fall asleep again? Man, that was deep."

The sound of the alarm clock registers. He looks to the clock as the monkeys mount another assault.

"Shit."

The monkeys pause.

"Shit! We're gonna be late!" He springs to his feet and discards the monkeys, who quickly realign in attack formation.

"Yeah," says Zeus. "Why do you think we're attacking you?"

Just kidding. This isn't that type of story. The monkeys don't speak, though they are remarkably intuitive. And adorable. I'm going to hammer that point, so watch your thumbs.

Littlethumb shoots through the cabin, wondering how in the hell he managed to screw up setting his alarm again (if this keeps up, he may have to reconsider his pre-mission meditations…). Knocking inconsequential bric-a-brac aside and to the ground along the way, he stumbles more than once over animal toys not left where they belong until he stubs his toe so fiercely, the pain sends him tumbling through a doorway into a room full of computers. He finishes the forward roll of his tumble by gracefully rotating and flopping into a rolling chair. At the last second, the chair decides not to participate and squirts out from underneath him. The monkeys cackle.

"Very funny," says the human as he stands and recovers the chair. Zeus and Sir Alister Pickney shake their heads in agreement. Stevie Two Sharks smiles and holds up a thin headset for his master.

"Thank you, sir." Littlethumb dons the headset and takes a seat in front of an array of monitors, stabbing at a keyboard with controlled urgency. Commands entered, he cracks the knuckles in his fingers and reaches for a computer mouse stylized as an old-fashioned telegraph key. "Zeus, a little traveling music please." The household's monkey minister of music presses play on a nearby stereo. The opening drum roll from "Hot for Teacher" by Van Halen announces Littlethumb's arrival to the airwaves.

"Thanks for joining us." The voice in Littlethumb's ear belongs to his uncle, currently halfway around the world, uncomfortably bobbing up and down on a camel suffering from intestinal issues.

"My pleasure," says the nephew. "Sound off."

"One, in position." Irish accent.

"Two, in position." Armenian accent.

"Three, in position." Greek accent.

"Four, in position." Portuguese accent, I think.

"Five, in position." Definitely American.

"Thirteen, almost in position." The madman, Samoset Daring Bird Jones, speaking as he drops down from atop the gassy camel. Littlethumb's uncle. Shaman, seer, troublemaker, and de facto leader of an obstreperous international cabal. Ladies and gentlemen, the Electric Medicine Men.

The Electric Medicine Men is an extended underground network of wrong-righters, do-gooders, and wayward rabble-rousers, either born with pure hearts or at least a little bit crazy, in the best way. Also called the E2M, the Electric Medicine Men travel the world fighting the sins of aristocracy from the bottom up. Known for hijacking black market shipments, toppling evil dark web networks, sabotaging fast food processing facilities, obfuscating corporate marketing initiatives, supporting liberal arts educations, destroying oil pump jacks, protecting indigenous peoples, freeing caged animals, and in general, being an all-around pain in the ass to the evil forces in this world who unscrupulously seek power and wealth.

The gang is in Western Sahara preparing to hijack a shipment of ivory headed north to Morocco. This caper is almost a no-win scenario. On one hand, stealing a shipment of poached ivory will screw some jerks out of making evil money. On the other hand, if the heist is successful, the E2M will remove inventory from a market whose players won't stop their evil trade, resulting in more dead animals. Damned if you do, more damned if you don't.

Take solace in the ivory's purpose if successfully stolen. Though it will still be sold, proceeds will go toward further protecting animals from poachers, creating a spiritual circle. Circles are strong.

"Cutting into satellite relay." Littlethumb serves from afar as the eyes, ears, and organizational force of the Electric Medicine Men. "Mark is a quarter-mile out. Tagging now."

"Escorts?" Daring Bird occupies the final intercept position, with their target not yet in view.

"Three confirmed. Two civilian rides, one cargo truck, reinforced ballistic glass. Arms in question."

"Copy that."

"Hey, Bodhi, you're operational jingo jango has gotten very smooth." That's Silas the Entertainer, purveyor of the Irish accent. Jokingly referred to as Mick or Mick the Dick. Lovingly referred to as Sal. A man of many nicknames and vices, though most of his vices are women.

"Thank you, One," responds Littlethumb. "The manual you sent has been helpful."

"Hold the chatter," says Daring Bird.

"Chatter holding."

"Chatter holding."

"Copy chatter hold."

"Copy chatter hold."

"Copy chat…"

"Goddammit, shut up," Daring Bird snaps. "Three, Four, Five, fall in behind target."

"Falling in."

"On Three."

"On Four, literally."

Titus the Nazarene, Bebiana "The Brazilian Bitch" Belo, and Jimmy the Tweaker all move into position behind the motorcade of contraband. Bebiana and Jimmy share a motorcycle. Bebiana drives. Jimmy keeps one arm wrapped around her waist and the other up across her torso, gripping her shoulder, like a seatbelt.

Silas the Entertainer watches their left flank from behind a sand dune. Hiding behind a dune on the right flank is Garo Kasabian, the Armenian Butcher.

"Okay gang," Littlethumb says. "Target in position in ten seconds."

"One, Two, that's your mark." Daring Bird takes a silent three count. "Engage." His Captain Picard impersonation falls distinctly flat, though his team delights in the effort for that very reason.

Personally, I think he overworks the accent. A little goes a long way in a single word impersonation. After years of practice, Daring Bird sounds like a Scottish serial killer with a mouth full of marbles.

Bebiana screams, "You're so bad at that!" as she guns her bike toward the motorcade.

On cue with his team's assault, Daring Bird says, "You love it," then triggers explosions to block the motorcade.

All of the motorcade's vehicles slam on their brakes amid a temporary sand cloud. Titus, Bebiana, and Jimmy take out the escorts, tossing low-impact charges under the SUVs as they breeze past on their bikes. The charges explode with non-lethal force but flip two of the vehicles. The third SUV shoots up a few feet and drops straight back down. A single member of the security force stumbles out, attempting to gain his bearings. Titus circles back, bonks the man on his head with a rubber mallet, and kicks closed the door the man exited. Bebiana and Jimmy weave through the vehicles tossing magnetic devices at them. The devices interface with the vehicles electronically, allowing Littlethumb to control the door locks and trap the passengers inside.

Silas and Garo take out two guards riding on the rear of the target vehicle, a cargo truck. As the sand cloud settles, the cargo truck driver sees a lone man standing in front of him, aiming a rocket launcher in his direction. Daring Bird is tall and lean, his frame strapped with wiry muscles and covered in the highest quality faux leather a modern-day medicine man can purchase. Hot for the desert, yes, but fashion is mastered by form, not function. A patch covers his left eye, with multiple scars sneaking out from underneath the patch and its strap.

The desperado shaman might appear less intimidating if he weren't holding a rocket launcher, but not by much.

With a twitch of the rocket launcher, Daring Bird motions for the driver to exit the vehicle. The driver spills out of the truck and scurries off into the desert. "I was gonna loan you the camel," mutters Daring Bird.

Bebiana pulls up next to the cargo truck's empty cab. Jimmy hops inside and takes the wheel.

"Alright, let's get that truck off the road and wrap this up," says Daring Bird.

"You guys are two minutes ahead of schedule," says Littlethumb. "Nice work."

"Makes up for the late start," Daring Bird snorts.

"What late start? We were late into position."

"Semantics."

"And while we're at it, how'd you wind up on a camel?"

"Bacchantics."

"Ha!"

The others join in the laughter, except Silas, who says, "Bacchantics? What's that mean, Thirteen?"

"I like to party."

A frequent yet peculiar phenomenon of a world trapped in linear chronology is the coincidental timing of certain occurrences. While our heroes are busy living their best Good Guy lives, another heist of significant proportion occurs somewhere in Western Europe. In an undisclosed major city, a famous art collection is loaded onto a large truck. The collection tours the world, moving from museum to museum on a regularly scheduled basis.

A security detail travels with the collection. Not unheard of when moving artwork of significant value, but in this instance, there is a level of pomp and circumstance specifically employed for marketing purposes. After all, the easiest way to make sure people know how interested they should be in something is to tell them.

The security detail is led by a stern older gentleman with bowler hat wearing and cane tapping sensibilities. A gentleman of lesser birth and chosen nobleness. An even hand. An impeccably dressed soldier.

In ten minutes, the gentleman will lie naked, tied up in an alley in the center of our undisclosed city. The art collection will have been stolen. The police will have arrived.

Ten minutes have passed. A band of extreme art thieves has fulfilled the prophecy of my previous paragraph (sufferin' succotash…?). The heist was sponsored by Nuclear Extreme Caffeine Sport Drinks. Go Extreme. Go Nuclear.

Two police inspectors exit their vehicle into a nasty storm. The taller man holds an umbrella. The shorter man stands halfway under his partner's umbrella and halfway in the rain. A young patrol officer approaches.

"Inspectors."

"What's the status?" asks the taller man as they walk into the heart of the crime scene.

"Stolen truck carrying an art collection on its way to the airport. Eight man security detail left behind, all down, but none of them appear critically injured."

"Witnesses, I presume?" asks the shorter man.

"The entire neighborhood, sir. We're gathering statements. Early indication is fifteen to twenty gunmen. This was a large-scale assault."

"An art collection in the middle of the day, in the middle of the city," says the taller man.

"This was a show," says the shorter man.

"Agreed."

"Shots fired?"

"Yes sir," replies the patrolman. "Odd detail there, sir, for a robbery. So far all we've found is non-lethal ammunition."

"Shrewd," the tall inspector responds. "Minimizes the potential charges against them."

"Hmph," grunts the shorter man. "Practical art thieves." (The short guy's rocking a mustache, by the way. I thought about calling the inspectors Mustache and Jerry, but didn't bother. I invite you to think of them as such, for the rest of this passage. Remember, short guy is Mustache and tall guy is Jerry.)

"Inspectors!" Another patrol officer shouts out. "I've got another man over here!"

Half a block away and around a corner, in an offshoot from the main alley, the inspectors find the officer standing near a cluster of garbage bins, shouting to his compatriots for a blanket and gurney. The inspectors line up next to him, along with the patrolman they were already speaking to. There, behind the rubbish, lies our noble head of the security detail, face down, naked, bruised, and battered.

"A nine man security detail, as it were," says the taller man. "This one must have given them a fight."

"I think so," agrees the shorter man. "Curious they stripped him."

"Indeed."

"Oh, they stripped them all, sir," says the lead patrolman.

The inspectors exchange a glance, and the shorter fellow considers admonishing the patrolman for not sharing this detail sooner. Before he can decide, medical aids arrive with blankets and a gurney to retrieve the naked man. They cut the zip ties binding the naked man's wrists, then roll him over and secure his neck for movement.

"My lord," says the shorter man, before the victim is covered.

"Yours and mine both! It's a wonder he didn't use that thing to untie himself."

"Well, he is unconscious…"

The taller man shrugs his shoulders. A gesture implying a multitude of potential responses to his partner's dry retort, without saying a word. I would have said, "I'm pretty sure that thing's a separate lifeform."

"So," the shorter inspector continues, "they initiate the attack around the corner there. Occupy the truck with the art shipment, exit this way, and our phenomenally endowed friend here makes one last attempt to stop them."

"Agreed."

"Why strip the security detail?"

"Perhaps they were looking for something. Something hidden in their clothes or on their body. A key or document, maybe. Whatever the thieves were looking for, it was faster to strip the security team and take the clothes to search later, rather than search them here on the street. Or, they were attempting to delay identification of the security detail's members for some reason."

"I wonder…were they merely trying to confuse the situation?"

"I suppose we'll find out soon enough."

"Most likely. I'll call a team down to collect the prints."

"I'll start the report."

We're back in the desert, where the Electric Medicine Men have moved to a secure location, hidden within a caravan. The camp is settled around an oasis and obscured from long-distance observation by the surrounding dunes. This nomadic tribe, like many others, appreciates the E2M's work and welcomes them with open arms.

Underneath a large tent, Jimmy the Tweaker is standing on the back of the cargo truck, staring inside. "Boss, you need to see this. Pronto."

"Almost there."

"Hurry," says Jimmy.

"Salvador does not hurry."

"You named the camel?" asks Jimmy.

"You named the camel after me?" asks Silas.

"Don't flatter yourself, my friend. His face reminds me of Dalí."

"What is it, Five?" asks Littlethumb. "What's in the truck?"

"Radio silent on this one, Bodhi. Will update when Thirteen has arrived."

"Copy that." Littlethumb turns to Zeus. "Coffee break, then?"

Zeus agrees.

Littlethumb retrieves a cup of coffee. In Western Sahara, Daring Bird arrives at the cargo truck atop Salvador the camel. Bebiana has also made her way to the rear of the truck and stands beside Jimmy the Tweaker.

"What's all the fuss?" Daring Bird asks, stepping off Salvador and directly onto the rear liftgate of the truck.

Bebiana holds a single finger to her lips, requesting Daring Bird not react verbally to what he will see. Peering into the truck, the old salty-dog yelps anyway.

"Oh, fuck me."

To ensure the Electric Medicine Men's communications remain private, Littlethumb has engineered a satellite hopping, channel bouncing, and radio frequency alternating encrypted satphone network. The team has also developed its own cryptographic cipher for any situation where a member feels compelled to send a secure written message. Thus, after Daring Bird discovers the true contents of their stolen truck, he sends Littlethumb the following cryptogram via digital photo of a code handwritten in the desert sand: *Bad intel. No ivory. Truck full of kids. And strange device.* Littlethumb responds with: *Kids, Morocco, consulate? Device me.*

Anonymously delivering stolen children to the American consulate is tricky but doable. Smuggling the mysterious device to Littlethumb will require more effort. The device must be analyzed for traceable elements and tracking technology. Can it be shipped? Taken on a plane? Is the device itself somehow physically dangerous to have in their possession, containing a chemical or explosive volatility or any number of other potential harmful mechanisms, like electric shock or shooting rusty darts? We'll find out soon.

In the meantime, now that we've knocked our action-packed opening sequence out of the park, we should get to know Littlethumb Brooks. Let's "tell don't show" this knucklehead all throughout his extremely roomy cabin in the Canadian wilderness. What do you say?

Littlethumb logs out of the team's network and powers down his computer. Next to the computer lies a piece of paper with the coded response he sent Daring Bird. Striking a match, he sets the paper on fire and drops it into an empty metal trash can, so located for this very purpose. Then he softly tosses his operations headset onto the desk in front of him.

A leery scan of the room follows. There's a window in each of the three exterior walls. The windows all have blackout curtains and are highly reinforced against outside entry. The room's lone doorway is in the interior wall to his right.

A computer server rests inside a thoroughly locked cage in the northeast corner of the room. One side of the cage is painted like a Sasquatch dressed as a sumo wrestler. I wouldn't say the cage is impenetrable, but a series of booby traps makes the locks nearly impossible to break or pick without damaging the server.

Content with his review of the room, Littlethumb exits into the main cabin. Originally a single-space domicile, the cabin has an open kitchen and decent sized common area, likely eight hundred square feet or so. A loft with two bedrooms runs the length of the main building. Many years earlier, during an extended stay when Littlethumb was a child, he and Daring Bird put in the loft and built an additional room off the rear of the cabin. Littlethumb has since added his meditation chamber and the server room off the sides of the original structure.

Littlethumb walks over to the kitchen and refills his coffee before heading into the back room. Turning on the lights reveals a large art studio, nearly half the size of the main house. Outside, the cabin backs up to thick tree coverage, obscuring the natural light despite the brightness of the day, leaving the studio both cool and dim throughout daylight hours. Along with stacks of paintings, both finished and incomplete, there are numerous easels in the room. In one corner, an original Vox Continental electric organ sits against the wall collecting dust. Opposite the organ is a sculpting station.

Among the stacks of paintings are portraits of a small child, following the child's life from newborn to toddler. Stylistically, the portraits represent all known – and several unknown – movements, from cubism to brutalism to knowism and everything in between. After a few minutes surveying the paintings, tapping keys on the Vox, and wiping dust from the sculpting station, he returns to the entrance of the studio. Littlethumb pauses in the doorway, taking one more look around the room, then switches the lights back off.

A creative block has plagued our hero for the last six months. Being creatively blocked as an artist is akin to death, or being in a coma, or a bad marriage, or a shitty job, or consumed with politics, or the constant pursuit of money, or any other vegetative state. An artist blocked from creation isn't fully alive, and may only be resuscitated by Mother Nature's grace. You can't fight your way out of a block.

You can, however, fight your own status quo. Shake things up and hope for the best. Try something new. Learn something new. Create your own catalyst.

And that, my friends, is another instantly rewarded foreshadow. For as Littlethumb reenters the main chamber to his fortress of near solitude, a dark blur whips past his face, narrowly missing his nose but successfully launching the coffee cup at his mouth across the room. So much for a character driven walk through the cabin. Instead: Enter, the dragon.

❋ ❋ ❋

Several weeks into his artistic block, after a couch-bender weekend of binge-watching Peter Sellers movies, Littlethumb decided to implement Cato and Clouseau's training method from *The Pink Panther* films. Littlethumb was bored, he wasn't creating, and he thought a touch of insanity might rattle him out of the nasty funk in which he was mired. Not to mention, spontaneous attack simulations looked like fun.

❋ ❋ ❋

As the coffee cup flies, the dark blur rotates on its axis, sending a human leg and foot whirling around for another strike. Littlethumb squats at the knees, ducking the assailant's kick and lunging into a forward roll. In one motion, he rises out of the forward roll and dives past the assailant and over the back of a couch. Jumping to his feet, he turns to face his opponent and is met by a flying kick to the chest.

The kick knocks Littlethumb stumbling backward. Another jumping sidekick immediately follows, sending Littlethumb through a front window. Every window in the room has been shattered since the training began. This one is already twice-repaired.

Littlethumb lands in a heap on the front porch of the cabin. Woofus Maximus, the coydog, scrambles to his feet and low-tails his way to safety. Woof's loyalty for Littlethumb is pure. His training as a guard dog is still in the works.

Lifting his head, Littlethumb sees all three monkeys sitting on the windowsill, bobbing up and down with delight. He quiets his mind and listens intently, feeling the vibration of footsteps. A rap is heard on the front door. Master Kim Chee is knocking on the inside of the door, as if requesting permission to enter the outside world. Yes, he's taunting his student. What great, cinematic quality martial arts master doesn't taunt and humiliate their student at every possible turn? Exactly.

While Master Chee toys with our hero, let's take a minute to look backward in time. Say, six months? Because synchronicity and whatnot, synchronicity being an early theme in this little fighter of a story. We'll see if the theme holds up throughout or survives the final editorial cuts. I tend to prefer chaos over fate.

Our flashback begins with a classic 1963 Buick Wildcat cruising through the Adirondacks on Highway 87. The red convertible's destination is Federal Correctional Institution Ray Brook, not far from Lake Placid. A young journalist controls the steering wheel. I haven't discovered his name yet. I'll fill you in when I do.

This is not his first journey from Manhattan to Ray Brook. His first trip was two or three weeks earlier. I suppose I could have started the flashback there. Let's do that. Back we go, two or three more weeks. We'll skip the drive through the mountains and get straight to the meat and bones.

"I appreciate your willingness to speak with me," says the journalist.

"Anything for my fans. And that's the truth. You don't just say that shit. You live that shit or you don't deserve to have fans." Imagine hearing this voice while still looking at the journalist's face (a redhead, by the way…). Then the camera rotates to view the man behind the "bad person" side of the glass, prisoner 06A1976: Tommy Toxic. Famed punk rocker. Lunatic. Murderer. Convict.

On this first meeting, the scars and violently reconfigured bone structure of Tommy Toxic's face make the journalist heartsick. No matter his misdeeds, this man should be pitied, his disfigurement serving as a stark representation of what life has done to him in general. Tommy Toxic is, after all and irrefutably, a victim in his own right. A victim of life's absurd cruelty, and an example of the unforgiving reality that a creature born of hell will most likely grow into a demon.

"So, what brings you out to my little castle?" asks Tommy.

"Your story. I'm sure you're aware, the anniversary of the concert is coming up again soon. I'm writing a…"

"Which concert?"

Our redheaded journalist is briefly rattled. All the research in the world can't prepare you to deal with insanity. Like so many aspects of life, insanity requires a tactile understanding. You must touch, feel, and embrace insanity's perspective if you hope to comprehend. Immerse yourself in the lunatic's reality. Just know that even then, the best you can hope for is to learn the necessary coping mechanisms for working with a subject who will never be fully understood, unless you go crazy too.

"The last concert, Tommy. In Philadelphia. The one that put you here."

"Oh, man. What a great show. Great show."

Referencing an infamous concert that ended in murder as a "great show" indicates that portions of this conversation would be wildly misinformative without continual interjection, making the retelling a laborious exercise as the journalist asks his questions, Tommy explains his distorted recollections, and I contradict them with reality. We'll jump to the reason why we're here.

"Tell me more about your relationship with Littlethumb Brooks."

"That's simple, bro. He's my best friend. Probably my only friend on the outside. Couple of decent fuckers in here, for sure, but L.T. is my guy worldwide. Inside or out."

"Interesting."

"What? Having friends? Most people have friends, bro. You're a strange cat, aren't you?"

The journalist chuckles. Is a madman calling you strange ironic? Doesn't matter. Ironic or not, Red finds the comment funny. (By the way, I'm giving our redheaded journalist the nickname Red, for the time being. We'll see how it feels.)

"I meant, and forgive me for being presumptuous, I find it interesting you would describe Littlethumb Brooks as a friend."

"Oh. Okay, then. I don't know what to tell you. He's my best friend. I mean, we don't get to see each other as often as we used to, for sure. But no one knows me as good as L.T. And, I bet you the socks on your feet, no one knows him like I do."

"Can you tell me about him?"

"Sure I can." Tommy opens his mouth to continue but hesitates. Consternation invades his face. His head shakes with malice, scolding himself. If not for the dense glass between them, Red would be duly frightened. All things being equal, the journalist is still rattled by the display.

"Why don't you ask Littlethumb?" Tommy finally says. "If he's the one you're so interested in, ask him." A change of tone in Tommy's voice confirms he's not the same person he was just moments before.

Tommy's transition requires Red to regain his bearings. A little shifting in the seat, some clearing of the throat, and a few sips of water to loosen the vocal cords. "Honestly, I would try, if anyone knew where he was. But I'm more interested in your perspective. Not so much Littlethumb's life story, but your relationship with him."

"What do you mean, if anyone knew where he was?"

"You don't know?"

"Know what?"

"Littlethumb Brooks has been missing since your trial. No one knows where to find him."

"That's stupid. He's famous."

"No, I'm sorry, but it's true. He's disappeared."

"Ha! That clever motherfucker." At this, Tommy begins a hefty laughter and knee slap performance. Eventually, his exuberance for the routine wanes and Red chimes back in.

"I'm sorry, what do you mean? Clever in what way?"

"I said clever motherfucker."

"My apologies. Clever motherfucker in what way?"

"Hmm. You said the whole world thinks my pal has disappeared, but he hasn't. That means the sneaky prick has tricked the whole world. I will call him a clever motherfucker in that way. How does that sound?"

"It sounds like you know where Littlethumb Brooks is hiding. Can you tell me where?"

"Nope. I didn't know he was hiding. How can I tell you where he's hiding if I didn't know he was hiding? That's crazy!" Tommy crosses his eyes, sticks his tongue out, and makes a twirling motion with a finger near his head, the universal sign for cuckoo. When the visitor doesn't laugh, Tommy abandons the bit and leans in close to the glass, speaking conspiratorially. "But, I might know where you can find him." Tommy leans back in his seat and crosses his arms, sporting a demon's grin.

The journalist sits quietly, waiting for Tommy to elucidate the matter. Instead, Tommy grows impatient, shaking his hands at Red as if expecting something. He wants to be asked. Prisoner 06A1976 may not need the information aggressively coerced from him, but he wants Red to at least indulge him a little bit more, despite having already been asked a variation of the necessary question.

"Oh, sorry," says Red, realizing what Tommy is waiting for. "Tommy, do you know where I can find Littlethumb Brooks?"

"Right here!"

Tommy jumps out of his seat with the admission. The murderous edge retreats, replaced by the playfulness of a child who's happily been discovered while playing hide and seek. Bouncing back and forth from foot to foot, Tommy laughs and laughs. "Right here," he repeats joyfully, banging his forehead against the glass with a smile. "Right here, right here, right here…" Bang, bang, bang…

Once Tommy started the headbanging nonsense, security put an end to the visitation and peacefully dragged Tommy back to his cell as he sang, "right here, right here, right here" over and over again. Sometime later, "Right Here, Right Here, Right Here" becomes a number one hit on prison radio.

Our redheaded journalist made several more trips up to Ray Brook to learn more about the supposed visits of Littlethumb Brooks. No one named Littlethumb or Brooks had ever signed in to visit Tommy Toxic. Explaining this to Tommy was fruitless. He continued insisting Littlethumb visited him, but Red couldn't pry any substantial information out of Tommy with regard to when or how often.

An epiphany regarding the visitation logs changed his luck. Red's initial review of the logs had been a quick scan for the names Littlethumb and Brooks. On the second pass, he more thoroughly reviewed all the names of the visitors registered to Tommy Toxic, including the dates they signed in. Was there a pattern to the visits, or to the names of the people? Honestly, who in the world would come to visit Tommy Toxic? There's no family, and yet, Tommy was visited with relative frequency. Who were these people? Legal counsel? Interviewers? Fans?

Tommy had been at Ray Brook for almost three years, and the visitation logs showed consistent visits by random people since his incarceration. Once or twice a month at first, then every few months, then every six months or so. Other than the declining frequency of the visits, there was no substantial pattern to discern. The last visit was five months prior to Red's investigation of the logs, and the one before that, almost a year.

Almost a year… A ton of bricks hit Red like a startling recognition (or maybe the other way around…). What was the date of that visit?

My god, the concert.

Red thumbed a page backward and confirmed his suspicion. Someone had visited Tommy on the anniversary of the concert in both the previous two years, with the third anniversary coming soon. This discovery inspired Red to notice something oddly similar in the names of that date's registered visitors. They were anagrams. Each name was made of the same letters. Upon further review, he realized almost every name registered to visit Tommy Toxic, while not always the full anagram, consisted of the same subset of letters from the alphabet. Don Sims, Dr. Brian Gant, and Jon Masters to name a few.

With this piece of intrigue firmly in place, let's catch back up to where our flashback initially began. The red convertible Wildcat cruises up Highway 87 with the top down. The sun shines, music blares, and the driver wears a conquer-the-world smile on his face. Guess what day it is.

3

Lyon, France (AP) – Famed art collection *The Marias* has been stolen. The collection was hijacked in broad daylight while in transit to the Lyon-Saint Exupéry Airport from La Sucrière Contemporary Art Museum in the Confluence quarter (district) of Lyon. The Police Nationale in Lyon confirmed the collection was stolen but have not yet released an official statement on the robbery. Numerous eyewitnesses of the event described an elaborate, mid-city heist perpetrated by up to twenty masked women and men. Members of the security detail tasked with transporting *The Marias* were left naked, bound, and gagged. Most, if not all, of the security detail suffered minor injuries. Others incurred more severe injuries, including major head wounds and broken bones. One security guard lost an ear. No deaths have been reported.

The Marias exhibit displayed at La Sucrière for three months and was scheduled to relocate to the Teloglion Foundation of Art in Thessaloniki, Greece. Inclusion of the collection in the Teloglion Foundation gallery would have been a relatively distinct honor for works produced by an artist born outside of Greece. Officials at the Teloglion Foundation have already made a public statement expressing their dismay at the loss of the collection.

Worth hundreds of millions, if not billions, of U.S. dollars, *The Marias* is a collection of dozens of paintings created by renowned artist and philanthropist Littlethumb Brooks. The subject of the collection is Maria Holguín-Brooks, the artist's deceased wife. The collection rose to fame after the infamous murder of Holguín-Brooks, who was killed on stage by musician Tommy Toxic in Philadelphia during a joint concert held by Toxic and Littlethumb Brooks. Whether an uncanny twist of fate or an intentional wink from the thieves, the collection was stolen on the deceased subject's birthday. The widower Brooks, having famously disappeared after the death of his wife, has not been reached for comment. His whereabouts remain a mystery.

4

We're back in the present in Canada. The scene opens on the front porch of our rural cabin a few moments after our hero was kicked through the front window. The monkeys still sit on the window sill enjoying the show.

Littlethumb Brooks is around six feet tall with one-hundred and ninety pounds of solid weight. Dark haired, dark complected, and generally received as handsome, his handsome ass is currently re-shaped as a human pretzel under the control of a five-foot seven-inch tall Chinese fella. All one-hundred and fifty-five pounds of Master Kim Chee sits on top of Littlethumb. The enigmatic kung-fu master playfully strokes a non-existent beard with one hand and peacefully controls his knotted-up pupil through a single pressure point with the other. Somewhere in here, I envision him toking on a stereotypical kung-fu master's pipe as well. If you roll with obvious tropes, then I say trope the kaboodle out of that noodle…

Master Kim Chee stops the fake beard stroking and retrieves a cellphone from his pocket. Holding the phone at arm's length, he snaps a few pictures of himself and Littlethumb, then releases his student. The tension in Littlethumb's body clearly eases before Master Chee hops to his feet.

"I'm hungry."

In response, an exaggerated groan escapes Littlethumb. Definitely a pain groan, but I'm not certain if the sound is a "sweet relief" *from* pain groan or a "holy shit this still hurts so bad" *in* pain groan.

"Hungry," Master Chee repeats, heading back inside the cabin.

Littlethumb remains on his back until the expression of pain on his face changes to a smile. With the terrifying human no longer present, Woofus trots over and licks his dad on the cheek. "Thanks, buddy," Littlethumb says, giving the coydog a scratch under the chin.

You may ask, how does one find and hire a martial arts master to conduct personalized surprise combat training? The short answer is to involve oneself with an obstreperous international cabal like the Electric Medicine Men. The long answer is all the varied ways you might find yourself in such an organization, all the other ways you might find yourself in a different organizational situation providing you similar opportunities, and of course, a deep dive into what in Shakyamuni Buddha's name you're doing with your life if hiring a martial arts master for surprise attack training makes any sense for your life at all.

Logic and reason aside, Littlethumb remotely interviewed several candidates who were recommended to him through E2M connections, and a few who had excellent customer satisfaction ratings on the dark web. Nothing felt right. All those dudes and ladies were devoted to training killers. Why were they all so severe, and why did honor have to be so tightly wound up in death with those folks? At some point in their interview, damn near every one of them asked Littlethumb who he was trying to kill. When he answered, "No one," many of them immediately hung up the call. Others berated him for wasting their time, then hung up the call. Several expressed their confusion before hanging up the call. A few immediately doubled their price, at which point Littlethumb politely said, "No thank you," and ended the call with appropriate decorum.

Thus, he was on the verge of letting the idea go when he received a surprise phone call from Master Kim Chee. I'm not trying to write Master Chee's accent, as he enunciates his English with great care. Feel free to imagine any potentially racist garbage for yourself, though if you're so inclined, this may not be the story for you.

"I understand you seek training."

"I do. May I ask who's calling?"

"My name is Master Kim Chee."

"Like the dish?"

"The dish is Korean. I am Chinese."

"Have you considered changing your name?" Littlethumb spoke too quickly, before his brain could send a cat to catch his tongue. "I'm very sorry. Please forgive me. I meant no offense. It's an excellent name. I was only thinking about cutting down on confusion, or jokes, or, you know what I mean."

"Name used to be Dim Sum." After Master Chee had enthusiastically snickered at his own joke, Littlethumb knew he'd found his man. Or, more accurately, his man had found him.

Believe it or not, Littlethumb never asked how Master Chee became aware of the open position. He decided the mystery of the situation would enhance the training. A continued sense of genuine potential danger would keep him on a different type of edge. But, once their training ends, Littlethumb looks forward to having Master

Chee sit for a portrait and learning more about who his enigmatic master truly is. (Pssst. That last line there is important…)

Back inside the cabin, Littlethumb finds Master Chee patiently waiting in the kitchen. Ingredients for a healthy brunch lay on the counter.

"Cook," says Master Chee without raising his head or removing his headphones to check the volume of his voice.

Though I prefer to let you paint much of your own picture, I will tell you that Master Chee is younger than what you may have initially envisioned based on the details provided. In fact, he may be younger than Littlethumb, though I'm not certain. What I do know is that he has what many would describe as an "old soul." I would say very old. Ancient.

Yet not so ancient as to forego the enjoyment of modern contrivances, such as digital music and mobile phone gaming. In other words, his eyes are locked on a video game on his phone while his head bops to aggressive orchestrations. I'm pretty sure he's listening to rap music.

One, two, three, four eggs are tossed in the air to land and crack in the pan that Littlethumb holds with his left hand. The cracked eggshells are emptied and removed before the yokes are beaten and the pan is placed on the stove. Next is a flashy demonstration of fruit slicing, intended to impress his master. Chee scarcely notices.

"You know," says Littlethumb. "I've been thinking it might be fun to add another layer to our game. Expand the parameters."

Master Chee ignores his student, intent on the video game.

"So, I was thinking," Littlethumb continues, "maybe I start hunting, too, and attacking." He jots something down on a pad of paper as he speaks. "Maybe we take the training off the reservation, so to speak."

Still no reaction from Master Chee. Littlethumb reaches for his instructor's headphones and snaps one of the earpieces. Chee jumps back into a defensive position, swirling his arms in an impressive kung fu movement. Littlethumb responds by robustly mocking the kung fu motion before flowing into sign language, stating he simply wants to talk.

A short aside, aka expositionous minimalous vomitous: Littlethumb taught himself sign language as an extremely bored youngster. This random decision later proved extremely useful, as his wife, Maria, was deaf. About two months into his training with Master Chee, he was pleasantly surprised to discover his unusual instructor also knows what Littlethumb considers to be the quiet language of love. In keeping with the established aspects of their relationship, Littlethumb has no idea why Master Chee learned how to sign.

Master Chee calmly retakes his seat as Littlethumb slides the pad of paper across the counter. On the paper are the words: *I know where you live.* This gets Master Chee's full attention.

"No, you do not," says Master Chee.

"No, I don't. I don't know where you live, but I needed to get your attention."

"Attention is an addictive drug for the childish mind."

"Yes! That's great. That one's going in the notebook." Littlethumb finishes breakfast preparations with toast, applying butter and jam with a drunkard's enthusiasm before tossing the toast onto a pile of eggs. "So, what I was thinking is maybe we expand my training off the compound. Possibly into town. I can hunt for you. Go on the attack. Maybe try to find out where you live for real. And we have to fight in complete secret. No one in town can ever see us tangle. I really think it would benefit my training."

"No."

"What do you mean, no?"

"I mean no."

"Why?"

"No why. Only no."

"Unacceptable." This incites a staring contest Littlethumb is not equipped to win. Not against Master Chee, whose stubbornness is born of a life dedicated to the arts of fighting, teaching, and forever maintaining the stoic posture of the immovable prick. Prick as in jerk, that is, not prick as in penis. Though a penis can certainly be a jerk and quite possibly immovable, depending on age or medication.

"Do you paint?" asks Master Chee, taking a plate of food.

"No," says Littlethumb, wincing at the notion.

"That is your purpose. Attack your purpose."

"But that's what our training is for. To help me find my way back."

"Back where? You are where you are meant to be, only standing still. You must move forward."

Littlethumb opens his mouth to argue but pauses, clamping his teeth back together with an audible clack. The master takes a mouthful of eggs and chews patiently, studying the look of consternation on his student's face. The student's mouth opens again, another failing attempt at words. Chee holds a finger in the air, signaling for Littlethumb to abandon his efforts, so Littlethumb takes an impatient drink of coffee and watches Master Chee laboriously chew his food in silence.

When Littlethumb's impatience gives way to peace, Master Chee swallows his food, wipes his mouth, and speaks. "A wise man once said, the blind man may spend his entire life wishing for sight, all the while never understanding he was born into a world of darkness." A large clump of food stuck to Master Chee's front teeth removes a good deal of the shine from his words. I'm certain he's aware.

Covering his eyes with one hand and holding a mysteriously appearing toothpick with the other, Littlethumb says, "That's great. I mean great. Really fantastic. I will ponder your words, master. Perhaps, in the meantime, thou wouldst picketh thy wise teeth."

Master Chee swipes the toothpick from Littlethumb. I won't tell you where the projectile clump of food lands. Choose your own adventure.

"May I ask who the wise man was?" asks Littlethumb.

Master Chee stares.

A coy, upward tick to one side of Littlethumb's mouth betrays his question's facetious intentions.

"Me," says Master Chee, knowing damn well he didn't need to.

"You just made that up."

Master Chee takes an intentionally slurpy drink of orange juice, eyes locked on his student.

"Who the hell are you, dude?"

As slowly as possible, Master Chee lowers the glass of orange juice from his lips to the counter. I mean achingly slow. Meticulously slow. A snail would have been jealous. Slower than you finishing this redundant paragraph until the glass gently settles onto the counter and Master Chee says, "Who the hell are you?"

Another long pause unfolds, this one shared, as the expression on each man's face relays the holding back of laughter or a bowel movement (or both, or one of each…), before Littlethumb breaks the silence.

"That's fair."

5

Delivering the stolen children to the United States Consulate in Morocco is a reasonably simple task. The trick, of course, is making sure the Electric Medicine Men remain anonymous. In spite of Daring Bird's enjoyment of theatrics, his organization has successfully maintained an urban legend status for several decades. Much of this can be attributed to supporters of the E2M cause. The Electric Medicine Men have a ridiculously loyal fan base. Like, professional wrestling fans loyal. Fútbol fans loyal. Pearl Jam fans loyal.

The Electric Medicine Men's supporters are the common folk, the oppressed. The ragtag masses, deemed expendable by the universe, their fellow humans and at the end of the day, one way or another, collar-tugging compassionate rhetoric aside, their own governments. I digress.

Dropping the kids off at the Consulate happens without issue. Handling the strange device is more complicated. Littlethumb wants to analyze the device, but shipping is off the table until it is tested for radiation, traceable chemical signatures, energy output, or anything at all that might get the package flagged by a freight company or customs.

This means someone will most likely have to smuggle the device to Littlethumb. A course of action that comes with its own set of issues, but those are issues that can wait. Daring Bird's number one concern right now is the safety of his team, who will be on lockdown protocol with the device in their possession for at least a month.

The Electric Medicine Men operate under a few simple organizational rules instituted by Littlethumb and Daring Bird. Rule number one is no killing. The E2M are thieves and troublemakers in the name of cosmic decency, not glorified murderous antiheroes. To be a force of righteousness in this world, they must remain righteous. Killing is off the table, period. There is no more slippery a slope into moral hypocrisy than a hero justifying homicide.

On down the short list of organizational rules are post-operational procedures, which starts with the entire team bedding down together for safety. According to Daring Bird's personal theory, on average, life will always provide some new calamity, heartbreak, or wonderful distraction within a calendar month, even for the forces of evil. Thus, the Electric Medicine Men always hide together for at least one full month. Protecting everyone and maintaining the group's anonymity post-operation is much easier if they're all together. If something happens and they're found, they might all die together, but at least no one on the team will have to live in fear while being hunted alone, or suffer from survivor syndrome.

After leaving Morocco, the Electric Medicine Men travel to an underground facility in Barcelona, where they contact a scientist and inventor in their network. Parthos the Drunk and Horny Monk is his codename. His real name is whatever the Spanish version of Doug might be. I'm kidding, but I do have to keep Parthos' identity a secret.

Once Parthos determines that the device is free of any standard tracking mechanisms and appears safe from imminent explosion, Daring Bird and the team head for a safe house in Marseille, France. If you're ever looking to set up a safe house for hiding out, plotting, or generally remaining "underground," coastal cities that have public and private airports and commuter trains are the way to go. You have escape routes accessible by land, air, and water, with multiple modes of transportation for each route.

In this instance, the mode of transportation is a dilapidated houseboat, as our band of hero crusaders piddles through the Mediterranean Sea, achingly making their way toward the coast of Marseille. From what I understand, Marseille is an extremely beautiful city. I've never been, though I have taken a virtual tour.

"I know you said nothing flashy," says Silas the Entertainer, "but this tub is a bit ridiculous."

"Almost there, Sal," replies Daring Bird.

"I hear you, boss, but you know how I feel about the sea."

"Yeah, I do."

"So imagine how I feel about the sea with an unusually large jack-in-the-box that could be a bomb on our boat."

"Maybe not so much different than me, or the rest of the team."

"You know, my father used to say, always walk straight lines, son. Always walks straight lines. You can't walk a straight line at sea, D.B."

"Almost there."

That's all of their conversation that I'm showing you because I like stopping at Daring Bird repeating himself. In real life, they go on to discuss the implications of the jack-in-the-box more thoroughly, what in the hell Silas's father meant by his vaguely sage advice, Silas's affinity for French cuisine, and his voracious appetite after an extended period of fear. Which is what being at sea always is for him, an extended period of fear. Silas does most of the talking.

Oh, yeah. The mysterious device has an outer shell designed to look like an oversized jack-in-the-box. Sort of slipped the jack-in-the-box in on you back there in the dialogue. So what we're dealing with is a slightly oversized jack-in-the-box with a friendly and not at all frightening clown painted on the sides. We don't know if the physical design has a functional role in the operation of the device or if it's purely a disguise, which means we also don't know what happens if you turn the jack-in-the-box's crank. Daring Bird cautioned against doing so and no one has had the nerve to argue with him. Not even Parthos, who was desperately curious.

The houseboat docks south of Marseille's Old Port, on the coast of the Endoume quarter. Silas is the first ashore, kissing the planks of the dock as if he's survived a tornado inside a hurricane inside a tsunami on a trip through the Bermuda Triangle, rather than a leisurely, uneventful cruise across the Mediterranean.

"I love the land," he says, followed by, "muah, muah, muah," as he kisses the dock thrice more. "And I love France!" Silas turns to his compatriots, who're still unloading from the boat. "Have I ever told you how much I love France?" he offers to anyone who will respond.

Garo Kasabian, the Armenian Butcher, happily takes the bait. "It's not France you love, my friend," he says with a smirk, patting Silas on the shoulder. "It's French women."

"Tomato, potato, Butch. And yes. I. do."

"Your promiscuity is a sin," offers Titus the Nazarene. "Joyful to your flesh but not to your soul."

"Oh, I don't know about that, T. Unless she's lying to me, my soul thoroughly enjoys a nice romp in the sheets with an enthusiastic lass."

"I will pray for you," replies Titus.

"You do not have a female soul," says Bebi. "I promise you."

"You don't miss a beat, Bebi," says Silas. "That's what I'm talking about. I bet none of the rest of you dopes picked up on that."

"Sal," offers Jimmy the Tweaker. "I don't think anyone on this team doubts there's a powerful anima in you craving the opportunity to belt out a few show tunes. That's why your little warrior, and I mean tiny, tiny pecker, is constantly running around overcompensating."

"I'll take the powerful animal comment and walk away," says Silas.

"Not animal, knucklehead. Anima."

"What's that?"

"Look it up."

"Let's go," Daring Bird interrupts. "Off the streets, asap. You can talk more shit once we're in the dark. I'll happily roast all you sons-of-bitches around a fire tonight after we're locked down."

"Alright everybody, you heard the old man," says Jimmy.

"You're older than me, jagoff," replies Daring Bird.

If you're picking up what I'm laying down regarding group dynamics, you might guess this is a common refrain between these two friends, along with the group's jabs at Silas the Entertainer's frequently comical dalliances. There's more hilarious banter on the way, but I encourage you to fill in your own punchlines when you feel I haven't massaged a joke to its full release. Send me an email or a letter with suggestions, if you like.

The team makes its way through the city to the Bompard quarter, not too far inland from the coast. The safe house is a historic home on a small estate surrounded by trees, in an area filled by similar, semi-secluded properties. Supposedly, the house was once owned by poet and playwright Edmond Rostand, a native of Marseille.

This safe house isn't exclusively for the E2M's usage. Divided into sections for privacy, consider the house a multi-unit "underground" timeshare, owned and operated by an extremely wealthy benefactor to the secretive forces of good. Not even Daring Bird knows who this person is. He or she is way, way up the food chain. Hell, I don't know who this person is, though I'm determined to find them out.

Only once has the team been turned away from a network safe house due to full occupancy. Honestly, there just aren't a ton of underground do-gooders running around looking for secret places to hide. Many people are trying to make this world a better place, for sure, but most of them are doing their work right out in the open for the rest of us to see, if we're willing to look. I bet they're easier to find than the secret entrance to a safe house.

The safe house's secret entrance is hidden inside a yard shed under a lawnmower facade. A digital keypad disguised as a family crest unlocks the door to the shed. Once inside, you push down on the lawnmower handle, lifting the mower body to reveal a ladder. Down the ladder you go, into a tunnel leading to the house's basement and the official front desk check-in of hotel *Don't Let the Bad Guys Get Me.*

An extremely thick iron door waits at the end of the tunnel. No ultra-modern technology here. An old-fashioned, coded knock on the door by Jimmy the Tweaker initiates check-in.

"Vacancy." A modulated voice spews from a rusty speaker on the tunnel wall.

"Six pilgrims, indefinitely," responds Daring Bird.

Without another word, the team hears sliding bolts and creaking hinges as the door is unlocked and opened. Standing inside the door, to Daring Bird's surprise, is a beautiful woman. The woman bows hello, arms firmly pressed to her sides.

"Hello. I am your host, Kumiko."

"Where's Laurent?" asks Daring Bird.

"Sir, Laurent has retired."

"Peacefully?"

"That is my understanding."

"How long ago?"

"I've served as host for eight months."

"You the first replacement?"

"Yes."

"Permanent residency?"

"I hope so, if my work is approved of."

"We'll need five rooms."

At this, Kumiko scans the team, finishing with a non-judgmental glance at Bebiana, who, if I haven't previously mentioned, has a slightly lopsided, Picasso-esque face graciously mounted atop the neck of a gloriously curvy and powerful physique. Five rooms for six people? Which one of these men is the eye of the beholder, laying with this confusingly sexy creature? Kumiko places odds on the leader, internally referencing alpha male nonsense. Then again, maybe two of the men find comfort in one another. This is a humanist network, after all.

"Please input your key," says Kumiko, holding up a computer tablet. Daring Bird types in a security key, anonymously verifying network membership.

If your security key doesn't work, the host is quietly alerted. Check-in moves forward normally without any indication you've been excommunicated or given yourself away as an imposter. You get a room, perhaps a meal, fair treatment, etcetera, and the next time you fall asleep, you wake up in chains.

"Please, follow me," says Kumiko.

No other guests occupy the safe house, giving our smart-ass heroes their run of the facility. Everyone drops gear in their rooms and reports for a team meeting. The device is not to be discussed in front of their host. No slips. Daring Bird isn't overly suspicious of her yet, but they must be careful. Play it normal and cool, but be cautious.

I say physician heal thyself, because I know Daring Bird, and I can tell you without a doubt that Kumiko's presence stokes a long-dormant, smoldering flame in his blah blah blah…Daring Bird is horny. Horny is an opposite state of being to cautious.

Let's move on to dinner and introductions. The team is in a spacious kitchen, cooking and making merry. Garo Kasabian mans the stove, working several sauté pans. Jimmy stands at a wet bar mixing drinks. Everyone else sits around a large harvest table in the center of the room. The gang falls conspicuously silent when Kumiko enters.

"I apologize for the interruption," she says, on her way to the refrigerator. "I will only be a moment."

With his feet on the table and a heavily chewed cigar in his mouth, Daring Bird says, "Please, don't rush. Join us for dinner."

Kumiko looks hesitantly at him, then the rest of the team.

"We're going to be here a while," Daring Bird continues. "Might as well get comfortable with one another." (I told you he was horny.)

"Thank you. I sincerely appreciate the invitation. Regretfully, I must decline. I have work." Kumiko holds up a container of food and bows her head, turning to exit the room.

"You should stay." Daring Bird's tone is a perfect blend of subversively threatening and subversively flirtatious.

Kumiko stops. If she felt threatened, she would retreat to her quarters, file a report, and arm herself. Instead, she turns around and stares intently at Daring Bird. The scarred-up medicine man's feet are still on the table and the cigar still proudly jutting from his mouth, which happens to be wearing a devil's pointy-tailed grin. Kumiko tilts her head and damn near knocks him over with an expression that clearly states if he doesn't watch his step, he might get what he doesn't even realize he's asking for. Between you and me, the options are sex or a knife in the chest.

Garo breaks the ice. "You will bring great shame to my family if you don't try my chicken cutlet."

Turning around, Kumiko sees the Armenian Butcher wearing a broad smile, gently rocking a sauté pan back and forth in each hand. An off-kilter chef's hat decorates his head.

"Madame Kumiko," says Jimmy, as he crosses back to the table, handing Bebi her drink and placing his on the table next to her. "May I call you Madame Kumiko?"

Kumiko gives an affirmative nod and Jimmy continues speaking as he takes a seat.

"The gentleman handling the pots and pans is Garo Kasabian, the Armenian Butcher. Soldier, chef de cuisine de magnifique, and uniquely qualified explosives expert." Garo sets a pan back on its burner and waves innocently.

"That knucklehead over there is Silas the Entertainer," Jimmy continues. "We're not sure what he does."

Polishing off a cocktail, Silas stands and holds his left hand out to receive Kumiko's, who politely obliges. The kiss he smacks on the back of her hand might have been skeezy, save for the fact Silas is actually a surprisingly smooth operator, born with an undeserved amount of charm. They don't call him Mick the Dick for nothing.

"My lady," he says. "Please, call me Sal."

"Whatever you prefer."

In response, Silas promptly jumps the shark from charming to cheesy, wielding a lazy technique, rarely effective on anyone but ignoramuses or the inebriated. Raising Kumiko's hand to his nose, he smells it lasciviously and says, "Are you an Aries?"

To which Kumiko beautifully feigns confusion and replies, "No, Okinawan."

The entire team howls laughter, including Silas. Extremely pleased with himself as always, he takes the container of leftovers from Kumiko and ushers her into a seat at the table. Jimmy continues introductions as the chuckles die off.

"This here is Bebiana Belo, the…"

Before Jimmy can finish, Bebiana jumps in to add, "The Brazilian Bitch," with a snarl. Kumiko isn't certain if the snarl was playful or aggressive. Neither is Jimmy, and for that matter neither is Bebi, yet.

"I was going to say love of my life," says Jimmy, pleasantly.

Bebiana lays a hand over one of his and says, "But you may call me Bebi."

"Brazil is a beautiful country," says Kumiko. "What city are you from?"

"I'm from Portugal."

"Oh. Then why…"

"Because if I was from Brazil," explains Bebiana, "I would be a bitch." Another round of laughter from everyone except the author of the joke, who mutters under her breath, "Country full of bitches."

"Okay. Next up, me, Jimmy the Tweaker. American. Boring. Feel free to call me J.T. if it suits you." Kumiko gives a seated bow, tilting her shoulders and head. "Last but not least, the handsome, surprisingly quiet bugger over there is Titus the Nazarene. Pilot, kitten enthusiast, and harbinger of spiritual litigation."

"I am Desposyni," Titus exclaims. "Child of Mary!"

"You're drunk," says Silas.

"Yes, I am!" Titus is a frequent, lightweight drunk, and a curiosity to his compatriots, who can't understand why he's never developed a tolerance. Silas is convinced Titus is an alien. No one else has ascribed to that theory, though Daring Bird is on the fence. Luckily, despite his drunkenness, Titus is as tight-lipped as they come. Neither alcohol nor sodium pentothal has ever pried an E2M secret from his judgmental mouth.

"I don't understand," says Kumiko. "What is Desposyni?"

"Generally speaking, the blood relatives of Jesus Christ," says Daring Bird. "Our friend believes he is a direct descendent of the children Jesus had with Mary Magdalene."

"I did not know Jesus had children."

"Neither does anyone else," says Jimmy. "But Titus is determined to sue the Catholic Church for misappropriation of the family name."

"Why the Catholic Church?" asks Kumiko.

"I don't know," says Jimmy. "They're the biggest, or the worst, or something."

"I am Desposyni," Titus mumbles. "Without age. Without name. Impossible to kill."

Kumiko tries to fight back a laugh but can't resist, so she hides it with the back of her hand.

"To be fair," says Daring Bird. "He is very hard to kill."

"And we don't know if Titus is his real name, or how old he is," says Jimmy.

"He's a goddamn alien," says Silas, at which point Garo Kasabian loudly tings a fork against a glass.

"Ladies and gentlemen, dinner is served."

*　　*　　*

Later in the evening, everyone relaxes around the harvest table, dirty plates shoved away from themselves as they continue to drink and chatter. The entire group is intoxicated save for Daring Bird, though he is suspicious of Kumiko. She seems to be faking drunkenness. Easy enough to discard as an effort to be a jovial host, I suppose…

"Though I have not been in my position for long, I must admit you are the most unusual guests I've hosted," says Kumiko.

"We'll take that as a compliment," says Daring Bird.

"Oh, yes." Kumiko hoots. "My apologies. I meant this in a good way."

"Madame," says Jimmy. "I promise you that's the only way anyone on this team would take it. Unusual is our game."

"So, you admit it is intentional. Is this why you introduce yourself with your funny names?"

"Oh, I like this one," says Silas, smacking the table and surveying his teammates for agreement. "She's quick! Yes, she is." Silas turns to Kumiko. "They are fun! Right? Besides, what's the point in having them if we don't use them?"

"Ha. Very true. I believe I understand why they call you the entertainer."

"Bear witness, momma."

"But why are you the Butcher? That is a killer's name. This seems out of place, or maybe, violent for your team's…" she pauses, searching for the correct word before settling on, "…I don't know. Mystique. Yes. The name seems more violent than your presence."

"I own a deli."

"You own a deli?"

"Yes, I own a deli and butcher shop. When I am home, I am a butcher. And, in our mission, the scary name is useful."

"He owns a deli." Kumiko laughs, consorting with the smiling faces around the table before landing on Daring Bird, who's watching her intently. Her laughter ends, punctuated by flushed cheeks, and she turns to Jimmy. "And what about you, mister tweaker? How did you get your nickname?"

"I am a hypnotist. I tweak people's minds. Hence the name, Jimmy the Tweaker."

Kumiko leans forward and playfully says to Bebi, "Has he ever hypnotized you?"

"How do you think I got her to fall in love with me?" He's joking, but Jimmy is extremely aware of the fact that he's no physical specimen. Obviously, physical attraction isn't a singular necessary component for successful coupling, but it certainly helps get things going. I teased about Bebi's odd sexiness earlier, but she's well above Jimmy's paygrade. Jimmy's few remaining assets in the attracting a lover department are a decent head of middle-aged hair, middle-aged emotional calm, and a cool job. Jimmy's no Harry Hamlin, and he knows damn well how blessed he is to have won Bebi's heart.

Kumiko turns her playful expression to Jimmy, then back to Bebiana, who winks and blows a kiss in Kumiko's direction. During the exchange, a stumbly drunken Titus wobbles over to the kitchen counter and turns on a small television, cranking the volume up so loud he interrupts the conversation.

"Hey, Titus, come on man, shut that damn thing off," says Silas.

"No," says Daring Bird. "Leave it."

On the television, a dashingly handsome anchorwoman discusses a familiar portrait displayed in the corner of the screen. I don't know

French, but I do know all Daring Bird needs to hear is, "...toute nouvelle information sur l'extraordinaire vol de la collection *The Marias* à Lyon, il y a plusieurs jours."

6

Adolph Hitler was born in April of 1889. He died, unironically, in April of 1945. He was a friend of mine.

Don't worry, this passage isn't about my and Adolf's friendship. I was simply obsessed with the above lead-in. The key element is Hitler died, and coincidentally in the same month he was born. There's the synchronicity again, and I didn't have to make that fact up. Also, I've never met Hitler and we're not friends. Our association would require a time machine, and if I had a time machine, I wouldn't waste my time palling around with a piece of shit like Hitler. Besides, I'm all about the future, baby. You gotta be a self-serving jerk to meddle with the past. Onward!

I restate, Hitler definitely died. He didn't go live out his days as a quiet sheep farmer in a secret mountain valley of Austria, nor turn into an immortal being hatefully guarding the lost Ark of the Covenant in a cave somewhere in the deserts of Terblakispan. Nor could you have accidentally met and befriended him in a small town supermarket in the States, hiding out and working as a kind, elderly grocery clerk. No. He died in the bunker. What happened to Hitler isn't the question. The question is, what happened to the baby?

Wait. What? Baby? What baby?

Hang on, hang on. We're going to massage this for a minute. In January of 1945, Hitler took permanent residency in the Führerbunker, an air raid shelter near Berlin. Including various other notorious pieces of shit, Adolph was joined by his main squeeze, Eva Braun, and his best pal, a racist scumbag German Shepherd named Blondi. This is common knowledge, along with the fact that Hitler and Eva Braun married shortly before their Romeo and Juliette-esque commitment to love and death. The unanswered question is, why bother? Why marry right before you die?

The baby.

Eva was secretly pregnant, giving birth during their last days in the Führerbunker. I have no idea why Hitler didn't marry her sooner. Doesn't matter. What matters is that Hitler's grandfather was a bastard child, and this fact deeply embarrassed young Adolph during his formative years. His own child would not be a bastard. Sure, his plan was for all of them to die, but not until he made an honest woman of Eva. They would greet the afterlife as an unholy family unit. Hitler, Eva Braun Hitler, Baby Satan Hitler, and Blondi the racist scumbag German Shepherd, all bound by God's institutional glory.

As Maxwell Smart would say, Hitler "missed it by that much." I think Hitler underestimated a mother's compassion for her children. Even an evil bitch like his unscrupulous paramour had an instinctual reticence to kill what she had created. Thus, Eva convinced her newlywed husband to let her murder the baby.

"You've killed so many," she said. "Let me kill this one."

Now, as history tells us, Hitler shot himself first, then Eva popped a cyanide capsule and chased him to hell. I find this theory hard to believe. Perhaps Adolph was crazy enough to feel certain his bride would murder their child and kill herself. Maybe he was a man of large-penised confidence, convinced his magic wand had cast a spell so powerful Braun could not live without him, but I think it's more likely he was plagued by tiny dick frustration, which leaves us but one choice. Eva Braun is still alive!

No, no. That's ridiculous. She would be dead from old age long before now, and this is about saving the baby.

Perhaps Eva shot Hitler. There was a struggle. She somehow managed to wrestle the gun away from Adolph and shoot him in the head. Then, immediately grief stricken, having killed her one true love, she followed through with the plan and ate the pill.

Too contrived? Whatever. The more I consider the situation, there are hundreds of hilarious ways the scene could have played out. The key element is they didn't kill their baby. A baby no one knew existed.

Hold that thought and I will circle back very soon. First, let's chat about Russia for a minute.

Several years before the end of World War II, Russia created an organization to oversee three separate counterintelligence agencies. Stalin named the organization Smersh. That's correct. Smersh. A logical portmanteau of words from a Russian phrase meaning "death to spies," but when translated to English sounds incredibly stupid. Seriously. Smersh!?

One of the first recruits to Smersh's counter-espionage branch was a young go-getter named Andrei Somvinslodkin. Handpicked by the agency's top official, Somvinslodkin made a name for himself as a successful assassin, scoring numerous eliminations of enemy spies early in Smersh's existence, which helped solidify the organization's standing.

On April 30th, 1945, guess who was the first Russian soldier to enter the Führerbunker's lower levels and discover the dead bodies of Braun and Hitler? Disguised as an SS officer, Andrei Somvinslodkin had successfully infiltrated the Führerbunker and attended Hitler's wedding the night before. During the following day's raid, he snuck down to the lower levels to ensure Hitler would be captured. Upon discovering the bodies of Hitler and Eva, Andrei heard an out of place sound. There, in the dampness of the evacuated bunker, amongst the fancy bunker décor and sophisticated furnishings, lay the baby, swaddled in Nazi regalia. Somvinslodkin would hide the child to raise as his own.

Many in the Russian army held great respect for Hitler's accomplishments. Reverence for a worthy enemy, if you will. Andrei Somvinslodkin counted himself among these ranks. Considering all he'd learned in his counterintelligence efforts, as far as Andrei was concerned, the one factor separating Hitler from the leaders of the Allied forces, in terms of personal character, was destiny. Destiny had determined the role Hitler would play in life and destiny had delivered this baby to Andrei. There were brilliance and defiance in this swaddling's genes. Greatness. The child would live to claim his true birthright.

I know what you're probably feeling in reaction to all this historical exposition. Before you get yourself worked up into an, "Ah, man, really? Historical fiction sucks!" underwear knot, rest assured this is not historical fiction. For all we know, Hitler and Eva may have indeed had a secret lovechild who survived long after their deaths. We have no proof this isn't true. This is not historical fiction, this is a legend.

The legend of a child birthed from the deranged seed and spoiled womb of unfettered evil. The legend of that child's descendant family tree, told much more reverently by said family than I. The legend of a modern-day villainous megalomaniac with designs on conquering the world. This is the legend of Comrade Somethingrussian.

A man approaching the middle of his lifespan, lost in the emotional miasma of anticipation, sits with pencil in hand, spiritlessly attempting to draft a trademarkable symbol for his evil despot organizational brand. The room around him is filled with dark wood and books. The desk he's hunched over is monolithic. The portrait on the wall behind him, soon to be replaced. Hopefully.

Designing should be a labor of love. The excitement of creation and an unbridled enthusiasm for advancing his schemes would normally instill high levels of joy in this particular human. Today, there's a listlessness, a stagnance brought on by the exhausting nervousness of expectations. The unparalleled weariness of prolonged determination. The fear of not achieving doggedly pursued goals. Thankfully for this minion of evil, and you, dear reader, who deserves a bad guy worthy of your interest, this is all about to change.

We're about to witness this man's final turn from heinous employee to diabolical entrepreneur. Say hello to Conrad Somvinslodkin, or as I like to call him, Comrade Somethingrussian, aka Stalin's Ghost, aka The Bear Führer, aka Hammer and Sickle Hitler, and, as he will most often be referred to throughout the rest of this story, Xander Bowfly, his chosen moniker as the evil head of an evil, yet-to-be-titled organization.

I will trust you to remember that Xander is Conrad, the grandson of Hitler and adopted grandson of Andrei Somvinslodkin. Conrad's father was Viktor Adolphus Somvinslodkin, secret lovechild of

Adolph Hitler and Eva Braun, who was raised by Andrei. A pilot in the Russian army, Viktor died unceremoniously in 1970 from an accident while training North Vietnamese MiG pilots, proving that sometimes the genes for legendary evil skip a generation.

Before he died, Viktor dumped his legendary evil bearing seed into a fetching young Polish bride named—you're not gonna believe this—Eva Braun Primskanelium (…that's right…), who was strangled to death by her father-in-law after Viktor's funeral. This lineage is a lot to absorb, I know, but as I mentioned before, you deserve a bad guy worthy of your interest. Xander and I shall do our very best.

❀ ❀ ❀

Okay. You've learned his names and his birthright. Shall we get to know the man?

To understand how he became Xander Bowfly, we must further explore Conrad Somvinslodkin. Conrad grew up an enthusiastic Russian, taking immense pride in his father's admirable death as a soldier. Immense pride further inflated by tales of his legendary bloodline. Every night when tucking young Conrad into bed, Grandpa Andrei whispered stories of Hitler's exploits, instilling in the child a great sense of responsibility for his life and his place in this world. Some might call this inflated sense of responsibility a classic case of narcissistic egomania, though never to Conrad's face.

As a youth Conrad excelled at academics and non-team-oriented athletics. He was particularly brilliant at mathematics, chemistry, and physics, idolizing scientific brilliance from the minds of Einstein, Tesla, and their contemporaries. Genius level intelligence might have confined Conrad to the role of a mad scientist and evil inventor, if not for his gifted athleticism and strikingly sinister handsomeness.

After graduating with honors from prep school, Conrad enlisted in the Russian army, where the young man appeared destined for greatness. A life of military success followed by a political career leading to extreme wealth and power. A life accomplished by many lesser men. No, this would not be the end game for Conrad. Though military success factored into his plans, Conrad's ultimate goal was the glory of subversive infamy, not some commonly achieved, public success story.

Step one in making a name for himself as a military cadet? Murder his commanding officer. There was no malice involved. The assassination was tactical. During the military trial, when the Prosecutor General asked him why he committed the murder, Conrad replied, "I want you to know what I'm capable of, so we don't waste our time." His gambit was successful.

The powers that be fast-tracked Conrad into their most clandestine operations. Creative intellect and lusty despicableness positioned him as a high-ranking operative whose communication channels flowed directly to the ear of the President himself. In short order, Conrad Somvinslodkin earned command over a secretive division of the Ministry of Defense.

Conrad's directive was international mischief. The President was a man of vision (or so Conrad thought), whose intentions were to destroy the stranglehold Western democratic powers had on international politics and the global economy. The mission was chaos, plain and simple. Pull the threads and watch the fabric unravel.

Innovation was the key. Humanity had entered an era of technological advancement rife with possibilities for unprecedented warfare. The very first team of Russian Internet Misinformation Experts, or RIME, was created by Conrad, and though one of his most successful campaigns, it only scratches the surface of the numerous advancements he made in espionage.

Government tensions were stoked on an international level by actively exasperating global conditions that incite mass immigration. Leisure platforms like video games and competitive dance were utilized for political radicalization. Operatives were installed in the States disguised as crazy evangelical preachers who, thanks to the internet, are still selling their messages of hate to millions of people.

Conrad produced white-nationalist rock and roll bands throughout Europe, writing most of their lyrics. He developed indoctrination methodology for terrorist organizations in Middle Eastern countries. He laundered oligarchy money through legitimate international financial institutions, criminalizing them forever.

These are merely a handful of examples. Trust me, they get worse. You don't want to know the pots he stirred in Australia.

Throughout his military success, Conrad remained devoted to his personal ambitions. The President was short-sighted, and honestly, though conniving on a savantish level, not super smart. True, the President was, is, bent on global upheaval, but to this day his vision is confined to established parameters. The President wants to destabilize the world within its current socio-political construct, to revamp the balance of power in the current world order. Conrad could bring the whole system down in the name of Mother Russia. Instead, the President gets off on toying with the system, like a cat batting a goddamn ball of string around. Conrad wants to set the ball of string on fire.

Which brings us to the present. Operations are underway. Military doppelgänger trained and in place. Manifesto written.

Xander Bowfly has emerged from Conrad Somvinslodkin's villainous soldier's cocoon a despotic fallen dark angel champion merchant of death. Mix your own metaphors, if you like. Shake them vigorously and serve them over ice. Just make sure each one summarizes a man bent on the insane task of reorganizing the socio-political structure of all humanity. A man whose plots and schemes are founded in the unwavering operational self-awareness that the purpose of his venture isn't the destination, it's the journey. Xander may never successfully install himself as godhead of the human race, but he will damn sure enjoy trying. "My life and times for the sake of pain, baby. For the sake of pain."

In accordance with his autocratic ascendency, Xander has employed an extended underground network of right-wrongers, do-badders, and obedient terrorists, either born with dark hearts or hearts weak enough to easily manipulate in a destructive way. The as-yet unnamed organization travels the world encouraging the sins of aristocracy from the top down. Known for managing black market operations, proliferating evil dark web networks, constructing fast food processing facilities, designing successful corporate marketing initiatives, locating new oil reserves, encouraging gentrification of indigenous lands, sponsoring unethical zoos, and in general, being an all-around pain in the ass to the righteous forces in this world who unapologetically seek equality and peace.

You know what? We're going to do that again. I don't want you to think I'm lazy, drawing an easy dichotomy between the good guys and the bad guys through an obvious and potentially hackish presentation of blatant oppositism. The heroes will have way more page count. Let's give the villains their due while we can, which means at least one more paragraph of…

The as-yet unnamed evil organization has begun destabilizing traditional currency in emerging economic markets. Countless man hours will be devoted to the promotion of quack holistic gurus, to proliferating the propagation of scientific falsehoods, and to purposefully obfuscating the accurate use of language. Underground labs secretly develop unnecessary entertainment products designed to exacerbate humanity's continual distraction from the quest for genuine internal peace, not to mention how absurdly easy these products make it for corporations and governments to spy on us in our own homes. They're working on new infectious diseases to sell for profit, new poisons to sell for profit, and new cures for the designer infectious diseases and poisons to sell for profit. All of this while constantly posting bogus recipes online for the simple pleasure of ruining a family's dinner.

Their most recent product launch went splendidly, but Xander still hasn't decided on the perfect name and logo for his organization. They are currently operating as Der Iron Meatloaf. Purposefully humorous in effort to confound investigators tracking their deeds. The issue is, Xander needs his organization to announce its true presence with insidious authority. This means a grand evil plot, which he's already devised and set underway. The problem is, his plans are in motion and he's completely at a loss for branding ideas.

Xander hoped he would be inspired by a deadline. By the pressure of creating a name and logo before his plan reaches a successful conclusion. Instead, his anticipation for a successful outcome has further stifled his creativity, leading us to find him doodling and dawdling in frustration, anxiously awaiting a phone call regarding the success of a concurrent, secondary scheme. A scheme for which Xander has no intention of taking credit.

The phone rings. Xander answers, "Yes," as slimy as you can imagine. The pitch, the tone, the accent, every bit. Slimy.

The voice on the other end of the phone says, "The mission is complete sir. Cargo is en route to the holding facility."

"Excellent. Prepare for our departure."

"Sir, there's something else." You know what happens to employees who tell bad news to the head of an evil organization, don't you? I thought so, but since you can't read the fear in his voice, let me tell you this bad guy is shitting his pants at the prospect of telling his boss what he's about to tell him. The one saving grace is their conversation being held over the phone. If they were face to face, the dude would likely have his tongue split down the middle.

"What?"

"Our other shipment, sir, to the south. It was hijacked."

"This is confirmed?" The emotional void in Xander's voice serves as the most frightening diction he could choose.

"Yes sir."

"We leave in one hour." Fury explodes in Xander, boiling his blood and setting his brain on fire with murderous exclamations. Suddenly, he's feeling very creative. Yes. Very, very creative. Oh, someone is going to get it. Probably multiple someones. Oh, they're definitely going to get it.

Jesus Christ! The amount of effort he put forth keeping his construction of the device hidden from his own government. Now this! Motherfucker! Three years! Three very long years designing and keeping the damn thing a secret from the President. Not to mention the ridiculous stroke of programming luck. That device is the key to everything. The goddamn key! Mother fuck, fuck, fucking fuck! FUCK!

The internal tantrum slowly calms and Xander returns to his sketches, freshly inspired. Though mostly childish drawings of him stabbing people in their brains and eyes and crotches, his fire has been stoked by antithetical conclusions, leaving him simultaneously fueled by anger and joy. Something gained, something lost. This is a place of emotional conflict he can work from, artistically. Oh yes. His new logo will be designed posthaste. I promise you I will discover it by the end of this book.

7

Time does not heal all wounds. For many injuries, time serves only as a mildly effective painkiller. A salve to make the pain bearable. Preventing infection, but never quite allowing the wound to dry up and fully heal.

This is the torture of loss and heartbreak, a cancer for the human soul, and a species-wide communicable disease born and bred into every last one of us, the inescapable grasp of sadness. Sadness will come for a visit when it damn well pleases, will not leave until it sees fit, and will make the rest of your dinner guests uncomfortable throughout the evening. Fuck sadness. Whoever designed this grand scheme of things can suck a fat sad…little thumb?

Littlethumb Brooks drives his faded blue pickup truck into town. Woofus lays on the front seat next to him, perfectly relaxed for a spell, without fear of his monkey tormentors. The monkeys never come into town with Woofus and his dad. They can't be trusted.

Tears leak down Littlethumb's cheeks. Maria. Always Maria.

There was a period after her death when he felt the emotional adjustment had been made. Life would go on, like it or not. He would honor her by living accordingly, including trips to visit Tommy. The visits offered emotional clarity to Littlethumb's efforts in forgiving the murderer, and Tommy's mangled face reminded Littlethumb of just how close he'd been to becoming a murderer himself, having beaten Tommy near to death in the melee that took Maria.

For a while, the methodology appeared successful. The universe had seen fit to restore Littlethumb's ability to paint his spiritual portraits. Though never of her.

I suppose right here is as appropriate a place as any to discuss all of the blood on Tommy Toxic's hands. You know Tommy killed Maria. Tommy convinced Littlethumb to hold a joint concert for charity which was, in actuality, a plot to murder Littlethumb in public. Instead, the show ended with Tommy accidentally shooting Maria. But Tommy was a killer long before he shot her. Fifteen years earlier, as a teenage boy, Tommy Toxic killed Littlethumb's entire family. Several hundred other people as well, including Tommy's own adoptive father.

Say what?

I said, Tommy Toxic killed Littlethumb's entire family. Mother Elisabeth, father Walter, brother Freddy, and sister Heather. Murdered by a teenage boy at the relentless behest of unhinged jealousy and undeniable madness. The explosion, though an unsolved mystery at the time, was a dour proclamation of Tommy's and Littlethumb's numinous entanglement. Diametrically opposed forces bound to one another against their own will. Sacrificial lambs to the slaughter of existence and the eternal insistence our species learn every goddamn way possible that life can devise to hurt us.

How much more devastating was the loss of his wife after Littlethumb learned he had befriended the man who killed his family? To have that same man murder the woman he adored!? Impossible to tell, although I would think the revelation made an already devastating loss intensely more profound.

What's more important to consider is the path Littlethumb chose in the face of such devastation, striving to forgive Tommy and be at peace with his loss. You must choose whether or not to believe such grace is possible, but I promise you, Littlethumb Brooks is a human. A human who is currently driving and crying, lamenting his recent lack of ability to use these feelings for creation. To give them more value than their present market viability as blatant emotional indulgence.

Littlethumb isn't likely to find the renewal of his gift by driving into town, but he will find supplies, fellowship, and the chance for a temporary respite from his internal turbulence. When not acting as the omniscient eyes and ears of the Electric Medicine Men, Littlethumb spends a considerable number of hours at a men's shelter he helped establish. Even in a small, rural Canadian town, resolute hardship is suffered. Personal destitution. Folks without homes or futures. Thus, Littlethumb finances the First Church of Good Deeds men's shelter and visits regularly, playing chess and training the men to run a charitable website named Onedollarprayers.com. Though not an actual church, of course, the shelter is so named for the amazing tax benefits. Also, a touch of sarcasm, being the "first" church of good deeds among thousands of years' worth of churches.

A women's shelter is currently in the works, with a Program Director already hired and financial negotiations for a facility underway. The need for the woman's shelter being an unfortunate example of the wrong type of equality. Destitution, hardship, and abandonment have no preferred gender.

Onedollarprayers.com is a longstanding charity project of Littlethumb's. The website was created to act as a spiritual circle. Patrons donate money, make prayer requests, and are encouraged to follow online meditation sessions meant to honor the prayer requests. At the end of each month, the Onedollarprayers.com patrons are asked to vote on charities to receive the collected donations, sending thousands of dollars to progressive charitable enterprises.

The meditation sessions were formerly hosted by Littlethumb. After Maria's death, his heart in shambles, he could no longer conduct the sessions in good faith. Currently, the meditations are hosted by a rotating assortment of wayward but loving souls from the men's shelter.

Littlethumb pulls into the shelter's parking lot. The streaks of tears have solidified into thin crusty layers on his cheeks, like dried up tributaries whose waters never reached their destination. He scrubs the flaky residue from his face as he applies the finishing touches to his costume. Today he's a mad scientist, donning protective goggles, a lab coat, and a crazy-haired wig.

In his earliest trips to town for supplies, Littlethumb wore disguises as a matter of necessity. Or so he thought. Worldwide fame still has its limitations. One of which is the passage of fifteen minutes. The people in this town didn't give two healthy poops about Littlethumb Brooks, his plight, or his fame. At least not on face value. Many now care a great deal, and the costumes are expected, having become part of his social contract with the community that helps keep his whereabouts unknown. Everyone enjoys a laugh, and Littlethumb maintains his skills as a master of disguise.

Inside the shelter, Woofus takes off to make his rounds and collect his treats as Littlethumb heads for the common area, where a sign over the entrance reads *The Friendship Center*. One rule is posted in large letters on the eastern wall of the room: LOVE.

Littlethumb's paintings line the walls of the shelter, including numerous portraits of past and present residents. From conceptual pieces to abstract still-lifes and everything in between, there's an unexplainable quality in every one of his genre-bending paintings that defies all logic and reason. Yet, of all his work, his greatest creations are his portraits of humans.

Most of the current residents of the shelter have sat for and been given their own portraits. Typically pinned to the wall of their sleeping area, these images show you who the men once were, or who they were meant to be, before life ruined them. Solace is found in the paintings, reminding the men of their virtue, their humanity.

Remember, we're discussing an artist whose works regularly command six-figure price tags, and while he's still alive! The *Shelter Collection* is worth millions, quietly hanging on the First Church of Good Deeds' cinderblock walls. Thus, the paintings serve to liven up the place and ensure the organization's financial security. If the shelter ever stumbles financially, paintings can be sold to keep the doors open.

To which, someone might ask, why don't the homeless dudes sell the extremely valuable artwork they've been given and get their lives back on track? Valid question. Honestly, a few have tried. The gains were short lived. The end results predictable.

This is the truth about homelessness that the pick-yourself-up bootstrappers refuse to understand. Homelessness is almost always about functionality, not laziness or delinquency. While many of these men are too far gone mentally to understand how much money their paintings might earn them if sold, those who do understand are too emotionally damaged to attempt reentry to "normal" society based solely on finances. One of these men specifically told me he knew what his portrait was worth, and that alone made him feel worthwhile. If he sold the portrait, he had no idea what the future would hold, and he would no longer have the one thing he could look at every day to recognize his value. To know he is beautiful.

Today is a Wednesday, and Wednesday is art class day. Littlethumb teaches painting to those who are ready to learn. Recently, teaching has led to snarky internal jabs at himself. Those who can't do… You know the rest.

Self-defeating jokes aside, watching these weary-souled men escape their own weary souls through the discovery of expression is a welcome pacifier for Littlethumb's recent inability to create. Each lesson he gives, he attempts to learn. To rediscover some hidden or forgotten path to his place of inspiration, where the world falls away and he becomes an entity of singular vision and purpose. Perhaps he is trying too hard. Perhaps water quenches thirst.

"Well, well, well, who are we today?" The voice of Willy Peete. Willy runs the shelter for Littlethumb. He was also the shelter's first guest. Willy's life fell apart after suffering a nervous breakdown over the loss of his young son and the subsequent divorce from his wife.

Losing his son put Willy in a cell to which his wife no longer held a key. The torment of his inescapable detachment — and having caused her further pain — landed Willy in a gutter. Nearly two years ago, Littlethumb and Willy found one another in a verifiable nick of time situation, both near death in the wilderness. That's another story for another day, which also involves the discovery and rescue of young Woofus, who was barely a month old at the time. Needless to say, all three share a special bond, commemorated by a portrait of Willy and Woofus proudly hanging on the wall in Willy's office.

Two items: First, whenever a Canadian speaks throughout the story, feel free to add "ehs" and other stereotypical Canadian patois as you like, you hosers. I refuse to. I'm not sure if doing so would be racist or not, but it's annoying as hell to continuously type, you're never sure how much to include, and honestly, if you spend enough time around these dudes you tune out their slang.

Item number two: Though the path to reconciliation, if discoverable, will be long and hard, guess who Littlethumb has hired as the Program Director for the new women's shelter, a position that will occasionally require working in conjunction with Willy?

Willy's ex-wife, you goofballs. C'mon, that was an easy one.

"You may call me, Dr. Cheevago, master of the infinite infinitesimal," says Littlethumb.

"I'ma go with Doc, Doc," says Willy, "and leave the fancy wordplay for the master."

"Ha. Fair enough."

The two men hug and slap backs, a hearty, earnest embrace. "How's everything going this week?" asks Littlethumb.

"Not bad, not bad. Though I will say, the fellas miss having you around more often."

"Yeah, me too."

Before the exchange turns melodramatic, Willy says, "Okay. Now that's out of the way." Then he claps his hands and turns his face into a purposefully forced expression of manic excitement. "Let's have some fun, Doc!"

The two friends work their way around the room, a typically packed house on art class day. Willy introduces everyone to the Good Doctor Cheevago. Most of the men play along, yucking it up and energetically sucking down coffee, as if Littlethumb's presence somehow encourages them to get all buzzed out in the brain and run in circles like a child.

There's Paul Tremblay. Paul was a mill worker whose left hand got crushed. Without the use of both hands, Paul lost his job, causing the rest of his life to fall apart. Littlethumb gives Paul a hug then whips out a pink balloon, inflating it with fervor.

"Doc, I know we just met, but I'm warning you," says Paul.

"But it is too late, Paul," says Littlethumb in a terribly generic western European accent. "I can't stop myself. It's happening. It's happening…" Littlethumb makes Paul a balloon "animal" shaped like a hand.

"You son of a bitch." Paul wears an exaggerated expression of insult before transitioning into knee slapping laughter. Right hand of course, on those knee slaps. Paul uses the balloon to give Littlethumb the middle finger before the good doctor leaves.

Insert a mad scientist laugh as Littlethumb moves on to Remi Fournier. Remi is a drinker. No excuses, but he does have his reasons. Fill in a scenario you find comfortable. Something providing you empathy toward a man who's chosen to drink his life away. (If you can't immediately think of a reasonable justification, stop reading and keep trying. I'll wait.)

Littlethumb makes Remi a balloon noose, shoving it over Remi's head and around his neck, then pantomimes a big glug-glug-glug and points at Remi to make sure he understands. Remi tosses Littlethumb a scattered-tooth smile and says, "One can only hope."

There's Monty Bergeron, Sid Cameron, and Bruce Gerard. Ducky Bell. Father Leblanc, who's not a preacher, but after a hallucinogenic-induced excursion through his own mind believes himself to be. Over there tossing dominoes are Norville Lapointe and Henry Clarke, both born into such poor luck it's amazing one of them will win the game. All of these men have stories that led them here, and none of those stories begin with the words, "I'm going to petulantly make choices I know are bad for me and ruin my own life on purpose."

Littlethumb twists an insulting balloon for each man as he and Willy cavort with their tribe of rabble and riffraff, laughter being one of the most effective medicines for deeply-seated pain, and comedy being the one form of expression inherently authorized to lampoon any subject, no matter how painful or sacred.

Most of the guys will join Littlethumb for art class, art being another effective medicine for their pain, but not all the men are ready. Lately, Littlethumb has had a crystal-clear understanding of what those men who aren't ready are going through. Those who can't do…

About two-thirds of the way around the room, Littlethumb notices a younger fella at a table in the corner, playing chess against a gentle giant named Samuel Wood.

"Who's the guy with Sam?"

"Oh, that's Sinclair," says Willy, who maintains an organizational chart in his mind based on surnames. "Been coming around quite a bit for a few months. Didn't realize you haven't met him yet. Funny you haven't."

Littlethumb recognizes the not-so-subtle jab at his recent absence from the shelter. A punch thrown out of love, he knows, but the truth is he's been around enough to have seen a new regular visitor. A new regular visitor who, by the looks of his clothes and tightly groomed head, does not suffer the downtrodden lifestyle of the shelter's regular clientele. "Yeah," he says. "Funny."

8

Did I mention the classic, cherry red Buick Wildcat convertible resting in the shelter's parking lot when Littlethumb arrived? The car Littlethumb definitely noticed, and admired, and wondered to whom the magnificent machine belonged? I didn't?

Littlethumb and Willy make their way across the room toward the redheaded, smartly-dressed young man playing chess. Having dispensed of Samuel Wood and moved on to another opponent, the redhead tipped his king in submission while they watched, offering an earnest handshake to his newest challenger, Arthur Girard. Arthur plays chess like an impatient lover, racing to the climax, swapping pieces until the board is clean and each player's king smokes an after-battle cigarette. At which point, almost anyone who plays Arthur tips their king and takes the loss, rather than declare the obvious stalemate. At which point Arthur, exultant in victory, will bounce around the room ensuring everyone bears witness to his triumph. Arthur took some accidental buckshot to the head about twenty years ago.

"Very gracious of you," says Littlethumb in Dr. Cheevago's accent.

"Oh, thanks," says Red, our mysterious red-headed journalist. "Nothing really. Watching a victorious Arthur is food for the soul."

"Indeed it is."

"Awesome costume. Willy, did I miss an announcement or something?"

"Ha, not unless we all did young fellow. Not unless we all did." All three men swap grins and eye contact. None of them know what the other two are waiting for, inciting an awkward moment of silence and study.

I can tell you I paused them to tell you this: Red, our mysterious young red-headed journalist's real name is…

"Hi, I'm Redmond Sinclair." The man stands and extends his hand. "Call me Redy, if you like. Most everyone does."

Littlethumb takes his hand and gives a firm, friendly shake. "Hi Redy, I'm Smith," he says.

"Just Smith?"

"Just Smith. Though today you may also refer to me as Doctor Cheevago, master of the infinite infinitesimal."

Redy Sinclair sprays laughter like he's spitting out a mouth full of drink.

"Redy," says Willy. "Mr. Smith here is the shelter's founder."

"Oh, *the* Mr. Smith!" The playful recognition is obvious. Redy knows who he's speaking to. He's been waiting. "I've looked forward to meeting you."

"Thanks. The pleasure is all mine."

"Tell you what," says Willy. "I'm going to see what's on the menu for lunch this afternoon. Let you two get acquainted."

"Meatloaf, Willy," says Littlethumb. "Wednesdays are meatloaf. You better not be messing with my dog or my belly. Cause Woofus and ol' Tum Tum here didn't drive all this way to find out there's no meatloaf."

"You'll be lucky I don't serve you pigeon feed gruel over rat leg confit, Doc." With that, Willy slaps Littlethumb on the back and heads for the dining hall.

"Shall I take a seat?"

"Please. Please do."

Both men sit. Nervous energy insists Redy begin resetting chess pieces. Littlethumb resets the pieces on his side of the board, studying the other man. Redy understands he's being observed. His anxious state is both natural and contrived. Natural because he's genuinely anxious. Contrived because he planned for this moment. And here he is, staring at a famous, reclusive, millionaire artist dressed as a mad scientist for no other reason than Wednesday. Yes, as you might imagine, Redy knows who "Smith" really is.

"I understand you're the reigning champ," says Redy.

"You know, I do love to humblebrag, so I will bashfully answer 'yeah, I am,' and hopefully I'll blush. Am I blushing?"

Redy hesitates, then says, "Not quite. But you are very suntanned for Canada."

"Nice! The will to survive. Ladies and gentlemen, this man swims."

"As opposed to sinks?"

"Bingo. You'll forgive me, please, my uncontrollable impulse for banter. It's one of the ways I hide my pain."

"From this day forth, all is forgiven. I know that game too."

"I'm sorry to hear that for you," says Littlethumb. "And happy for you as well." A moment of silence, as Redy expresses his understanding for the sentiment with flowing eyebrows, pursed lips, and messages from several other members of his face's communications team. "Speaking of games," Littlethumb continues, "shall we have one? Somehow this board has magically reset."

"Ha, ha. It does appear to be calling to us. I accept your challenge, sir."

"Excellent." Littlethumb extends both fists over the table, clenched tightly. "Pick your poison."

Upon review, a white pawn is missing from the ranks on Redy's side of the board. *When did he do that?* thinks Redy. *That's pretty good.* Redy taps Littlethumb's left hand, which opens to reveal the white pawn.

"Your honors," says Littlethumb.

"I'll play white," says Redy.

"Aggressive."

"Eh, they're already right here."

Littlethumb reaches across the board and places the white pawn back in its rank.

"Shall we set the clock?" asks Redy.

"Why not? Time binds all mortal lives, whether measured or ignored."

"Keats?"

"My uncle."

"Sounds like Keats."

"Uncle may have stolen it. What do you think, fifteen minutes a side?"

"Oh, I'd say fifteen is more than enough for you to shatter my delusions of grandeur."

"Ha. I suppose we shall see," says Littlethumb, setting the two-sided clock and returning it to the table. "At your leisure, sir."

I won't be overly descriptive or gluttonously use chess jargon here, but please enjoy the following snippet: Redy Sinclair opens his maneuvers with a Queen's Gambit. Littlethumb presents a Stonewall

Defense, declining a pawn exchange at the center of the board. After a few moves, Littlethumb abandons the Stonewall, performing a queen's side castle of his king. Meanwhile, Redy adds layers of defense to his pawns, opting for long term control of the center board, or so he thinks.

If you aren't familiar with chess strategy, one of the most common basics in theory is controlling the center of the board. This means having as many pieces attacking or defending the center squares as possible. However, you will frequently sit down across from some jackass who opens the game by advancing their pawns up the outside ranks. You will also meet jackasses who take their queen out early in the game and run her all over the board, constantly attacking and retreating but never developing her subordinates. Both are shock and awe tactics, in my opinion, of players typically less skilled than they believe themselves to be. Every so often you face an opponent who is exactly as skilled as they need to be, and they will utilize one of these annoying approaches to run you off the table.

You don't know Redy well enough to make assumptions, but you might suspect Littlethumb for an unorthodox player based on what you've learned of our hero thus far. What unfolds between the two men is a game of measured routine. Redy controls the center of the board (again, or so he thinks…). Littlethumb presents the beginning of several aggressive defenses, deftly starting one recognizable line then transitioning to another, yet maintaining his true focus on building an impenetrable fortress around his king. Littlethumb's king, by the way, is always named Hector the Invisible, which has nothing to do with chess.

After a series of turns by each player, all pieces remain on the board. The move is Redy's. The clock is ticking.

"Man," says Redy. "Been a while since I've played a board this log-jammed."

"Yeah, most of our friends in here are impetuous by nature. Slowly developing, best laid plans aren't really in their wheelhouse."

"Ha. I suppose not." Redy studies the board, thoughtfully rubbing his chin as he ponders his next move. The game's development insists its players commence swapping pieces. The question is, where to begin?

In the game of chess, much like the game of life, one of the greatest skills to have is the ability to see as many moves ahead as possible. If I do this, what are all the outcomes I can possibly envision? Where do the choices lead? A reasonable analogy, visually, is how a family tree grows and splinters. The main difference being, you must attempt to envision all the other people your parents each *might* have married, and how the tree would look several generations down the line based on those many nuptial scenarios. The possibilities are mind-boggling. As a child, I could stare at the board visualizing moves for lengthy periods, all of my body's natural fidgety energy transferring to my brain to power extended analysis. As an adult, I have lost my patience for the long game and rarely play. A shame.

My personal failings as a chess player aside, please take note: As you hold this book, you can feel in your hands the significant portion you've currently read. We're almost a fourth of the way in. All the pieces are on the board. The players engaged. The tone established. The game afoot. Redy takes a knight.

"Nice move," says Littlethumb.

Before Redy sets the captured knight aside or says, "Thank you," he realizes Littlethumb has already returned fire. A white pawn is missing. *What the hell? That was fast,* thinks Redy. This isn't simply a reference to Littlethumb's move selection, but also the physical speed used to make the move. Redy didn't see Littlethumb's body move at all, yet the clock has been returned to him and there is a black bishop resting where Redy's pawn sat moments before. *Did I look away? I must have.*

Not to be outdone, Redy opts for speed of his own. Pieces rapidly disappear from the board as both men put sleight of hand skill on display, eyes locked in silent conversation. Hands fly, attacking the board and smacking the clock. A crowd of healthy vagrants and honest ne'er-do-wells gather around the combatants as Redy employs the distraction of dialogue.

"It's a wonderful thing you've done here, Mr. Smith, opening this shelter."

"Thank you. It's a blessing to have the opportunity."

"Also a blessing to be able to afford the opportunity, I should think," replies Redy.

"Absolutely," agrees Littlethumb. "A blessing. One your shoes appear familiar with."

Redy nods humility. They are expensive-ass shoes on his feet. "Yeah, I'm lucky that way. Not so much in others."

"The plight of man," says Littlethumb. "The plight of man."

A crucial error by Redy effectively ends the game. Overreaching with his queen, Redy attempts to sacrifice her in hopes of advancing a pawn to the eighth rank, promoting said pawn to queenhood in position for a checkmate. The misstep leaves Redy's queen exposed and catches

Littlethumb off guard. Was the blunder intentional? Littlethumb is suspicious. I believe the error to be an honest miscalculation on Redy's part, perhaps due to the speed with which they were playing. Whatever the reason, Redy instantly recognizes what he's done.

Littlethumb responds by making a purposeful gaffe. A gift, inciting a loud gasp from the audience. None of the folks who are watching should doubt for a second Littlethumb's mistake is intentional, as they've all witnessed his advanced skill at the game. But they're also a bunch of goofy lunatics, so they walk away bewildered, discussing their surprise with conspiracy theories as to how the mis-take occurred, never accounting for the fact that Littlethumb always loses his first game against a new opponent. Not to mention, he consistently lets the rest of them win games on days when they obviously need the ego boost. These men are too far off the reser-vation to notice or call into question the irrational dichotomy of Littlethumb consistently losing games to lesser opponents and his otherwise brilliant play.

Though Redmond Sinclair may turn out to be crazy, he is no fool, and absolutely understands the gift Mr. Smith, Mr. Littlethumb Brooks "Smith," has given. The gift is accepted with silent contrition. Redy takes a knight that Littlethumb should have used to block checkmate, instead creating a checkmate, and humbly extends his hand across the board. You can tell the handshake offer is humble because his face is emoting humility super hard.

"Good game," he says.

"Good game," Littlethumb responds.

"Want to run 'em back?"

"Oh, I think we'll have the opportunity for another game down the road."

"Raincheck then."

"Absolutely." An extended moment of silence ensues as both men comfortably stare at the other. Eyes locked in "who will be the first to twitch" combat. Littlethumb breaks the silence.

"Why are you here, Mr. Sinclair?" The tone of the question is neither antagonistic nor suspicious. Littlethumb is a master of disguise on multiple levels, including dialogue. Curiously, though he lives to expect the unexpected, he is surprised by Redy's answer.

"I'm trying to find Littlethumb Brooks."

The words don't surprise him. Littlethumb might easily have guessed Redy's answer. The surprise is Redy's enthusiastic honesty. Redy admits his mission with a child's glee for revealing a big secret.

"Interesting. How come?"

"I hope to interview him. I'm a journalist."

"Oh. That's pretty cool. I've always wanted to write more. What makes you want to interview Littlethumb Brooks? Seems like his fifteen minutes were up years ago."

"To be honest, I started on a mission to do a piece on Tommy Toxic. I thought learning how prison has affected him would be interesting. Whether or not he's receiving treatment. If he's healing or growing more detached from the world. An in-depth exploration of a tragic life. But once I interviewed Tommy, I realized I had to find Littlethumb. I mean, what a story!"

"Yeah, I suppose so." Littlethumb's tone walks a fine line between disinterest and not behaving like a killjoy dick. "But what brought you all the way up here?"

"Tommy Toxic. He told me Littlethumb Brooks still comes to visit him, and that he lives here. I know it's a crapshoot. Tommy's clinically insane. But I figured, what the hell? Nothing to lose by seeing if Tommy is correct, and everything to gain."

This is a lie. You know it, I know it, and Littlethumb immediately knows it too. Not once in his visits with Tommy has Littlethumb mentioned living in Canada. The question is motivation. Is this a good-natured fib intended to hide a mildly uncomfortable detail, told by Redy to keep his subject at ease? Or is this a dark-hearted lie used to hide malicious intent?

The trick is, Redy understood before their meeting that Littlethumb would likely recognize his lie, and if so, might also recognize the possibility that Redy assumed Littlethumb would recognize the lie. But does Littlethumb realize that Redy may know that Littlethumb recognized what Redy assumed? The catting and moussing begins, but to what end? To what end?

9

"Something is wrong?" says Kumiko, as much a statement as a question. We're back at the safe house in Marseille, where the Electric Medicine Men have learned *The Marias* were stolen and Daring Bird has abruptly exited the room.

Kumiko searches for a face willing to respond. In a group performance worthy of vaudeville, the Electric Medicine Men trip and fall all over themselves in an effort to conceal the obvious. Happy creases in the corners of her eyes display Kumiko's appreciation for the bit.

"I understand if it is none of my business."

"Eh, D.B. really loves art is all," says Silas, who didn't have to say anything but can't help himself.

"I'm sorry, I wasn't clear. Obviously, something is wrong. I suppose the more accurate question is, will this be affecting your stay?"

"What's obvious? That?" asks Silas, tossing a thumb in the general direction of Daring Bird's exit. "That's nothing. He always does stuff like that." Silas gives a dismissive wave, then leans back in his chair and proudly takes a cold bite of chicken cutlet.

"Forgive our friend," says Jimmy. "Bullshit is a birthright for him."

"No need to forgive. As I said, guests here are expected to have secrets. I take no offense."

"Thank you," says Jimmy.

"You're welcome, though I must say, I don't understand. Everyone knows who Daring Bird Jones is. His nephew's story is very famous. The trial exposing his nephew's identity was international news."

"Oh," says Bebiana, her tone dryer than the skin on her elbows.

"How is it we keep this organization a secret, again?" Jimmy asks his compatriots.

"It's the eyepatch," offers Garo.

"Yes!" agrees Titus. "The eyepatch!"

As mentioned earlier, the Electric Medicine Men have largely maintained their anonymity through the loyalty of their supporters. The other most important factors, obviously, are never getting caught or seen while performing their secretive deeds. Missions are meticulously planned around lack of visibility, including from satellite imaging, unless they've hijacked a satellite for their own purposes.

The trial Kumiko referenced is a lawsuit from several years ago. An identity theft and trademark infringement suit was filed by Littlethumb's former art teacher and mentor, Sawyer Pettimore, who we will meet shortly. Though Daring Bird made a surprise appearance in court, Kumiko's spoken opinion of his fame says more about who she may be as a person (smart…excellent memory…working an angle…?) than what "everyone" knows or remembers about Daring Bird Jones. The rest of humanity — except for you, me, and our heroes, of course, of course — currently has the short-term memory of a mosquito rapidly devolving into that of a gnat, feverishly batting its wings against the soul crushing winds of the age of infinite media. Hoo-ah!

❀　❀　❀

"Okay, then," says Jimmy, "seeing how there's no need for us to keep lying to you unsuccessfully, I'm not certain if this will affect our stay or not, so I think I might wander off and see if I can find out." Jimmy stands to exit, shooting a wink at Bebiana before leaving the room.

A brisk trip through the house brings Jimmy to Daring Bird's quarters, where he finds their leader hunched over a laptop computer. "Find anything?"

"Not much to find," replies Daring Bird. "Looks like Cross and his team were taken to a hospital in Lyon." Mortimer Cross is the stern, sharp dressing leader of *The Marias* security detail who was left naked and beaten at the scene of the crime. He's also an adjunct member of the Electric Medicine Men.

"What's the next step?" asks Jimmy.

"Gonna call Pettimore, see what he knows."

"Should I prep the team for relocation?"

"No, not yet. No reason to break procedure right now. This will take time. Whoever did this, my gut tells me tracking them down will be hard. The middle of the friggin' day?"

"Ballsy, and thoroughly executed." Jimmy is leaning over Daring Bird's shoulder, reading a recount of the heist. "And strange. I mean, I know the paintings are valuable, but what do you do with all of them? That's a lot of art to move on the black-market."

"Yeah. There has to be a plan for long term storage."

"And protection."

"Yep."

"It doesn't make sense," Jimmy says, rocking his head in disbelief. "One or two, maybe a handful, but the entire collection? In the middle of town. It feels…unnecessarily grandiose."

"I agree. Whoever did this was showing off."

"Right. Which begs the next question, were they showing off because they could, or was another motivation in play. Was the heist misdirection? A trick?"

"Excellent question. I say we presume there is a grander scheme afoot and move forward accordingly. In the end, if whoever orchestrated this was merely putting on a show, good. Our job is less complicated. Either way, the mission is clear. Recover the paintings. One way or another."

"Copy that."

"I'm gonna call Pettimore. Have the gang start digging for any intel they can find. You know the drill. I'll come find you after the call."

"Copy that. Will do."

Jimmy leaves the room and Daring Bird takes a moment for an exhausted sigh. Imagine you're a Robin Hood-esque leader of a secretive organization who travels the world fighting evil, filled with boundless enthusiasm for the specific task at hand and for the overall glory of your lifelong mission. That doesn't mean you don't get weary.

There's an ocean of water under the bridge between Daring Bird Jones and Sawyer Pettimore. An ocean.

"The Sky Is Falling" by rapper Trip History, aka Mista Trip, blasts from Sawyer Pettimore's mobile phone. Caller ID shows the name Chicken Little. Daring Bird would not find this amusing. Sawyer finds the label hilarious, but with love, not animosity. He waits for three rings, allowing his wandering mind to fully report to the present, then answers the phone.

"Hey," says Sawyer.

"Hello." Daring Bird's voice is modulated, for safety. The perverted sound is off-putting at first, but Sawyer has gotten used to it over the years.

"Everybody safe?" asks Sawyer.

"For the time being."

"Calling about the news?"

"Yep."

The waters under the bridge of Daring Bird and Sawyer Pettimore's relationship contain a troubled, turbulent history. One where Daring Bird had wanted to hurt Sawyer, badly. That's a long way from a loving friendship.

Honestly, there wasn't much Sawyer could have done about the situation, and to be fair, Daring Bird's contempt was earned. As a young man, Sawyer had an immature, bitter spirit. Daring Bird had sensed this, making him leery of the art teacher's motivations, though Littlethumb eventually broke his uncle's grudge. Daring Bird couldn't hate someone his nephew cared for so dearly.

"You talk to the kid yet?" Daring Bird asks.

"No. Had a feeling you would call. Thought I would see what you know first. Also, I may be monitored."

"Good. Good thinking."

"You think he knows?" asks Sawyer.

"I doubt it. He would have already contacted me, and I figured I would gather any information I can before telling him. At least I might be able to answer a few questions."

"Right."

"Speaking of which, I'm guessing you've already gotten calls from authorities?"

"Yep. FBI, French secret service, Lyon police department. A CIA contact who knows Cross from his service days. Oh, and some guy from the Department of Agriculture."

"The Department of Agriculture?" For all the governmental nonsense Daring Bird witnesses on a regular basis, this still catches him off guard.

"Yeah, weird huh?"

"Yes. And no weird stone goes unturned. You got any rich and famous friends with government contacts you've been hiding from me?"

"You know I do."

"Dig around. See what you can find out. Will be considered perfectly reasonable under the circumstances, since you manage the collection."

"What are you going to do?"

"First thing, I'm going to check on the old fella, see if he remembers anything." Old fella isn't an official team nickname for Mortimer Cross, but Sawyer knows exactly who Daring Bird is referencing.

"Why not call him? Would be quicker."

"I'm guessing he's under surveillance. Gotta go in person. Scope the situation out."

"I suppose 'be careful' isn't necessary?"

"No, but appreciated." On the verge of ending the call, Daring Bird realizes he almost forgot something. He takes a second to scold himself, then says, "Hey, how's my girl?"

"She's fantastic, as always."

"Good."

"Needs her daddy, though. She's growing fast, Bird. Only gets faster."

"I'm working on that."

"Let me know if I can help."

"Will do." Dramatic pause right here, as both men consider the same subject from different angles, taking different paths to the same destination.

"Alright," says Daring Bird. "Give the squirt a hug from me. I'm off to it."

"Will do. Good luck and safe travels."

"I'll do my best."

10

At some point, you deserve a more intimate understanding of our mystery might-be-a-journalist man. How about right now? Who is Redmond Sinclair?

Redmond Bartholomew Sinclair the Fourth. Young. Early- to mid-twenties. Not much younger than Littlethumb, who's south of, yet barreling headlong toward, the continuously redefined benchmark of human life we call thirty years old. (Thirty was once a high-water mark for a human's survivability in this perilous world, with expectations of emotional adulthood. Today, thirty is the new twenty, and to be frank, dangerously close to the new fifteen, but I digress…)

You may have already surmised a man so young as Redy wearing expensive clothes and driving a perfectly restored classic automobile might come from affluence, and you would be correct. Redy is more than rich enough to have completely avoided our most recent and widespread form of indentured servitude: student loans. A trust fund kid, for sure, but he's also living proof of the timeless adage, "money doesn't buy happiness." Fleeting moments of joy, money can purchase the hell out of. True happiness? Not so much. Though an argument can be made that if you string enough fleeting moments of joy together, your life will happily be over before you know it.

Sadly, stringing moments of joy together hasn't been Redy's deal. Orphaned before he reached his fifth birthday, Redy was on the verge of being a never-had-a-chancer, and still is, despite his plentiful inheritance. Just like Littlethumb, Redy's parents were stolen from him by the illogical, misguided cruelty of a psychopath. The end result of that trauma is a young man with infinitely conflicting emotions, cultivated by outward lessons of pain and hardship terrorizing the inherently loving child within. We're talking nature versus nurture when the nurturer is a ham-fisted, chaotic, cold-hearted son-of-a-bitch named human existence. Or, in this specific, non-metaphorical instance, Uncle Carmine. Uncle Carmine isn't a blood relative, but he is an abusive geriatric bastard who took Redy under his inappropriately touchy wing.

The Sinclair family's finances had been in the care of Carmine Strotham, Esquire for decades. Redy's father had inherited generational wealth. The type of family money that can turn you into a socialite philanthropist or a worthless, self-indulgent gadabout. Fine examples of the former, Rita and Bartholomew Sinclair were loving, decent humans.

After Redy's parents were killed, Carmine was the executor of the Sinclair estate. With Redy's aunt and uncle persistently off on mission work, having Uncle Carmine steward Redy through his schooling made sense. Carmine is a deeply trusted member of the entire Sinclair family. He's also a fine example of humanity's age-old "trusted but not actual blood member of the family who is actually a piece of shit dirtbag" trope, noodled here and in other tales of history or fiction and destined to be kaboodled tomorrow, the next day, the day after that, and indefinitely on into the future of our reality.

Redy hasn't dealt with Uncle Carmine yet. Emotionally or legally. The young man barely summoned enough strength to stay alive. Not enough to air his hurtful dirty laundry to the world in a quest for imaginary justice.

I will admit it's a powerful shame more kids must suffer the same fate as Redy due to his lack of strength for action. Please don't judge him. There's no happy ending in this story for you, dear reader, with regard to Uncle Carmine. Unfortunately, there are many for him, and yes, that's a smartass line about a disgusting piece of shit child molester, but I'm not joking around here. I'm not laughing. I'm begging you for empathy, and empathy can be hard to develop unless you force yourself to consider things in very intimate, uncomfortable terms. So, consider daily on your life's journey, happy or sad as each of your days may be, that somewhere out there is a piece of shit named Uncle Carmine living affluently and happily molesting his way through the world. Imagine the hurt and confusion, the general non-stop cavalcade of horrible emotions preventing you, if in Redy Sinclair's young, tormented shoes, from being capable of anything other than escape.

Imagine the cavalcade of hurtful emotions includes thoughts of those other youngsters out there being preyed upon by pieces of shit like Uncle Carmine, and your own lack of strength to fight for them. To save them. To conquer the monster who stole your innocence and is coming for theirs. How do you live with that? How?

I will tell you how Redy Sinclair lives with it. His brain played a game called self-preservation. Brain rewrote the narrative. Brain altered reality. Brain suppressed all those terrible thoughts down into a deep, dark, unhealthy chasm, forcing a confused and angry phoenix of revenge to emerge. Remember, dear friends, our relationship with our mind is quite possibly the greatest example of Stockholm syndrome this life presents us. We have no greater force to trust to get us through all this madness than our brains, and they simply can't always be trusted. If you're hungry for some food for thought, chew on that. Chew it well, at least one-hundred times before swallowing. Otherwise, it can be hard to digest.

We're spying on Redy in his hotel room. He's just returned from meeting Littlethumb Brooks and is high as a kite. No drugs are necessary. This is the elation of long held dreams being born into reality. Until recently, Redy never thought he would have this opportunity.

Honestly, he's been in a haze since his discovery at Ray Brook. Redy can barely remember following Littlethumb up to Canada. Or going back to New York to prepare for his mission. Or the month he spent in Toronto, driving back and forth to scout the town and Littlethumb's movements before he finally took the leap and checked into this hotel.

An audit of his rented domicile reveals a guest of meticulous nature. Several months of usage and there's scarcely a clue the hotel room has been utilized. No dirty towels. No food containers or luggage in sight. No pile of clothes. The few signs of occupancy are a large spiral sketch pad resting on a table by the window and, next to the sketch pad, a weathered straight razor. Engraved on the razor's handle are the initials R.B.S. III. If not for the sketch pad and razor, housekeeping would think the room is unoccupied.

Redy scans the intensively organized environment. Maintaining order has been his survival. Whether at home, the interior of his badass vehicle, or in this small hotel room in the middle of Canadian nowhere, meticulous control of his personal environment centers him, gives him peace.

A peace you can't find when participating in the outside world. The outside world, he understands, is the arena. The inescapable battleground for physical and mental survival. The playing field with no boundaries, where you don't get to choose the game, make the rules, or control whether or not you win. No matter the self-determination, there are so many intangible factors influencing each day for each human, success or failure is a goddamned coin toss in a world insistent on forever skirting the precipice of chaos and fate. Those two lusty concepts, forever entwined by the timeless adage *opposites attract*. Or, in this instance, become one.

Chaos and fate are expressions of the same mechanism. Anything possible may happen in this life. Chaos. Once any possible said thing has occurred? Fate.

Obviously, many successful humans would argue the level of control we have for our own destinies, and I'm not going to tell you they're wrong. What I'm going to tell you is, if you boil our existence down to its primordial inception, whether you put the effort forth and succeed or put the effort forth and fail is, in many ways, written in the stars, the fabric of time, your DNA, or quite possibly some unknown deity's plan. Nevertheless, what other option do we have than to take action, even if said action be inaction?

Do you see? Because Redy does, and Redy suddenly realizes he can't further his plans if he doesn't lose his mind a little bit (quickly noting to himself that he already has, and thinking, *More. A little bit more.*). There is nothing sane about this path he's chosen. Sanity won't get the job done. This is a job for unchecked emotion. This is a messy job for irrational hands unafraid to be dirtied. This is a job for crazy.

Accepting this notion with a resolute smile, Redy Sinclair nods to himself in agreement, strips himself nude, and trashes his hotel room.

Several hours later, Redy's feet are propped up on the table as he enjoys the disheveled life-scape in front of him. The television is going to cost a few bucks to replace. Whatever, he's rich.

Our man remains unclothed, enjoying the coolness of the air on his skin, still warm and damp from a hot shower. His muscles are taut and twitchy, reeling from the glorious tossing of his hotel room. The nakedness is a beastly, self-indulgent expression, honoring the wild animal he set free to wreak havoc.

On the table, the straight razor lays open, a trickle of blood on its edge. The sketch pad is in our naked beast's lap. Redy is staring at the room's large mirror, his own body the featured reflection, drawing a picture of himself drawing a picture of himself in the midst of a gigantic mess. What else would you do if you had nothing but revenge on the mind and hands full of time?

The last flames of his internal combustion are quietly burning themselves out through artistic expression as he sketches himself for posterity. The elation he felt earlier has passed, replaced by his normal sense of self, though freshly renewed and invigorated. Redy passed the test with flying colors. Though he can't live this turbulence daily, the animal can be unleashed, and will be.

To this point, Redy wasn't certain, but the vengeance-seeking demon living inside him has had its first taste of the outside world, and the outside world tastes like fried chicken. Delicious. Speaking of which, Redy's hungry. Time to order dinner and clean up this mess.

II

Littlethumb Brooks sleeps on his front porch, slouching against the wall. His wrists and ankles are loosely tied. A paper sack with a smiley face drawn on the front covers his head. A handwritten note lies in his lap.

Woofus Maximus licks his daddy's hands and whines. Dad's head looks scary, but everything smells fine. Woof isn't concerned. He's bored. Dad needs to wake up and play. Licking the hands that feed him works, as Littlethumb slowly stirs.

Naturally hunched to his left during slumber, Littlethumb straightens his shoulders and slowly realizes there's a bag over his head. *What the hell?* He attempts to remove the bag and realizes his hands are tied to his ankles. *Seriously?*

Recognition sets in. He was making a few more stops in town before heading back out to the cabin. The last thing he remembers is walking out of the hardware store.

I suppose I get what I deserve.

Lightly bound and easy enough to escape, the ropes fall from his wrists. Removing the sack from his head leads to the discovery of the note in his lap, which reads: *Master Chee 1, Smith 0. Remember, was your idea.*

Chuckling as he unties his ankles, he leans back against the wall and happily sighs. Then he looks down at the sack on the ground and sees the smiley face mocking him. *Nice touch, Master Chee,* he thinks. *Nice touch.* Even when all is not right with the world, all may still be right with the world, if only for a moment. The sun is fading on this day.

A thermos of coffee sits to his right. Another nice touch. Littlethumb tests the coffee. Still warm. No more than an hour could have passed since Master Chee left. Littlethumb stands and takes a look around. His truck sits in the drive. Assuming Master Chee ambushed him in town, then drove him and Woof back out to the cabin, how the hell did Chee get back to town? Hitchhike? Not likely. Hours could pass in between vehicles driving on the main road to the cabin. Jog? Perhaps. Great exercise, but the cabin is at least twenty kilometers from town (we're in Canada, so we're gonna metric system this business…). Almost a damn half marathon. Then again, maybe Chee doesn't need to get back to town. For all Littlethumb knows, the dude could be living in the woods somewhere near the cabin. Hell, the diminutive monster could still be hiding somewhere on the property, which would not surprise Littlethumb one iota. Such is the way of the Chee.

Littlethumb heads indoors, in need of a healthy distraction. Normally this would lead to creation. Painting or playing. One way or another, putting his soul on display for the world, the spirits, and the gods. Not today.

If we're going to help Littlethumb figure out why he's blocked artistically, you need to know more about Littlethumb Brooks' early life, the past being an important indicator of all that may come next. Littlethumb is a full-blooded Wampanoag. From what I can find, the Wampanoag were one of the first tribes to greet the Pilgrims. I'm not going to delve into the tribe historically at this juncture, but you should read about them. Fascinating people with a rich history.

Littlethumb was the tribal name bestowed upon him by his grandfather Kicking Rocks. Raised in New York City, Littlethumb's parents came from a family unit who left the tribal lands, yet maintained respect for the dignity of their ancestral ways. They were "modern" folk, blending the sacred teachings and moral fiber of their DNA with the metropolitan culture of the day. Littlethumb's father was a man of stern spine, with an open, loving heart. His mother, an angel who floated on her feet and sang in her sleep. And as I type these words, Littlethumb places a photo of his family back on an end-table in the living room of the cabin. The photo includes his brother, Freddy, and sister, Heather, lost in their youth to the fabric of whatever we become in death, another hardship woven into the unfinished tapestry of Littlethumb Brooks' life.

Baby of the family, Littlethumb was a quiet, playful child who preferred thoughtful observation over the sound of his own voice. Odd? Sure, but no certain indicator for his genius. Though at the end of the day, when you decide how this all works, nature versus nurture, God's plan, chaos, fate, universal existential coding, or some weird but completely possible combination of all the above, it's reasonable to assume his unusually quiet nature as a child may have been a signal he was meant for an unusual life.

To wit, Littlethumb's artistic brilliance came on the backbone of unique, metaphysical, spiritual experience. I will leave the particulars for Littlethumb to explain later, in his own words. Got to keep you hungry for the entree, after all, though I will serve the following appetizer: As a ten-year-old boy, post unique metaphysical spiritual experience, Littlethumb Brooks painted an exact replica of Leonardo da Vinci's *Mona Lisa*.

Stop. Confirm. I said what I said. An *exact* replica of the *Mona Lisa*. Painted by a ten-year-old boy.

Several art critics have argued Littlethumb's version is more flawless than the original. I tend to agree, but we can hold that debate another day. Right now, I want to discuss his meteoric rise to fame and his ruinous association with fellow childhood star, punk-rocker Tommy Toxic.

What you have here, in Littlethumb Brooks, is a man blessed by a gift and burdened by tragic loss. A man filled with instinctual joy and a dreadfully cultivated, deeply-rooted sadness. A man caught dead center in the great compromise known as the balance of existence. The cosmic sway of good, evil, and the neither in between, where our hero is a blinding light. The shining example of how virtuous we all could be if we really gave a damn. Ever-enduring kindness, that's the soul of our man, the heart of his matter.

In his youth, Littlethumb's identity was kept secret, making a mystery out of who was creating his paintings. The plan was orchestrated by his grade school art teacher and mentor, Sawyer Pettimore. Sawyer turned the intrigue behind Littlethumb's amazing talent into a national phenomenon, and the first public exhibit of Littlethumb's artwork was deemed the perfect occasion to reveal the youngster's true identity. In accordance with life's cataclysmic nature, this was also the perfect opportunity for an expression of Tommy Toxic's psychotic rage.

The attention Littlethumb's talent garnered infuriated Tommy, who is a few years older than Littlethumb and at the time was succumbing to the fear of losing his own childhood stardom and therefore, in Tommy's juvenile mind, his relevance as a human. Littlethumb Brooks was a shiny new toy for American pop-culture. Jealousy demanded Tommy break the new shiny toy, and he did. The explosive device Tommy unleashed at Littlethumb's art exhibit cemented the inescapable connectivity of Tommy's and Littlethumb's lives. Though one could argue their entanglement was written in stone by the birth of the universe. Chaos or fate, chaos or fate…

Alright, almost enough of the horrible recollecting, though you do need to know one more piece of important information about Littlethumb's tragic art show. Once Tommy left the building and detonated his bomb, four people survived the explosion and ensuing fire. Littlethumb, Daring Bird, Sawyer Pettimore, and a kindhearted art groupie whom a young Sawyer Pettimore — feeling himself because he thought he was about to become a big deal — had taken as his date.

Horniness and a touch of cowardice provided Sawyer and his date their escape (i.e., they were having sex in the elevator and fled when the bomb went off). Littlethumb and Daring Bird escaped through the medicine man's hardwired grit and determination. Afterwards, suspicious the explosion was retaliation for the Electric Medicine Men's international mischief, Daring Bird took Littlethumb to Canada, where he raised his nephew in hiding.

Littlethumb sits on the couch. A monkey rests on each shoulder, with the third calmly nested atop Littlethumb's head. Tamarins are very small creatures. Littlethumb barely noticed Zeus mount his noggin. He rarely does.

Woofus is pressed in next to Littlethumb's left leg, cleaning a paw. A cup of tea steams on the coffee table. Next to the tea is an open laptop computer, displaying the surveillance feed of a child's bedroom.

Eyes closed, Littlethumb's mind is chasing feelings disguised as thoughts that don't want to be caught. Trying to chase down an emotion on the run is exhausting. "Come here, unsettled feeling," your mind will gasp, huffing and puffing, out of breath. "I'm not going to hurt you. I only want to know what you want from me," but the emotion wants nothing, my friend, except to exist.

His ruminations lead to thoughts of Maria. Always Maria. There she is, a multitude of images at once. Tossing her hair, laughing, shedding a tear, making love to him, pulling his hand as she joyfully bounds forward through the world. Surely you recognize this montage from television and movies, but hopefully, you have these loving memories of your own. Oh, and hopefully they are happy memories, experienced while the one you love is sitting across the room and you're staring at him, or her, or them, waxing nostalgic, feeling the warmth of a satisfied heart flush your skin. Because one of life's nasty little tricks is the fact that this slide show may bring you pain or joy. These exact same thoughts may warm your heart or drive you mad with grief. You pick.

In this moment, Littlethumb chooses stoic consideration. Channeling emotional energy toward rational analyzation. The sociopathic disassociation of critical thought. Pondering how the clock works. Is the clock's body full of gears, or a simple tiny motherboard of digital impulse? Is the burden of his gift the death of so many he loved? Could he have had one without the other? Must another bad thing happen for his abilities to return?

There it is! *Is that what I'm afraid of? Is this fear-based?* Maybe, Littlethumb, maybe, but what was the catalyst? What specifically inspired your block? His mind races back to the last time he remembers painting, but before he can get there, his phone rings. Zeus abandons his post atop Littlethumb's head to retrieve the phone. Sir Alister Pickney and Stevie Two Sharks give chase. Woofus dives under the coffee table, head low and tail hiding, always prepared for the worst.

12

Regarding Daring Bird's supposed fame, the trial Kumiko mentioned earlier involved Littlethumb's rediscovery as an adult. Though Daring Bird suffered about five minutes of almost-fame, after the proceedings he quietly went back to his mysterious life. Despite Kumiko's cagey press for information from the team, the average person would have no idea who Daring Bird Jones was if they passed him on the street.

Some of you will remember the court case well, having closely followed the proceedings. Most of you didn't watch the trial, though you may remember general details from the broadcast news, daily papers, and the internet. You might know that Uncle Daring Bird showed up dressed like an old lady and brought the entire trial to a screeching halt, but knowing this doesn't mean you can pick the real Daring Bird Jones out of a lineup. Yes, he took off the wig, but there was still the makeup and the fake boobs, and a bad floral-patterned dress. Not to mention the chaotic scene, when the courtroom devolved into madness following the revelation that Littlethumb Brooks was still alive.

The situation wasn't about Daring Bird, and his speedy retreat back into the shadows ensured that all the attention was focused on Littlethumb.

Enough jogging down memory lane. Let's settle back into the present, where Daring Bird is presently staring at a slightly oversized jack-in-the-box. Learning of *The Marias* theft was a surprising kick to the nut-sack, and if you've ever had your testicles so much as grazed, you will woefully recall the nauseating pain. (Ladies, I have no idea how to relay the horrible sensation for your intimate understanding, nor can I compare the misery to other painful phenomena such as birthing a child, which I, of course, can't imagine. I merely ask you to trust me. Being kicked in the nuts is shockingly awful.) For Daring Bird, *The Marias* collection is a spiritual artifact of an amazing human. An amazing human who completed a powerful spiritual circle with his nephew.

Although he once had to physically assault a grieving Littlethumb to prevent the paintings from being destroyed, Daring Bird believes their existence provides Littlethumb great strength. These portraits of a saintly woman travel the world, placing a vision of wide-open love on display. That once in a blue moon, some people really do have soulmates, written in the stars, reincarnated throughout the generations to find each other once again for one more once-in-a-blue-moon love. That "most will never have but all must believe is possible and should at least get a taste of" love.

Oh, I lied. Speaking of blue-moon love, there's one more store on memory lane where we should stop outside and window shop. Peering through the figurative glass, we see Daring Bird had true love in his past, stolen from him by the same devil who stole his nephew's. Daring Bird's secret paramour, C.C. Constantine, died in the fire the night of Littlethumb's childhood exhibit. The repercussions from calamitous events prove endless. See the Big Bang for further examples.

The medicine man has spent many hours pondering his choices in life, wondering if he should've left his self-imposed personal duty to the world behind and devoted himself to the love he was so lucky to have discovered. It's a tough conversation. Would she still have died, or might they have lived out their lives in an unencumbered unity of souls? Did he realize they had true love when she was alive? Or is this a trick his brain plays on him, rewriting his personal history, amplifying his loss for the sake of God knows what? Maybe their relationship was purely an awesome fling. Or is that the real trick? Convincing himself his mind is playing tricks on him with regard to the depth of his feelings for C.C., so he can more easily accept his loss?

Nonsense, all of it. Did he really love her? You're goddamn right he did. Goddamn right. For this particular subject, that's the one thought that matters. The rest are bullshit, exercises in futility, yet unavoidable, and consistently reoccurring. He can't control the ability of these thoughts to spring forth within him, all he can control is how he reacts to them. In an effort to boil all the nuance and emotional discourse of life down to a simple creed, Daring Bird will frequently offer the following piece of advice: Head down, feet forward.

Keep plugging away. Next steps. Focus your mind on what's next and let the rest wash away. Heal thyself, oh wise medicine man, heal thyself.

Speaking of plugging away, Daring Bird's next step is an unpleasant phone call to his nephew. Numbers are dialed and he hears the phone ring. You already know the monkeys are racing for the phone on Littlethumb's end, from last we left them. Zeus got the head start, but Sir Alister Pickney wins, returning the phone to his master with a triumphant screech.

"Hello," says Littlethumb.

"You sleeping?" asks Daring Bird. "You sound asleep."

"Nah, just thinking. Trying not to think."

"Waste of energy."

"Yup. What's up?"

"Tough news, kid."

"Awesome."

Comfortable silence rests between them. Whatever comes next may suck, but from thousands of miles away, and connected electronically, each man still feeds off the presence of the other.

"C'mon," Littlethumb restarts. "Out with it."

"The collection was stolen."

"Which collection?" Littlethumb speaks before really thinking.

"The collection."

"The whole thing?"

"The collection, kid. The whole damn thing."

"Right. Dumb question." There's a world record-level sigh right here, originating on Littlethumb's end of the line and wrapping its way around the world to die in Daring Bird's lungs, as he refills them to speak again.

"Okay, band-aid yanked. I feel better, so thanks for taking that off my plate."

"You're welcome. Glad I could help."

As I've quite recently begun to overexplain, there's a deluge of thought and emotional discourse coming for Littlethumb here, with regard to the stolen collection. At this juncture, I will spare you that gobbledygook, as Littlethumb chooses to spare himself. He takes a deep mental breath and tells himself to, *Stick to the facts, man, just the facts.* Fine. Ask a relevant question, brain.

"What the fuck?" he says.

"Yeah, I know."

"When?"

"About forty-eight hours ago, or so. There's been news coverage, but I figured you probably weren't watching or reading or you would have called."

"Where? Does Sawyer know?"

"France. Yes."

"C'mon. Don't make me keep asking questions. Lay it on me."

"Don't know much yet, I'm afraid," replies Daring Bird. "News reported a sophisticated heist in broad daylight. In the heart of Lyon."

Littlethumb abruptly realizes Mortimer Cross might be in trouble. "The old fella?"

"Minor injuries. Hospitalized locally, but according to Sawyer, he's sick from exposure. The entire security team was left stripped, bound, and gagged."

"That's putting on a show."

"Exactly what I thought. Which, I suppose, makes sense for an art heist."

"What about Saw? What's he know?"

"Not much. Multiple authorities have contacted him but not with any real information yet. Mostly asking him questions."

"Of course. Jesus. What are the odds they investigate this as an insurance fraud case?" Not a question from Littlethumb, so much as a reflection of an instinctual disrespect for the mechanics of law enforcement and the insurance industry.

"Less likely if no claim is filed, I suppose."

"Right. Hopefully. So what's next?"

"I'm gonna scoot up to Lyon, find out what Cross remembers. Go from there."

"Gotcha. Any news on our cousin?" Littlethumb and Daring Bird definitely have cousins, but in this instance, cousin is code for the curious jack-in-the-box sitting in front of Daring Bird. Honestly, the codeword is unnecessary here, as they're on a secure line and scarcely maintaining a secretive conversational tone as it is. I could lie and tell you their communications are always brilliantly secure through impeccably coded dialogue but, despite their fully developed system, flawless adherence to protocol ain't realistically human. Besides, you're willing to buy inconsistencies in half-assed filmmaking on a regular basis. Including documentaries. Reasonable, then, you should purchase some here. Get a giant real-sugar soda and a tub of butter-smothered popcorn for a snack while you read, if it helps.

"Nope," Daring Bird replies. "Other than he likes to travel."

"Copy that."

"Anything new in your world?"

"Actually, yes. A curiosity, but we'll save that for later. I haven't quite taken its pulse yet."

"Fair enough. Heads on swivels, I always say."

"Since when?"

"Hmph. Since now. I mean, I'm pretty sure I've said it before, but damn, Silas is beginning to rub off on me, I think."

"You know, my daddy always told me…" Littlethumb starts, then Daring Bird finishes with…

"…never let yourself be anything other than what you may already be."

An earnest chuckle helps clear the air in each man's room. Life is nothing but hard times, laughter, and the spaces in between. I love laughter, but those spaces in between may be the actual best parts.

"Alright, I'm gonna get moving," Daring Bird says. "Stay safe." *I love you, kid.*

"Copy that, you too." *I love you too.*

Daring Bird ends the call and sets down the satphone. A few seconds pass, and he realizes he forgot to mention Hope. *Dammit,* he thinks, but before he starts beating himself up or debating whether or not to call his nephew back, there's a rap at the door.

"Yeah?"

Jimmy the Tweaker enters the room. "What's the scoop?"

"I've got to sneak up to Lyon. Find out what Cross knows."

"I know this goes without saying, but I'ma do it anyway. Breaking your own rules, boss."

"I suppose that's what they're made for, life being so melodramatic and silly."

"What do I tell the gang?"

"Whatever you want. Truth is fine with me. But no one leaves."

"Not a chance. I'll hypnotize everyone of 'em if I have to, but I won't." Jimmy, so you know, has a very slick instantaneous hypnosis technique he created and refined during years spent as a successful con artist. I would describe the technique to you here, but in doing so you would effectively be under my control, and I can't have that on my conscience. Just don't be surprised if you start barking at squirrels.

"What about that thing?" Jimmy nods at the device.

"Stays with you until I get back."

"Great. Remind me again how it's not a bomb."

"It's not a bomb."

"Thanks. Much better. Feel much better now."

13

Among the many life choices our evil despot makes in reverence of his Grandpa Adolph, Xander Blowfly owns a secret underground bunker. The bunker was designed by Parsnook Kronen, a Swede, and one of the world's most sought-after design architects by evil syndicates. Kronen's bunkers, lairs, and torture chambers are renowned for their elegant yet utilitarian Feng Shui.

Located south of Sirte, Libya, the land purchase was negotiated by Xander's secret identity, Conrad Somvinslodkin, with the late Muammar Gaddafi. Due to Conrad's work for Russian Intelligence, Conrad and Muammar were friendly. The notorious dictator had been more than happy to facilitate the sale of a worthless swath of desert to Conrad's associate. Noting, of course, the various strings attached, including but not limited to monthly taxation, quarterly inspection, and potential confiscation. Offering to double the tax payment successfully squashed the quarterly inspection clause, while tolerating potential confiscation is simply the price of doing business with a dictator, whose agreements are always tenuous. Although, from time to time, you get lucky. Upon Gaddafi's death, with Libya embroiled in a civil war, Xander has doubled his operations and his profits in the region.

Anticipating the arrival of his most recent prize, Xander travels from his domestic residence in Denmark to the bunker, where his shipment from their facility in Guinea-Bissau should have already been waiting for him. What in the hell was he thinking, sending the shipment by that route? The rhino horns and elephant tusks in Tifariti could have been shipped on their own. Why didn't he send the slaves and his device on a more direct path? Such precious cargo. But nooooooo. Instead, he sent them to pick up the crates of ivory in Tifariti. Stupid efficiency obsession.

Forget the cost savings! I'm telling you, saving money held no bearing. He's got money coming out of his ears! It was his damn compulsive need for efficiency! Whatever. He will take his mistake out on someone else at a later date. Most likely the entire squadron who lost D-13. (D-13 is the name I've discovered in my notes for Xander's device, representing successful completion of the invention on his thirteenth attempt.)

The loss of D-13 is a bitter pill to swallow, tapping at Xander's good humor like an angry sculptor's chisel. Perusing his new collection should at the very least provide a temporary distraction from his frustrations, and there's business at hand. To juice the market before his auction, Xander made a limited number of the *Marias* available for presale. The pre-ordered works must be prepped for delivery, which includes the installation of imperceptible surveillance devices in their frames. These buyers were specifically chosen due to Xander's interest in spying on them.

Among them is a cattle tycooning hedge fund manager looking to class up his midwestern climate-catastrophe bunker. There's a sheik who will hang his purchase in the main sexy chamber of a small harem palace, built far away from his main palace out of respect for his honorable wife. There's a fossil fuel baron who's reserved space on a wall in the panic room of his solar-powered yacht. Of course the yacht is solar powered. You've got to do the simple things to offset all the self-enriching, purposeful destruction of a planet.

A painting will hang in the mansion of a murderous drug kingpin, specific location of the stereotypical South American drug cartel compound unknown, and I'm not sure who purchased the painting headed for the South Pacific. I daydream about an *Island of Doctor Moreau* scenario, but the book version. Not the godawful Marlon "Buckethead" Brando film version.

One more shining example, and a relatively new entry into the annals of human douchebaggery. There's a brilliant Silicon Valley tech superstar engineer social media mogul waiting on his purchase. This self-fellating edgelord will stash his painting in the cargo area of the spaceship he's building so he can winter in orbit and live his sociopathic disassociated sentient human robot persona to the fullest degree.

Along with having constructed his own Bear Führer bunker, Xander wears a tooth around his neck in honor of his grandfather. The tooth currently twists in the fingers of his left hand as he stares at the first specimen in three long rows of paintings.

Magnificent, he thinks. *They're all so beautiful.*

But where is the one? One of these masterpieces excels above all the others and is destined for the highest honor: adornment on the wall of the office from which the complete alteration of the modern world will be planned and executed.

Where is she?

Clear your head, Xander, and enjoy the splendor before you. Clear your head, and heed the call. One of these portraits is speaking to you. One of these portraits announces its supremacy. Do you hear it? Don't worry, you will. In a few minutes, she will steal the breath from your lungs for a second time, as she did not long ago.

Xander Bowfly's first in-person viewing of *The Marias* came early in the collection's tour of Europe. The paintings were on display at the Rijksmuseum in Amsterdam. A vigorous art enthusiast, Xander had followed the story of the collection and its enigmatic creator very closely. Littlethumb Brooks' disappearance, shortly after the death of his wife, had generated fresh intrigue around the young painter's work and captured the fascination of our villain sophisticate.

This is a flashback recounting Xander's first trip to view the collection in person, described here in a two-step process. Step one, he stood for an extended period with his jaw hung open, damn near in a pleasure-induced coma. Step two, he recovered the ability to speak and uttered the words, "Breathtaking. Simply, breathtaking." He was surprised, but not startled, to receive a response.

"Yes, she is." The author of the response didn't plan on speaking to a stranger. The words blurted forth on their own.

Xander turns to see a roguishly handsome figure gazing at the artwork. "I've forgotten time, and may easily have grown old where I stand."

"Yeah, this guy's work tends to do that to you." How serendipitous to have been passing through town while his nephew's artwork was on display. That's right…

"Your accent. You're American?"

"Yes. Wampanoag."

"Ah. A lovely people."

"Yes, they are." Daring Bird offers a curious expression to the stranger, question implied.

"History buff," says Xander.

"I would say so." Both men return their gaze to the beautiful woman, whose heart appears to beat right out of the portrait in front of them.

"It feels a silly game, to measure these works against one another, but I do believe this one is my very favorite. I'm not quite sure why, any more than I could express what makes any of this work so profound, but this one seems to have stolen my will to walk away."

"I suppose, at the end of the day, that's what it was created to do."

"Hmph. Yes. I suppose so."

Another quiet moment as both men bask in the glow of holy beauty, then Daring Bird says, "Well, I should make my escape while I can, before I wind up glued to the floor next to you."

"If you happen across someone in pain, tell them where to find the cure."

"Indeed. Will do, sir. Good day to you."

"Good day to you."

❀ ❀ ❀

There are two reasons I shared the previous flashback, twos being a theme in this chapter. The first is to reinforce this message: Among the many amazing portraits on display in our evil villain's underground lair, there is one he covets above all others. There is one painting that made his black heart sing hallelujah and put this whole scheme in motion. I don't recall the second reason for the flashback, but here we are anyway, as Xander walks along the first row of *Marias*.

My god, he thinks. *I had already forgotten their effect in person. How did he do this?*

Xander hasn't genuinely forgotten their effect. The memory of his reaction to their splendor is what drove him to steal the collection in the first place. What Xander alludes to is the heavenly physiological reaction he feels in the presence of the paintings. Once removed, your memory can recall the profound sensation, but the pleasing chemical dump is not produced by memory. It's produced by presence. Kind of like remembering sex feels incredible, but you don't make the goofy expressions or grunty noises when you're recollecting, the way you do when physically connecting. You smoking from my bowl here? Picking up what I'm laying down?

I'm going to fill in some details on ol' D-13 while Xander makes his way through the stolen art collection. We've got a few minutes until Xander finds the specific portrait he's looking for. I figure discussing his invention is more useful than blubbering on about a villain's appreciation for art.

D-13 was a happy accident. Don't get me wrong, Xander built the device on purpose. However, its ability to function developed by chance (*chaos or fate or fate or fate…*), the end result of intense mathematical effort over the course of multiple sleepless days spent under the influence of very powerful designer drugs. Drugs of Xander's own creation, chemical mixology having been one of his most revered talents while employed as a government stooge. In this instance, the drug of choice was a neurosteroid designed to enhance the brain circuitry responsible for processing numbers. Compounded with methamphetamine for energy and hallucinogens for creativity, and you've got a mathematician's dream cocktail, if said mathematician is insane and willing to risk forever losing the use of a functional brain.

After crashing from his drug induced mathematical bender, Xander woke several days later to discover he had written a randomized algorithm for quantifying the probability of creating a unique invention.

D-13 is the artificial intelligence running this algorithm. In other words, Xander built an invention designed to figure out how to build another invention.

The trick is, he doesn't know how D-13's algorithm works. The sequence of instructions is so expansive, retracing his steps was next to impossible. The fact that he wrote the algorithm on a whiteboard, carrying over onto the walls of his lab, carrying over onto tabletops, empty food containers, into notebooks, and ultimately onto his own skin, doesn't help. I'm not sure how in the hell he managed to input the whole mess into a computer.

What I do know, and what Xander has ascertained, is that somewhere in the algorithm a mathematical error must exist. An impossible to find mathematical error. Somehow, when he entered the algorithmic "ifs, ands, or buts" into his program, he made a mistake that caused D-13 to work. Which I suppose is an accident, rather than a mistake. Call it what you will, Xander can't duplicate his efforts. But…what if…but…

No. He can't. Which means the stolen device is one of a kind, both in form and function. A self-contained singularity. A singularity with a sole purpose, whose self-improvement cycles are bent toward one specific outcome, one specific "find."

Perhaps Xander's invention isn't a singularity in the manner classically defined by real-world scientists or science fiction writers, but it damn sure will be if ever connected to another intelligent machine and exposed to knowledge outside its own programming. Thus, for all other intents and purposes, Xander is giving himself credit as such. To his knowledge, in his drug-induced creative frenzy, he invented a scientific dream baby, and now his dream baby is gone.

Suddenly, so is the negative emotional residue affecting his enjoyment of the spectacular art before him. There she is. Four spots down from the end of the third row, her angelic beckoning an irresistible force in Xander's mind. Come to me, child, and lay thine eyes upon the meaning of the world, the beating heart of woman, mother of all nature and wonder.

Each of these paintings depicts the same woman in all her glory, yet for Xander, this one is the most glorious. Behold, Maria.

For a moment, everything washes away. His grand schemes, the loss of his device, the comparatively disappointing loveliness of his own wife. (A physically beautiful woman possessing an exceptional capacity for coping with her husband's evil, despotic ways. Pray, spend money, pray, spend money, pray…spend more money.)

In case you're wondering, I have a distinct purpose for not describing these paintings. I know exactly what they look like, so don't be snarky. I have a very clear memory of them, in my mind's eye. I'm not being lazy. And if you're upset because I'm not spoon-feeding you mental imagery, then I ask you, who's really being lazy?

Imagine on your own the most exquisite painting you can, the euphoria viewing said painting creates, and the unyielding adoration and desire the artist had for his subject. Then, go out and find something to make you feel the same way. That is my wish for you, fellow human. Find the object of your heart's desire. Do so in a fair, ethical, lawful way, and then cherish what you've found for the rest of your days. I've missed my boat and have nothing left but to tell these stories. I don't want you suffering the same misfortune.

Oh, the tooth. Yes. Forgot for a second. The tooth around Xander's neck I mentioned earlier.

The tooth is supposedly Hitler's first bicuspid. There's no way to prove this, as the Führer's body was repeatedly burned to the point of nothingness. This is a fact. I assume the repeated burnings were understandably grotesque entertainment, performed by Russian soldiers far from home, plagued by the misery of war-torn brains and vodka-tainted blood. Whether my assumption is correct or not, history confirms Hitler's and Eva's bodies were either thrown in a bomb crater and incinerated or set aflame in another similar variation of this scenario. What history doesn't tell you is that Andrei Somvinslodkin had pulled one of Hitler's teeth as a memento for the Führer's secret lovechild.

Xander can't prove the tooth belonged to his grandfather. The rest of Hitler's remains were destroyed beyond any possible hope of DNA testing. Thus, the tooth is merely a symbol, a totem of his evil lineage that serves as a rubbing stone for contemplative moments, when the use of a habitual physical movement suits the type of person Xander wants to be, and who he wants to be seen as: the thinking man's villain. And yet, this thinking man still can't settle on the perfect name for his organization. Maybe the Iron Tornado? The name doesn't quite have the same phonetic ring as The Iron Waffle, but it does make more sense, especially if you consider the violent, innate malevolence of a tornado as analogous to the machinations of an evil organization seeking global dominance. Also, the acronym for The Iron Tornado spells T.I.T., which Xander finds hilarious. After all, who's afraid of a tit?

Is that irony? I think that might be irony.

So, I looked up the meaning of irony again. From what I can tell, irony is basically sarcastic oppositism, so I don't think the concept of being afraid of a titty is ironic so much as silly. Either way, I'm going to abstain from using the word irony until I have a better handle on its proper application. Ahem. Cough.

14

Who are we if other people don't hear our innermost thoughts? Imagined versions of ourselves? How do we trust these inner-knowings without external validation? These questions boggle Daring Bird's mind as he tries to fall asleep, denying him the rest and rejuvenation he needs.

Is our self-perception honest?

Ha! Not always. There's lunacy, and addiction, and self-preservation, and all other manner of outward or inward forces that influence a person's understanding of their inner-being. Self-awareness will travel so far, to the edge of the cliff, if you will, before we're forced to turn back and save ourselves from the fall. The deep plummet into a frightening, dark ravine of everything we are, which includes unmistakably broken pieces. The horrific, scattered remains of our stable self. A graveyard of broken toys, lost friendships, tattered dreams, and irrevocable real-world mistakes. All the unavoidable failures and character flaws our existence insists we must live with, locked away somewhere deep in the psychiatric ward of our mind, protected under lock and key by an imaginary synaptic nurse named Ms. Keep Me Sane.

We share ourselves as best we can, our boundaries often set by the role we've chosen to play in life. Daring Bird is a hero, which means he must operate with an open heart. These are the rules of the game. To stand in the eye of the storm wielding abundant, courageous love.

A restless mind switches to thoughts of trees and their stoic nature. Two meters into a poem Daring Bird is creating and reciting to himself against his own will, his eyes roll back in his head and he starts to tremor. Stout convulsions are followed by high-level twitching and one stiff-legged kick straight up into the air.

I'm going to wait for Daring Bird to discuss the vision he's having. Right here, we're going to focus on how all his thrashing about wakes up Kumiko. She rolls over on her stomach and raises her naked torso off the bed, resting on her forearms, staring down at the medicine man as he shivers. I told you Daring Bird was horny. Turns out, Kumiko was too.

The team was upset with Daring Bird for having broken his own rules, and rightfully so. They understood the need to visit Mortimer Cross and would admit this sort of behavior from Daring Bird is uncommon, but they still didn't appreciate the precedent set by his actions. No one, and I mean no one, enjoys "do as I say and not as I do" leadership. If you're a youngster taking in this tale, I beg you to remember this as you age into a leader. Please, be honest and diligent in your duties, and play by the same rules you impose upon others.

Moving along…after appearing as the bound, gagged, and unconscious leader of a security detail earlier in the book, there will be no more cameo appearances for Mortimer Cross. Please know he's a trustworthy friend and willing cohort, and will fully recover from the pneumonia he's suffering. Fortunately, despite his illness, the old soldier was able to provide some useful information. For instance, as you already know, the assailants used non-lethal ammunition. A rare, albeit intelligent, maneuver. If caught, limiting the possibility for murder charges was no small thing.

Another curiosity, though not necessarily uncommon for evil organizations, is a matching tattoo Cross noticed on the thieves he fought. And what were the tattoos of, you might ask? Obviously, as part of this narrative nonsense, the tattoos were of a single word: Trope. (Noodles and kaboodles!)

Just kidding. Just kidding. The tattoos Cross saw were a sinister variation of the familiar theatrical comedy and tragedy masks, neatly hidden behind the left ears of his attackers. Between you and me, the tattoo was an early option for the gang's logo, during a period of consideration for naming Xander's organization the Theatre of Pain. Though Xander scrapped the idea for the name, he decided the logo was an excellent, ubiquitous mark for his employees to recognize one another, while not being so unusual when viewed by outsiders as to be seen for anything more than a poor choice of personal style.

FYI, though we're still fairly early in the story, moving forward, while continuing to gracefully (and not so gracefully…) utilize many of your favorite rhetorical devices, I will be leaving behind the explicitly fourth wall breaking, "Hey everyone! Look! Here's a trope!" jokes, having binged through the trilogy faster than expected. You're welcome.

Several weeks have passed since Kumiko's and Daring Bird's first squishy tango (a generously affective coupling of genitals and souls).

Their first dance came as a matter of presumed contrivance, a convenience, where each partner thought they had taken the lead. Here's how the sticky-get-down went down:

Upon returning to the safe house from his trip to see Cross, Daring Bird found Kumiko awake and alone. In an attempt to distract her from his sneaking around, he seduced her. Or so he thought. Turns out, the sharper blade to their double-edged seduction belongs to Kumiko, who decided after their first meeting that she would readily employ her most satisfying interrogation technique on the handsome, curious devil. What better opportunity than when the man thinks he's marshaling the parade?

Playful arguments can be had about who seduced whom, but the answer doesn't matter. What matters is they discovered a true affinity for one another, exposed through a feverish display of passion during what was supposed to be a pragmatic yet physically pleasing exercise. I'm not going to go so far as to call the situation love at first coitus, but I will say they both immediately recognized what they had done. Can o' worms opened, ladies and gentlemen. If either of them saw this coming before they were cumming, they had effortlessly lied to themselves about the potential outcomes of their potential actions.

To be blunt, the sex was so good, just thinking about it, I can't talk right after neither. Have a smoke. I am. A voyeur smoke. A jealousy smoke. A "what am I doing with my introverted storytelling non-relations-having life" smoke.

You can't hide the intense afterglow inspired by phenomenal sex. Hell, trying to hide the "I'm somewhat better than I was yesterday" twinkle from average sex is near impossible (let alone the dank residue smeared all over your aura from disappointing sex…). The rest of the Electric Medicine Men immediately caught wind of the affair. In a unit this tight, there isn't much any member can successfully hide from the others, and Daring Bird's attraction to Kumiko was impossible to conceal. After the required period of safe house confinement came to an end, the team wasn't surprised to see Daring Bird wish them farewell without having packed his own bags. Frankly, his mates silently encouraged their leader to lay a little hay and roll around in it. Lord knows the man needed some loving.

The rest of the team went their separate ways to await further instructions. Garo Kasabian headed back to his family and deli, and the happy confines of domestic life. His next assignment likely to arrive in the nick of time, when he's desperate to get the hell out of there and satisfy his recurring need for adventure.

Silas took off to find someplace to party where there are plenty of women and no boats. First stop, the prolific nightlife and pale-skinned wonders of Prague. As the old saying goes, "What happens in Vegas may stay in Vegas, but only in Prague is what happens in Prague."

Speaking of Las Vegas, Jimmy the Tweaker and Bebiana traveled to the City of Sin. Jimmy has a son there who's a fellow hypnotist, currently on a "rise" portion in the rise and fall of his life. This would be the first chance for Bebiana to meet Jimmy's son, and despite her tough as nails persona, the Brazilian Bitch was nervous.

Lastly, no one has a clue where Titus the Nazarene dashed off to. God knows where to do God knows what. I swear the Nazarene may actually be an alien, or an angel, or an as-yet-unnamed immortal Earthly creature neither science nor fiction has discovered.

Back to the present. A Daring Bird Jones and a Kumiko Something-Or-Other are presently in between sweaty sheets. They've huffed and puffed and blown each other's houses down. Had some sex. Some good, kind, bangin' of the bedposts. That's what was done. Healthy. Yes ma'am. Oh to not suffer from irrational sexual hang-ups brought on by the mendacious religious programming of your childhood…

Kumiko lights a cigarette as she watches Daring Bird have what we know to be a vision. For the most part, he looks like he's having a mild seizure, though Kumiko somehow instinctually knows this is something else. Perhaps because the dude's freaking name is Daring Bird.

The trembling stops and Daring Bird opens his eyes, looking up to see Kumiko staring down at him. Disorientation is followed by a satisfied smile. May everything wrong with this world be damned, when waking up to a human so lovely.

"Bad dream?" she asks.

"Something like that," he lies. Daring Bird pushes himself up in the bed and borrows Kumiko's cigarette for a drag. "Sorry if I woke you."

"That's okay. It's been a while since I was kicked in bed. I don't mind."

Daring Bird places the cigarette back between Kumiko's lips and strokes her hair. Several days and nights of making whoopie have broken the ice for personal revelations. This is dangerous. He knows, and so does she. They're both compromised, and the revealing of secrets begins.

"I work for the Department of Agriculture," says Kumiko, stabbing the cigarette out in a tray on the bedside table.

"Oh. I suppose that makes sense."

Kumiko raises her head to study Daring Bird. Not a hint of sarcasm in his eyes. *He's good,* she thinks. *This man would never break.* "You aren't surprised?"

"Of course I'm surprised," he admits. "Not that you're an agent. That was fifty-fifty."

"Fifty-fifty?"

"Take no offense, please. I assume everyone is working for someone. It's one of the reasons I'm not dead. You have a fantastic cover."

"I'm still insulted." She pinches his left nipple, harder than one might find tantalizing.

"What the hell is the Department of Agriculture doing operating a safe house in France?"

"I'm a Special Agent for the Office of the Inspector General. Undercover the last seven years."

"And several days."

"That was terrible." Another nipple squeeze, this one more playful. Daring Bird pulls her hand away and kisses it, then wraps her arm across his chest.

"Do you know the first Commissioner of the Department of Agriculture was named Isaac Newton?" he asks.

"Yes, I do, but why do you?"

"I read a lot." A moment of silence as he thoughtlessly strokes Kumiko's skin. Of all the sex all the humans have had since the beginning of existence, I am boggled by the countless subjects addressed during pillow talk. Stop and imagine for yourself the absurd nature of humping like craven beasts... — I know, I know, sex can be gentle and romantic and boring — ...like craven beasts, then casually discussing how you might actually feel about one another, personal spiritual philosophy, the mechanics of politics, what you might like for lunch, or who is taking which child where that afternoon. To be clear, this is not a negative commentary. I simply find the whole goddamn deal, our lives in all their facets, abundantly comical. Including the pain.

"It's funny though, right?" Daring Bird continues. "The first Department of Agriculture Commissioner has the same name as the guy who realized gravity existed by watching fruit."

"Yes. It is funny. Maybe not laugh out loud funny, but I am laughing on the inside. I promise."

"Hmph. I think I like the smart-ass version of you."

"I hope so. She's the one you've been sleeping with."

"We ain't been sleeping, darlin'." There's more sex right here. I'm sure you know how the Carolina Sunrise goes. You're welcome to cover your eyes.

Man, that early combination of lust and possible love. Though I'm not particularly a huge fan myself, I will readily admit there's nothing quite like it. My discomfort with the situation is a me problem, not a grand statement on the dichotomy of humans as instinctual animals versus humans as creatures gifted with the ability and self-awareness to rise above their animal nature toward something greater. Or whether those two concepts are mutually exclusive.

Imagine how clinical and insincere sex might become if we approached intercourse with nothing but a stoic, scientific mind. Yet, to counter my own point, research has already shown a little scientific study of pleasure and anatomy might assist many humans in better lovemaking. Of course, better lovemaking is a tiny factor in what I mean about rising above our animal nature. I'm talking about everything we can accomplish if we train ourselves to control our base desires for pleasure and seek something of greater significance within. But with thoughts like that, we're diverging from science to spirituality and belief in an inner-being capable of elevation, where one might operate from a higher level of existence, and suddenly I'm reminded of the real problem here. Do you see?

"We've got to stop overthinking the simple things," a middle-aged man says to himself, halfway through the game, standing there with the damn ball in his hands, frozen in place by indecision. Call a damn timeout and set up a play, dummy!

The previous aside was brought to you by my lack of interest for intimately describing a sex scene. You may uncover your eyes, we're safe. Kumiko and Daring Bird have taken a break from their workout to catch their breath. The conversation resumes. Daring Bird speaks first.

"Why are you here? I'm aware the Ag Department has an unusual purview, but any guessing how you wound up here, that's an exercise in futility."

"Happenstance. I made choices to maintain my cover, and eventually those choices led me here."

"But what's your assignment? I mean, as long as we're exposing ourselves."

"General inquiry. My principal duty is to root out corruption inside the department. With the import and export of international goods, and our efforts to end food insecurity in other countries, we have thousands of agents involved in economies around the world. The system is rife with corruption."

"Of course. And I presume a wealth of information can be gathered when operating an underground safe house."

"You presume correctly."

"So why are you telling me any of this?"

"I've known about your team for several years. I enjoy your work."

"No kidding." Daring Bird is admittedly surprised, and a bit concerned. "When you say known?"

"Don't worry, yet. Although your team is on our government's radar, they haven't identified you, and for the most part they aren't trying very hard. Every action traced back to you and your team has generally played into our hands. Basically, from what anyone back home can tell, you're harmless."

"Eh. That doesn't exactly make me feel great. Don't get me wrong, I assumed we were on someone's radar." A lightbulb goes off right here. "How did you know?"

"Know what?"

"Who we are. How did you know?"

"I didn't."

Son of a bitch! You just confirmed it, dickhead. You just told her! Fucking. Rookie.

The expression of recognition on Daring Bird's face is like a giant neon sign. Kumiko almost feels guilty. "Don't be upset," she says. "I'm excellent at my job."

"Yes, yes you are. Well played."

"You didn't give it away. I meant I didn't know when you arrived, but I placed wires after your team did their sweep. I heard enough...before." Kumiko's pause is a touch of playful bashfulness, as her use of the word "before" references their gorging on one another's erogenous buffets.

"Again, why are you telling me this?" There is a not-so-gentle, foreboding squeeze of Kumiko's body from Daring Bird right here. A subconscious act and unfortunate threat he did not intend on making.

"Why do you think?" she replies, squeezing herself even more tightly into him. "I'm alone and I've compromised myself. You tell me?"

Daring Bird could offer a myriad of potential explanations for her admission, with varying degrees of lies or truths, fitting into three categories: trying to help, trying to trick him, or because telling him is of zero consequence to her. He chooses, "Surprise, physically satisfied confessional?"

"My God, the ego of man. I'm not telling you this because you're decent in the sack." It's a playful jab. She knows his response was flip. He's fishing for the answer from her because there are so many possibilities, including the one answer so simple it's difficult for a man in his position to accept.

"Decent!?" The icy look of confirmation lets Daring Bird know Kumiko is pushing his buttons. He can assume he's more than decent and move on. Let it go, phallic pride. Let it go. "Decent!?" He couldn't help himself. "Alright, alright. You're trying to help us. I appreciate it, sincerely."

"You're welcome."

"Not so fast. You forced me to say it, instead of saying it yourself. I respect that. Now I want to hear you tell me why."

"People believe things more when the words come out of their own mouths."

"Uh uh. Nice try, but that's not the 'why' I'm looking for and you know it. I'm invoking quid pro quo. Why are you trying to help us?"

"I respect your work. This world is covered in a blanket of gray compromise. You can't defeat evil with compromise, and you can't fight darkness with a flickering candle. We're in a constant war and most of the good guys are gray. Governments are gray. My job is gray. Your team, you, others like you, you're the bright light in the interrogation room. You're the light. The world needs you."

"Fuck me, lady, I…I don't know what to say."

"Say thank you. Then say 'fuck me, lady' again."

"I can do both those things."

More sex. Fifty-three minutes later, more cigarettes, fresh coffee, and more chit chat. We listen back in as Kumiko speaks. "There's a double agent in our department. We haven't identified who the person is, but I've been gathering data on them. I believe they're taking orders, at least some of their orders, from whoever built the device you stole."

"Did you know about that thing before we got here?"

"Theoretically. We intercepted communications about something having been built and placed in transit, but we couldn't trace the communications. We don't know what the device is or who built it."

"Of course not. I'm rarely that lucky."

"I don't know," says Kumiko, "I think you're very lucky." There's a moment for an extremely delicate kiss right here, finished off with a bite of his bottom lip, reminding Daring Bird of just how lucky he is. Then she rolls over on her back and says, "It would be foolish not to assume the mole is aware the device exists, or that whoever built it knows your team stole it from them. Everyone will be looking for you."

"I figured as much." There's a pause right here as recognition sets in, then Daring Bird says, "Exactly who do you mean, everyone?"

End scene. Lights out. Exeunt stage left. All the world being a stage and whatnot…

15

While Daring Bird shacks up with Kumiko, Littlethumb endures several weeks of chess and bullshit with Redy Sinclair, not to mention a handful of excellent sparring sessions versus Master Chee. Pieces fly from the chessboard, bruises accumulate, and days are exed off the calendar.

The relationship between Littlethumb and Redy develops in the same manner as the armies on the checkered battlefield are deployed: intentionally. Meticulously. And though I said chess and bullshit, the truth is Littlethumb and Redy discuss all facets of life but their intimate personal lives. Both are perceptive of the game the other is playing. A veiled march toward familiarity, where abject emotional truths and general philosophic beliefs are openly shared without any context of personal history. Each may know how the other feels about the deliberate scam of trickle-down economics, but neither has said a word nor asked the other about family or childhood. The challenge of who will drop the pretense first is as eager as the battles between the tiny black and white soldiers. Redy is plotting a crime.

Littlethumb is biding time. Until what or when, I do not know, and neither does he.

Whether an interview is Redy's true motivation or not, Littlethumb enjoys his company. The guy is intelligent and thoughtful and has a quick wit that isn't afraid of taking a sharp left turn. Yet, there's an edge to him. An aggressiveness to Redy's opinions that doesn't sit comfortably with Littlethumb, though such behavior can easily be written off as youthful passion.

This situation is similar to his friendship with Tommy, who casually forced his way into Littlethumb's adult life, though Tommy had at least been a childhood acquaintance. Redy is a complete unknown. Then again, on the plus side, the odds of Redy having murdered several hundred people before he was fifteen are pretty slim.

I suppose the biggest difference between this situation and his relationship with Tommy Toxic is Littlethumb's current frame of mind. Our guy is treading water, both emotionally and spiritually, and has been doing so for a dangerous amount of time. Inescapable sadness can wreak havoc on our rational processes.

Does Littlethumb realize he's reached this place emotionally? Does he understand the full extent to which his mental distress is affecting his behavior? Of course not. How could he, when these very things are preventing him from operating at nominal capacity?

Even the wise may be shortsighted in the present, as wisdom is often the apprentice of hindsight.

And now there's the theft of his paintings to deal with. Esta vida es muy complicado, or something like that…

For Redy, the gamesmanship serves to moisten his monster's wolf-ish lips. Assuming there's no logic in the thought processes of crazy is a mistake. Insanity can be very logical, but the logic always initiates from an incorrect (or unstable, if you will…) starting place. The hunter has cornered his prey. What comes next is inevitable. Why not savor this moment? I've no argument against doing so, young Redy, save for the countless occasions when savoring the moment has bitten a villain in the ass. Then again, who said you were a villain?

Here we are again at the First Church of Good Deeds on a quiet afternoon. Most of the shelter's regular guests are out enjoying pleasant weather, doing whatever they do. The chessboard is freshly reset. Redy opens the game by advancing his king's pawn to center.

Not for nothing, the win-loss record is consistently balanced or tilted in Redy's favor. On occasion, Littlethumb will take a small lead. Perhaps to serve notice as to who is really in control of this situation. More often than not, however, Littlethumb allows Redy the advantage. Or so he thinks. For all we know, Redy is allowing Littlethumb to think he is allowing Redy the advantage. For all we know, God is a donut and the universe is his hole. Such is the nature of mortal conflict and pastries.

"You know," Littlethumb says, "I applaud your patience. These last few weeks must have been annoying."

"I'm not sure I understand," replies Redy. "I've thoroughly enjoyed our games and our conversations."

"Yes, but you came here with a purpose." Littlethumb fianchettos his bishop to square g2. "I feel like I've been a bit of a jerk."

"How so?"

"Well, I'm ashamed to admit it, but I haven't been completely forthright. I have an idea you already know this, and you've been very patient about the whole situation."

I'll be damned, thinks Redy. *I did it. He's breaking.*

To be frank, over the last few days, Redy's patience was in peril of giving out. Phase two, the second and final phase of his not-quite-completely-thought-out plan, has been scratching at his door, begging to move forward. This surprising turn by his adversary catches Redy off guard. How to respond, how to respond?

"Honestly, I was surprised you introduced yourself as Smith." Here comes the queen again, as Redy moves his most powerful piece off the back line of the board and into attack position.

"Yeah, old habits die hard."

"But why Smith? I mean, your identity trial was what, three or four years ago? And pretty highly publicized. Anyone who knows who you are probably knows you were using the name Smith."

"Would it have mattered if I had said Tom Jones? You already knew who I was."

Before answering Littlethumb's question, Redy backs his queen away from a trap, then looks up to see Littlethumb grinning. "What?"

"Tom Jones makes me laugh."

"Who's Tom Jones?"

"Uhm, possibly the most bad-ass crooner of his generation. Look him up."

"What's a crooner?"

"Fuck you, buddy."

"Ha! I'm messing with you, man. I know who Tom Jones is. 'What's Up Pussycat,' right?"

"'What's New Pussycat,' but yes. Thinking about it makes me laugh every time. And I don't care if it was written for a movie. The song is absurd, and this dude sang it with such ridiculous bravado and made it a massive hit."

"This is a cruel and stupid world."

"Yes, it is."

"But I still don't understand. Why Smith? Why an alias at all, if you presumed I knew who you were?"

"Well, I'm in hiding. I meet a stranger. I use my secret identity. Everyone around here calls me Smith as it is."

"But it's not a secret. Your trial, and the live painting shows, and the concert with Tommy…" Redy trails off here. The hesitancy is contrived.

"It's okay, Redy. I know. If nothing else about my life stuck with people, when Maria died, I know it was a big deal in the news. But fame is very fleeting, and it's not like I was famous for a long time anyway. I promise you, a few years out of the public eye and I can walk down a crowded street and almost no one sees Littlethumb Brooks. All they see is a man. Or, for some, unfortunately, a dark-skinned man they aren't too sure about, so they better be careful of."

"I guess I have to take your word for it, it being your life and your experience."

"Probably for the best."

"But if that's the case, if you're correct, why are you hiding up here? What's the point?"

"Jesus, skipping the foreplay and straight to the bedroom, aye?"

"Dude, we've been at this for weeks."

"And you still aren't getting my panties off this easy."

"Lame."

Littlethumb concedes with a tilt of the head.

"Just 'cause you agree, doesn't make it better," says Redy, exercising lighthearted indignation. "What's it gonna take?"

"I'm not sure." Littlethumb advances a pawn to Redy's eighth rank, turns the pawn into a queen, and declares, "Checkmate."

"Good game." Redy studies the board, trying to figure out where he screwed up.

"Good game," says Littlethumb. "You overplayed your rook early. Once you opened up that line, I knew I was sacking my queen to advance the pawn. Was a simple matter of execution, and how much I could get out of the queen exchange."

"Hmm. Your queen exchange looks oddly familiar." Redy knows exactly where he's seen the play before. He and Littlethumb's first game. "You know, sometimes I feel like every game I've won, you've let me win."

"Yeah, life can be funny that way."

"Geez. Thanks for reassuring me."

"You're a whizbang player, my friend. Super whizbang. Feel better?"

"No, but mostly because I can't trust anyone your age who uses the word whizbang."

"You probably shouldn't." Littlethumb finishes resetting the black pieces on his side of the board then sits back in his chair, hands clasped behind his head. "So, what's the deal, Redy? Why me? What odd little nuance of life has led Mr. Redmond Sinclair on his wild goose chase into rural Canada for the chance to interview a recluse who no one cares about anymore?"

Odd little nuance? Redy thinks. *I'll show you an odd little nuance, you fucking asshole.* "Damn, you work that question up in advance? You're writing my story for me."

Littlethumb's response is silence. A silence implying he's done with banter for the day. His question stands fast as a locked gate, to which only a perceived honest answer is the key.

Redy concedes and answers Littlethumb's previous question. "Alright. The answer is pain." Truth! If all else fails, truth!

"How so?"

"I've suffered mine, and I figure there's more to come. I'm curious about survival. You're not much older than me, and you've already dealt with so much. I want to know how you've survived. Don't take this the wrong way, but I'm not certain I wouldn't have killed myself."

The comment momentarily throws Littlethumb. Was that an earnest revelation? Is the kid in danger? "Tell me, then, what you've suffered," he says. "Not for any need to prove yourself to me. Please don't take it that way. I ask for the sake of empathy. Shared experience."

"Oh no. I'm the interview-*er*. This story is about you, and you've been making me dance around for weeks. I'll keep dancing, but I'm not dropping my drawers until you do, if mine come off at all."

"Then I guess we're at an impasse. I hope you understand. It's nothing personal. You already know quite a bit more about me than I do you. Enough so you could write your story about these last few weeks. Maybe even sell it, if anyone still cares about me, which I'm not completely sure of. Maybe an art magazine or something, but please know my reticence is nothing personal. You seem like an earnest fellow, Redy. A nice guy. So, I will give you this one honest quote before we call it quits for the day. The reason I don't care to discuss my life is because I'm not up here in the middle of nowhere hiding from the world. I'm up here in the middle of nowhere hiding from myself."

The kooks and crazies arrive for dinner, shuffling into the shelter's rumpus room with hungry bellies and delusional stories of the day. So as not to feel like a jerk, having flatly refused Redy's request for a genuine interview, Littlethumb insists Redy stay and help him serve dinner to this gaggle of almost forgotten souls, these discarded and hungry pawns in a dispassionate universe.

Evening gloom has settled on the two men as they shake hands in the parking lot of the shelter. Littlethumb makes every effort to ensure Redy hasn't taken offense at their earlier conversation. His refusal to give the interview has nothing to do with Redy, he promises, but it does, and he drives away feeling like a jerk for lying.

I mean, we know Redy wants to hurt him, and Littlethumb's aware that something is off with this dude, something not quite right. To have wasted months living here, waiting to meet him? Then weeks pretending he didn't know Smith was Littlethumb? Never mentioning a thing about his own life? At all? The fact that Redy hasn't been more forthright is exactly why Littlethumb shouldn't feel like a jerk, yet he still does.

Let it go, dude. Let it go.

He can't.

Overthinking knots his brain as Littlethumb pulls into a gas station before reaching the outskirts of town. What's the end game to all this? And why now, when the team just got themselves tangled up in whatever the hell they found on that truck? And the paintings. The paintings! How the hell are they gonna get them back?

Leaning against the truck while the gas tank refills, pondering life's complicated nonsense, Littlethumb notices Woof stand up inside the truck's cab. The coydog circles around and stares out the back window, sniffing at the air with a soft whimper. Littlethumb turns to investigate, but there's nothing there. That's when he gets bonked on the head.

16

In case I haven't been abundantly clear (wink, wink), several years ago, Littlethumb was involved in two separate major litigations. The first was a lawsuit filed against him, which I have previously discussed as the "identity trial." The second was Tommy Toxic's murder trial.

During the identity trial, a mysterious Coney Island boardwalk caricature artist named Smith was discovered to indeed be the long-missing Littlethumb Brooks, whom the world had presumed dead since he was a young boy. Obviously, Littlethumb wasn't dead, though at the time, he didn't know he was alive either. I know, I know, but it's true.

The shock from the art exhibit fire that killed his family gave Littlethumb amnesia, and while the amnesia was a blessing that lasted for several years, as a teenager his memory of the event returned. Littlethumb's anguish was devastating. The poor child could not stop reliving the nightmare of his family's deaths. He begged his uncle to help him make the pain go away. Not knowing what else to do, Daring Bird agreed to assist Littlethumb in having his memory suppressed through hypnosis. What was supposed to be a short-term solution turned into a decade of living without the full memory of his former life.

At the beginning of the identity trial. Littlethumb, quite purposefully, didn't know who he really was. By the end of the trial, the hypnosis had been lifted, Smith was back to being Littlethumb, his and Maria's first date was scheduled, and the art world had to completely reassess the value of the formerly dead painter's work.

Littlethumb and Maria dove heart first into a whirlwind romance and would marry soon after. Barely a year later, she was dead. Hence, Tommy Toxic's murder trial. And now you know the rest of the…eep, boop, Harvey, warning, Paul Harvey, plagiarism warning…

Oh, to be clear, Jimmy the Tweaker is not the hypnotist who suppressed Littlethumb's memory. No reason for any mystery there. It was another hypnotist dude, but he died. Natural causes. However, Littlethumb's ordeal gave Daring Bird the notion that a hypnotist would be an asset for the Electric Medicine Men, which led to the hiring of Jimmy.

We're back at the cabin. Littlethumb startles awake and blurts, "Motherfucker!"

The slightly muffled sound of his words, and breathing, beg curiosity. Eyes are open, but there's no sight. Everything is dark. *Am I blind?!* Not genuine panic. A joke to self.

Sticking his tongue out as far as possible, he feels the tip scrape against the twiney dry coarseness of burlap. Couple this with the recognition that his hands and feet are once again bound, and Littlethumb understands what has happened. *I've unleashed a tiny monster on my life.*

In a flash. the burlap sack is removed and a small note floats into Littlethumb's lap. The note reads: *Master Chee 2, Smith 0.*

"Found that on the floor there next to you," says Daring Bird.

Instant cheer explodes with the sound of his uncle's voice. Littlethumb jerks his head left to right as Daring Bird steps into view, out from a shadow in the dimly lit room. "Uncle!" Littlethumb frees his wrists from the knotted rope and stands to embrace his uncle. Forgetting his feet are bound to the legs of the chair, he attempts a step forward and falls into his uncle's arms. Wearing a huge smile, he looks up and says, "Why did you leave me tied up?"

"I didn't want you waking up and surprising me." As he speaks, Daring Bird rights Littlethumb, then settles him back down into the chair so his nephew can finish untying himself.

"What? How?"

"You know, if I was in the other room or something."

"Seriously?"

"Hey, bud, you're the one who hired the guy. Didn't want to spoil your fun."

"Touché." Ankles unbound, Littlethumb practically leaps out of the chair to enthusiastically wrap his arms around Daring Bird. "It's so great to see you!"

Daring Bird receives and returns the hug with equal enthusiasm. "You too, kid. You too." He pats his nephew on the back, letting him know their loving greeting has been duly fulfilled. Littlethumb holds on a few seconds longer.

"When did you get here? How long was I out?" asks Littlethumb in rapid fire succession, releasing his uncle from the bear hug and resting his hands on Daring Bird's shoulders. Confusion remodels Littlethumb's face. "What's with the eyepatch?"

"Huh? Oh. Ha. I suppose I've gotten used to it. Forgot to take it off."

Daring Bird removes the eyepatch to reveal a completely functional eyeball resting in a fire-scarred socket. "Parthos made it for me. Check it out." He gives the eyepatch to Littlethumb, who turns it over in his hands, inspecting the digital imaging and readout on the inside of the patch. "Pretty cool, right? The patch has built in heat signature tracking, night vision, GPS, and can zoom in up to a hundred yards away with total image clarity."

"And it's a bold style choice for the modern, middle-aged, danger-seeking medicine man."

"You're damn right it is."

"I want one."

"No caping my style, Grasshopper." Daring Bird plucks the eyepatch from Littlethumb's hands and tucks it into the chest pocket of his jacket.

"Ha. It's so great to see you." Littlethumb goes in for another hug, squeezing his uncle tightly and feeling the return on his investment. Once satisfied, he pushes away and repeats, "When did you get here?" as he turns to walk somewhere.

"Half an hour ago." Daring Bird reaches for his nephew, grabbing his shoulder and insisting he turn back around. "Ahem."

Littlethumb rotates, wearing a sheepish grin. "What?"

Daring Bird raises his eyebrows and tilts his head. "You're good, kid, but you're not that good."

Littlethumb chuckles and politely returns the eyepatch to Daring Bird's lapel pocket.

"So, what's up with the Friday night bondage?" Daring Bird asks. "You really that bored?"

"Nah, this is just a bad idea gone bad. I accidentally talked Master Chee into training off the property. This is the end result."

"Oh, it's a result for sure, but you might want to be careful calling it the 'end'."

"Fair advice, wise uncle. Fair advice." Littlethumb takes a beat, staring at his mentor, then says, "Man, I'm so glad you're here."

"Me too."

"How long was the commute?"

"Couple of days."

"Who made the trip?"

This question, my friends, to be clear, is the apprentice's delight. To revel in the skill and ingenuity of his teacher. For if Littlethumb be a Master of Disguise, who do you think deemed him so? By what officiality of credentialed expertise was the young man certified? You guessed it. The University of Uncle Daring Bird, of course.

"Dr. Archibald Gravely, research scholar and renowned lecturer on the mechanics of light synthesis in deep sea dwelling creatures, left France after a semester-long residency at Le Frenchy Shmug Face Academy, traveling to Great Britain where he 'met' Adelay Clements, old-world cobbler and clock repairman, who was conveniently heading to the see-through waters of the North Caribbean for a long overdue vacation. Once Adelay arrived in Nassau, he bumped into his longtime friend Mateo Doukas. Mateo, heir to a family fortune established in the sponging industry, made Adelay's acquaintance in London many years ago during the acquisition of a beautiful eighteenth century clock."

"Fantastic."

"Of course, Adelay's arrival in Nassau had nothing to do with the coincidental timing of Mateo's need to travel to the United States the next day, where he would meet his business associate David Sandelgo before David left for his hunting trip, all the way up in the peaceful confines of the Canadian wilderness."

"And were the travels of these fine men safe? Any harrowing tales of derring-do or Sturm und Drang?"

"Considering the cargo? I would say the entire commute."

Eyes light up and youthful brow rises. "The mysterious device! I'd almost forgotten. Where is it!?"

"The other room."

"C'mon then, let me get a look."

"Tomorrow, kid. Plenty of time for that tomorrow."

"Are you serious?"

"Yes. I had a long trip, and I'm tired. Exhausted, to be frank."

In his excitement, Littlethumb hasn't absorbed the full measure of his uncle's posture and palette. Weariness announces its presence in the form of sagging shoulders and darkly sunken eyes. The type of deep down tired that ages you twenty years, and even with a long night's rest, you only get back nineteen.

This more focused observance of Daring Bird's fatigue sobers Littlethumb's mind from the elation he received by the surprise presence of his uncle. Now he feels like an asshole. Forget the device, you jerk. Your loved one is exhausted and there are other loved ones to account for. "How's the team? Mortimer?"

"Team's fine. On break. Safe. Cross is down with pneumonia. He looked like shit, but he'll make it. Ornery bastard."

"Was he able to speak? You get any relative info?"

"Yeah, but not much."

"You know what, in the morning. We'll talk in the morning. Let me get you some food or something. What time is it?"

"Late. No food. Sleep. But isn't there someone else you want to ask about first?"

"That goes without saying."

"You should say it anyway."

"Have you talked to Sawyer? How's Hope? Is she doing okay?"

"Yes, I have, and she's doing great. You should give them a call."

"Yeah, I know."

"Well…" Normally, Daring Bird would lean in on Littlethumb here about the choices he's making, but he's too damn tired to have any confidence he would deliver the lesson correctly. Instead, he cuts his nephew, and himself, a break. "You know what, my bad. This can wait until the morning, too. I've got to hit the rack. Sleep. Must have sleep."

"I hear you. Despite my little nap, I think I could nod off pretty easily myself."

"Alright, kid, I'll see you in the morn."

"Yep. Goodnight, dear uncle madman."

"Goodnight."

Occasionally, exhaustion can be a blessing. For example, Daring Bird goes to bed feeling a touch sanctimonious, having cornered his nephew emotionally by mentioning Hope. You can add a smidge of guilt on top of the sanctimony for not telling Littlethumb about his recent vision. After all, the visions come for a reason, and this one is clearly a message for the kid. Luckily for Daring Bird, he's too damn tired to lament any of this, falling asleep shortly after he lays down.

Littlethumb isn't so lucky. About an hour is spent waffling between mentally beating himself up and the notion of going into the bedroom and physically punching his uncle in the stomach. Why'd he have to do that right before bed?

Make no mistake, Littlethumb knows his uncle's intentions are always honorable, but dammit. So much for sleep. Brain isn't going to let this one go. Nope. Too much unresolved doopity-doop to sleep on. Instead, our bleary-eyed hero makes coffee and puts on his lab coat. (Okay, he doesn't actually put on a lab coat. That's a "doing science" metaphor.)

Littlethumb finds the device buried deep in his uncle's rucksack, swaddled in dirty socks and underwear. *Oh, sweet. Middle-aged man smell. Awesome.*

No shit, he almost holds a pair of the underwear up to his nose to take a huge deep exaggerated smell, like a teenage boy with his neighbor's panties in a movie. As a joke to self, you know? One of those personal gags you only share with god or the universe (whatever your beliefs may be). At the last moment, he remembers that no matter how funny the thought is, these are his uncle's dirty tighty-whities, not some hot neighbor's panties. Then he goes to wash his hands.

Once the evil is washed off, Littlethumb retrieves the device and his coffee and heads into the server room. Nothing like investigating a mysterious device to keep your mind off uncomfortable subjects. I mean, he could go for a run, but who wants to exercise in the middle of the night? Not me, or Littlethumb. Nope. A run-on sentence I could go for, but not a midnight run. Inspecting a mysterious device of unknown origin and purpose that might be a bomb or some other form of destructive and deadly implement disguised as a jack-in-the-box is way better than going for a midnight run.

17

In the morning, Daring Bird finds Littlethumb slumped over a workbench in the server room. The device is on the table not far from Littlethumb's head. Both head and device are still in one piece. There are screwdrivers, pliers, magnifying glasses of varying strengths, miniature telescoping cameras, and other assorted tools scattered on the table. Rather than wake his nephew, Daring Bird leaves him be and heads for the kitchen to cook breakfast.

About twenty minutes into the frying of the bacon, Littlethumb emerges from the doorway of the server room and plods across the cabin to the kitchen, managing to simultaneously scratch his ass and his head in a cinematically stereotypical fashion. You can toss an exaggerated yawn in there too, if you like. He sits at the counter and Daring Bird slides a cup of coffee to him.

"Get some rest?" asks the uncle.

"Apparently. You?"

"Slept like the dead."

"Good."

Daring Bird returns to the bacon as Littlethumb quietly sips his coffee, waking to the world. The younger man muses with silent appreciation as his senior tends to the food. Processing nothing but observation, Littlethumb records this moment for future usage, when uncle is no more and his presence only found in memory or projection.

For a moment, the rest of his family is there. Mom and dad are setting the table for breakfast, stealing happy glances from each other as sister Heather and brother Freddy chatter with Daring Bird, who's back from some adventure and completely lying about where he's been and what he's been up to. Grandpa Kicking Rocks is in the corner, sipping chicory tea and cheerfully observing his brood. Then Maria walks in, baby in arm. Littlethumb shakes his head free of this delusion immediately. Words. Use words to speak and get out of your own head, boyo.

"Any word on when the food will be ready?" he asks.

"When it's ready," says Daring Bird. "You know I like to slow cook the bacon."

"Slow-cooked bacon, that's a band name."

"Ha. Not bad." Daring Bird turns and very slowly, with melodramatic flair, enjoys a piece of bacon for his nephew to watch.

Littlethumb holds his hands palm up and says, "What the hell? I will come across this counter."

Daring Bird's response is to toss a piece to his nephew. "Whet your appetite."

"Hmm. It's good. It's so good."

Eggs are fried and the two men adjourn to the dining table for conversation and sustenance. Little is said in the first few minutes as they attend to their bellies, but the plates are cleared in short order and the moment arrives for dealing with all the subjects they were both too tired to discuss the previous evening.

"You making shit?" asks Daring Bird.

"No. Oh, I am currently working on an impressive dust installation. Does that count?

"What's the problem?"

"Seriously? If I knew…"

"Alright. What's on your mind?"

"Same thing as always."

"Look, I wouldn't ask you to let her go. I don't want you to. But," Daring Bird struggles for the correct words until his facial expression confirms he's found them. "You don't have to let her go, but you've got to let her go."

"What is that supposed to mean?"

"I don't know. I thought you would. You're smarter than me."

How do you describe a physical gesture used to proclaim you sort of agree with what someone else has said? For example, in this instance, if Littlethumb accepts the notion he's smarter than his uncle, he's not exactly certain how smart that means he is. The gesture Littlethumb makes is a humble yet *smart*-assed acceptance. Picture that as best as you can.

"Jimmy told me to say it," responds Daring Bird.

"Well at least it wasn't Silas!"

Daring Bird snorts into his coffee. "Ha!"

"Did you ask Jimmy what he meant?"

"Yes. He said you would get it, then reminded me I'm a seer and told me to figure it out."

"Hmm. I suppose we'll have to ponder on it. I think I may understand, but due to ambiguity, I call for an immediate subject change."

"I second the motion. It's too early for head games. We can get back to your personal problems later in the day."

"You brought it up, ya nerd."

"Yeah, yeah." On this, Daring Bird returns to the kitchen for a second helping of food, speaking along the way. "So, you picking the next item up for bid or you want me to."

"Go for it. You're already on a roll."

"Yes, I am. Let's see. Early in the day. International mischief to deal with. Mysterious device. Your fucked-up painter problems. Oh, I know. What's up with the book?" he asks, returning to his seat.

Before Littlethumb can answer, a dramatic scuffle ensues under the table. The monkeys steal a piece of bacon Daring Bird tosses to Woofus Maximus. Woof chides the monkeys for their thievery, but his courage fails as our three simian ninjas gleefully chase the young coydog from the room.

"I like the new recruit," says Daring Bird, "but he's got a lot to learn about living with monkeys."

"You have no idea."

"So, the book? Anything new?"

"Yep. The first draft was not positively received by the publishers. Also, for some reason, they keep trying to figure out where I'm living. It's really annoying. I'm beginning to wonder why I agreed to write the damn thing."

"You thought it would be healthy for you."

Speculation sours Littlethumb's face.

"You were right," says Daring Bird. He waits for Littlethumb's face to soften, then follows with, "What didn't they like? Was it the title?"

"What? No, it wasn't the title. Apparently, the publishers don't like what they consider to be a fantasy biography concept. They said it's over-romanticized. They want rewrites."

"Are you going to tell them it's not a fantasy?"

"Of course not. What's the point? They'll probably think I'm furthering my shtick."

"I suppose. So what are you going to do?"

"I don't know."

"Good. I'll tell you. Publish it yourself and don't change a damn word. Except the title."

"They already paid me."

"Give 'em the money back."

"Huh." Not a question, huh. A thoughtful, huh. "Yeah. I could do that. Actually, I would enjoy that."

"There you go."

"I guess so."

"And change the title."

"For the love of…what the hell is wrong with the title!?"

Employing a healthy dose of chewy pragmatism, Daring Bird finishes off a mouthful of food, washes it down with some coffee, then matter-of-factly states, "You already spoke."

The working title of Littlethumb Brooks' first memoir is *Littlethumb Speaks*. Littlethumb stares at his uncle, a lightbulb of recognition switching on in the brain, face blanked in defeat. "Now? Now you tell me?"

"I figured you would eventually see it for yourself. I mean, you did all those talk shows. The cat's out of the bag. You've spoken."

"Fine, smart guy. What would you call it?"

"I don't know. Off the top of my head? How about *Littlethumb Sneezed*? I mean, the sneeze is the…what's the word?"

"What word?"

"You know, about stories. The thing that makes the story or whatever."

"A MacGuffin?"

"Yeah, MacGuffin. The sneeze is yours. Sets the whole coaster in motion."

"I'm not sure that's right."

"Look it up."

At this, Littlethumb leaves the table and retrieves his laptop. He brings the computer to life and keys in his search, then says, "Welp, what do you know. I guess you're right. According to Merriam-Webster, a MacGuffin is 'an object, event, or character in a film or story that serves to set and keep the plot in motion despite usually lacking intrinsic importance'."

"See, that's the sneeze."

"Yeah, I guess so. And I have to admit, I like the way it sounds better. *Littlethumb Sneezed.*"

"There you go. Problem solved."

"Thank you, old wise one."

"You're welcome."

"Old, old, wise one."

"Fuck off."

"Ha! I think I will. I will fuck right off right now." Littlethumb stands up with dirty plate in hand and pats his uncle on the shoulder. "I'm gonna shower, get cleaned up."

"We wish you would."

After Littlethumb has showered and dressed, he finds Daring Bird in his art studio. Daring Bird has unstacked a pile of paintings and dusted their edges, leaving them resting against the wall single-file, so each can be viewed. I mentioned these before. The portraits are a series of a child, a girl, showing the history of her life from her first moments of blind, newly-birthed cold and confusion up until what one might presume are representations of her first steps.

Presently, Daring Bird is polishing an unfinished stone sculpture of a tiny monkey, an homage Littlethumb was creating to honor his uncle's first rescued tamarin, Jojo. Littlethumb notices the Vox Continental has also received a thorough dusting.

"Feel better?" asks Daring Bird.

"Top notch," says Littlethumb, still toweling at wet hair.

A final wipe of stone Jojo and Daring Bird turns, folding the rag in on itself as he steps to the center of the room. He faces the paintings of the child, soaking in the wonder of his nephew's abilities, and the abject adorableness of his great-niece. "I had a vision." The words are spoken with stoic sincerity. No need to add weight by using any sort of emotionally charged delivery. Daring Bird's visions don't occur on a regular basis. The importance is understood. Pay attention.

"You don't say."

"I do."

Littlethumb straps the towel across his shoulder and crosses the room to face his uncle. He stares at Daring Bird. Daring Bird stares at the paintings. "So…you gonna tell me what you saw, or make me beg for it?"

"Turn and face your creation." Daring Bird tilts his head and darts his eyes to insist Littlethumb follow his instructions.

"I know how beautiful she is," Littlethumb says, eyes still locked on his uncle.

Both men are avoiding discomfort here. Daring Bird, from describing a vision he fears. Littlethumb from laying eyes on the image of his daughter, for reasons you likely already understand.

"The vision," says Littlethumb. "Tell me about the vision."

A deep breath and Daring Bird finally capitulates. "You were dancing."

"Odd. Was I poppin' and lockin', or doing the robot…?" The attempt at levity rings hollow in Littlethumb's own ears and doesn't scratch the surface of Daring Bird's grave expression.

"With Maria. You were dancing with Maria."

Littlethumb faces his paintings, reflexively looking away from his uncle, accidentally punching himself in the stomach with the images of his daughter, mind and heart instantly split between sadness for his current state of affairs with Hope and sadness for his dead wife. "Was there anything else?" he asks, a quiver in his chin.

"That was pretty much the gist."

"So, what do you think?"

"You know how this goes. It can mean any number of things. Or nothing." This last bit here is hopeful nonsense. Daring Bird knows the visions always mean something. The problem is, the most obvious interpretation of this one, at least to him, is that his nephew is going to die. Dancing with his dead wife in the spirit world? What would you think the vision means?

"Right." *Why did you wait to tell me something this important? You're scared. Oh man, you think I'm dead meat. That's why. I'm whining about my life and you're walking around thinking you've doomed me.* Littlethumb puts an arm across his uncle's shoulders, searching for the correct words, but how do you reassure someone else when you're suddenly wondering if you're going to die?

Daring Bird relieves the pressure by speaking first. "Anything unusual happen lately up here?"

18

Let's spend some quality time with Redmond Sinclair, whadaya say? What's it like, a day in the life of a man committed to murder, who has no previous murderous experience? You might be surprised to find out, not much different than yours.

Don't get me wrong. Odds are you have a job to deal with. Family and friends, too. Our boy Redy was born to independent wealth and is currently wandering this world untethered, safe from any relationships of true emotional depth (or so he thinks). My comparison isn't so much about how you and our wannabe killer physically spend your days as it is a comparison between emotional states of being and their cycles. Cycles of energy and fatigue, and boredom, and the fleeting, flirtatious but often unfaithful concept of self-love. Every mirror in the world a person may love or hate, depending on the moment in which to it they thoughtfully gaze.

Whether you enjoy mirrors or not, we see Redy's reflection moving up and down inside one. He's on the hotel room floor doing pushups next to the room's lone table. On top of the table sits a stack of sketch pads. The budding artist has been busy.

After his morning exercise, he'll head to K's Diner for his usual breakfast, where he'll order ten minute's worth of food in exchange for an hour's worth of conversational fellowship. The truth is, Redy enjoys this peaceful little town, quietly tucked away from the rest of the world, far from the pain of his real life. This is a place he could stay, if not for the reason he came.

The people here are hearty, filled with elan for their fellow humans and life in general. Toil and comradery make fulfilling days, free of the excess and unnecessary manmade dangers confronting people in areas of denser population. Don't get me wrong. This isn't a blanket condemnation of big city living. I've done both. I dig peace and quiet, yet still find myself comfortably nestled inside the walls of a city where activities abound, despite my reticence to regularly participate in said activities.

No, this isn't a personal literary comment on being a city mouse versus a country mouse. This is a very specific note on the psychology of Redy Sinclair, who holds his past in contempt, and therefore the city in which said past occurred. Guilt by association entwines the conditions, locations, and all the other connective tissue of an existence that has broken him.

I once left a city with my tail between my legs, having made a fool of myself there, over and again, in my youth. To this day I hate that place, and despite knowing most of the wounds suffered there were self-inflicted, I still harbor resentment for the town. As if it somehow created the circumstance for me to be such an extravagant, childish jackass.

Redy's situation is very different, to be sure, as the damage done to him was heinous and not by his own hand. He was a child thrust into horror by the unmerciful chaos of existence. But, the overwhelming sense of "this is a bad place where bad things happened to me" is similar. Redy knows the city didn't create his personal circumstances, but emotions do what they do.

Speaking of murder, Redy has managed to compartmentalize his intentions. His monster self has been locked away inside the hotel room, caged in the pages of his sketch pads. Countless scenarios reflecting pain and unfettered rage are inked on their pages, but that's where all the crazy stays. For the time being.

Someday all those sketches may piece together to form an airtight case of premeditated murder for a District Attorney, or a best-selling graphic novel. Or both. Whatever happens down the line, the notebooks currently act as a magical prison for a broken young man's vengeful animosity.

Thus, monster safely locked away, the smiling, handsome young fellow who ventures out into public has been warmly received by this friendly town. Truth be told, he's genuinely a nice guy. A nice guy on an unfortunate, insidious mission. There is guilt to be had. These people he's begun to care for, their love for his enemy is obvious. There is guilt to be had in taking something they care for from them, but what must be done must be done. They simply don't understand all of the pain and misery for which Littlethumb Brooks is responsible.

My belabored point here being, under normal circumstances, Redmond Sinclair is a likable, affable, decent-hearted guy, suffering enormous pain (…sound familiar?). Sadly, life has thrust the opportunity for vengeance before him. A tough call to ignore. Especially when we live in a world populated by thoughtful, sentient creatures who are convinced there's such a thing as justice.

The scales must be leveled. The universe insists, having presented Redy with this opportunity. The memory of his parents insists. His aggrieved heart insists.

Speaking of all the ways one might kill another person, Redy has labored in contemplating different methods. As mentioned above, many of his sketches are depictions of ways he might exact his revenge. To be frank, the drawings have been an exercise in speculation and acceptance. Could he perform the horrible act he's depicted? Could he do those things to another living, breathing creature? Is he capable?

Either way, an appropriate course of action has presented itself. An idea so obvious it hid in plain sight. Now he must prepare, both emotionally and functionally.

After breakfast at K's, Redy wanders a few blocks downtown. There's a center square surrounded by shops, offices, and a few pubs. Enough places to pop in and people to see for a person to happily fill their entire day with hellos, conversation, and goodbyes. That's how a smiling stranger grows familiar.

By lunchtime, he's at Jacque's Taproom, nestled into a booth and working a crossword puzzle. Having never been much of a drinker before this current chapter in his life, afternoon pints have become a daily phenomenon. Fizzy lager whispers to him in a room so quiet he can hear the carbonated bubbles climb to the surface of the beer and gently pop.

Willy Peete enters the pub, receiving a loud hello from bartender Gertie. "Light crowd today, I see," says Willy.

"Yeah. Did you tell everyone you were coming?" Gertie sets an iced tea on the counter for Willy, accompanied by a playfully flirtatious squinch of the nose.

Stirring lemon into his tea, Willy turns to scan the room and sees Redy, who graciously pats the top of his table. "C'mon, Willy. Come have a seat with me."

"I think I will, my friend. I think I will." Willy makes his way to the table and slides into the booth. "You eat yet?"

"No, no. Still working off breakfast, so I settled on an appetizer." Redy taps the glass of beer with a wink.

"Wish I could join you, but I'm gonna have to order something more substantial, if you promise not to think I'm rude."

"I promise not to think it, but I'm gonna tell everyone in town you are anyway."

"Ha. You realize I've lived in this town my whole life. They already know!" Willy's enthusiasm for his own jokes is infectious, easily pulling earnest chuckles from Redy. "You sure you don't want anything?"

"I'm good," says Redy. "I may have something here in a bit."

"Gertie, can I have a half club and a cup of whatever soup you've got today?"

"Sure thing. Have it out in a few minutes."

"Thank you, dear." Willy turns to Redy, conspicuously, and then leans over the table. Waiting for Gertie to turn her back, he whispers, "You know, I had such a crush on her when we were younger."

"You don't say?"

This is a regular interaction and response. Willy thinks it's hilarious to tell people he once had a crush on Gertrude Chamberland. Perhaps the secret isn't what he finds so funny, more so the over-romanticized delivery of admitting the long-held crush.

"You ever consider doing something about that?" asks Redy, already knowing the most likely options for Willy's answer.

Today, Willy chooses, "Oh for heaven's sake, I'm too old," easily his third or fourth most frequent response. No one ever bothers to remind him Gertie is the same damn age. "Just like to make sure people know I was alive once." Of course, the truth is, he will never fully let go of his ex-wife. Someday, maybe, they will each heal enough to give themselves another chance together.

Redy smiles and takes a drink of his beer, tilting his head in appreciation for Willy's bit. Willy begins every interpersonal interaction in a manner destined to bring a smile to your face. An excellent skill to possess for a person committed to helping the downtrodden.

"Any big plans for the day?" asks Willy.

"Nope. Thought I might swing by later for dinner with the guys. Otherwise, I'm mostly twiddling my thumbs."

"Not such a bad way to spend a day. This world's always trying to keep us busy. Gets worse and worse for the younger generations."

"Yes, it does."

"Oh, by the way, if you're doing more twiddling tomorrow, we might could use a hand out at Thomas and Sharon Barnett's house. Me and several of the boys are going to help them repair a stretch of fence." Willy has a way of sneaking up on you with requests for assistance, another excellent skill for a person running a shelter for the homeless and afflicted.

"Sounds like fun. I should be able to help, though I've been told I'm dangerous to have around construction projects. Something about throwing hammers."

"Why doesn't that surprise me?" asks Willy, chuckling as Gertie swings by and drops off his lunch. "Thanks, Gert."

"My pleasure. Either you gents need anything else?"

"No thanks."

"This is perfect, thank you." As Gertie walks away, Willy tests the soup for heat, sipping a touch from the spoon. "Damn, that's hot. We're gonna let that cool for a minute."

"What type of soup is it?" asks Redy.

"I'm not sure. Tastes like potato or something. Too damn hot to tell!" Willy sets the spoon down and fusses with his sandwich, checking for mayonnaise, removing excess lettuce and tomato (which he promptly stuffs in his mouth and chews, ala carte), and smashing the whole pile down to better fit his mouth. He takes a large bite, then, speaking through clenched teeth, he says, "So, I've been meaning to ask you something."

"Okay," says Redy, his tone amenable yet curious.

"I don't want you to take offense."

"Willy, you know how it goes when someone leads with a statement like that?"

"I do, I do. That's why it felt necessary. I like you, Sinclair. And I don't mean to pry, but I'm curious."

"Oh, for goodness sake, out with it." Playful exaggeration, to be sure, but Redy definitely wants to know what comes next.

"Since you insist… You've been around town here for several months. And everyone has really taken to you."

"I appreciate that…"

"But we know why you're here. So, I'm wondering, how long are you going to stick around? If you don't get what you came for, that is. How long will you stay?"

"Are you guys running an over-under on me or something?"

"What's an over-under?"

"Are you serious?"

Willy doubles-down with a facial expression insisting he knoweth not of whatever Redy speaketh.

"It's a gambling term. I was asking if you guys were betting on how long I would be here."

"Oh. Ha. No. We're just curious, that's all. Small town and whatnot. Like I said, folks here have taken a liking to you. We're wondering what happens if you don't get what you came for."

"I don't know. I guess I haven't really thought about it. I've just been focused on getting the story."

"Sure, sure. That makes sense, but what happens if you never get your interview? Smith is a different kind of person. Hard to read, you know? How long are you willing to wait?"

"I don't know." Redy takes another drink of beer. "Don't you think it's odd he runs around town calling himself Smith? And you all, you all call him Smith, but everyone knows the guy is Littlethumb Brooks?"

"Maybe. A little. But we all know what happened to him. Who am I, or any of us, to judge someone who needs a quiet place to hide?"

"Hide from what, though? The guy's loaded. He's famous. Everyone pretty much loves him. What the hell does he have to hide from?"

"I think you're leaving out the most important piece of the puzzle, Redy. Why would you do that?"

"I don't mean to. I mean, I'm not. I, I'm only leaving it out, outloud. Not in my consideration of the situation. I understand running from the pain, believe me. But, don't you see why it's such an interesting story to tell? To try and write?"

Willy lets Redy's questions hang in the air for a moment, then responds with a question of his own. "What don't you trust about him?"

"What do you mean?"

"I've watched you two since you met and you're both keeping one another at arm's length. It's obvious to me why he's doing so. What I don't understand is why you are. You're trying to get the guy to talk to you. What are you hiding from him?"

"I'm not hiding anything."

"Yes, you are. And if it's obvious to me, then it's obvious to him."

"No, no. I'm not. I mean, I'm not intentionally hiding anything. Sure, there's stuff about my life I'm not sharing, but that's…I don't know, happenstance? I'm not the kind of person to volunteer stuff, Willy. It's not my nature. I don't mind talking about me, per se, but it's not my preference, you know? So, I've been trying to follow his lead. In my mind, I've ceded control of our conversations to him. I'm trying to make him comfortable, so he'll talk to me."

"I see. I understand your thinking, but if I may offer you a piece of unsolicited advice, stop doing that. If you want someone to open up to you, you need to open up to them. I understand it may not be your nature. You two are a lot alike that way, I think. But you're the one trying to get something here. If you want the guy to trust you, stop playing his game and give him a real reason to trust you."

19

"You mentioned something before, on the phone. A curiosity?"

We're back at the cabin, right where we previously left things. Daring Bird has asked Littlethumb if anything unusual is going on, then follows up with the above question.

"Do we have to talk?" responds Littlethumb. "I wanna go play with my new toy."

"We need to get all the rest of this shit out of the way first."

"All the rest of what shit?"

Daring Bird pulls a piece of paper from a pocket and unfolds it, holding it up for Littlethumb to see a list.

"You made a list?"

"Of course I made a list."

"You're a madman. Can it wait? Do we have to do the whole list right now?"

"I figure we should get all this other shit out of the way first, in case that thing blows us up."

"If it blows us up, what difference will any of this other shit make?" The transition from recognition to defeat on Daring Bird's face would have been comical, if not for the…you know what. If not for nothing. The expression was comical, though his nephew was polite enough not to laugh. Instead, Littlethumb says, "How about we compromise and do two things at once?"

"Alright. Alright," says Daring Bird, refolding and returning the list to his pocket. "I'ma take a leak and I'll meet you in there."

Daring Bird takes a piss. Littlethumb goes for a glass of water and to quietly shed a few tears he fought back while observing his paintings of Hope. They reconvene in the server room, and I suddenly realize the Electric Medicine Men's Canadian Command Center, where Littlethumb keeps his E2M computers and other various implements of secret and not-so-secret technology, needs a better name than "server room." How about the command room? Much better, I think. More inclusive of the entire scope of the room's holdings. Oh, and we'll capitalize the name, to relay its proper-nouny importance.

So, we're in the Command Room and Littlethumb says, "Last night I examined the box for booby traps. I didn't see anything, but to be honest, I was so tired I should check again before we fiddle with it. Better safe than sorry."

"I concur. Always. Though my guess is, whoever built this intended on using it. Which means it's unlikely they booby-trapped it from themselves."

"Yeah, probably not. Any security measure they may have put in place for transit or storage would probably be easy to disarm, if you're the one who installed them."

"Makes sense. Now, two things at once, so listen up, knucklehead. I'm about to preach to the choir."

"Please don't."

"Has to be done. You're singing off key."

"Okay, that's a fantastic metaphor." Littlethumb uses an exaggerated tone, implying the metaphor is not fantastic. In fact, his tone overtly suggests his uncle employed a very cheesy, terrible metaphor. I know I said I was going to stay away from using the word irony, but I'm almost certain Littlethumb's remark was ironic.

Whether a successful use of irony or not, Daring Bird ignores Littlethumb and says, "Let me remind you, happiness is not designed to be constant. If we were constantly happy, there would be no happiness. We can't be happy without also being sad, because without sadness, there would be no barometer."

"That's a lot of happies."

"Har har. My point is, you can't have one without the other, so you keep your pain in perspective and leave your joy unbound. That's how you survive all this madness. Keep the bad in line and let the good run wild."

"I can do that," says Littlethumb, his back to Daring Bird. "How about this. Does this bring you unbound joy?" Littlethumb straightens up from his examination of the jack-in-the-box and turns toward his uncle. He's holding a pair of pliers and wearing magnifying glasses. The type a jeweler wears, with the protruding, tubular-shaped magnifier. A set of fake buck teeth is sticking out of his mouth.

The medicine man can't help but laugh. "Yes. Yes, it does, but this is exactly what I…take those stupid-ass teeth out, will you?"

Littlethumb does a "What teeth, these teeth?" routine, then pulls them out of his mouth and shoves them in a pocket. Daring Bird continues.

"You've got to stop avoiding all the pain and find the beauty in it. It's the only way."

"The only way for what?"

"The only way to live. To keep living. You have to embrace the hurt. It's already a part of you, whether you like it or not. Let it make you stronger. Let your pain stand, not as the opposite of your happiness, but as its companion. I'm not telling you to wallow in misery, that's different. I'm telling you to accept your pain as part of the joy of life. We all suffer and overcome and move forward, and the ones we lose along the way, they never leave us. They just get to rest before us, until it's our turn to be welcomed home."

"I know." Littlethumb stops and removes the magnifying glasses. "I'm sorry. Bad choice of words from the student. Better I should say, I understand. In theory. I thought I had this figured out. I mean, up until what, six or seven months ago maybe, I felt like I was moving forward. That's what's so confusing. I was creating. Then it stopped, and I can't figure out why."

"Stop trying. Stop trying to figure it out."

Littlethumb shrugs his shoulders in concession to an unspoken fact. He can't stop trying. Such is his nature, to understand, and his uncle knows this.

"What's going to do more damage?" continues Daring Bird. "If she gets to be with you and love you as her father, as she should, and something goes wrong? Or, if something goes wrong, and she never had the opportunity?"

"You know I'm not worried about something happening to me. It's what happens to the people who love me, who I love."

"I love you, kid, and I'm right here."

Rather than conceding the point, Littlethumb is struck by the notion that until now, he had somehow managed not to stress-out about his uncle suffering from his death curse. So much for that.

The expression on Littlethumb's face is an easy read. "Listen," Daring Bird continues. "You can't be afraid to lose someone you love, or you'll never love all the way. And if you believe this life is chaos...well, you know chaos doesn't do patterns. So, either you accept what happened was the impartial nature of reality, a random occurrence, which means there is no curse upon you and no precedent for assuming something bad will happen to Hope. Or, you're going to have to set about the task of completely rearranging your personal philosophical beliefs on human existence. At least, as they appear. As you've explained them to me."

This is an argument whose bones are covered in meat, and tough for Littlethumb to ignore. I suppose he could argue that chaos, being chaos, could throw a few patterns into the mix to complicate philosophies and pre-conceived notions, but what's the point? Daring Bird's right. If Littlethumb's going to be who he wants to be, as a man, as a human, as an artist, as a father for Christ's sake, is there anything more important than living up to his own personal philosophies? Or, can one believe things should be a certain way, are a certain way, but not have the emotional capacity to, for lack of better words, practice what one preaches? I mean, are you swimming upstream for no reason if you perpetually force feed yourself a belief system you can't actualize in your real life? Should you instead adopt a doctrine based solely on behavior for which you are capable? "This is what I'm capable of, so this is what I believe in," feels limited to me. Therefore, I vote "no." This court rules in favor of holding beliefs and philosophies on life that an individual belief holder is not physically or emotionally capable of fulfilling or acting on. Case closed. Man, if Judge Harold Lograve could see me now.

"Uncle, I have no choice but to concede. You know you're correct."

"What did you say?"

"Oh fuck you. Don't act like it's the first time, you old shit heel." Both men belt out laughter they were desperate for, breaking the heavy mood. "Okay, now that I've received the gospel, can we move on down your list?"

"Alright. What's next?"

"You're the one with the list."

Daring Bird reaches back into an empty pocket to retrieve the piece of paper. Then another pocket. Then another.

"Or are you?" says Littlethumb, holding the piece of paper up for his uncle to see.

"Jesus, kid. Either you've gotten way better or I'm slipping."

"I refuse to believe you're slipping."

"Me too."

"Though you did feel the need to write all this stuff down."

"There's a lot going on."

Littlethumb wads the paper and tosses it into a garbage can, turning back to his inspection of the jack-in-the-box. "How about you tell me what Cross had to say? Maybe we can focus on this real-world stuff, stay off the psycho-babble train for a bit."

That last line from Littlethumb could have been a command or a request, depending on its delivery. Emotionally, his words are a desperate plea to end their mawkish discourse. Thankfully, his uncle is similarly inclined.

"Yeah, that works for me," says Daring Bird. "According to Cross, these were mid-level hires using expensive equipment. A well-funded, well-organized assault team made of average skilled labor, at best. Was a numbers game, way more bodies than needed to overpower his security detail."

"Maybe a big show of force for publicity, too, then. News splash." Littlethumb is bent over the device as he speaks.

"Most likely. You don't steal a famous art collection in the middle of a major city for no reason. Could have been done once the collection was further in transit."

"Did he see anything traceable? Any clues?"

"You want to let me tell you what I know or you wanna keep asking questions?"

"Sorry."

"Don't be, just slow down that brain of yours and listen, Grasshopper." Daring Bird jabs Littlethumb sharply with a finger to the ribs.

Littlethumb stiffens straight up, blurting, "Jesus!" and glares jokingly over his shoulder at his uncle, who is standing very proudly as he folds his arms across his chest.

"Now you're focused," says Daring Bird. "There were two important details Cross gave me. The first is, the assault team was using non-lethal ammo. Second, during the fight, he noticed the thieves all had the same tattoo behind their left ear."

"Interesting. What was the tattoo?"

"The comedy and tragedy masks."

"So, they're a gang of theater enthusiasts stealing art. Makes perfect sense."

"Kind of hard to steal a theater..."

"Touché."

"All jokes aside, these guys are either some sort of gang or lackeys for a larger organization. Or both."

"Man," says Littlethumb, "either way, who steals an entire art collection? It doesn't make sense. That's so many paintings to try and move underground if they did it for the money. And otherwise, what's the point? You love art so much you're going to steal a bunch of paintings and hide them from the rest of the world forever? Why would you do that? Who would do that?"

"Apparently, we would. I thought you agreed to stop asking questions and listen?"

"What?" asks Littlethumb. Daring Bird starts to repeat himself and Littlethumb waves him off. "What do you mean, 'we would'?"

"I guess you were listening. I followed up with Sawyer after I met with Cross. He got a curious piece of information from a client in France with connections in Lyon's local police force. A member of our security detail reported that the thief who attacked him claimed they were the Electric Medicine Men."

"Curious indeed. I guess that explains the rubber bullets."

"Was a shrewd move, however you slice it. Keeps murder off the list of crimes and fits our M.O."

"But an art heist doesn't."

"You and I know that," says Daring Bird, "but not the cops."

"Right. Right. So, assuming somebody out there is tracking our work and trying to figure out who we are…"

"No need to assume. I have confirmation, we're on multiple radars."

"How do you have confirmation?"

"The concierge at the safe house, in Marseille. You're not gonna believe this, she's an undercover agent for the…wait for it…"

A staring contest ensues. Daring Bird isn't kidding.

Wait for it.

Wait for it.

Wait for it.

And right as Littlethumb opens his mouth to pejoratively encourage his uncle to finish the damn sentence, Daring Bird beats him to the punch and says, "Wait for it…"

Littlethumb signs the words, "Oh screw you" as aggressively as possible, wearing a chiseled smirk. Daring Bird doesn't know sign language, but he gets the drift.

"The Department of Agriculture," says Daring Bird, finally.

"The Department of Agriculture?"

"I know, right!?"

"Hang on, let's do that again, but now I'm a villain." Littlethumb holds his arm out in front of him, elbow bent, and slowly clenches his fist as he says, "The Department of Agriculture, I knew it!"

"Not bad."

"Now I'm confused again, but way more. The Department of Agriculture?!"

"Alright, alright. Seriously. You know you didn't see that coming."

"Nope, and that's why you deserve the trifecta." Littlethumb belts, "The Department of Agriculture!" like a superhero announcing his arrival.

"Stop."

"That's what you get for making me 'wait for it.' What the hell is the Department of Agriculture doing in an underground safe house in France?"

"Exactly what I thought. Apparently, they do all kinds of weird shit. My guess is using the Ag Department is an easy way to hide budgets for secretive international espionage."

"Man, this world is so stupid and convoluted." Littlethumb shakes his head in befuddlement, then another thought occurs to him. "Hey, exactly how did you ply this information out of an undercover government agent?"

"Easy. She seduced me."

"She seduced you to give you government secrets? That doesn't make any sense."

"It does if I seduced her right back."

The incredulousness of the expression on Littlethumb's face breaks the record for most incredulous expression ever. There's no plaque or blue ribbon or anything, but if anyone ever asks you, you tell them the world record holder for the most incredulous facial expression ever — past, present, and future — is Littlethumb motherfuckin' Brooks.

"That's absurd," he says. "How did you seduce her right back?"

"I'm incredible in the sack."

"We both know better than that."

"Ha, ha, yeah. She figured us out. It was the device. They pegged us for recovering the stolen kids, and apparently, the device was already on their radar. When we showed up at the safe house, she saw the box on hidden surveillance and did the math. Then we both did things. Me and her. You know? We did a lot of things."

Fingers are shoved in ears as Littlethumb says, "La, la, la, la, la, la, no thank you. No thank you."

"Alright, alright. I'm done. Her name's Kumiko, by the way. I think. Actually, that's probably not her real name. Definitely not her real name. Anyway, she said there's a double agent in her department. She figures that's how they knew about the device, but she doesn't know why the double would leak the intel."

"To help flush us out?"

"Maybe, but she didn't think so. Apparently, from what she can tell, most of the government agencies that know about us are fine with leaving us in place. Doing the good lord's work, after all."

"And we know how governments love that." Both men agree without speaking that governments and altruism don't always mix. "I'm skeptical," Littlethumb continues, "but I suppose if the general impression among the rat fucks of this world is that governments and law enforcement are allowing us to operate, that could explain why someone decided to try and pin stealing the collection on us."

"Yep. The bad guys haven't been able to figure out who we are, so they're putting the law on us."

"Goddamn. Remember when this all seemed so simple and fun."

"Nope."

"Me neither. So, what's next?"

"You figure out what the hell that crazy ass jack-in-the-box is while me and the team find your paintings. We knock all that shit out, then I get to go have more sex." Daring Bird enthusiastically wiggles his brow at his nephew and wistfully says, "A lot more."

20

Too many pages have turned, I feel, since last we visited Conrad Somvinslodkin, aka the Wretched Eye, aka Baron Von Killstain, aka the Winter Lament, aka Count Faustian Scourge, aka Comrade Somethingrussian, aka Xander Bowfly.

Xander has been busy! If only people understood the subtlety and nuance involved in being an evil despot. Sure, sure, devising schemes of global anarchy requires a lot of effort, but it's the minutiae, the countless daily decisions, that are truly exhausting.

Honestly, the work never ends for any head of an entire organization, whether said organization be your favorite daughter's beekeeping troupe or an as-yet unnamed villainous syndicate. Amazing to consider how most of our species is born with similar capacities for energy creation and expenditure throughout their life, when taking into consideration the end result of all that energy may be managing a bake sale or attempting global domination. Genetics and luck, I suppose, are the difference-makers in the outcome of aspirations where, for many people, with all the hard work comes power, and with power prestige, and with prestige, well, somewhere in there also comes lots of money. Which is as much a reason as any for a human to eschew sleep and good intentions. Even a madman like Xander Bowfly will admit the seductive allure of money is a fierce desire to oppose, despite having given his will over to a greater calling, the auspicious insistence of villainy. Of course, with successful high-end villainy comes lots of money, so, you know, two birds with one stone.

Our wannabe despot has returned to his home in Denmark. One can only spend so many days and nights in a bunker, especially a bunker in Libya. Sure, the bunker's amenities are top-notch for the Big Cheese, but there's a crispness to the air in Denmark you don't find in the desert, and Xander is in the mood for a decent snuggle. Air that cracks the lungs and sex with someone who loves him. I figure most people can relate to those things.

As for Xander's wife, I find conflict in her resembling any poorly written excuse for the beleaguered domestic partner of a bad guy, whether male or female. She's loved Conrad since they first met, and he's a great father, but she's never really known how he makes so much money, and he comes and goes a lot, and she's suspicious of his activity but doesn't want to risk losing everything she has by dealing with reality. Consequently, she chooses to live in a dream bubble with her children and blah, blah, blah, blah. She's a human caricature, to be sure, but a stereotypical paramour for an evil villain is much more realistic than a delicately nuanced, "how could this person seriously be in love with an evil villain," genteel doll.

Besides, we don't have time for her to be dynamic, with regard to my relaying this story to you. She may be dynamic, but we don't have time. Her friends and family can defend her character and intelligence later. They can slander me in the press for slandering her. Whatever.

As far as I can tell, she has more than enough reason to suspect her husband is something awful. She can take all her prayers for his soul and shove 'em up her stupid, yoga-sculpted butt.

No, I don't hate women. I feel the same way about Xander's wife as I do the musclely, butch, sex-toy prick that Xander screws in London. Him's also reaping the lifestyle benefits of guilt by association without care or concern for the pain and misery of others, so to hell with him too. Come to think of it, my phone was made by children in a foreign country and your petrol for the auto comes from a war-torn region populated by oligarchy and destitution, so fuck you and fuck me, too.

Sorry, sorry. The news was on. The story. Back to the story. Just like the last time we saw him, Xander stands in awe of Maria. Presently, we're in his office. The bare spot on the wall behind his giant desk has been filled with the most beautiful portrait he's ever seen. To have had this woman, to have lost her, Xander can't imagine the pain Littlethumb Brooks must have felt.

Wonderful.

Seriously. He can't imagine. Being a sociopath, what Xander equates as love is really an expression of his lust for control. For power and possession. What makes this particular sociopath particularly dangerous is his keen self-awareness. Xander knows he can't feel the depth of love for anything in this world the way Littlethumb Brooks felt love for this woman. Reason three for stealing the collection. Yes, stealing art serves to honor his great-grandpa Adolph and the quality of work in *The Marias* made for an obvious target, but Xander also stole the collection out of resounding jealousy for another human's talent.

Make no mistake, Xander has no interest in trading his destiny for a brilliant artist's romantic existence. No thank you. The die has been cast in Xander's favor, but he is jealous of Littlethumb's talent all the same. Normally, he might kill the artist, but seeing Littlethumb's creations exist is worth the jealousy, and persistently stealing Littlethumb's work will surely plague the artist more than even the most prolonged horrible death possibly could. How torturous.

Ah, the perfect segue, and a potential foreshadowy snack. Xander hasn't decided to steal the rest of Littlethumb's publicly displayed work yet. I jumped ahead by accident. That's your sneak peek, though it may not happen unless the studio picks us up for a second season. The perfect segue is discussing a *potential* evil scheme as preamble to discussing a few of the *actual* current evil schemes our man Xander has in development. You should not be surprised to learn Xander is a Type A personality. Rather, you should have already guessed as much. And I'm certain you know how those Type A personalities must always have something to do, running in circles until they're exhausted and crash harder than anyone ever. Crash so hard.

Seriously, those people. Go, go, go, crash. Go, go, go, crash. And if they're not physically go, go, going, it's an intellectually ego-feeding go, go, going until their brain can't go, go, go anymore and they crash. The kind of person who can't sit still and watch a movie unless they've already tired themselves out, at which point they always fall asleep less than five minutes into the film.

By the by, and so you know, I prefer lighthearted movies that run under two hours. I'm probably a Type A-minus, or maybe a B plus. The slight step down from hardcore Type A behavior, mostly due to controlled substances and the martial arts.

Xander, on the other hand, hasn't watched a movie since childhood. He's a full-on Type A, son-of-a-bitch piece-of-shit bad guy with a never-ending To-Do list. Thus, he always has numerous evil schemes in different stages of development. Let's take a look.

As you already know, he's still working on a catchy name, possibly an acronym, and a logo for his organization. We've touched on this more than once, so we'll move along and revisit again later if a new idea pops up. Besides, branding his organization isn't a scheme. I'm stalling. Don't judge me. I never got a close look at Xander's actual To-Do list in real life, so I have to make up this junk.

I kid, I kid. I was waiting for Xander to finish staring at Maria and sit down. Now we can peek over his shoulder at what's on his desk.

Plans for a deep-water submersible look cool. Apparently, Xander has designed a single pilot attack submarine capable of traveling farther into the depths of the Earth's waters than ever before. We're not yet sure what sort of trouble he may cause with the sub, and probably won't know until his people get down into the ocean and poke around a bit. I've heard rumor there may be an ancient alien species living in a vessel at the Earth's core, secretly controlling the arc of human existence. Nonexistent-Heaven help us if Xander manages to infiltrate those assholes.

Next up, there's an invitation design on the desk for a secret criminal slave auction. The invitations were supposed to go out last week, but the lost shipment of children has forced him to push back the date. No point in holding a large sale without a premium inventory, which means he can put more thought into the invitation design for his slave market before he sends the official invites out to potential buyers. The good news is, he recently got a tip on a remote village in India that is chock-full of children he can steal.

Ooh, there's something interesting. A manilla envelope labeled ICE (an acronym for *In Case of Emergency*). Inside are designs for a satellite scrambler. Production is already underway at his shop in North Korea. The satellite scrambler does exactly what you might think, and if used to its fullest extreme, can bring every satellite in space crashing back to Earth, effectively destroying the Earth's global communications and surveillance abilities. Of course, Xander has no interest in doing that, considering he constantly utilizes the satellites. Hence the folder's *In Case of Emergency* label.

North Korea is funding the machine's development through a wholly-owned subsidiary of Xander's organization. The North Koreans hope to target the satellites of specific enemies, of course. They'll never have the opportunity. Once finished, Xander will take the machine, destroy the development facility, and blame the espionage on another negative entity. Quite possibly Cuba. Cuba's been coasting along lately, living off the reputation built in Castro's youth amongst the evil, and slowly trying to legitimize themselves as a peaceful entity amongst the good. No reason to allow that nonsense to continue.

Also, no reason to blame the theft on a liberal democracy like Great Britain or the United States. The North Koreans already hate them. As I've mentioned before, Xander isn't becoming an evil villain iconoclast simply to undermine Western Democracy. This is about sowing division between everyone. This, this is about messing with the whole world, man. Yeah.

(Sorry. A hippy briefly invaded my narrative voice. Won't happen again.)

Moving on to our next item... Let's see. Oh, right. The outing of the Electric Medicine Men. Xander discovered the existence of the E2M near the end of his career working for the Kremlin. Rather than alert his bosses, he kept the knowledge to himself. His schemes for private enterprise were already in motion, and he recognized the E2M as a valuable force on the playing field. Xander isn't concerned with their destruction, though he is concerned with their success rate.

The ease with which the Electric Medicine Men are operating is clearly unacceptable, given they have managed to accumulate a near perfect record of successful missions. Including, apparently, the theft of Xander's device. Yes, he's convinced the Electric Medicine Men stole his device and rescued the slave children. Details of the operation scream their name. They may as well have left a note scrawled in the desert sand.

I understand if you assumed Xander's goal is to ruin the E2M. A logical assertion, considering his attempt to frame them for stealing *The Marias,* but when your explicit goal is to create havoc and reap the potential rewards a chaotic environment allows, having a rogue team of good guys in play is beneficial. Covertly manipulating an active force like the Electric Medicine Men can make them an asset. After all, Xander has plenty of criminal enemies for the wannabe heroes to antagonize. A dash of disinformation leaked here, a pinch of backstabbing his evil cohorts there, and Xander will use the good guys to unwittingly help him consolidate power.

All of that said, the E2M has operated without interference from legal authorities for far too long. Xander's ability to wield the group to his own liking requires boxing them in. Limiting their freedom of movement. Hence, Xander's attempt to pin the *Marias* heist on them. Moving forward, the Electric Medicine Men will forever be looking over both of their shoulders.

But, and this is an elephant-sized but, the stealing of his device calls for retribution, meaning someone has to die. Fortuitously, a self-proclaimed "hero" has been loitering around Vatican City. The man appears to be an intoxicated fool, but his repetitive mumblings and grumblings have triggered reports from Xander's spies, provoking suspicion the man is potentially connected to the Electric Medicine Men.

The connection is thin, but with the drunkard's unusual behavior and no other current leads on the location of his device, Xander orders the man captured for interrogation. If he is an associate of the Electric Medicine Men, whether a full-fledged member or an ancillary ally, the gruesome death of this drunken "hero," coupled with the perfect clue as to why he was killed, will send the appropriate message. *Someone knows who you are, little children of the light. Someone born of darkness, lurking in the shadows.*

It's me, it's me.

21

We're going to pick up the pace here, as we barrel toward an explosive, action-packed climax and our downward resolution. Here's where we start bringing all our people together under one metaphorical narrative roof. Before we get back to Littlethumb and Daring Bird solving the world's problems, or delve into Redy Sinclair finalizing his plans for revenge, a few important developments with the rest of the team should be discussed.

As I mentioned earlier, after the safe house stay in Marseille, everyone went their separate ways. Silas went to Prague, ostensibly for the women and nightlife. Prague is a reasonably safe locale, regarding domestic crime, but anywhere you find an exclusive club scene and expansive nightlife. you will find the criminal element. Everyone knows how fancy bad guys enjoy fancy clubs. And who would be the clientele for the purchase of famous stolen art? Fancy bad guys.

Our man Silas the Entertainer has a history with fancy bad guys. They adore him. Mostly for his unabashed, lecherous nature and free-wheeling quest for inebriation, but also because of his legacy membership to a famed international jewel thieving and smuggling ring known as the Five Fingers. I mean, you didn't think Daring Bird simply plucked his team off the street, did you?

Silas' great-great-grandfather was one of the original Five Fingers. The organization is still thriving, mostly staffed by the direct lineage of the five founding fathers and mothers, including numerous relatives of Silas. Choosing not to follow in his ancestor's footsteps has distinguished him throughout the precious stone underworld as his family's puckish black sheep. Make no mistake, he is a beloved black sheep (something he and Daring Bird have in common), but with regard to striking out on his own rather than participating in the family business, a black sheep none the less.

Why does this matter? Because on his first night in Prague, Silas runs into a cousin who *did* join the family business. A cousin who happens to be in town celebrating the theft of fifteen rare black rubies, so named due to the absurdly dark, deep red center of the stones.

These two goofballs get all butter-faced, catching up on old times, and frolic their way to an exclusive party inside a castle in District 21. At said party, Silas meets the young trophy wife of an aged billionaire douchebag who more than dabbles in the for-profit financing of criminal enterprise. A young trophy wife who is very annoyed with her husband for hanging another beautiful woman's portrait in the smoking parlor of his super-secluded hunting lodge.

How does Silas extrapolate this information from the pissed off trophy wife? Easy. He takes one for the team. No, by takes one for the team, I don't mean he sleeps with her. Silas is a philanderer, but he ain't no adulterer. Baking someone else's potato is outside his personal code of hero ethics. By takes one for the team, I mean he suffers her incessant babbling. This chick is a talker, and though her chatter isn't all bitching and fussing, she eventually weaves her way to the blatant disrespect of a husband hanging a portrait of another woman in his goddamn hunting lodge. To be frank, she has a fair point.

As Silas is stumbling across a lead in Prague, Jimmy and Bebiana have their own accidental success in Las Vegas. Jimmy's son, whose name I won't reveal for his safety, has recently scammed a room full of rich assholes in a closed-door, high-stakes poker game. Excited to see his dad and to meet Bebiana, he jabbers incessantly about his recent exploits and how fantastic he's doing in Vegas. The poker playing is temporary, to pay the rent and to make connections. Soon he's gonna have his own live hypnosis show. (Between you and me, he does get his own show, rises to fame, pisses the opportunity away when his ego runs wild, and then winds up on the smoking cessation hypnosis circuit. I'm working on the screenplay. I have a title and everything: *Messing with My Head*.)

By the way, the National Guild of Hypnotists claims over fourteen thousand members, and that's only one organization among many others worldwide. Without further research, I'm assuming at least one-hundred thousand hypnotists exist around the world. This may not seem like a huge number, but it's enough. They could be anywhere, messing with people's heads, including yours. By the time you realize something's wrong, it's way too late. One minute you're enjoying your morning commute to work on the train, the next thing you know your wallet is missing and you cluck like a chicken whenever someone says, "excuse me."

Back to the recent poker game. If you're wondering how to cheat at cards by utilizing hypnosis, the process is simple when you have a secret, instantaneous hypnosis technique passed down to you from your father. You plant subconscious tells in your opponents, then watch them pick their ears, tug their noses, and blink in Morse Code as you rake pot after pot after pot. As long as your opponents are shitheads, no moral discourse is needed.

The game Jimmy's son infiltrated was a big shithead table, and these big shitheads did a lot of bragging about luxury items they owned and famous women they would bang, as big shitheads are wont to do. Especially when some young anonymous hotshot like Jimmy's son is robbing them all blind at poker. Well, during the game, to deflect people's attention from the poker hand, this one particular shithead mouthed off about how he was going to buy a rare portrait at a super exclusive underground auction. I'm sure you can see where this is going. That's lead number two on the stolen *Marias*.

Don't worry, despite work invading their vacation, Jimmy and Bebiana still make a few decent shows. *15,000 Horses* is excellent. Jimmy also introduces Bebiana to the best prime rib in Las Vegas, served daily at Jerry's Famous Coffee Shop, which is tucked neatly inside the smoky, wheelchair-bound, oxygen tank-filled glory of Jerry's Nugget Casino. You've never seen more wheezing at Keno tables in your life. Truly glorious.

Most importantly, Bebiana and Jimmy's son get along like aces. This is a big deal for the Brazilian Bitch. Hardcore abrasive outward demeanor or no, she cares deeply for Jimmy and wants his son to like her. These are human beings, people. Hearts matter.

Next up, Garo Kasabian, the Armenian Butcher. As previously mentioned, Garo goes home to his family and deli in Queens. Garo's off-duty routine includes hanging out with his wife, playing board games with his kids, and lying about his travels (who would have known there are so many conferences for people in the deli business…). He's not really an intel guy. Business to run, you know? Speaking of which, during his visit home he gets a great deal on locally raised meat for his shop.

Funny story, a great deal on meat is how Garo landed a membership in the Electric Medicine Men. Yep. That one's a funny story.

And then there's the Nazarene. The boastful, drunken Titus. In case you were wondering, yes, he's the drunk who's been mouthing off in Vatican City. Before Xander's men can capture him, this goofball manages to get himself arrested trying to climb the wall around the Vatican. Which, if you aren't familiar, is completely unnecessary. The modern Vatican has a very large public entrance.

Normally, Titus' epic drunken jail cell ramble, crowing about his lineage and destroying the Catholic Church, would have been ignored. Vatican City has its fair share of protestors. However, Titus' caterwauling about "saving the children" raises the eyebrow of an associate inside the police force, who was previously notified about Xander's lost shipment of slaves. Xander has been assured his agents will have the opportunity to brutally interrogate the prisoner.

People talk. Whether inebriated, or nervous, or completely full of themselves, or tied to a chair, or self-conscious to the point of information dealing as an act of over-compensation, or an ancillary character in a film used to move the plot forward, or any number of countless other reasons, people...talk. Not everyone, you say? Many people are naturally quiet and introverted and don't need to perpetually hear their own voice, you say? Fine. Show me a naturally quiet person and I'll show you how that same person would vomit their thoughts all over the place under the correct circumstances.

For the sake of acknowledging chaos, I concede there are exceptions to this general rule of thumb I've so haphazardly outlined above. Please, carry on.

We're back in the Command Room with Littlethumb and Daring Bird, not long since we left them. An hour at most. Littlethumb is finishing his inspection of the mysterious jack-in-the-box and Daring Bird is reviewing communications from Silas and Jimmy.

"There's some interesting news," says Daring Bird.

"What?"

"Team Bebi and Jimmy have a lead on the collection, and apparently so does Silas."

"Awesome. How'd that happen? I thought you put everyone on break."

"Well, Jimmy and Bebiana are in Vegas, and Sal's in Prague, so…"

"Ha. Enough said." Littlethumb turns to Daring Bird and pulls a latex glove off his left hand, stretching several of the fingers until the glove shoots off his hand with a snap. The glove on the right hand is removed in less dramatic fashion after he realizes his uncle isn't watching.

Daring Bird turns away from the computer and motions to the jack-in-the-box. "What's up with that thing?"

"I think we're all set. If it's booby trapped, I can't find anything."

"Great. Let's break and go take a look at lunch. I'm already getting hungry again. Too much coffee, I think."

"Sounds good to me. If we're going to get blown up, we should definitely have a final meal."

"Right. You got any porterhouse steak?"

"Oh yeah. Fresh lobster tails, too. We'll do surf and turf, and I think I have twice baked potatoes already prepped. The Brussels sprouts will take five minutes. You can whip up the red velvet cake."

"Right. So, grilled chicken and greens?"

"Leftover salmon."

"Works for me."

As they make their way to the kitchen, Daring Bird breaks formation and returns to the Command Room, reappearing a few seconds later with the crumpled-up list of talking points that Littlethumb tossed in the garbage.

"You kidding me?" says Littlethumb, watching his uncle un-wad the paper.

"No. I keep forgetting…" Daring Bird pulls out a pair of reading glasses and scans the list.

"I will never get used to those," says Littlethumb.

"Shut it." Daring Bird finishes his review of the list and says, "Oh, right," then folds the paper and removes his glasses. "Man. Either I'm extremely distracted by something or my memory is beginning to slip at way too young an age."

Littlethumb opens his mouth for smartass commentary, but Daring Bird cuts him off.

"Don't say it."

"What?"

"You know what."

"Actually I don't. I was going to wing it, but you interrupted my thoughts."

"Good. Now hush and let me ask you a question. You made a comment while I was in Marseille about something going on here. I was trying to ask you before. What's the deal?"

"Hey, close your eyes and tell me what you see."

"No."

"I bet you it's that spy lady."

Daring Bird's face betrays him.

"Ha! I knew it. You're thinking about her right now! You're not suffering early onset anything yet, old man, except early onset horny. You've caught a love bug. That's what your problem is. Distracted by the spy lady's booty. I can't believe I didn't notice it the minute you told me about her. Jesus, I can smell it on you."

"Quit changing the subject."

"I'm not. It's nothing."

"Then why do you keep changing the subject."

"Why do you keep changing the subject?" The look Daring Bird shoots his nephew tells Littlethumb his uncle has had enough playful banter. Daring Bird isn't one to lose his patience, but he's never been above patiently knocking his nephew to his nephew's ass when necessary.

"Alright, alright. Sorry. It's nothing, really. Just this kid. Supposedly a journalist trying to get me to do an interview. When I mentioned it to you before we had just met. I was curious but not super concerned. That's why I didn't say more."

"Has anything changed?"

"Eh. Not really. I can't get a bead on him. Whether I trust him or not, which is odd. And I'm not sure I believe he's a journalist, so I guess that's odd too. He hangs around the shelter, helps out with the guys. We play chess. Lots of conversation but nothing substantial, you know? I'm not sure what to do. I mean, I can't make him go away, whether he's uncomfortable for me or not. He's done nothing wrong."

"Have you done any research on him? Find out if he's telling the truth about who he is?"

"Nah, not with everything else going on. I guess mentally I kind of put him on the back burner. Besides, if I was that concerned, normally I'd have Cross look into him." Littlethumb's speaking with his back turned, pulling containers from the refrigerator.

"Put it on the back burner, huh?"

"Yep." Turning around to unload goods from the refrigerator onto the counter, Littlethumb catches on to Daring Bird's disbelief.

"Really?" asks Daring Bird.

"What?"

"Alright," Daring Bird relents. "Fair enough. But, if you aren't truly concerned, why not give the interview and be done with him?"

"I'm not sure. Honestly, that never really crossed my mind."

"Seriously?"

"Oh, not the giving the interview part. The being done with him part. I have no idea what he's really after, but I can't shake the feeling it's not about doing a 'where is he now' story about me."

"So, this dude gives you an off-putting gut reaction, you ignore your intuition, and continue hanging out with him?"

"Well, when you put it like that, yeah." Littlethumb shrugs his shoulders with a humble, "I don't know what else to tell you" expression.

All three monkeys leap onto the kitchen's island counter, strutting in tight formation around Littlethumb and Daring Bird's lunch ingredients. "Alright, knuckleheads. Alright." Littlethumb takes a handful of nuts and evenly disperses them into three small bowls at the end of the counter, then adds berries and carrot.

"You know," says Daring Bird. "There's an easy way for you to figure out what's up with this guy. Won't matter if he's lying about who he is or not. What's his name, anyway?"

"Redmond Sinclair. Goes by Redy."

"Interesting. Excellent name."

"Yeah."

"You know what I'm going to say. Why haven't you already done it?" Daring Bird is implying Littlethumb should paint a portrait of Redmond Sinclair, to elucidate the young man's intentions as harmless, or potentially devious. The notion of painting Redy is exactly why Littlethumb's been avoiding this conversation.

"You know why. I'm blocked."

"You're chasing your tail, kid. You've spent months trying to figure out the reason you're blocked."

"Yes. I know. It's been very frustrating."

"I'm sure it has. Maybe, instead of wasting so much time trying to figure out why you're blocked, you should be looking for an irresistible reason to paint."

Trumpets. Fireworks. One thousand doves released into the air at once. The famed nuclear mushroom cloud over the New Mexican desert. Any of these works as an adequate descriptive analogy for Littlethumb's internal recognition that his uncle is correct. "Son of a bitch," he mumbles.

"I know," says Daring Bird. "What can I say? I'm good."

22

After his conversation with Willy Peete at Jacque's Taproom, Redy Sinclair wanders the sidewalks, placing one foot after the other, walking off a two-pint lunch with no forward thought other than right-foot, left-foot, right-foot, left-foot, smile at the person coming toward you, wave through the window to the lady at the register in there, don't think, don't think, don't think, don't think. His subconscious mind is battling for his sanity, doing everything possible to quiet the monster, to keep the monster locked in its cage while the bag of flesh wrapped around all this crazy is don't think, don't think, don't thinking his way through the world until he finds himself in the downtown grocery.

Although their conversation ended on a different subject, Willy tapped a nerve. The issue is the concept of opening up to Littlethumb. Willy's suggestion that Redy expose himself to another. What is there to expose, save for the pain and anguish suffered at the fiddling hands of Uncle Carmine? Nothing. The end result of Littlethumb Brooks' fame, with regard to the life of Redmond Sinclair, could have been the title of a Tommy Toxic album: *Uncle Carmine and the Damage Done.*

Which means, despite Willy's good intentions, the monster is shaking its cage, and the subconscious struggle to quiet the beast has left Redy in a dreamy state. Why is he holding this tiny mirror and these hotdogs? A cashier asks if he needs a bag for his purchases. Why is he standing at the counter of the grocery buying a makeup mirror and a pack of hotdogs? He doesn't wear makeup. Or eat hotdogs.

I'll tell you why, because you know who does eat hotdogs? Who desperately drools over hotdogs, or any other type of people food containing the sweet, sweet meat of former animals? Dogs. In this instance, I'm specifically thinking about a particular coydog one might want to keep quiet if one were spying on a certain cabin in rural Canada.

Master Chee is in a coffee shop eating donuts and reading a book about Solomon Hand. Hand was a serial killer and cannibal who murdered and ate an entire small town in Kentucky sometime in the early 1900s. The book Master Chee reads is a comedic cookbook titled *Town to Table: The Recipes of Solomon Hand,* detailing the ingredients and cooking styles Hand may have used on his neighbors, written because humanity, and particularly American culture, is equally as fuckbrained as it is full of potential. I assume Master Chee's reading this garbage as an exercise in misanthropy, as he persistently scoffs in disgust with every turned page after page after page. Don't worry, Master Chee, the copy of *God is a Donut and the Universe is His Hole* you're planning to read next, while eating donuts, will make everything better.

Oh, I mention the enigmatic Master Chee right here for the following reason. Upon entering a formal agreement for surprise attack training, Littlethumb disengaged all of the cabin's perimeter defenses. No tripwires, video cameras, or motion sensors were allowed to operate for the duration of the training, if the purpose of the training were to be fulfilled.

Making his way out to the cabin unnoticed shouldn't be too tricky for Redy. The main road north from town is scarcely driven, as most the commercial traffic heads southwest toward Toronto or east toward Ottawa, and there's nothing else off the dirt road to Littlethumb's current home but hunting land.

The trip is made on a bicycle. Whether Redy likes it or not, the beast is engaged, and his dreamy transitional state of being has given way to coldblooded calculation. Depending on how his final plans shake out, a bicycle's silent approach and escape might wind up being more crucial than speed. Plus, if a motorized vehicle does happen along, he should be able to hear them coming from a distance, allowing him to get off the road unseen. In the end, if he winds up using a car, fine. No reason not to be prepared for multiple scenarios.

About one and a half kilometers from the cabin, Redy stashes the bike and tromps the rest of the way through the woods on foot. Yes, I said tromps. Dude ain't a ninja. Ain't no Master Chee. Though, by the time he reaches the cabin, he is a fully different creature. Out here, in the woods, it's safe to let the monster speak to him.

Once the cabin is in view, he snoops around more effectively. Super quiet-like, hotdogs locked and loaded. Woofus Maximus is outdoors "on duty." Woof hasn't quite grown into his role as a guard dog. The will is there, but the skill is not. Any defensive barks are preemptively quashed by flying tubular meat-stuff. When Redy appears, Woof quickly says hello and returns to his dirty, hotdog-gorging business.

Slinking around the house, Redy cases the perimeter, committing the lay of the land to memory and sketching the exterior of the cabin from multiple vantage points. Three offshoot rooms extend from the main building. One on each side and one off the back. Though most likely inconsequential to Redy's eventual plans, he notes an array of solar panels scattered across each section of the roof. There's also a large elevated water reservoir tucked into the exterior's northwest corner. Once the sketches are finished, he decides to take a closer look. What's the worst that can happen? He gets caught spying and claims he was trying to gather information for the article he's writing?

There's a thrill to be had, in sneaking. We all felt the exhilaration in our youth. You may have forgotten. I haven't. I sneak as much as possible, as I'm convinced that prudently employed childish behavior helps one maintain a youthful mind and body. Want to keep your spirit young? Try stomping around your house like a T-Rex every other Thursday. Roar in frustration then laugh your ass off when your tiny T-Rex arms won't let you reach the delicious leftovers in the back of your refrigerator.

Redy may not be indulging his inner child, but in an effort to obtain the cabin's interior layout, he is peering in windows from viewpoints any twelve-year-old will tell you are safe spying angles. Most of the windows have open blinds or curtains, or at least enough of a gap in whatever may be covering the window so that Redy can get a glimpse of what's inside. There's a small room that appears to be a meditation area (or something similar), an art studio, an open-air kitchen, and a common area with a loft overhead. One more room, however, is impossible to see inside.

From a window in the front of the cabin, Redy sees what must be the doorway to the uninspected room. Two humans emerge from that doorway and Redy hastily ducks out of view. *Ah*, he thinks. *The mirror. Of course.* He pulls the mirror from his pocket and holds it up to see the reflection of two men walking through the cabin.

When the coast is clear, Redy rolls back over and lifts his head again, barely enough so he can peek through the window. There's Littlethumb, standing in the kitchen pulling food out of the refrigerator. The other dude has his back turned. *Who the hell is that guy?*

"You're not that good," says Littlethumb. We're back inside the cabin, where Littlethumb prepares lunch and responds to his uncle's suggestion of painting Redy Sinclair's portrait. "You had to dig through the garbage to remember what the hell you wanted to talk about."

"Distraction does not equal quality degradation. I got you cornered, nephew. Tell me I'm wrong."

"You aren't. Painting Redy is the most logical solution, though you do realize it's possible nothing happens? I wind up just staring at the canvas, or even worse, painting some godawful piece of realism."

"What's your problem again, with realism?"

"Realism is merely a reflection. Not an explanation."

"You make that up yourself?"

"No, that's Benoit Leclercq, my favorite Belgian expressionist."

"Dear God. Belgium, the schizophrenic middle sibling of France and Germany."

"Yep. That's why I like his work."

"Yeah, yeah. All jokes aside, what's the worst that can happen? You don't paint for shit, and you're right back where you already are?"

"Pretty much."

"Okay then. Problem solved. Let's eat."

Redy ducks again as the men turn his direction carrying plates of food. Time to go. Pretty much has what he came for. Except…that room. Why the hell is that room so buttoned up?

Take another look, Redy. See if you missed anything. Should take them at least ten minutes or so to eat. You can check the exterior again. Maybe there's a peek-through spot after all.

There isn't. Each of the room's exterior walls has a single window. Every one of the windows is locked and blacked out tightly. There are plenty of logical reasons for having curtains tightly drawn, including no particular reason at all. Perhaps it's a dark room for photo processing. Or, the room could be used for storing any number of other items they don't want the sunlight to damage. Or, the curtains are left closed because the room is rarely used. Plenty of logical explanations.

What there aren't plenty of logical explanations for is what Redy sees after he returns to the window in the front of the cabin. Littlethumb and the other dude are standing in the kitchen area attaching cookware to their bodies. Small metal pans have been taped to the front of their legs. Small cutting boards are attached to their arms. The man Redy doesn't recognize is currently duct-taping a cookie sheet to Littlethumb's torso, already wearing one himself. Both appear to be fitted with bulletproof vests underneath the cookie sheets.

What the fuck? thinks Redy.

Once they've finished attaching kitchen implements to their bodies, each man grabs a saucepan and heads toward the mysterious room. Before they reach the room, Woofus Maximus trots in, emerging from a secret doggie tunnel that runs under the front porch and up through an interior floorboard doggie-door. If you've ever had a canine housemate, you're acquainted with the apparently random, out of character decisions a dog may periodically make. This isn't so much out of character for Woofus as delayed. The initial excitement he felt over the hotdogs, this manna from heaven, temporarily short-circuited his instinctual instructions to deliver his kills to his master. To seek approval for consumption. After gorging through all but one of the hotdogs metered out to him by Redy, Woof's instincts finally reminded him to see if his dad might also want a bite of hotdog.

"Oh shit," says Redy.

Inside the cabin, Littlethumb notices Woofus as he and Daring Bird are crossing the room.

"Hey buddy," he says. Then he stops walking. "What the hell is that?"

Damn near sick from tube-meat, wagging tail slowed by nitrate satisfaction, Woof sets the hotdog on the floor and pokes at it with his nose, rolling it closer to his dad.

"Hotdog," says Daring Bird.

"Hotdog?" asks Littlethumb. "Where'd you get a hotdog, bud?"

Redy ducks and crawls away from the window as fast as he can. Once outside the window's frame, he scrambles to his feet and leaps off the front porch, dashing toward the woods. Reaching cover from the tree line, he turns around to see Littlethumb and the other dude exit the front door of the cabin.

Definitely time to go, he thinks, backing further into the woods as quietly as possible.

"Wanna stay here for the flush out while I circle the house?" asks Littlethumb, scanning the land in front of the cabin.

"Sure thing. Go take a look," says Daring Bird.

With clanking metal attached to his body, Littlethumb heads to the right side of the front porch, opposite the side Redy escaped from. The saucepan in Littlethumb's hand is moved to an assault position as he disappears off the side of the porch and around the house. Daring Bird closes his eyes and breaths deeply, slowing his thoughts. Listening carefully, he reopens his eyes and searches the edges of the woods. Rustling branches. Crunchy leaves. Any telltale sign of movement.

Nothing.

A few moments pass before Littlethumb emerges from the left side of the cabin, hopping back up onto the front porch.

"Nothing, I take it?" asks Daring Bird.

"A couple of tracks around the house, but that's all."

"What do you think? Your sensei for hire?"

"Yeah, most likely. Funny timing though."

"Funny? That's one way to put it."

"Not ha ha funny. You know what I mean. It was probably Master Chee. The hotdog and footprints are outliers, but he likes to mix shit up. And he appears to be crazy as hell, so I wouldn't put much past him. It's highly possible he had an attack planned, saw you were here, and bailed."

"Fair enough." The words float off into the wind as both men stand quietly, each deciding whether they believe the snoop was Master Chee. Each coming to the same conclusion: There's no way to know. "Back to it then?" says Daring Bird.

"Yeah, I think so." They head back inside and make their way to the Command Room. In preparation for the turning of the crank, Littlethumb and Daring Bird move all the computers and other high-end electronics to one side of the room, placing them on the floor against a wall. Tables are flipped on their sides in front of the damageables to act as shields. Daring Bird and Littlethumb previously considered taking the device outside to turn its crank, but decided against the possibility of being seen, despite the rural locale. A decision thoroughly reinforced by the presence of an unwanted guest, whether the unwanted guest was Master Chee or not.

Preparations complete, they stand in front of the mysterious, slightly oversized jack-in-the-box with a non-frightening clown painted on the side. Sauce pots rest calmly on each man's head. Gas masks cover their faces.

"Luke," says Daring Bird, mimicking the respiratory exuberance of cinema's most famous Darth. "Is this really necessary?" He's referencing their cookware body armor, holding his arms out for observation.

"Yes," says Littlethumb. "Better safe than sorry."

"But the force."

Littlethumb chuckles. "I was expecting, 'but I'm your father.'"

"Felt perfunctory."

"Ha! You're on your game today."

"Yeah, the possibility of getting blown-up does that."

"And yet, you question our multipurpose body armor."

"I question the usefulness, not the intentions."

"And on that note…" Littlethumb turns to his uncle, who gives a solemn nod of the head – doesn't any nod of the head feel solemn when the head-nodder is wearing a gas mask? Whatever. Killing my own moment…

And on that note, Littlethumb turns the crank.

23

Rolling off his naked wife, despotic copulation successful, Xander closes his eyes for an early night's rest. Instead, right as he's dozing off, the very moment his mind flips off its light switch, a vibration pulses from the watch on his bedside table.

The watch is a prototype home network device, exceedingly more advanced than any similar product already in the marketplace. Xander hasn't decided whether or not he'll sell the design to a technology firm or manufacture the watch in-house. Or, he may keep the design for himself and let the world continue advancing at the snail's pace currently approved by governments and the corporate hacks who worship the world's stock markets. Tiny incremental profit-driven steps in consumerism being the dominant force behind technological improvement and whatnot.

The vibration grows more aggressive. Xander's mind accepts its fate and turns the lights back on, opening his eyes to inspect the watch. *Interesting*, he thinks, before an explosion of recognition blasts him fully awake. *Very interesting!*

Hastily unknotting himself from sheets and covers, he practically leaps out of bed. Pants are gracefully legged as Xander hop-steps across the room, grabbing a tee shirt on his way out. Wifey rolls over and sleepily asks where he's going, but he ignores her. She's nameless and faceless for a reason, folks, and she knows it too.

Xander attaches the watch to his wrist as he shuffles down the hallway to his office. There's a Tea application on the touch screen. He selects black with spiced cloves. The butler will arrive shortly to deliver his liquid caffeine. In the meantime, a nice toot from the amphetamine inhaler sitting in the top right drawer of his desk will do the trick. Wakey wakey!

As his brain shoots chemically induced fireworks through his body, Xander brings his computer to life and logs in. Username: Lord Bowfly. Password not shown. Don't bother trying to guess the password. The answer is too obvious for you to ever stumble across, there being an endless amount of potential obvious answers.

Seriously, stop trying to guess his password and pay attention. I'm certain you know what's going on here. Yes, Xander's watch has alerted him to the activation of D-13. The jack is out of the box.

Shortly before Xander Bowfly receives notification that his device has been activated, Littlethumb and Daring Bird brace themselves for impact as Littlethumb turns the jack-in-the-box's crank. Keeping with tradition, Pop Goes the Weasel emanates from a built-in music box. I suppose the anticipation would have been equally unnerving in silence.

On the penultimate click of the crank, both men flinch dramatically. Nothing happens. Each man looks at the other, gas masks hiding chuckle-faced expressions mixed with varying degrees of other simultaneous emotions. Whimsy, relief, and snark, to name a few.

"I guess our timing was off, huh?" says Littlethumb.

"I guess so," says Daring Bird, who whistles the tune and counts the beat on his fingers. "Does it go to the end of the song, or is it supposed to spring on the 'pop'?"

"I don't know but we jumped early either way."

"Oh, fuck it." Daring Bird abruptly reaches for the crank.

"Jesus, shit!" says Littlethumb, as Daring Bird twists the crank forward one more click.

The jack-in-the-box pops open, sending the contents bursting forth, though a jack puppet does not emerge. Instead, a geometric object bobs and sways on the end of a metal spring. The object appears to be made of bronze and has twelve flat, pentagonal sides. At each intersecting corner of the object's body is a small round knob, formed from the bronze. In the center of each side is a circular pattern composed of decorative amethyst flakes. There is a faint internal glow showing through the amethyst.

"That's different," says Daring Bird.

"Unusual for sure. I think it's a Roman dodecahedron," says Littlethumb. "Or, more accurately, a replica of one. This isn't an artifact."

Daring Bird stares at Littlethumb, who's staring in fascination at the dodecahedron, until he notices his uncle is staring at him.

"What?" asks Littlethumb.

"This is the part where you tell me what a Roman dodamajig is so I don't have to look it up."

"Oh. No sweat. I didn't want to be presumptuous..."

"Be presumptuous."

"Right. Basically, no one knows what they're for. Maybe a hundred or so have been discovered throughout Europe. They date back to the Roman Empire, hence the name, but no one knows what they were used for, if anything. They may have been strictly decorative, but it's much more likely they had some form of utility."

"And how, exactly…actually, no. Why, exactly, do you know about these things?"

"I read a lot."

"That's my line."

"Bacchantics?"

"That's mine too."

"Man, I never realized how selfish you are."

Daring Bird shrugs his shoulders nonchalantly. "Don't know what to tell you, kid. I'm kind of a jerk. I like to think of it as artistic license." With that, Daring Bird takes the pot off his head, knocks the crap out of his nephew, takes the device, and disappears.

Okay, okay. That doesn't happen at all. Sorry. My mind went off on a "what if Daring Bird had betrayed Littlethumb" tangent, so I decided to tease you. Daring Bird never betrays his nephew. You can do the research yourself or save the effort and trust me. I told you before, this isn't historical fiction. Historical fiction sucks.

Daring Bird takes the pot off his head, then removes his gas mask. "Either we take this stuff off or cook ourselves for dinner. What do you think?"

"I think you would be very gamey," replies Littlethumb, removing his own saucepan-helmet and gasmask. After setting them down, he locates a pair of scissors. Daring Bird opens a pocket knife and they both cut away the tape holding on their homemade armor.

"So," says Daring Bird. "If no one knows what these things are for, why does our guy make a device to look like one? More importantly, what does this doda-whatchama-doohickey do? I'm assuming there's at least speculation as to what they may have been used for?"

"Yeah, there are numerous theories. Now say it with me, do-deca-he-dron."

Ignoring Littlethumb's pronunciation lesson, Daring Bird says, "Was this built in an analogous fashion to one of those theories, or purely for fun? Or as a disguise? Or because whoever built it likes history? And does it matter?"

"I have a suspicion it doesn't matter." Make-shift body armor removed, Littlethumb takes a closer look at the dodecahedron. "You see these circles here?"

"Yes."

"On a typical dodecahedron, most, if not all, of these circles were open, exposing a hollow body."

"Interesting. Whoever built this went to a lot of trouble to cast the bronze. Hard to believe the effort was purely for artistic purposes."

"Right?"

"Is the bronze design functional? Does the shape serve a purpose?"

"Maybe it's symbolism."

"But to what end, when no one knows what these things were used for?"

"Good point. Maybe it has something to do with the compositional properties of bronze."

"Or maybe it is random. Because they like history, or they're a big fan of the Roman Empire. Or just because they know these things exist. Maybe whoever built this needed something to put guts inside, so they chose this *dodecahedron* shape for the hell of it."

"Guts! Yes!" Littlethumb makes a hesitant face as he reaches for the device, apprehensively tapping one of the corner knobs with his right pointer finger.

As Littlethumb touches the device, Daring Bird says, "Bzzzzzzzzz!"

You knew that was coming, right? I mean, I would have done the same. I'm guessing you would have too, as I'm assuming the best in you.

Littlethumb busts out laughing and says, "Fuck you, man. For real. Suck a butt."

"I got you." I'm sure you understand how pleased Daring Bird is with himself.

"Yeah, that was solid."

"Touch it again."

"I'm going to. Shut up." Littlethumb reaches again, tapping at the corner knob, then probing the rest of the device. "Apparently it isn't dangerous to touch."

"Until someone turns on the anti-theft shock blast."

"Would you stop? Seriously. Not making this any easier, ya jerk." A side-eye shot off the bow from Littlethumb has no effect on Daring Bird as he smiles heartily, extremely proud of teasing his nephew, who says, "I hate you."

"Me too."

The examination continues in silence as Littlethumb inspects the dodecahedron from all angles until he finds a micro-port for electronic connectivity, discretely located at the base of the device near the spring. "There it is," he says.

"Access point?"

"Yep. Micro-USB port. I'm guessing dual purpose, charging and programming. There's gotta be a rechargeable battery inside, and I'm betting this thing will talk to a computer."

"Then let's plug that fucker up and see what it has to say."

Who in the hell are these two? Those are Xander's first thoughts after the video relay on the dodecahedron activates, as he stares at the image of two gasmask-covered faces on his computer screen. Positioned in one of the corner knobs of the dodecahedron is a single tiny camera. A lamentable design flaw, internally noted by Xander as both the figures step outside the camera's range.

On a side note, when discussing Xander's device, most of the time we're going to use the abbreviation "dodeca," because I like the way it sounds and typing dodecahedron over and over is cumbersome. I could use Xander's label, D-13, but seeing how only the bad guys know that name and the good guys will most likely continue referring to the device in a variety of ways, dodeca feels more inclusive of you, dear friend and confidant. Our own special descriptor. Thus, when Xander's around we will use the name D-13. Otherwise, you and I will most often refer to the device as the dodeca.

Back to the tiny camera. Xander housed the camera inside one of the knobs located on the northern hemisphere of the dodeca. Appearing to be solid bronze like the others, this knob is formed of a translucent bronze compound, allowing the camera to function without being visible to an observer. Similar in effect to a two-way mirror in a police station's interrogation chamber or a pervert's bathroom. In other words, Littlethumb isn't going to find the camera and our heroes aren't going to know they're being watched.

Regrettably for Xander, the single camera extremely limits his surveillance perspective. Xander assumes he included the camera to spy on whoever might purchase D-13. Potential theft of the device would not have been considered in his design plans. Not when raging on confidence fueled by powerful drugs. Besides, presumptive failure doesn't fit within the narrative of a winner's mindset. Otherwise, Xander would have included a tracking device.

Why didn't I put a fucking tracking device in the damn thing? And for fuck's sake, why one camera? Such is life, Xander, such is life. Just like a work of art, an invention is never perfect.

Before he can thoroughly beat himself up over design flaws, Xander sees a face he recognizes on his monitor. Daring Bird, who is no longer wearing a gasmask, has stepped back into the camera's view, but he moves away again before Xander can capture his image. *Dammit. Almost got you.* A second of frustration and then, *That face looked familiar. Where have I seen him before?* Unable to remember, after several minutes of consideration, Xander lets it go. *It'll come to me. Always does.*

Xander sets the video feed to record then switches away from the camera monitor, opening the diagnostic software for D-13. The program is running successfully. That's why he didn't install a tracker! *Of course.* The simplicity of design paradigm. A dedicated tracking device wasn't necessary, as he should be able to trace the coded radio signal transmitting D-13's status updates, bouncing from satellite to satellite and decoded by his computer.

The victory is short lived, as Xander quickly presumes he won't be able to trace the signal. Under these circumstances, intuition suggests a successful trace will be too easy. He's correct. As we've previously discussed, our heroes' cabin is a telecommunications blackhole. Any wifi or alternate radio signal emitting from the cabin is immediately scrambled into countless "pieces," to be reconstituted by thousands of separate signals on its path to wherever the original signal is going. If Xander attempts to trace D-13's signal, it will appear to originate from thousands of different locations at once.

Don't get me wrong. Despite his suspicions for a successful trace, Xander tries anyway. A thorough mind takes thorough action. Exhaustive due diligence, this is the way of the transcendent evil genius.

Several days trudge by as Littlethumb attempts to determine the dodeca's function. He's figured out the bronze shell houses a self-contained artificial intelligence utilizing an internal database (most likely a digital version of the *Encyclopedia Britannica*...). The artificial intelligence is running a non-sequential program, designed to process an infi-nitely complicated algorithm. An infinitely complicated algorithm most likely designed to solve a very sophisticated unknown problem. This is a verbose effort to say they still have no clue as to the dodeca's purpose because Littlethumb can't figure out what the algorithm is attempting to calculate.

Meanwhile, Daring Bird receives updates from the team. Silas had his fill of wine and women and has taken off to further investigate the trophy wife's husband. He couldn't extract coordinates for the hunting lodge from the disgruntled spouse, but he did get her money-hoarding prick of a husband's name. In Vegas, Jimmy and Bebiana have acquired intel on several upcoming black-market auctions, and Bebiana had a hell of a run at the craps tables. Equally as important, Jimmy's son took a huge shining to Bebiana, so Vegas was an all-around success.

Garo sent a melodramatic, two-word update via email. Subject line: Stir Crazy. Message: Cabin fever!

Last but not least, Titus is missing.

24

"Wake up!"

Daring Bird is snoozing on the couch in the cabin's living room. There may be no rest for the wicked, but the righteous know well the enduring importance of an afternoon nap. Particularly an afternoon nap from which slow escape is the only path to freedom. A solid minute is required for Daring Bird to wake up and gather his senses before opening his eyes to find an enthusiastic nephew practically hopping up and down in excitement.

"I figured it out!"

"Figured what out?" Daring Bird sleepily asks.

"What do you think?"

"I don't think. Bring me a cup of coffee or a tea or something."

"Get your ass up! This is exciting!"

"Alright, alright. Fine. Fuck. Fine. I'm coming." Daring Bird sits up on the couch and collects his thoughts. A pleasant memory adds a smile to his face. As he stands, he says, "You have no idea how nice my dream was."

"Yeah, I think I do," says Littlethumb. Daring Bird looks at Littlethumb with an appropriately quizzical expression, to which Littlethumb responds by raising his eyebrows and nonchalantly pointing to his uncle's crotch.

Daring Bird looks down and says, "I'll be damned."

"Not yet you aren't," replies Littlethumb. "For no man lay truly damned, so long as his penis doth yet function. Third Fuckalonians, chapter five, verse four, the Cyrenaic Bible."

Still too sleepy headed to enjoy the joke, Daring Bird blinks obvious confusion and says, "Let me take a leak."

"Hurry up!" responds Littlethumb, smacking his uncle on the ass. "This is exciting!"

They reconvene in the Command Room a few moments later. Daring Bird walks in, piss-boner successfully relieved, carrying a cup of leftover, microwaved coffee. Leftover coffee tastes like mud, but it does the trick.

Littlethumb leans against the table where the dodeca is connected to one of the room's many computers. Arms folded across his chest, he's extremely pleased with himself. Stevie Two Sharks and Zeus are standing on the table on either side of the computer in the exact same pose as Littlethumb. Sir Alister Pickney is sitting on top of the dodeca, feeling very regal. Woofus Maximus' hotdog eating ass is god knows where, anywhere but wherever those damn monkey devils are. Arf.

"Alright," says Daring Bird. "You look extremely proud of yourself. Whatcha got?"

"What *we've* got is something amazing. I don't know where to begin!"

"Keep it simple. Does that help?"

"Nope!"

"Then begin from the beginning and keep it slow."

"I'll try." Littlethumb takes a deep breath and scratches his chin. Not thoughtfully. It's an itch. "So, the other day we figured out this device is running a program, right?"

"Yes. You plugged it into the computer and it was doing something."

"Exactly. What it was doing, is doing, is processing an algorithm. What appears to be called an undecidable problem."

"Which means the algorithm never stops running until the answer to whatever question the algorithm was designed around is yes."

"Very good, uncle. You were paying attention."

"Don't let the fake leather pants fool you."

"If those are fake, they already have." Beat. Staring contest. Daring Bird loses and sports a tightlipped, corner of the mouth smirk. Littlethumb continues. "Anyway, I think I figured out the question. Or, not me, I should say, but the program I'm running to analyze the algorithm seems to have figured out the question."

"What's the question?"

"Do you watch *Star Trek*?"

"That's the question this thing is trying to answer?"

"No, that's my question."

"You've known me your entire life, kid."

"And yet, I'm still asking. So do you watch *Star Trek* or not?"

"How in the world do you not know I'm a *Star Trek* fan? My amazing Captain Picard impersonation?"

"Oh, he's *Star Trek*?" This right here is a desert-dry, exasperated fakeroo. Littlethumb knows Captain Picard is from *Star Trek*. You'd have to be a completely off-the-grid psychopath like Harrison Crutcher (look him up) to not know the name Jean-Luc Picard.

"Yes. *The Next Generation*." Daring Bird looks at Littlethumb like he should know what he's talking about. Littlethumb masterfully feigns ignorance.

"I'm not really a fan. I've only seen the movies."

"*The Next Generation* made movies too. You know what, never mind, but please know I'm deeply disturbed by this conversation."

"Fair enough." Littlethumb holds a poker face as long as he can before cracking into laughter.

"It was a rhetorical question."

"It was a rhetorical question."

"Hardy fuckin' har," says Daring Bird. "You got me. Now will you tell me the damn question? The actual question. How can you be this excited and not just tell me what the hell you're so excited about…?"

"I was trying to set up a cool reveal! All you had to do was say, 'Why yes, nephew, I do enjoy *Star Trek*'. I didn't know you would ruin it!"

Daring Bird shoves a playfully aggressive finger into the air and says, "What the hell is the damn thing doing?!"

"Trying to invent a replicator!"

"What!?"

"I said…!"

"Wait! Wait…" Daring Bird resets the conversational tone. "Okay. No more shouting. Now, how is that thing going to invent a replicator."

"The *device* appears to be trying to determine whether or not it is scientifically possible."

"To invent a replicator?"

"Yes."

"You mean, like a *Star Trek* replicator?"

Littlethumb takes his turn sporting a jokingly contemptuous facial expression, jutting his chin forward with eyes flared open, holding both hands palms-up, clearly stating that his rhetorical question, 'Do you watch *Star Trek*?,' was asked for a very specific reason.

"Alright, alright," says Daring Bird. "So, this *device* is trying to figure out if building a replicator is really possible."

"Precisely. And I believe the presumption is, if the algorithm determines inventing a replicator is scientifically possible…" There's a moment of recognition here. "You know what, maybe we shouldn't be saying replicator. I bet it's trademarked, or copywritten, or both."

"I think you can still say it in real life."

"Eh, let's go with duplicator, to be safe. Not one-hundred percent accurate, but I don't think either of us wants to be tied up in court litigating a copyright or trademark infringement case."

"Ha!" The coffee has done its business and Daring Bird immediately gets this joke. Do you remember? The trial to prove Littlethumb's identity? The proceedings began as a trademark infringement suit. "So, to restate, the device is trying to answer the question, is a *duplicator*," Daring Bird tosses a wink at Littlethumb, "is a duplicator scientifically possible, and the presumption is?"

"The presumption is, if the algorithm determines a duplicator is scientifically possible, you will find a general understanding of how the machine would function within the algorithm's calculations, which could also explain the mechanics for building the actual machine."

"Then what we may have here, in the end, is the basic design for a machine that would change the course of humanity."

"Absolutely."

"Do you think it's possible?"

"Yes. In some form or fashion. We already have three-dimensional printing technology and those capabilities are advancing rapidly."

"This would be different though. We're talking about making things out of thin air, if you're comparing the machine to the one on," Daring Bird whispers, playfully, "*that T.V. show.*"

"Ha. No. Not out of thin air. Not likely. Any practical application would probably require organic matter. Or maybe inorganic, but I don't think we would want to eat inorganic matter. Either way, I wouldn't expect a *duplicator* to be able to make something out of nothing. I'm pretty sure making something from nothing is scientifically impossible."

"Is it though? Does what we consider 'nothing' really exist?"

"Odd phrasing, but I get your question. I guess maybe not. We perceive empty spaces that aren't really empty. Atoms are everywhere, and I'm pretty sure that's what the device," Littlethumb whispers here, hand covering his mouth, matching his uncle, "*on that T.V. show*, did. Instantaneously rearrange atoms."

"Not to *Star Trek* nerd you here, but I'm pretty sure they had several different iterations of similarly capable devices, depending on the technological era a particular storyline was set in." Daring Bird doesn't give his nephew the opportunity for a smart-ass retort on this one. "Never mind. Not the point. I'll punch myself later."

"If you don't, I will."

"Fine. So, this device could figure out how to rearrange atoms readily available in the air. Or potentially, rearrange the composition of the atoms themselves?"

"I suppose, yeah. Or at least, that's what the algorithm is trying to decide. Or something along those lines. Honestly, I'm assuming there are possibilities we can't begin to fathom."

"Right. Most likely. So how long do we wait?"

"There's no telling. This program could run for years. We could actually stumble across the technology to create a duplicator while the program is still trying to calculate if it's possible. Whatever database it's using is fixed, to keep the device self-contained. Any breakthroughs in technology after this was built aren't likely to factor into its calculations."

"Unless the program somehow predicts those technological break-throughs as a result of trying to solve the grander problem. Or if the database gets updated externally."

"Exactamundo, dear uncle."

"Now my head hurts."

"Your face is killing me."

Littlethumb and Daring Bird have adjourned to the living room. Daring Bird sits on the couch with a computer in his lap, checking communications from the team. Littlethumb is pacing around the room and mumbling to himself. The quiet one man show ends when Littlethumb says, "It would change everything," loud enough for Daring Bird to respond.

"Huh?" asks Daring Bird, still focused on the computer.

"Nothing," says Littlethumb. "Everything. Do you realize…that thing. If that thing is successful, it would change the course of humanity. Forever."

"Wait. It's a thing again?"

"Fuck off."

"Sorry. Couldn't help myself. Yes, it would change the world. I thought I said that earlier?"

"You did. I'm just thinking about all the ramifications."

"Well, don't get a cramp. No need to hurt yourself. It's a very big 'if'."

"I know, I know."

Daring Bird closes and sets the laptop aside, then removes his spectacles and tucks them into the chest pocket of his shirt. "It's time for me to go."

"Now?"

"Yes. I mean, not this very moment. I'll leave tomorrow."

"Where to?"

"I'm going to visit my lady friend, relay the information the team has gathered on your stolen collection, see if she can help us track down the paintings."

"Ah yes, your mistress del departamento de agricultura — holy shit!"

"What?!"

"The Department of Agriculture! That's what!" Littlethumb stares at his uncle, waiting for the recognition, which doesn't come fast enough, so he points emphatically toward the Command Room door.

"Oh." Daring Bird says, purposefully feigning understanding at his nephew's herky-jerky pointing, then the recognition honestly sets in. "Oh!"

"Exactly! If the algorithm proves we can synthesize food at the drop of a hat, I suspect the Department of Agriculture would be very interested."

"So would corporate agriculture. They wouldn't need to exist anymore."

"Of course! Man. Sure doesn't take long to reach the part where a bunch of rich people would lose tons of money and would most likely do whatever they could to prevent the advancement of useful technology toward a better world."

"Unless they're the ones who hold the patent."

"Right. Do you think she knows?"

"No, I don't. Or if she does, she's playing a different game. I'm pretty sure I can trust her."

"So, what's next?"

"What's next is we find the collection. And you deal with this Redy character. Don't get sidetracked by the science fiction in the other room."

"Man, that's tough."

"I know, but we have no idea how long the program will run or if a 'yes' answer is even achievable. My guess is, the odds are much more likely the device ages and dies before it discovers inventing a duplicator is possible. Besides, you've got a potentially dangerous, secretive presence inserting himself into your life, and I've had a potentially ominous vision. We need focus." This last bit is spoken with a soberness teetering on internal dismay. One of the quirks about being a receiver of visions is the visions don't come with a manual for interpretation, or a list of instructions for how to respond. Over many years, Daring Bird has learned the best he can do is try not to overreact. You stay mindful and maintain a steady course. Head down, feet forward.

And before you ask, yes, of course the thought of a potentially dangerous stranger hurting his nephew frightens him, but a stoic mind recognizes the presence of the shadow of death on a daily basis. We have no control. Period. We may lose anyone at any given moment, making every day an opportunity for indescribable agony if we aren't duly prepared. And even then, no matter how grounded we are in the reality of life's precious fragility, death often surprises us with a fierce onslaught of pain and anguish.

Our wise uncle understands this. Each lesson he gives Littlethumb on overcoming the fear of losing people is as much for himself as for his nephew. Daring Bird could stay to watch over Littlethumb until the situation with this stranger plays out, but what happens afterward? Any number of other potential reasons to remain nearby until the end result is never leaving your loved one's side, living a life dominated by fear and the hopeful prevention of loss. That is no way to live. Besides, all this human nature-induced emotional gobbledie-goo-goo-goo aside, his nephew can take care of himself. The kid is kind of a badass.

25

If you're a normal person, you may not realize how easily you can make an effective date rape drug in the safe confines of your own home. I had a buddy in college who could make the concoction in his dorm room. Don't worry, we only raped ourselves. We were all about getting chemically obliterated, not terrorizing other humans.

The mixture requires a few simple ingredients, a source of heat, and for several recipes a simple, inexpensive centrifuge, readily available in local hobby shops. Redy's centrifuge arrived in the mail this morning. I resist naming the drug, and certainly won't list the ingredients, out of fear some young knucklehead will read this story and try to figure out how the devil's brew is made. Mischievousness lives a half-step from harmfulness, whether exercised by the innocent at heart or a willful bastard.

Have you ever halfheartedly continued forward with plans you weren't certain you could see through to completion? I ask because Redy Sinclair's been operating in this state of being for a while, and will continue for the foreseeable future. His foray into the woods to scope out the cabin, for example, was performed with a detachment from reality allowing him to ignore the underlying purpose of his scouting mission and focus solely on the reconnaissance itself. I mention this because Redy is currently whipping up a knock-out cocktail in his hotel room, still uncertain he will have the nerve to see this through. You'll know if his level of resolve changes.

Ingredients are mixed and poured into glass test tubes. The tubes go into the 'fuge, switch the power on, and voilà, in an undisclosed amount of time you've got easy bake date rape. A simple, elegant solution for a troubled young man bent on revenge, or for any modern-day evil piece of rapey shit.

Rather than wait on the results, Redy goes about the rest of his day, which leads him to the First Church of Good Deeds. The hallway inside the entrance is lined with damaged umbrellas, standard issue equipment for the poor urban forager. Have I mentioned the survivalist miracle that is duct tape?

The rows of umbrellas put a smile on Redy's rain-wet face. He was hopeful the shelter would be packed on such a dreary day. No matter his purpose for being in this odd little town, Redy truly cares for the shelter's band of broken men (or band of broken brothers, if you will, for those of you possessing maniacal alliterate leanings).

Redy throws his jacket on a hook in the hall, then enters the common room to witness a display of joyful madness. These knuckleheads are banging about the joint like a bunch of coked up two-year-olds let loose in a house made of bouncing floors and crayon-colored walls. He spots Willy and makes his way across the room.

"Hey," Willy says. "Mr. Sinclair! Glad you showed up."

"What the hell is going on?" asks Redy, continuing to soak up the irreverent scene before him.

"Today's Arthur's birthday."

"Oh, right! Dammit. I forgot. I meant to get him a gift."

"I wouldn't worry about a gift, Sinclair. We keep having to remind him today's his birthday as it is."

"Ha! Sounds about right."

"Let's get you a towel, help you dry off," says Willy, giving an encouraging tug to the underside of Redy's arm. "How'd you get so wet, anyway. Don't you own an umbrella?"

"I walked over from the square. Thought I would be fine with my hood on, but the wind picked up. Rain was coming in sideways." They enter a small pantry kitchen off the common area and Willy pulls a couple of large towels from a cabinet and hands them to Redy.

"Here you go."

"Thanks."

"Wanna throw your pants in the dryer? We've probably got something you can wear in the lost and found until they dry."

"Nah, they'll dry quick enough and I've got long johns underneath. I can't even feel it." As he speaks, Redy wipes his face and towels at his hair. Then he dabs at his pants, brushing away as much wet as possible.

"Long johns? On a warm day like this?"

"Warm? If it's in the forties, I'm layered. I don't mess around in the cold, Willy. Being cold is for suckers." The last line is delivered with an affirmative point of the finger, and Willy blurts surprised laughter.

"I suppose it is, young fella! I suppose it is."

They exit the pantry back into the common room and make their way over to a group huddled around Arthur, who's wearing a homemade crown. Arthur is holding court, telling his friends a story about Robin Hood blended with Jack and the Beanstalk, with an appearance from a few Transformers thrown in to boot. Like all the best stories, this one culminates in a glorious battle between the forces of good and evil, where the good guys win and everyone forgets all the death and destruction suffered along the way. I will say, one aspect of Arthur's storytelling I enjoy considerably is how each tale concludes with a triumphant feast. Today's main course is fried chicken. Mountains and mountains of fried chicken.

The group thins upon the completion of Arthur's epic adventure, and the birthday boy sees Redy. "Hey, Redy, do you know what today is?"

Redy gives a knowing look to Willy, who cheerfully shrugs.

"Sometimes he remembers," says Willy.

"It must be the crown," Redy says, then he turns to Arthur. "That's a great crown, Arthur. Let me guess…"

Arthur can't wait. "It's my birthday!"

"Of course! Happy Birthday!"

"What did you get me?"

Redy tosses another knowing look at Willy. "Close your eyes and I will show you."

What ensues is a laborious effort by Arthur to fake pinching his eyes closed while still keeping them open enough to see. The end result is a bunch of blinking and squinting mixed with an expression of dedicated seriousness, as Redy spins three-hundred and sixty degrees then holds up two curled fists.

"Alright, Arthur. Open up your eyes and pick a hand." After careful deliberation, Arthur chooses Redy's left hand, which opens to reveal a folded twenty-dollar bill. "Happy birthday, Arthur."

"Thanks, Redy!" Arthur takes the twenty and parades around the room, trumpeting his king's ransom.

A familiar blue pickup truck pulls into the shelter parking lot. Inside are Captain Wisecrack and his faithful coydog sidekick, Sidesplitter.

Captain Wisecrack is a comic book superhero published by Screwball Comics (© 1985 Gomicorp, Inc. All rights reserved), who has a superhuman ability to defeat his opponents using disarming, irresistible humor. There's no pun he can't deftly sling, no punchline he can't enunciate to its greatest potential. Mother Nature herself can't resist his impeccable comedic timing, and neither could Master Chee. For with Daring Bird back on the road, the Master is back in action, though quite taken by hilarious surprise when he descended upon the pun-iest man in foe-business. He's…Captain Wisecrack!

Seriously, before Littlethumb and Woof left the cabin in their costumes, Master Chee swooped in for an ambush. Sidesplitter's cowl and cape stopped Master Chee in his laughing tracks. After a quick explanation and several rapid fire one-liners, Captain Wisecrack avoided Master Chee's attack. Master Chee wanted no part of a sparring session filled with terrible puns. Moving on…

Of course Littlethumb dressed up as Arthur's favorite comic book character for Arthur's birthday. Would you expect anything less? I hope not.

Oh. Another item of note inside the truck, besides the begrudgingly costumed coydog sidekick, is a plastic tub full of paint supplies. It's time.

Everyone gets a kick out of the arrival of Captain Wisecrack, and Sidesplitter Woofus brings the house down. Arthur is awestruck by the bejeweled scepter Captain Wisecrack presents to him. A perfect match for his crown! Legend has it the scepter was crafted in the depths of the Canadian wilderness by three powerful warlock monkeys of the Tamarin Literatus coven. The scepter has magic, and protecting it is a solemn responsibility Arthur accepts in as solemn a manner as possible, once someone explains to him what the word solemn means. Honestly, Arthur would make a solid film actor, even after the buckshot to his brain.

Redy is enjoying himself, watching all these broken fellows temporarily piece themselves back together with laughter, but then the bastard artist has to go and make things uncomfortable. Talk about being caught off guard. One minute, you're happily socializing in a room full of wonderful miscreants, beautiful deviants, and exquisite misfits. The next, you've been put on the spot by your nemesis and all your so-called friends.

Littlethumb makes Redy an offer. Let him paint Redy, and Littlethumb will give the young journalist the interview he so desires. The offer itself isn't offensive. What infuriates Redy is Littlethumb's asking Arthur if he would like to see Littlethumb paint on his birthday. Arthur, in turn, asks everyone else in the shelter if they want to see Littlethumb paint Redy's portrait, firmly placing Redy on the proverbial spot.

It's tough to explain why the idea of having Littlethumb paint him in front of everyone feels so invasive. Or, perhaps I should say, tough to perceive. I can explain Redy's state of being, but once again, unless you experience and feel things for yourself, emotions can be difficult to vicariously digest. Consider this: If you've ever suffered anxiety or paranoia about a social gathering, take those feelings and dump a psychotic break on top.

Okay, most of you haven't suffered a psychotic break. Panic attack, anyone? Sigh. Just imagine being in a room full of demons and they're all trying to suck out your soul. Close your eyes and feel the hysteria. Oh, I know! Don't know why it took me this long, but imagine you've got an old friendly "uncle," wealthy and proper, tasked with raising you after your parents died, and this dirty evil shitbag likes to touch you, and shush you, and touch you again, all the while encouraging you and telling you everything is going to be okay. Everything is fine.

This is what happens to Redy. The connective emotional tissue between Uncle Carmine and Littlethumb Brooks is too powerful for him to deny in this moment, and in his mind, everyone in the room turns into Uncle Carmine. Encouraging him. Reaching for him. Telling him everything's going to be okay. Everything is fine.

Switch. Permanently. Flipped. Monster cage unlocked.

Mentally, Redy steps into the haze and pulls the door shut behind him. No more half-hearted plans. Señor Sinclair has vacated the hacienda. Nobody remain calm.

"Are you alright, son?" asks Willy. One of those questions where the look on the other person's face tells you they absolutely are not alright, but you ask anyway, hoping the other person says they're fine and you've misread them, and you're immediately reassured so you can go about your business. Don't mistake the innate desire to go about your business as a lack of empathy. No one *wants* to be bothered, not even people who care.

Redy blinks rapidly, then confidently states, "One hundred percent. Was just having a moment there. Flashback to the war."

"I didn't know you were a soldier."

"I wasn't. Sorry. Bad metaphor. I've been told I have an above average ability to disappear into my own head. Didn't mean to freak you guys out."

"No worries, my friend. No worries at all, so long as you're fine."

"Top notch."

"Redy, I apologize," says Littlethumb. "I didn't mean to put you on the spot."

Then why did you, liar? thinks Redy. *Because you did.*

"It was meant to be all in fun," Littlethumb continues.

"No need to apologize. Seriously. I spaced out, that's all. Happens sometimes. Something sparks a thought or a memory, and I get lost in my head."

"I can definitely understand that."

"You wouldn't believe how many dates I've ruined for myself."

"What's a date?" asks Littlethumb.

"Alright then," says Willy with a chuckle. "Maybe we go play chess or something, leave the painting for later." At this, the few men who are still paying attention mumble their discontent with Willy's recommendation.

Arthur groans loudly and says, "Ah, man."

"No, no," says Redy. "Don't worry, Arthur. It's your birthday. If you want to see Captain Wisecrack paint, that's what you're going to get." Redy claps his hands together and smiles at Littlethumb. "Let's do this."

26

"Would you prefer to stand or sit?" asks Littlethumb, setting up his easel and paints.

"Uh...I don't know," says Redy. "I've never imagined myself as the subject of a portrait."

"I think that's honorable, man. Not necessarily a humble line of thought, the portrait of oneself."

Redy politely bows a thank you.

"How about this?" Littlethumb takes a few strides and picks up an adult sized stool, then turns back toward Redy. "I like the in-between sitting and standing look. Frames nicely."

"Works for me."

Littlethumb places the stool in front of the eastern wall.

"Interesting choice," says Redy.

Littlethumb's response is a puzzled expression, and Redy motions toward the word "LOVE" painted on the wall in large, colorful letters.

"Oh, ha. Yeah, that may or may not wind up in the portrait," says Littlethumb, adjusting his easel to a perfect distance from where

Redy will pose.

Now Redy is briefly puzzled, but he dismisses the comment. *Whatever,* he thinks, then he pulls off his sweater.

With his back to Redy, Littlethumb is addressing the crowd. "So, I know it's been a while since we've done this. You guys can come in fairly close here, but maybe stay out from directly behind me. Stand over to the left or right, so you can see the work in progress. And if you prefer to wait and see the finished painting as a surprise, watch from the side over there, but I would say, stay five to six feet off the line between me and Redy. Okay?"

Eager faces respond with eager nods. Most of the gang has experienced a Littlethumb performance, prior to his current artistic block. Therefore, most of these unruly sons-of-bitches recognize the gift of pleasant euphoria they're about to receive.

Littlethumb turns back around and is surprised to see Redy has tossed his sweater and button-down shirt over the back of a chair. Despite the undershirt Redy is wearing, the young man's chiseled physique is on display. Short sleeves cling tightly to shoulders and arms rippled by the fault lines and sharp-edged cliffs of hard muscle, along with what looks like a moderate amount of scar tissue poking out from underneath the sleeves.

Jesus, thinks Littlethumb. *The kid is ripped.* I will finish Littlethumb's surprised thoughts by explaining that Redy wears loose clothing to hide a dedicated athlete's musculature. Not the most unusual choice in the world, though people who put maximum effort into their physical fitness often prefer showing off the fruits of their labor.

Our mischief-making painter instantly determines Redy's modesty is either genuine humility from a self-conscious person, or, a purposeful effort at hiding destructive strength. Some folks know damn well how dangerous they are, and some folks know damn well the art of concealing how dangerous they are to the rest of the world. Never let them see you coming…

Attempting to show no reaction to Redy's display, Littlethumb says, "You ready, Redy?" then scoffs at the accidental wordplay. "Ew. God, that was awful. Sorry."

A playful smirk from Redy accompanies the words, "You should be."

"Let's go with, 'you all set?'"

"Works for me, but if you don't mind…" Redy indicates the removal of his t-shirt.

Curious but unbothered, Littlethumb speaks in an accommodating tone. "It's your portrait Redy. However you want it."

The shelter's crew processes an assortment of emotions: shocked, impressed, bemused, saddened, disturbed, mildly confused. A few are surprisingly unmoved. Redy Sinclair rests comfortably on the stool, both feet on the ground, legs about half bent, his self-mutilated expression of a painful and angry childhood on display for gods and men. Do you remember his father's straight razor? What we see here is the naked truth. Redy's torso is covered in self-inflicted scars that stretch out across his shoulders and the tops of his arms. If you can stomach the sight, gazing long enough to truly absorb the damage done, you will notice the not so vague pattern of a bird taking flight. The clawed feet and dangling legs begin at Redy's belly, growing upward to form the body and fully spread wings across his chest and shoulders, the tips of the wings finishing below the shoulders on the upper biceps and triceps.

The scars vary in length, but none are more than an inch or so long. I can tell you with certainty the birdlike, mosaic pattern of the scars began unintentionally. The original cuts themselves, those were quite purposeful.

A desperate child, panicked for an end to the abuse he was suffering, decided his "uncle" might lose interest in him if he was damaged. Understandable, though a discerning psychopath might respond, "If you're gonna go that route, why not go all the way? Cut up your face?" To this I would explain because Redy was a child, and not yet that far gone, and scared, and desperate, and stuck between the rock of not wanting to believe any of this was truly happening, and the hard place of accepting it was. He did what he was capable of. He started cutting himself and hoped for dear life the damage would make his abuser leave him alone. Sadly, his plan didn't work. Ultimately, puberty would turn Uncle Carmine away and land Redy in a military boarding school.

You wouldn't expect the pain to end, merely because the abuse had, would you? Of course not. Redy's young mind had been so focused on escape, he hadn't considered the days to come. The nightmares and panic attacks. The desire to punish someone or something for his suffering. The constant internal torment. The programmed *need* for external abuse, because abuse is what he knew. What he understood. The poor kid didn't know what a life without terror felt like and certainly didn't understand how to be happy or how to trust happiness. Thus, he continued cutting, long after the abuse had ended, and eventually he noticed an obscure pattern to the gash marks on his belly and chest.

To be frank, recognizing this pattern significantly aided in his mental survival. The imagery of a bird taking flight and the potential for freedom, for escape, this comforted him. Yet, so much strife was sown and cultivated within Redy, the hate had to go somewhere. His subconscious mind, still so terrified by the demon who fed on the shattered remains of his tragically orphaned soul, was too frightened to confront his true enemy, instead searching anywhere and everywhere to find a new, comfortable outlet for the festering malice inside him, until one day…

You guys see where this is going, right?

Witnessing the gnarled landscape of Redy's body, Littlethumb is torn between appreciation for the beauty of the scars and empathy for the negative circumstances he presumes inspired their creation, assuming this type of cutting rarely happens without a traumatic catalyst. He could weep if not for the resolute, stoic posture of Redmond Sinclair. Rather than shed a tear, Littlethumb sends Captain Wisecrack home for the day. Though he planned for a lighthearted presentation to entertain a friend on his birthday, a sadness radiates from the subject before Littlethumb, insisting this performance be an expression of sober appreciation. Our painter gazes upon a grave communiqué of anguish, intent on finding hope and peace hidden within. Of course, at the end of the day, his intentions don't matter unless they happen to fall in line with what nature already demands.

As for the other members of the First Church of Good Deeds? They don't waste any mental energy pondering what caused the scars, they simply react emotionally to what they see. Each of these men is broken in their own way. If anything, learning Redy is damaged makes sense. He's already one of their own.

A few are impressed, don't get me wrong. "My guy is a wicked ass scarecrow," and, "Whoaaaaaaaaa," and, "Man oh man, I think Mr. Sinclair may be a super-secret agent or something," may have been said, and if not those exact words, equal exclamations of fascination.

A number of the men are sad, quietly getting choked up or retreating to a corner for a moment alone. Retreating is commonplace at the shelter, accepted and understood. The words, "Let's give him a moment," never needing to be spoken.

In this moment, King Arthur is moved by the plight of his subjects. Despite his excitement for Littlethumb's impending show, Arthur responds to those who've been wounded in battle with dignity. Placing a hand on the shoulders of the soldiers who are distraught at Redy's appearance is a royal gesture of somber, distinguished compassion. Fully embracing his embattled friend is an open expression of genuine concern. The surprised look on Redy's face is replaced by one of humble appreciation, and he returns Arthur's hug without reservation.

"Alright, alright," says Redy, patting Arthur on the back. "Let's have some fun."

"What do you say, birthday king?" asks Littlethumb, as Arthur makes his way back to his seat. "You ready to watch me paint?"

Arthur leaves his grave demeanor in the dust in favor of renewed excitement. Holding his scepter in the air, he says, "What say you, men?" His subjects cheer encouragement, and Arthur lowers his scepter, aiming at Littlethumb. "Our court has spoken, Sir Smith. Let the performance begin!"

When he paints, Littlethumb Brooks escapes our shared reality. You must understand, his abilities aren't merely exceptional, they're supernatural. A state of being is reached similar to one achieved in a sensory deprivation chamber, where unnecessary senses divert all available power to forward thrusters. You may speak, but he will not hear. You may touch, but he will not feel. He might smell. I'm not sure about that.

Imagine tunnel vision, where all you see is a canvas and a subject. Everything else around you is an amorphous swirl of colors, like you're floating in a long hallway where the floor and ceiling and walls are constantly rotating faster and faster around you into a blur of infinite hues, and the color you need for your next brush stroke is always in view. Almost as if you could dip your brush into the swirl of the physical world.

I don't mean to give the wrong impression. I've not waded this far into the sparkling waters of this recollection to boringly reveal Littlethumb Brooks as a comic book-style mutant (that will come later, tee hee, tee hee…). His eyes don't roll back and go all white, nor does an eyeball pop open on his forehead or in the palms of his hands, and certainly not on his butt. No, as I've stated previously, I will wait for Littlethumb to further explain his abilities when he's ready. What I'm trying to convey here is the experience. And the show.

Several years ago, as I've also mentioned previously, Littlethumb regularly performed his painting for live audiences. Part of his brilliance, if he's in the proper healthy condition, is the ability to phase in and out of his artistic trance at will. To jump back and forth between being with us and without us in the blink of an eye, or better yet, the stroke of a brush, if you will.

Seeing the show was like being at a rock concert. There was music, dancing, laughter, and romance. Maria would join him on stage to act as disc jockey, eternal muse, and dance partner supreme. They traveled the world together, performing in the most intimate of settings or stadiums filled with thousands. A theater in the round art studio was built on Coney Island to entertain tourists and raise money for charities. That was his life, a daily expression of profound creativity and love. Until Tommy Toxic destroyed everything, and for the second time no less. First his family. Then his wife. And still, the hero forgave.

I'm happy to report that Redmond Bartholomew Sinclair the Fourth proves to be such a compelling subject, Littlethumb's block is finally shaken. A deep breath and earnest trepidation accompany Littlethumb's approach to the easel, but the moment the first splotch of color hits the canvas, he's off and running. Literally. Running in place was a regular part of his act, back in the day. So much for the somber approach. Littlethumb gets going and can't help himself. The showman's chops are rusty, for sure, but he dips into his bag of tricks without hesitation, both to give the gang a festive show and out of pure excitement to once again be doing the thing he enjoys most.

Once the last stroke is taken, the last detailed effort of smudging made, and his thumbprint pressed into the bottom right corner of the matte (being his signature signature), the crowd cheers approval. Exclamations of another masterpiece burst forth from those who've previously witnessed his talent. The neophytes stand aghast.

Many moons have passed since Littlethumb has received this adulation. The response is humbling. He bows to the audience, a maestro holding his baton, then humbly calms his friends. "Okay. Okay, guys. I appreciate it. Seriously. Thank you."

"We done?" asks Redy, having exercised almost all of his patience for this situation.

"Yep, I think that does it," says Littlethumb.

"Cool." Redy pulls his tee-shirt on and then slips into the button down and sweater. Sitting for the portrait has emotionally exhausted him. On the verge of losing his composure, he makes a hurried round of farewells, circling back to say his final goodbyes to Littlethumb, Willy, Arthur, and several others still huddled around the portrait. The fact that Redy stands behind the easel isn't lost on Littlethumb.

"Don't you want to look?" he asks.

"No thanks."

"But it's yours."

"Give it to Arthur. His birthday." The look of shock on everyone's face is a genuine curiosity. Enough of a curiosity to make Redy want to see the painting. Still, he resists. Screw the painting, and fuck Littlethumb Brooks, whose stupid face Redy can't help but land on. *Look at him. Can't possibly understand how someone might not give a shit about how special he is. Fuckin' narcissist.* And while the monster seethes on the inside, on the outside, the man offers a self-conscious smile and says, "Please, don't take it personal. I don't care for mirrors either."

27

Flummoxed. An excellent word and exactly how Littlethumb feels. A subject not wanting to see their own picture? This is a first, although maybe Littlethumb shouldn't be surprised, factoring in his prior conversations with Redy Sinclair.

Anyone may gaze upon a painting by Littlethumb Brooks and recognize its magnificence. That's why his artwork demands an extremely high price tag and goes on exhibit tours around the world. Not everyone can gaze upon a portrait by Littlethumb Brooks and truly comprehend what they see. What is being revealed to them about the portrait's subject. Perhaps receiving the message requires an artist's heart. Perhaps, simply an open one.

Either way, in this instance, not even our openhearted artist can discern the message being sent. Littlethumb needs time alone to meditate over the portrait. Not a problem, as Arthur is more than happy for Littlethumb to take the portrait home under the guise of properly mounting it to a worthy frame.

Whatever Redy's intentions toward Littlethumb are, there is

definitely more to the situation than a simple interview. Of this, the portrait makes Littlethumb one-hundred percent certain. Unfortunately, that's about all he is certain of with regard to the young "journalist." Redy Sinclair is a puzzle.

Flummoxed. What a word.

A more direct commute is made on Daring Bird's return trip to Marseille. No longer carrying the dodeca, he's less concerned with taking the circuitous route he used on his way to Canada, time being of the essence. Bebi, Jimmy, and Silas are all chasing their leads. Daring Bird needs any potential intel from Kumiko as soon as possible, and he doesn't trust any external lines of communication for contacting her. Plus, the sex. The sex is way better in person.

Hopefully, Kumiko can also help locate their missing teammate, searching any available databases she's willing to utilize for information regarding their drunken zealot. Maybe the goofy son-of-a-bitch got himself into trouble with the law. If so, Kumiko might be able to discretely locate him.

Oh, speaking of Titus the Nazarene…

Our villain of many a whispered name sits behind his large desk in his home office in Denmark, trying to remember what life was like before children. That's right, Conrad Somvinslodkin, aka the Bloody Inventor, aka the Red Left Foot, aka the Interloper of Death, aka the Reaper's Cloak, aka Your Mom's New Shitty Boyfriend, aka Comrade Somethingrussian, aka Xander Bowfly, has children. Wifey declared a spa day and took the fleet of au pairs with her, so Xander was left to the whims of his brood. There's five or six of them, each no more than a year apart from the next, and none over the age of seven amazing years old. In other words, Xander's gonna be one of those stereotypical bald supervillains soon, once he's done pulling out his villainous flaxen hair.

Work time has become doodle time for Xander, as the kids are distracting him from focusing on his evil machinations. The sketches portray his kids in cages, rabid and mangy, snarling like feral dogs. Having affection for your progeny doesn't mean you can't let your imagination run wild if the kids are distracting you from work, and wait a minute. There's an idea. In the middle of applying an absurdly oversized set of canine teeth on one of the caged children, a potential name pops up for his as-yet unnamed evil organization. The Iron Fang! Decent ring to it. Could make for a cool logo. Ooh, and the name loosely connects to his grandfather Adolph's tooth that he's wearing around his neck. Yes, this idea has legs.

A buzz on his intercom interrupts his thoughts. "Yes," replies Xander, but he can't hear anything. "Hey! Children, quiet down. Daddy can't hear."

You guys got kids? If not, I'm guessing you're still familiar with how obediently most children quiet down when they're asked once. Or twice.

On the third attempt, Xander yells, "SHUT UP! Shut up, or I will have every one of you strung upside down from the roof of this house for the birds to peck out your eyes!"

That works. All five or six of his children shut up, though one begins to cry. A single tear and heartfelt sniffle escape this child's body before one stern look from Xander sends the tear retreating back up into the kid's eyeball. The sniffle runs and hides behind a sister, who shakes her head, emphatically pleading that the sound had not come from her.

"What was it you were saying?" asks Xander into his intercom.

"A report on the drunk, boss. I reviewed footage of the interview."

"Did he talk?"

"Yeah, he did plenty of talking. The crazy son of a bitch went on and on about suing the Catholic Church. Accused our agents of working for the Pope. Swore up and down he would never tell them anything while he was constantly blabbing about all kinds of stuff, except anything we want to know. I think that bit about the kids was a coincidence, boss. You know, with the church."

"Was he tortured?"

"Yes sir. Extensively. I've never seen anything like it. They beat the living shit out of him. Zapped his sack. Broke every damn toe he has. Nothing. He never stopped talking but didn't say anything of consequence."

"He's a professional then?"

"Yeah, or crazy. Honestly, boss, I'm leaning toward crazy on this one. I think he's a crazy, drunken zealot."

"Did we kill him yet?"

"Uhm…no… Actually, that's another reason I called." You can hear the trepidation in this despicable fellow's voice.

"What?"

Silence.

"Out with it, man. I don't have all day."

"He escaped."

"What!? How did he escape?"

"We don't know for sure. He was bound so tight. Our guess is a joint dislocation to loosen the bindings."

"Get your ass up here and bring someone with you. Someone cheap and easy to replace who I can stab in the eye." Xander isn't joking.

"Boss?"

"Now! That new guy. The one with the harelip. Get his ass in here! And send someone to remove these beautiful fucking children!"

There's only so much peering into the mystical void a person can take. A rough analogy, but suitable enough for my purposes here. Littlethumb has mentally exhausted himself in the presence of Redy's portrait. He's stared. He's sat facing the painting with his eyes closed. He's paced, turning on the portrait as if attempting to catch it red-handed in an act of chicanery. Nothing.

Don't get me wrong, there is plenty to learn from the portrait, as with each and every one of Littlethumb's paintings of a human subject. The issue here is conflict and conflict resolution, and if you find this derpity-doo confusing, I've accomplished my mission.

I promise I'm not being a dick for no reason. Littlethumb's flummoxed and I want you to feel it too. I'm begging you for empathy again. To put yourself in Littlethumb's exhausted and confused shoes as he tosses a drop cloth over the painting. He can't stare at Redy's portrait any longer, and he doesn't want the damn thing staring at him.

Or surprising him.

I'm joking. Once he's prepared to observe the work again, Littlethumb's hopeful a dramatic removal of the drop cloth will provide a startling new insight. We'll see.

One last frustrated look at the covered portrait, then Littlethumb walks over to the unstacked paintings of Hope left standing against the wall by Daring Bird. Without looking directly at the images of his daughter, he returns the canvases to their pile, a thoughtless act made for the sake of needing movement. After restacking the paintings, he wanders from his studio into the living room and considers what else he should do with himself. Nothing. Nothing…

Maria smiles to him from beyond. A punch to the gut, followed by Hope's beautiful face appearing in his mind's eye to throw a hard right hook. He should call Sawyer. Check on Hope. Talk to her. Instead, he chides himself for clinging to pain he's supposedly trying to run from. *Fuckin' chickenshit, dude,* he thinks as he walks to the dining room table and opens his laptop. She isn't there. Littlethumb stares at his daughter's bedroom on the computer screen, wishing he could get a glimpse of her smiling. Being happy. Being safe.

If wishes were ditches, Littlethumb. If wishes were ditches…you could lay down in one and die.

His lame attempt at checking on Hope unsuccessful, Littlethumb shuffles toward the Command Room to check on the dodeca and see if there are any new communications from the team. Don't take his lazy gait the wrong way. The shuffle is a genuine lack of energy. He's not feeling sorry for himself. His emotional state is more along the lines of wanting to punch himself in the face. Hopefully, you find this more acceptable than feeling sorry for oneself.

Inside the Command Room, he stops to marvel over the dodeca, faking enthusiastic curiosity for his own sanity's sake. Still operational. Yay…

Next, he checks the computer. The program appears to be running without any issues. Double yay…

Halfway around the world, a villain falls out of his chair.

Harelip's new nickname is Ol' Freddy One Eye. The poor fella. Don't get me wrong, he's a despicable sort who agreed to work for an evil villain, but the guy still had a very bad day. And no one could tell him what he'd done wrong.

Once Xander was done being furious, he sent the man to his lab for an upgrade. Ol' Freddy is a muscular specimen, worthy of a little investment. A prosthetic eye, similar to the technology in Daring Bird's eyepatch, will be installed. Basically, in exchange for Xander taking his anger out on him, the guy gets a promotion, a raise, a physical upgrade, and a healthy dose of Stockholm syndrome for his new boss. Loyalty bred through cruelty and reward.

The minute Ol' Freddy One Eye is dragged from the room, Xander's children return, launching an all-out assault on their father, turning the office into an inmate-led asylum. Spastic miniature demons crash about the room until one of them lets out a spectacular shriek, having discovered Freddy's amputated eyeball behind the leg of a chair. Xander quiets the child and is about to take them all outside and drown them in the river, aka treat them to ice cream, when he notices movement on D-13's surveillance camera monitor.

What's this? he thinks. "Run ahead, my little demons. Daddy will be right behind you." Turning to a henchman, he says, "Take my children out to their playground and keep an eye on them. I will be out shortly."

Xander sits back down behind his desk and enlarges the window containing D-13's monitor on his computer screen. The video relay has been recording indefinitely, but to this point, Xander hasn't seen any movement since the day D-13 was activated. He has a man on his tech staff checking the video daily, but no clear images have been recorded.

When Littlethumb hooked the dodeca up to a computer, the device got turned so the corner knob housing the camera pointed in an obscure direction, covering an area of the Command Room off the standard walking paths. Most of Littlethumb's checking on the dodeca is really checking the computer to see if there is progress in the algorithm's computations. There's no need for him to hover over the dodeca itself. Littlethumb randomly deciding to take a closer look, bending the dodeca back and forth on its spring while simmering in an emotional stew is…well, chaos or fate? You decide.

❀ ❀ ❀

Xander's tits are tingling. *I've got you now, you son of a bitch. I'm not even angry. I've enjoyed our little game, but I've got you now.* He rewinds the feed in slow motion, searching for a clear shot.

"There you are," he says, pausing the video. The only view he has of his enemy's face appears to be of the man (or woman) stepping away from the device, but the side of the face is there, in the top left corner of the screen. Xander clips the person's head and emails the picture to his marketing lab, immediately calling them on the phone.

"Joe here," says Joe, a member of Xander's marketing department. Don't forget, Comrade Somethingrussian has numerous legitimate financial holdings and free-market products. The role of worldwide evil villain isn't duly fulfilled without a completely absurd public life for your true identity. Several years ago, as a measure of control over both his public and secret initiatives, Xander moved all marketing in-house. The department has two divisions, public and private. Both divisions are run by off the grid tech mercenaries, bound by nerdy blood and loyal to the cause.

"Joe, I'm sending you a file I need cleaned. Resize and de-pixelate the picture immediately. I need to see this face."

"Yes, boss. I have the file. Should be no problem. Two minutes, please. Will have it right back to you."

I won't be so melodramatic as to tell you this is the longest two minutes of Xander's life, but Xander will. Oh, the horror. Two minutes!

My god, the entire world could change in two minutes. Galaxies collide! Universes are birthed into existence!

Rather than sit and watch Xander lament our ever-changing perception of the passage of time, I figure we should check on Redy Sinclair real quick. And I mean real quick. Dude is passed out in his hotel room.

Redy gave his knock-out cocktail a try, to make sure the drug is effective. As I mentioned earlier, I've taken this awful concoction. Certain bodies hate this chemical inside them much more than others. I've seen men of various shapes and sizes either happily enjoy a powerful buzz, pass out within minutes of consuming the liquid, or violently discharge the chemical from their body through their ignorant mouth holes.

Luckily for Redy, he passed out safely, without hitting his head. Having gone to the bathroom shortly after ingesting the concentrated liquid, he was already woozy when he flushed the toilet. On his way toward the bed, he fell, bouncing off the side of the mattress on his way to the floor.

Xander's jaw hangs open. The two minutes were up two minutes ago, and his face has been frozen like this since he laid eyes on the enlarged, cleaned-up image that Joe in marketing sent back to him. Once Xander recombobulates, he frenetically scrambles to verify what he sees.

Xander can't internet fast enough, despite his exceptional internetting skills. Still photos. Videos. This must be a look-alike. Proof that everyone has at least one doppelganger in this world. It can't be him. It can't be.

Ridiculous. Impossible. It's just too fucking much!

Melty brains ooze from Xander's eyes, ears, and nose. The despot slumps back in his chair, cranially jellified. Perhaps I spoke a bit too soon with regard to his recombobulation. Several more mind-blown minutes pass before his brain returns to service, as the lobotomized facial expression he wears survives a few more seconds before a memory resuscitates him.

That face. The one he saw in D-13's camera before. It was that guy from the museum. The Wampanoag! How did that not register before? THE WAMPANOAG!

A blistering search and Xander's suspicion is confirmed by courtroom footage of Littlethumb Brooks' identity trial. The "old lady" in disguise was the same man at the museum in Amsterdam. Littlethumb Brooks' uncle! Xander suffers another bout of dumbfounded thoughtlessness before moving on to the manic contemplations of a villain in ecstasy.

I'm going to need a new brain. My god. I…I can't tell anyone. No one else can know. It's too big a secret, and no matter if it wasn't, there's no one to tell who will understand. Who will truly understand the absurd beauty to all of this. Littlethumb Brooks, a goddamn painter, an Electric Medicine Man? Unbelievable. I can't…

My device was stolen by Littlethumb Brooks. And I met his fucking uncle staring at a collection of his work. A collection I stole! Oh, the irony. The irony!

Wait, is that irony?

Who cares!? Irony, coincidence, chaos, fate. Who gives a flying shit!? My life is complete. My favorite living artist is destined to be my greatest enemy. Unbelievable. My circle is complete.

Magnificent!

For what is the life of any arch-villain worth, without the perfect nemesis? A singular presence to devote oneself to. A marriage of heaven and hell.

Enough. Enough romance. I will find you, Mr. Brooks. You have something that belongs to me.

Refocused, Xander puts an Opportunity out to six of his most trusted and notorious mercenaries, all known for their impeccable success rate and one-hundred percent infallibility in keeping secrets. Never forget, information is one of the most valuable currencies in human existence. The one thing irrefutably more valuable than information is time. Speaking of which, Conrad Somvinslodkin is late for a conference call. Xander clicks *send*, activating Opportunity Five-Fourteen. The assignment is a seek and find, no contact.

Back at his favorite coffee shop, Master Chee polishes off a delicious blueberry donut, licking sticky fingers before reengaging his current read. Most of the dogeared pages of *God is a Donut and the Universe is His Hole* weigh heavily to the left in his hands. Master Chee will likely give the book four or five stars, depending on how everything comes together in the end. Next up on his reading list is *Wandering Aimlessly Through Fortune*.

A vibration courses through Chee's body. Reaching into a pocket, he pulls out a phone. Nope, wrong one. Another phone appears. Not that one either. On his fourth attempt, he opens the correct cellphone to an incoming message. With a surprised hmph and a head scratch, Master Chee takes a drink of his coffee and sends the following response: *Opportunity Five-Fourteen accepted.*

28

Most of our pages weigh heavily to the left, as this tale nears its completion. Where's the action-packed climax I promised? It's got to be in here somewhere. I bet the fun starts with a knock on a door.

Littlethumb is cleaning a bit. Putzing about the house to let the afternoon slip away. "Farting around," as my Jesus used to say. A day or so has passed, I think, since Xander discovered Littlethumb has the dodeca. Not long.

Any knock on the cabin door is a cause for suspicion. I mean, this is a somewhat secret hideout. People in town know where Littlethumb lives, but he doesn't entertain and almost no one shows up to the cabin unannounced. If someone does, it's typically for a package delivery. Something Littlethumb is halfway expecting.

Another knock as he makes his way toward the front of the cabin. There's a short, solid wood thumping stick resting against the wall next to the hinged side of the door. The staff has been stained and lacquered for longevity, and is perfectly balanced for striking. Littlethumb grabs the weapon before unlocking the door. He leaves the stout chain lock in place, reminding himself once again that he's been meaning to install a peephole since he moved back up to the cabin.

Opening the door as far as the chain allows, Littlethumb peaks through the crack to see the smiling face of Redy Sinclair.

"How's it going?" asks Redy.

"Good, good," says Littlethumb. "Bumming around, doing a little house cleaning." No invitation is made to enter. In an effort not to appear suspicious, Littlethumb says, "How's it going with you?"

"Doing alright. It's a beautiful day." Redy turns and takes in the vista as confirmation, then rotates back to Littlethumb, still smiling. There's a poker face dance here. Redy doesn't want to ask to be let inside. Conversely, Littlethumb is hesitant to invite Redy into his home.

Redy finally breaks the stalemate. "I'm sorry to show up unannounced. I hope I'm not a bother."

"No, no. No bother at all. Sorry, I'm just surprised. I don't get many visitors out here."

"I bet not. To tell you the truth, I didn't plan on invading your privacy today. I gave in to a whim."

To tell the truth, eh? I bet Silas' daddy has a saying about people who say that. "No worries, no worries at all, my friend. What brings you out on this whim?"

"I figured this was the best way to make sure you agree to do the interview in your home. Or at least part of it, anyway. Your environment is important to the story, to your present reality. People tend to be most comfortable and powerful in their own homes. Unless they're married."

A decent joke, but it doesn't break the ice.

"So, by agree," Littlethumb says with a smile, "you mean stop whatever I'm doing and sit down for an interview with you right now?"

"If you're free, and don't mind the company. If you don't feel like getting into the interview, no worries. We could hang out, maybe play a game or two of chess. I didn't come out here just to…that's a lie. That was almost a lie. Of course this is mostly about doing the interview. But if you aren't in the mood, I would still enjoy bullshitting over a game." Redy hesitates briefly, then plows forward. "I'm sorry. Bad form. I should have called or something. I was hoping you wouldn't mind if I surprised you, after you put me on the spot at the shelter the other day."

Make no mistake, Littlethumb sees this comment for what it is, an attack. Not an all-out assault, but definitely the advancement of a pawn. The plight of the empath, however, is to recognize your actions may have wounded another, in spite of your best intentions. Don't be ashamed of empathy in hindsight. It's one of the few acts of looking over our shoulder we can truly use to guide us forward. To that end, the ball bounces in Redy Sinclair's favor here, thanks to the gentleness in Littlethumb Brooks' heart.

"Damn, Sinclair," says Littlethumb, clearly being playful. "You didn't have to go all in on the guilt trip. I was just messing with you. Hang on a second." Littlethumb shuts the door and drops his thumping stick down into an antique butter-churn used for holding umbrellas.

The door swings fully open and Littlethumb stands inside, his right arm held out as an invitation to enter. "Come on in," he says.

Redy enters the cabin toting a backpack strapped to both shoulders. There was a loose Plan B if Littlethumb hadn't welcomed him in. Loose Plan B consisted of Redy forcing his way in and assaulting Littlethumb. The painting event at the shelter has locked his resolve in place. This is happening, one way or the other. Of course, Plan B might have been tough considering how Littlethumb controlled the front door and given the fact he appears to be in solid physical condition.

"Welcome to my humble abode," says Littlethumb. "Not much to look at, but it's out in the middle of nowhere and has running water."

"Not much to look at my ass." Having not been scouting for artwork when he was spying, inside the cabin, Redy finds an impressive assortment of homemade bric-a-brac and paintwork scattered throughout the space. Oddities. Sculptures. Woodwork. "Jesus, man. This place is amazing."

"Thank you."

"Is this all your handiwork?"

"Most of it. Not all, but most."

"Impressive."

"Eh, I'm alone a lot. Please, have a look around. Make yourself at home."

Redy, already on tour, stops at a piece near the harvest table. The remains of a spinal column hang on a wall, with the vertebrae painted in dull white and black hues to resemble aged piano keys. "I dig this a lot. Do you know what animal the spine came from?"

"Moose, I think. Would you like a cup of tea or something?"

"Yes, please. That would be great." Awestruck by the amount of art in the room, Redy makes his way from the piano spinal column to an antique camera installation, where the cameras hang to create the frame around a painting of a dark vortex with a minuscule point of light in the center. Redy escapes the piece's trap and moves on, touring the rest of the cabin like a museum.

"The tea or the something?' asks Littlethumb.

"Huh?"

"What would you like to drink?" Littlethumb says with a chuckle. "I've got almost any flavor of tea a normal person might ask for, or if there is something else you might prefer…I can brew coffee. Have a few sodas in the fridge."

"No, no. Whatever you're having is fine with me."

"Sounds good."

As Littlethumb preps a teapot and a couple of mugs, Redy continues his way around the cabin. The awe wears off as he remembers his mission. The small squeeze bottle, originally used for eyedrops, is in his pocket and ready to go. A stun gun rests in the top compartment of the backpack. The stun gun was a part of his potential Plan B and is pretty much all of Plan C.

Redy would prefer to avoid physical combat. Too many things can go wrong, and there is a lot of unknown with Littlethumb Brooks. Stun guns are extremely effective if they hit their target, but you've got to hit your target. You've got to get the shot off, for that matter, and Littlethumb has yet to fully turn his back on Redy since welcoming him inside. Redy has surmised, correctly, that his best plan of action is to slip the proverbial mickey.

"What's with this door, if you don't mind my asking?"

Littlethumb turns and sees Redy standing next to the Command Room door. "What do you mean?"

"I mean, those are some heavy duty deadbolts on an inside door. Kind of mysterious."

"No mystery at all. The locks are on there because I don't want the door to be easy to open."

Redy laughs casually, "You know what I mean. What are you hiding in there, Mr. Brooks?"

"A bunch of stuff I don't want seen or stolen. Obviously."

"Any little nugget you can give me for the write up, or is this strictly off limits?"

"We'll see," says Littlethumb. Obviously, he isn't telling Redy a damn thing about what's in there. "Gonna take a lot more foreplay to get me naked."

"Yikes. If it's gotta be like that, on second thought, I don't think I care anymore."

Littlethumb gives a nonchalant shrug. "Your loss. I'm a very considerate lover."

Redy gives the joke as much throw as he can, laughing as he makes his way to the kitchen counter. "I, on the other hand, have been told I'm extremely selfish. I don't agree, but you know, I don't really care."

"Ha! Nice." A whistle blows and Littlethumb reaches for the tea kettle without looking, eyes monitoring Redy.

Damn, thinks Redy. *He's not gonna take his eyes off me.*

Littlethumb pours the tea and returns the kettle, turning his body but monitoring Redy in his peripheral vision. "How do you take your tea?"

"What flavor we having?"

"Earl Grey."

"Uhm, a little milk or cream then, if you have any." *C'mon fucko, turn your back. Give me two seconds. That's all I need. Two seconds.*

"Absolutely. Milk in the fridge. Sugar in the cupboard there. Help yourself, then come have a seat."

Son-of-a-bitch. Maybe I put it in the milk or something and wait. But there's no telling how long he might have to wait, and he correctly assumes Littlethumb has eyes on him.

You might be asking yourself, and wishing you could scream at me or Littlethumb, "Why the fuck would you let Redy in the house!?" A fair question, I suppose, with Littlethumb already suspicious of Redy, but this situation has to come to a head. One way or the other. The kid has basically been stalking him for months, and Littlethumb is compelled to unravel the mystery. Considering his inability to find answers in the portrait, what other choice does he have than to confront the situation head on?

Only to delay the inevitable.

Besides, Daring Bird's vision may be directly related to circumstances with Redy. Time to get this over with. If a bad ending awaits Littlethumb, he can't stop it, or he would. Chaos or fate, either way, any negative result coming to fruition will prove to be outside of Littlethumb's control. Allowing Redy into his home, keeping his eye on him, these are methods of attempting control.

Yep. Control. Like chaining yourself to a palm tree in a hurricane.

Both men are seated on the couch, a full cushion apart, bodies halfway turned to face one another for conversational purposes. Their teas rest on the coffee table in front of them.

"So," Littlethumb says, "should I start rambling, or do you have a list of questions?"

"Oh. I have questions, for sure." Redy opens wide the main compartment of his backpack and thumbs through multiple sketchpads to find a notebook. Between you and I, several of these sketchpads are going to die alongside Littlethumb. They are a part of his life Redy Sinclair plans to leave behind, once the deed is done.

"Are you an artist, Mr. Sinclair?" asks Littlethumb, nodding at Redy's backpack.

"I wouldn't be so bold as to call myself an artist," says Redy, genuinely modest. "I sketch. Been a hobby since I was a teenager, but that's it. Just sketches."

"Don't sell yourself short. You appear to be toting around a sizable collection there. May I see?"

"Uhm, sure." Here's another opportunity, Redy. Maybe the sketches will distract him long enough. Why didn't you think of this? Redy thumbs through the pads, looking for one without any of his murder-death-kill scenarios featuring Littlethumb. He lifts the backpack up onto the couch between them and pretends to continue his search, then pulls out a particular sketchpad. "There may be a couple of decent pieces in this one. I don't know. It's not something I have a lot of confidence in, honestly. It's more like a compulsion."

"Look around this tacky ass cabin, my friend. I completely understand."

Redy hands the sketchpad to Littlethumb with one hand and reaches into his pocket to prep the squirt bottle with the other. The pad is eleven by fourteen inches in size. If Littlethumb will take a close look at a sketch, maybe pull the pad up to his face at the right angle, Redy can spike Littlethumb's tea under the guise of reaching for his own. A few seconds is all it will take.

Several unsuccessful attempts are made. Each one ends with Redy casually picking up his own mug and taking a drink. The numerous attempts deplete Redy's tea, and a new idea crosses his mind.

"Do you mind?" he asks, holding up the empty mug.

"No, not at all. There's more in the pot."

"Cool." Brilliant!

As Redy walks over to the kitchen, Littlethumb flips another page in the sketchpad and says, "Redy, I am very impressed by your work."

"Thank you. That's very kind of you to say."

"I'm not just saying it. I mean it. There's genuine vision here. Have you trained at all? Study art in school?"

"No. I mean, I had art class in elementary school, but nothing else." He fills his mug then holds the pot in the air. "Can I top you off?" The plan is to squirt the roofie into the pot, but not yet. Can't waste what little he has if Littlethumb doesn't accept.

"No thanks," says Littlethumb, doublechecking his mug. "Barely touched mine so far."

FUUUUUCK! Redy makes his way back over to the couch, the small squirt bottle magician-palmed in his right hand. He settles back down on the couch and observes Littlethumb as the artist continues to flip through his sketches. If this doesn't happen soon, Redy is switching to Plan C.

"This one is beautiful. Not that the others aren't, but I particularly enjoy this one." Littlethumb rotates the pad for Redy to see his own work, the drawing of a man in agony, shuffling his way toward a grave. The depiction is reminiscent of those evolution of man drawings with apes, cavemen, Cro-Mags, etcetera, except this one is the evolution of one man's pain and suffering through life to death.

Shortly after Littlethumb turns the pad back around and flips another page, Woofus Maximus comes barreling through his trapdoor in the floor, all three monkeys in glorious hot-pursuit. The game is called "Catch the Tail on the Doggie and Drive the Doggie Nuts."

"What the hell?" says Redy.

Littlethumb scarcely notices, accustomed to the random craziness of his roommates and highly engrossed in Redy's artwork. "Huh? I'm sorry, what?"

"You have monkeys?"

"Oh, ha. Yeah. You kind of get used to them. Learn how to tune them out."

"I think that's a personality quirk, man, whether people can tune stuff out or not. I tend to be on the 'or not' side of things."

As the humans speak, the monkeys have cornered their prey. Woof is against the back of the couch in a defensive attack posture.

Positioned in a triangular front, the monkeys have taken high ground atop various decorative implements (plants, shelves, lamps…anything you imagine works fine…).

"How in the world, with all our conversations at the shelter, have you never mentioned you own monkeys?" An opportunity has presented itself. The small squirt bottle is hidden in firing position.

"I don't know," says Littlethumb. "I'm surprised it hasn't come up, though living with monkeys doesn't exactly weave its way into normal conversation."

"Ha. I suppose that's true. So, what are their names?" *Be ready. Turn, motherfucker. Turn.*

"That guy over there to the left, rocking the mohawk, is the bohemian Stevie Two Sharks. Here in the middle is the authoritarian, Zeus." *Here we go. C'mon. Turn!*

"And over there to the right," says Littlethumb, rotating his upper body and turning his head, "is the gentleman Sir Alister Pickney." Littlethumb turns back toward Redy, wearing a proud poppa expression.

Redy leans back up with his mug of tea in hand and says, "Fantastic."

29

"It's not going to be okay." Those were the last words Littlethumb heard before passing out.

In a convenient turn of events for Redmond Sinclair, the natural cooling process of the tea compelled Littlethumb to guzzle his mug. Yes, Littlethumb is one of those. Some people sip, some people guzzle. You decide who you want to be. I'm a Gemini so I float where the wind finds me, or something like that.

Anyway, after a few minutes, Littlethumb becomes woozy, wondering what he missed and where he's gone wrong. He maintains a poker face, or so he thinks, refusing to give Redy the satisfaction of asking what has been done to him. Instead, Littlethumb attempts to excuse himself to the restroom before falling over the coffee table and landing on his back. His eyes are wide open, brain super cloudy, body completely immobile when Redmond Bartholomew Sinclair the Fourth leans over him wearing a hangman's grin and says, "It's not going to be okay."

I was initially going to let loose a diatribe here about the distracting na-
ture of love and pride and ownership. The essay was to be titled *For the
Love of Monkeys* and was going to be an esoteric explanation as to how
Littlethumb dropped his guard while introducing the monkeys to Redy
Sinclair, without ever specifically noting the present circumstances. Then
I considered telling the back story of how Littlethumb acquired the
troop. Again, a roundabout way of blaming his distraction on reverence.
Not a negative commentary on caring for things, so much as a satirically
presented pragmatic discourse on the reality of our existence, human
emotions, and efforts to move a plot forward. I scrapped both ideas.

A mind begs its owner to wake. Dragging awareness, against its will,
all the way to the frontal lobe then down an elevator to the ocular
control room. Before the shutters are opened, awareness throws one
last hissy fit, promising to remain the tight-lipped servant of confusion whether we turn the lights on or not.

Littlethumb stirs slowly, registering the throb in his head as painful. He's in pain. Did he get drunk last night? Pain tells the eyes not
to open. Something else stops an instinctive urge to place a hand on
his suffering head.

Are my hands tied? asks someone in his head who sounds exactly
like him, but very far away.

Master Chee again? asks the same voice, no longer so far away.

No, the voice answers, now front and center.

Littlethumb opens his eyes. Vision is still fuzzy as hell and his
head is slumped forward. Lifting his head is more difficult than normal, and the struggle results in his noggin lolling from side to side.
From this sunken posture, he sees blurry feet moving stuff around a
room in front of him. *Ugh. Fuck this.*

Eyes re-close. A long, deliberately slow breath enters the nose and heads for the brain, up and over, then down the spine, circling the body, turning the lights on throughout the house before slowly exiting his mouth. A few more of these to help ease the pain…no…not ease, to help accept and ignore the pain in his head. Then he re-opens his eyes.

Redy Sinclair is moving around the room, lining up what appear to be drawings. Sketches. All on the same stiff drawing paper as the pad he'd shown Littlethumb earlier. Earlier. How much earlier? *How long was I out?*

The sketches are being propped up, leaning against the wall in front of him and against the legs of easels scattered around the room. Littlethumb faces the western wall. The Vox sits in the northwest corner, where Redy is propping up drawings against the side of the organ's base. These are all the sketches Redy has made of killing Littlethumb. Evidence and legacy, to be destroyed alongside Redy's enemy. To be left behind forever once the circle is complete.

A fresh review of Littlethumb's bindings lets him know he isn't wiggling his way out of these. Don't forget, Redy has witnessed Littlethumb's sleight of hand skills and correctly assumes Littlethumb may be chock-full of surprises. His arms are tied behind the back of the chair, where the ropes tightly secure his wrists. Littlethumb's hands are also bound with his fingers outstretched and palms flat together. His legs are secured to the chair by ropes around his ankles and shins. Not so hard, really, to effectively tie a person to a chair and destroy one of the most successful and absurd plot contrivances in cinema history, the slipping free of the bindings. Unless, of course, the person can dislocate their own joints. Ahem. Cough.

Redy is whistling a tune as he works. Sounds like a Tommy Toxic song. I think maybe it's the rhythm to "When You Die, I Killed You," but that can't be right. "When You Die, I Killed You" was never released.

Bootlegged, maybe, I guess? Or was Redy there, that night in Philadelphia, when Maria was killed?

However Redy learned the tune, after noticing his captive is awake, he locks eyes with Littlethumb, tosses a sketch to the ground, and whistles a punctuating note. Then another one. Then another and another until the song is over, the spiral pad is empty, and a smattering of sketches decorates the floor.

"What are you doing?" asks Littlethumb, voice thin and scratchy.

"Setting the kindling," Redy answers. "Don't you know how to build a fire?" Then he crosses over to Littlethumb and zaps him in the neck with the stun gun, rendering him unconscious again. The preparations aren't quite finished.

How much can you take, Littlethumb? How much will you endure to finish the game? Can you play through the pain to earn a fair and honest death? A well-deserved rest? For every hero's journey eventually comes to the same end. The Reaper whispers, "Ready or not, here I come," and a life turns into a legend.

A cup of cold water splashes against Littlethumb's face. He stirs. Another cup is poured directly over his head. Mumbles and grumbles, the common noises a person might make as they're forced back into the active world.

Littlethumb opens his eyes to see water flying toward his face and pinches them shut again. He shakes his head like a dog tossing the wet off its coat and reopens his eyes.

"There he is," says Redy, pouring yet another cup of water over Littlethumb's head.

Rather than speak right away, Littlethumb looks around the room. There's an empty chair in front of him. Redy's sketches are scattered all over the place. He remembers seeing this before. The device. What's the device doing in here?

"What are you doing?"

"What does it look like I'm doing? I'm killing you." Redy tosses the cup aside nonchalantly, then steps out of view. He returns carrying a large box of matches, pacing back and forth behind the chair.

"Where are the animals?"

"I shut them in the room with all the locks, where I found that." Redy points to the dodeca, which is sitting on top of a stool. "I'll let 'em out later. I'm not going to hurt them. They're innocent."

"Why?" asks Littlethumb. "Why are you doing this?"

"Uh, uh, uh. I'll be asking the questions, but I promise you will understand before we're done. I want you to die knowing why you deserve this. But first, I want to know what that thing is."

"What difference does it make?"

Redy lights a match and tosses it to the floor. The match flames out before landing. "Nope. I told you, I ask the questions. Is it a bomb?"

"You know, setting me on fire might be difficult after soaking me in water." *Take this conversation east and west, Littlethumb. Keep him talking.*

"Oh, don't worry. That's the plan. I want you to burn slow."

"I mean, I get it, but I likely die of asphyxiation first anyway."

"I'm disappointed in your opinion of me, Mr. Brooks." Redy holds up a painter's mask. "It may not help for long, but it will definitely give you a little more time to think about what you've done. Now, quit changing the subject. Is that a bomb?"

"No, it's not a bomb. I'm a painter. Why would I have a bomb in my house?" *And why aren't I already dead, if that's really what you want?*

"Stop. Asking. Questions." Another match flames out on its way to the floor. "You have a room filled with a lot of very odd equipment for a painter. Especially a painter who's already killed hundreds of people." Redy takes a seat across from Littlethumb and lights another match, holding this one up between them, allowing the flame to burn until it dies singeing his fingers.

"What are you talking about? I've never killed anyone."

"Haven't you? I thought it was symbolic…but I see this…thing…and I think, did this motherfucker do it himself?"

"Do what?"

"Start the fire."

"What fire?" Littlethumb asks before he can stop himself from speaking. He knows what fire. There's only one.

Redy picks up the bucket of water he was using to fill the cup and tosses what's left on Littlethumb, then throws the bucket aside. "*The fire*, Littlethumb. You know the one. I've read everything there is to read about that night. The fire was started by an explosion. And here I find this thing in your goddamn secret computer room in there, and all I can wonder is, are you some kind of crazy fucking Unabomber serial killer, living up here in the middle of nowhere?"

"That's insane."

"That's insane?" Insulted, Redy instantaneously transitions from seething to blind rage. Jumping up from his seat, he rips his shirt open, tearing it from his scar covered body. "That's insane?" he repeats, spitting the words out of his mouth. "This is insane," he says, motioning toward his own body, then pounding his chest with his fist. "This! Is insane!" He reaches into his pocket and reveals his father's straight razor, opening it and digging a cut into his chest, seething again, calmly repeating as he works the blade. "This is insane."

Littlethumb winces sorrowfully, then speaks as calmly as possible, attempting any level of de-escalation to this situation that he can muster. "Redy, I was ten years old. I didn't build a bomb or start a fire at my own art exhibit. Tommy killed all those people. He killed my family."

"No. No. No! You killed those people. And your family killed themselves. Tommy may be crazy, but he's a victim. Just like me." Those last three words come out slowly as Redy punctuates them with one more cut on his chest. "This fucking world… Tommy had no one. He was kicked out into all of this cruelty, this shit, with no one to protect him. Just like me. The fire was your fault. Yours and your family's. They made everything about you. You! You were the one who was so special. You were the one that everyone, that my parents, had to go see! You ruined everything. You!"

Redy is stomping back and forth now, aggressively striking matches and tossing them to the floor as he speaks, straight razor still in the hand that's holding the matchbox. Working himself into the murderous fury he desires, Redy is twitching, huffing and puffing like an animal in distress, flexing the muscles throughout his body as he stomps around. There's a physical transition here. The monster, set free of its cage on the inside, is rising fully to the surface. Redy turns toward Littlethumb, eyes piercing, body flaring, and through clenched teeth he points and says, "You killed my parents. They were there. They were there to see the amazing Littlethumb Brooks and you killed them. You took everything from me."

"I…"

Have you ever felt the buzz of inspirational energy and brain activity a person may have under the pressure of a deadline? Whatever the assignment entails, at the last minute you find yourself brimming with ideas and the motivation to complete your task before it's too late? That's what happens right before you die an untimely death, if you have the advanced notice of knowing you're about to die an untimely death.

"I…"

Littlethumb can't finish his sentence, and it wouldn't matter if he could. Redy is ranting, marching around the room, tossing lit match after lit match to the floor and ranting about all of the pain and misery Littlethumb Brooks has caused. All the families who suffered because Littlethumb was *so* special. All the pain Redy himself has suffered. Revenge. Justice. Sweet revenge. A cruel world that rarely offers the aggrieved an opportunity such as this.

Justice!

The rant is background noise, muffled, like when Littlethumb is painting, as he's retreated into his own mind. Into the tunnel, where all these thoughts are swirling as fast as the colors run from his paintbrush to a canvas.

Jesus Christ, it's exactly what I told Uncle. My life is a death curse. This poor kid. No wonder he hates me. His parents died because of me. They died in the fire, and I got famous. I started all of this, whether I meant to or not. I'm the catalyst… My god, when I painted Tommy. All that darkness. I was so young. What if I misunderstood. I misunderstood and my painting drove Tommy over the edge. So many people died and he's right. It's my fault. Mine. Better he kills me now…

Daring Bird's vision! Of course! Redy kills me and I go to Maria, and no one else will suffer because of my fucking 'gift.'

Peace washes over him.

Hope will be safe. No more fear. No more sadness or confusion. I can watch over her from the other side, with Maria. She's safer if I'm dead. Redy will be set free, and Hope will be safe with Sawyer as her daddy.

Daddy…?

What? What about daddy?

In the same moment he accepts his impending death, Littlethumb realizes what blocked him artistically those many months ago. His racing mind screeches to a halt and slams into reverse, rocketing backward through a blur of events and faces and emotions until he's sitting on the couch watching his daughter on the computer. Through the surveillance camera in her bedroom, he watches Sawyer Pettimore read her a bedtime story. Befitting whose daughter she is, Hope had only recently spoken for the first time, her very first words being a variation on fried chicken. Littlethumb doesn't know this, but I'm telling you. I'm telling you because as Sawyer Pettimore closes the book and says goodnight, he gets up to leave and Hope says *the* word. The singular word every boy or man who dreams of being a father wants to hear someday: Daddy.

My daughter, thinks Littlethumb.

Littlethumb Brooks witnessed his child call another man daddy, and it broke his heart. Denial ain't just a river, etcetera, etcetera, as you certainly know. So, he locked the moment away. Didn't happen. Didn't see it, didn't hear it. But he had, and his artistic block was his subconscious mind's way of reminding him something was wrong. That something had to change.

How could I have been so blind?

You were afraid. And confused. And hurt.

But that doesn't explain uncle's vision. Or Redy…Am I supposed to die?

No.

No no no no no. It can't be like this. Whatever the vision means, killing me won't set Redy free. It's murder. You can't let him become a murderer. That's doom. That's crazy. Maria would want you to help him. The guy's in pain. You've got to help…

Figure it out. All that darkness. The kid's in pain.
Think! He's in pain...
Holy shit! The darkness!

30

"It's not a bomb. That device is an artificial intelligence that could save the world."

Redy stops marching back and forth and turns toward Littlethumb.

"What did you say?"

"I said, it's not a bomb. The device. It's an artificial intelligence working on a problem that could potentially change the course of humanity. It could save the world."

"Not mine. My world fell apart the night you killed my parents. There's no saving my world."

"That's not true. You can save yourself. You have a choice, just like I do."

"What choice do you think you have? You're about to die."

"I can choose to let you kill me. To let you become a murderer. Or I can tell you the truth, and maybe it sets you free. Maybe you rise above all of this pain and death and become the person you're meant to be."

"Who the fuck do you think you are?" Redy shakes his head in disgust. "The person I'm meant to be? You don't know anything about who I'm meant to be."

"Yes, I do. I've seen it. I didn't understand at first, but I do now. I've seen who you really are, Redy, and I can show you."

"No, let me show you." With violent speed, Redy suddenly looms over Littlethumb. He drops the matchbox down onto Littlethumb's lap, places the straight razor between his teeth, and rips Littlethumb's shirt open at the neck, exposing Littlethumb's chest. Then Redy takes the razor from his mouth and digs the blade into Littlethumb's flesh.

"Do you feel it?" His teeth are clenched, his face inches away from Littlethumb's. "This is who I am."

Littlethumb doesn't grunt. He winces, but he bites his damn tongue and holds his mouth shut with all his might, denying the urge to scream out in pain. Then, through gritted teeth, he says, "No. It's not. This is not who you are. I can show you."

Redy laughs incredulously. Straightening from his hunched position over Littlethumb, he swipes the razor free of blood on Littlethumb's pants, then folds and pockets the blade as he speaks.

"You can show me?" The matchbox is retrieved as he steps back. "Ladies and gentlemen, the great and powerful Littlethumb Brooks," he mumbles, slightly monotone, as if losing interest while he searches the floor for something. Redy bends over and picks up one of his sketches, then holds the drawing up to review a frighteningly detailed portrayal of Littlethumb's disembowelment. "Ah. This one is perfect." He turns the paper for Littlethumb to view, pointing at the picture. "See, that's you."

"Redy…"

"Shhhhhh." A match is struck and held to the corner of the sketch. The paper curls away from the heat, but after a moment, flames begin to dance at the edges. Redy tosses the sketch back to the ground and adjusts it with his foot, positioning it to contact another sketch and pass the fire along. Then he sets a path of sketches for the flames to further spread. Once finished, he turns back to Littlethumb.

"Time for me to go, Mr. Brooks."

"No. You don't want to do this."

"I'm certain I do."

"Dammit, Redy, I've got a daughter!"

"Where?" Redy looks around the room conspicuously, toying with his captive. Littlethumb ignores Redy's snark and motions to the paintings of Hope, stacked against the wall over his right shoulder.

"There. That stack of paintings. Go look. Go look at my daughter, Redy. Don't do the same thing to her that Tomm…that I did to you."

"I've never heard anything about a daughter. You're stalling."

"No, it's true. When Maria died, I kept her a secret. Go look. See for yourself."

"A secret daughter? Perfect. Absolutely perfect. I will have a look. And so will you. You can stare at her and think about what you've done while you burn." The paintings lie face down with drop cloths in between to protect them. Redy crosses the room and picks up the top painting on the stack, then sets it aside and sorts through several more. Littlethumb can barely see Redy in his periphery, but can tell Redy is staring at one of Hope's portraits.

"Do you see? Do you see her joy? I told you I can show you, Redy. All you have to do is look at your portrait. Just look."

"I don't think so." There's a vacancy in Redy's response, as he finishes selecting a painting of Hope. Stepping back over in front of Littlethumb, he holds the painting for Littlethumb to view. "Let me ask you, do you see it? Because I do. I see a little girl full of joy who's going to be very, very sad. Do you see that? Do you see how sad she's going to be?" He takes the painting and leans it against the wall facing Littlethumb.

"It's not the same when it's not you," Littlethumb says, more to himself than to Redy.

"What?" asks Redy, looking over his shoulder.

"I always forget, for everyone else. The feeling's not quite the same when it's not them. When it's not their painting."

Redy turns back around. "What the fuck are you…no. Doesn't matter. Goodbye, Littlethumb."

"Don't leave. Not yet. Let me tell you what happened. If I'm gonna die anyway, please, let me explain."

"I have no interest in anything you have to say. Our lives will no longer be tethered, Littlethumb Brooks. You will die by fire, like my parents. The circle will be complete, and I will be free."

"No, you won't. You won't be free, Redy, because I'm not the one. I'm not the one who hurt you, and if you kill me, you'll just be another murderer."

"This isn't murder. This is justice."

"Not if you kill me. Not if you leave another innocent child without her parents. Her mother was already taken from her. If you kill me… No, Redy. That's not justice. That's murder. That's darkness. And all the pain inside you will control you forever."

A long groan exits Redy's body as he puts both hands to the sides of his head, shaking in frustration. Then his left hand fishes for the straight razor in his pocket.

"If you kill me, you're doing the same thing to Hope that happened to you. It's your choice, Redy. Do you want her to suffer? Like you have? Are you going to do that to another child?"

Groaning again, pure frustration and confusion, Redy says, "Stop," holding onto the word, stretching it out as he pulls at the razor in his pocket with haphazard desperation. The razor tangles, and Redy struggles to free it. Finally tearing the razor loose, he opens the blade and digs a fresh cut into his abdomen.

"Look at her, Redy. Look at her. She doesn't deserve this. Don't do this to yourself."

"Stop. Talking." Redy turns to the portrait of Hope, then back to Littlethumb, pointing the straight razor at him, arm fully extended. He stabs at the air with the razor, grunting, then turns back to the portrait of Hope.

"Redy, please listen to me. Please. For Hope."

"Stop!" Rotating to face Littlethumb again, still pointing the razor as he speaks, Redy takes a deep breath and speaks through gritted teeth. "Two minutes, for her. I'm giving your daughter two minutes for you to repent, so you can die with a clean conscience. Then you burn."

"When I was a little kid, I sneezed and the world froze. But the sneeze didn't really matter. It was a coincidence, I guess. And the world wasn't really frozen."

"For fuck's sake." Redy is standing in front of Littlethumb, arms folded across his chest, impatiently honoring his benevolence toward Hope.

"Just listen, dammit."

Imagine Littlethumb speaking breathlessly and continually picking up steam as he tries to explain a metaphysical spiritual occurrence in less than two minutes. "The world wasn't frozen. I thought it was. My family, they appeared frozen in time. I could hear their hearts beating, but the sound was from very far away. I knew they were alive, but I was alone. Days went by and nothing changed. They were still alive but frozen. I didn't know what to do, and I didn't know how long they would be that way, so I left. I took off, and I started walking across the world, and the more I walked, the more I realized the world wasn't frozen. I wasn't in the world. I was somewhere in between life and death. And the longer I was there, the more I was connected, the more I could see. I saw positive and negative forces inside everything. Animals, people, plants. In the land and the mountains and the sea. There was light and dark in everything, but almost all of the dark was in people. And, as a child, in my head the light was good and the dark was bad. Evil. But most people were…dim…gray, they were gray. Some were more light, some more darkness, but most were gray, with the light and the dark blending, constantly struggling for control."

"You should hurry. Time's almost up."

Picking up more speed. "The longer I was in the spirit world, the more I was connected, the more I could see. And near the end I found my grandfather. Or he found me, really, but he was dead, of course, he had recently died. I forgot to say that earlier, but he was proof I was in the spirit world. Proof what I was seeing was real. He pulled me to the other side, by accident, when he died, and after I found him, we traveled together until we came back home. And I go to sleep in my bed, and I wake up on the same day I left, and everything is back to normal, but not really, and the next thing I know, I paint the Mona Lisa and everything changes forever."

"Two minutes," Redy says, making a show of checking his watch. "Time's up."

"No, no, no. Don't you understand? Don't you hear what I'm saying? I saw the good and evil in people, Redy, and I can still see them when I paint, only now I'm not sure it's that simple, but either way that's why I had to paint you. I was trying to see who you really are, on the inside. To get a better sense of your intentions. But I couldn't figure it out. I stared and stared at your portrait, but I couldn't understand what it was trying to tell me. I thought all of the darkness was evil, and you were torn between good and evil. Like you were born that way. In conflict. I didn't know what I was supposed to do. But I understand now, because the darkness isn't evil. It's pain. And the painting was never meant to speak to me. It's meant to speak to you."

"The painting is supposed to speak to me? About my darkness? I give you a chance for redemption, to die honorably, for the sake of your daughter, and you beg for your life with a bunch of crazy nonsense? You think you know about my darkness? About my pain?"

"Not me. The painting, and I can prove it. It's right there. Look at your portrait, and then if you don't believe me, if you don't see, you can leave me here to die."

"I'm already doing that."

"But you're still here, Redy. You're still here because you're fighting all that pain. This isn't who you are, who you're meant to be."

"Shut up."

"Just look at the painting, Redy. Just look at the painting and you'll see."

Wavering, Redy clutches the sides of his head again, hunching forward. Looking down at the ground. he repeats, "Shut! Up!"

Off to the left, Littlethumb sees the trail of fire connect with one of the sketches propped against the wall. "Redy, we're running out of time. You're running out of time. If you go through with this, you won't be a victim anymore. The kid inside you who suffered, who deserves to live free of all this madness, he'll be gone, Redy. He'll be gone, and you'll never get him back."

Redy looks up at Littlethumb, hands still clutching his head, a terrified child's expression on his face. Tears of anguish and confusion stream from bloodshot eyes as flames climb the wall behind him.

"Redy, I know you're confused and you're hurting, but all you've got to do is look. Just look at the painting and see for yourself who you really are."

The child inside Redy turns to the easel where his portrait sits hidden by a drop cloth. Then, Redy the man turns to Littlethumb, his face the distorted expression of a person burdened with insurmountable suffering. He looks over his shoulder at the fire beginning to spread. He jerks a half step toward the room's exit, as if fighting the monster's pull. Fighting the urge to run. To run and never look back. But he will look back. You know it. I know it. Littlethumb knows it.

"REDY LOOK AT THE GODDAMN PAINTING!"

The child wins, turning from the direction of the exit, refusing the monster and defiantly sending the man lurching toward the painting. Redy struggles physically, approaching the easel as a final act of resistance against the monster trying to forever enslave him. With shaky hands, reaching as if an invisible force is pulling against him, trying to hold back his arms, he summons the final bit of strength needed to sweep the covering up and away, releasing the drop cloth to land in a heap wherever it may.

Monster, man, and child are gobsmacked. Redy staggers backward a step or two, then plops down onto his butt, as if the portrait shoved him to the ground. Looking up at the truth of his being, tears that moments before contained frustration, anger, and all things bitter instantly represent the joy of understanding. An infinite hopefulness flowing throughout humanity's interconnected souls, as the portrait tells Redy the story of who he was meant to be, before the world got ahold of him: A gentle, loving person.

The story of who Redy may still become? Perhaps the best version of ourselves is one that empowers the person we were meant to be over the person we already are, after the cruel world has had its way with us. That's what Redy sees painted on the canvas before him. Not the monster he's envisioned, desperate to escape and wreak havoc. No, he sees a divine spirit, his inner child surviving to conquer the pain and hatred thrust upon him. Redy sees a courageous, virtuous man.

What you see on the canvas is a picture of Redy in the spirit world. There's no shelter wall in the background, and Redy isn't sitting on a stool. Instead, he floats in a thin haze, surrounded by the translucent "physical" world of a bustling city. The background people are faceless, blurred images of the dark, light, and gray that Littlethumb witnessed in the spirit world. Redy's body faces the viewer, but at an angle, as if he were moving from up-stage right to down-stage left in a play. His legs are together, shoulders and back arched, and arms spread wide at a downward angle, similar to a comic book superhero pose. Perhaps one where the hero is taking flight.

The depiction of Redy's face is an honest, handsome reflection of a healthy Redmond Sinclair, yet we can look through his skull to see the forces at work in his mind, including the flow of his blood, which can be traced incrementally throughout his body, as the painting depicts both his internal and external form. Sort of like a mashup of Slim Goodbody and the villain Two-Face from Batman comics, except beautiful. The depictions of Redy's internal systems are romantic, not clinical.

"Do you see?" asks Littlethumb.

Redy stares at the heart beating in his chest, pumping blood filled with white light into his body, but there's a darkness in his mind. The blood leaves his heart untainted but returns corrupted by the darkness. As the darkness spreads, it threatens to overcome the light, but the light is more powerful, depicted by a thinness to the black paint and a concentrated depth to the white.

The colors blend and take shape in the upper left portion of Redy's chest, blurring into talons that grip his heart. The talons connect to the outstretched legs of a phoenix, as if the phoenix is bursting forth from Redy's heart to escape the bird-patterned scarring of his body and be reborn.

The phoenix flies at the same angle as Redy's body, rising up and out to the side so the animal doesn't block your view of the man. The torso of the phoenix is covered in white scales with black trim. The wings and the rest of the body are also trimmed in black. On the skull, the black and white paint are equal in concentration. White paint wraps the head, creating a slatted helmet. Thick stripes of black feathers show through the slats in the helmet and blend into a black beak. The depiction culminates in piercing, oversized, bright white eyes that are askew of the angle of the bird, thinly trimmed in black and painted as if the phoenix was staring directly at the viewer. Staring directly at Redy. Staring directly at you.

31

Here's the part where you get to choose for yourself, in regards to this little fighter of a tale, between chaos and fate…

In the earliest hours of a new day, during the ante-meridiem quiet intended for slumber, our genius fiend wakes from a brilliant dream. At first groggy and unimpressed by the situation, Xander's resistance to his inspiration subsides as the idea kicking around in his head goes from room to room, flicking on all the lights. Close-eyed consternation slowly transitions to blinky-eyed recognition. *Fuck. That's a good idea.*

No going back to sleep now. Not without chemical assistance. Might as well get your ass up and enjoy the silence for a bit, Xander.

His body begrudgingly abides, exiting the bed and sliding into house shoes. First stop, the kitchen, for a glass of water and a cold chicken leg. Next stop, the office.

Upon reaching his sanctuary, the chicken leg is already whittled to the bone. Xander drops the remains into a trashcan and flicks on the office lights, then walks over to his desk, where he stands enthralled, yet again, by the stunning portrait of Maria. Loins stirred, Xander considers masturbation but immediately disregards the idea with contempt. First of all, this painting is far too distinguished for subjection to a mere catalyst of self-gratification. Secondly, Xander does not masturbate. One of the many benefits of evil villainy is copulation on demand.

No whores in the henhouse, Xander reminds himself, telling his loins to calm down. *Besides, I'm not in the mood.*

The idea that ruined his perfect night's rest needs recording, so he takes a seat and fires up his computer. The concept is a Ponzi scheme involving digital currency. Rather boring on first pass, as Xander doesn't need the money, but not so boring when Xander targets specific underground markets. Destabilization of criminal networks being as paramount to his vision of chaos as his fuckery in the civilized world.

There are computer coding notes and general scheme plans to write before they slip from his mind. The work doesn't take long. Once the file is created, notes taken and saved, Xander rocks back and forth in boredom. Middle of the night. Wide awake. What to do, what to do? Television? No, waste of cognitive resources. Read a book? Might help put him back to sleep…

I suppose I could review status updates from agents in daytime zones. Ooh. D-13. Let's see if you've got anything exciting to share.

Who needs television when you've got secret cameras installed in various objects located all over the world? Xander opens the surveillance program receiving D-13's video feed. A small window pops up, and Xander sees movement.

Well, well, well, he thinks, switching the window to full screen.

"What the fuck?!"

Xander shooshes himself and listens intently for any stir his voice may have caused, then leaves his desk and pokes his head into the hallway, looking both directions for any signs of life. No monstrous progeny stirring. Good. Satisfied that all remains calm, he gently closes the door and returns to his desk with a lighthearted swiftness. The same type of dexterous tiptoed swiftness my cane wielding grandmother used to employ while moving around her house when she thought no one else was watching. (Otherwise, she moved slowly and played up the need for assistance because she enjoyed the attention, may she rest in peace.)

Giddily confused, that's Xander's state of being. *Now this was worth getting out of bed for!*

To be clear, he's witnessing on his computer the dramatic confrontation between Redy Sinclair and Littlethumb Brooks. Talk about wishing he had installed a microphone! Xander would give away one of his children to hear what's being said. (Probably the third boy, that little shit…)

The angle of D-13's camera allows Xander to witness part of the action. The computer screen is mostly filled by wall and ceiling, with the image of Brooks to one side. He appears tied to a chair. An enraged, half-naked man keeps stomping in and out of the camera's view. Xander can't see the fire slowly spreading, and he can't see Redy's portrait. Obviously, he doesn't know what he can't see, but what he can see is fantastic. Blissfully entertained, he considers making himself popcorn but doesn't want to miss anything. Then he remembers he has servants and calls down to the overnight attendant for a large tub of popcorn smothered in butter and a giant real-sugar soda, like they sell at the movies.

The popcorn and soft drink arrive quietly as the action is heating up. Crazy dude hops into view and takes a razor to Brooks' chest. *Fascinating,* thinks Xander. *I wonder what he's done to piss this man off. I bet it's a woman. Artists can be such indiscriminate hounds.*

The attacker menacingly hovers over Brooks. Xander captures several screenshots for analyzation. Whoever this crazy redheaded bastard is, Xander has to have him identified. There's a solid chance he may steal D-13. *What a strange journey you've wound up on, my little creation.*

Several minutes pass as the artist blabs away from his captive position, then Xander sees the crazy guy lurch toward something out of view, apparently behind or off to the side of D-13. A portion of the right side of the guy's body is in a closeup view on the monitor when he suddenly appears to fall down.

What was that? A clear shot of Brooks opens back up and Xander can see him speaking toward the floor. Xander tosses popcorn into his mouth intently, chasing it with the cola, wishing he was a fluent lip reader. Copious amounts of bubbly liquid sugar tingle Xander's taste-buds, and a lesser man would spray his mouthful of soda all over his computer screen when he sees what happens next happen next:

A startling notification pops up on Xander's computer.

You have got to be fucking kidding me… There truly is no god.

D-13 has completed its assignment. The algorithm has success-fully finished its computation. Do you want to know what the program determined?

I knew it!

The program has determined it is scientifically possible for a matter reorganizer to gather free-range sub-atomic particles and use them to build previously defined materials. In other words, make something out of nothing. "All you have to do" is have the molecular composition of your desired outcome on file. Assuming, of course, the required machinery is technologically available.

So many questions! Although his software can alert him to the program's completion and basic findings, Xander can't analyze the results without having D-13 hardwired to a local computer. Thus, despite learning a replicator (Xander has no issue committing copyright or trademark infringement…) is scientifically possible, he can't see any of the mathematical data supporting this conclusion.

Hasty decision time, Xander. Leave your priceless device in the hands of someone else, risking their ability to discover its secret, or…? Or what? Destroy it? Destroy this one-of-a-kind example of your brilliance? Not to mention D-13's incalculable power, if the necessary materials exist for building the machinery to actualize its findings. For fuck's sake, why didn't he install a tracking device!?

Enough. 'There's no crying in baseball,' Xander. You know what you must do.

Inside the thin walls of the jack-in-the-box is an explosive compound of Xander's creation. A more stable, less volatile, yet equally powerful derivative of nitroglycerin, this semi-solid compound is undetectable. No one could have discovered it. You can't look for what you don't know exists.

Wait. Theoretically, I suppose you can. Though not in this instance, unless you dreamt up the exact same idea Xander had for creating this explosive compound so you could then search for said explosive compound. Never mind. Losing focus. What's important is that Xander faces the decision of destroying D-13 or potentially allowing someone else to capitalize on his invention's findings.

What type of evil villain do you want to be? he asks himself, but he knew the answer before he asked the question. The type of evil villain who readily sacrifices anything and everything to prove a point. To prove a point to himself, his friends, his enemies, and the entire world. The greatest secret evil villain in the history of mankind, that's what type.

Speaking of enemies, *What a shame,* thinks Xander, as he deactivates Opportunity 514. No sense paying out a contract with Littlethumb

Brooks about die. At least one of Xander's assets would wind up sending Brooks' obituary as proof he's been found and request payment, scoundrels that his assets are. Cancellation of the Op will prevent any nonsensical discourse, including the possible severing of relationships and/or asset body parts.

Despite Xander's stonehearted resolve, this entire situation is a massive disappointment. Since learning of Littlethumb Brooks' involvement, Xander has romantically envisioned an extended battle of wits and wills between himself and the artist. Alas, someone else appears to have beaten him to the punch. Oh well. Considering the circumstances under which he discovered Brooks' ties to the Electric Medicine Men, Xander should not be surprised this situation is ending poorly. In fact, if not beguiled by his enthusiasm for the idea of a brilliant artist unwittingly filling the role of arch-nemesis, Xander would have clearly seen there was no happy ending to the Electric Medicine Men possessing D-13.

C'est la vi, Xander. C'est la vi…

Then again, perhaps Brooks survives. What an amazing revelation that would be. Were their discord to continue, it might soften the blow of D-13's destruction. Nothing like setting yourself up for an improbable, marvelous surprise.

Maybe he lives, thinks Xander. *Maybe.*

Either way, D-13 cannot remain in the wrong hands. At least Xander can take solace in knowing his enemy will see D-13 and its remarkable knowledge destroyed. Whether Brooks survives or dies, Xander is certain that watching D-13 self-destruct will be a shocking disappointment.

"Farewell, my wonderful friend," Xander whispers to himself. "I wish we had more time together."

With that, Xander initiates D-13's self-destruct protocol.

❀ ❀ ❀

Master Chee arrives at the cabin and sees Redy's car parked out front. I'm assuming the presence of the vehicle is unexpected, and I'm not certain if Chee knows who the cherry red Buick Wildcat belongs to, but I'm positive it's familiar to him. Small town and whatnot. He has to have seen the vintage car before.

A cold hood indicates the car's been parked for a while. Informative if not paramount to Master Chee's movements. He skulks into the shadows of the trees lining the cabin, attaching camouflaged surveillance cameras to branches facing all the cabin's windows and doors. Any possible exit from the building. Once the cameras are set, he takes position behind a fallen tree stump in the woods, uphill from the left side of the front porch.

Master Chee pulls a small laptop from his backpack and powers it up, checking to ensure the cameras are functional and accurately positioned for comprehensive surveillance. Then he beds down for an apparent stakeout. Stars are out. Master Chee reads by the light of the moon. The book is titled *A Curious Passage of Time.*

Shortly before midnight, a vibration stirs Master Chee from his intent consumption of literature. On his second attempt, he finds the correct phone and reads the incoming message. Opportunity 514 has been canceled. Interesting, though, perhaps not so much for a secretive martial arts master.

Whether intrigued or supremely unfazed, Master Chee marks his book for closure and packs up camp. Before shutting down the computer, he notices odd heat signatures from one of the infrared cameras located behind the cabin. Still, he closes and packs the computer.

Master Chee is about to hike away, but hesitates, instead turning to sneak back down toward the cabin. I suppose even the Buddha was curious on occasion.

❊   ❊   ❊

We're back inside the cabin. Redy sits on the floor, staring up at Littlethumb's majestic representation of him. Observing yourself through the lens of a visionary artist can be a lot to absorb. Especially after suffering as Redy has. The portrait offers Redy an escape from the chains in which he is bound, locked and keyed by life in his own emotional prison. Whereas he once saw nothing but torment in his reflection, in the portrait he sees a vision of hope. For the first time in his life, Redmond Sinclair accepts his beauty, and the wonderous life he might yet still live, given the strength to see it through. Strength he most certainly possesses, if Littlethumb's painting has anything to say on the subject.

Littlethumb is silent now, allowing Redy to deliberate uninterrupted, but the fire is spreading. A manic debate wages in his head as he swaps glances back and forth between the flames and the young man seated on the floor, holding out as long as he can before speaking, hoping Redy will break the silence first. Littlethumb is near his wit's end when the dodeca breaks the silence for him.

Ding.

A few seconds pass before Redy acknowledges the sound. He shakes his head, returning to the present, then looks over his shoulder toward Littlethumb and says, "What was that?"

"I don't know. It sounded like it came from the device. It must have. Maybe it's finished running its program."

"What program?"

Ding.

"That's two," Redy says, ignoring his previous question and jumping to his feet. "Is there a three? Will there be three?"

"There almost always is."

"What happens on three?"

"I got a bad feeling about this, Redy. You better get out of here."

"I thought you said that thing isn't a bomb!"

"It isn't, but that doesn't mean it can't explode. Redy, get out of here. Now!"

Ding.

"Shit," says Redy.

"Fuck me again," says Littlethumb.

The dodeca's explosion is gentle, comparatively speaking, in regards to the typical glory of self-destruct mechanisms. The amount of explosive compound used was limited by the dodeca's structure, but more than sufficient to ensure destruction of the device. Due to proximity, the concussive force of the blast is enough to knock Littlethumb over in his chair. Redy, even closer to the dodeca than Littlethumb, is pierced with multiple pieces of bronze shrapnel and thrown backward several feet. Both men lay unconscious. Fire spreads.

Making his way to the back of the cabin, Master Chee is near the rear window of Littlethumb's art studio when the crack of an explosion emits from the house. Master Chee dives behind a nearby woodpile to avoid any successive blasts. Nothing occurs so he dashes to the window. The curtains are drawn. There's no view of the happenings inside, save for the flickering glow of a fire on the march showing through the tiniest of seams between the window's frame and the blackout curtains.

Sprinting around to the front of the house, Master Chee licks his fingers and taps at the handle to the front door. Cool to the touch, he thumbs the latch and pushes but the door is locked. Three steps back, distance perfectly calculated for efficacy, he flies sideways and kicks the door open with relative ease. Once inside, Chee takes a split second registry of the situation then dashes through the cabin.

Entering the art studio, Master Chee registers two bodies. One unknown and stirring, the other his employer who is tied to a chair. Smoke is filling the room. Flames have engulfed the lower half of the western wall, including the portrait of a child, and are spreading fast. Master Chee rights Littlethumb in the chair, tilts him onto the back legs and drags him out of the cabin to a safe distance away from the house, still assuming the possibility of another explosion.

When Master Chee reenters the art studio, the other body is gone, apparently through the room's northern window, now open. An empty canvas frame rests on an easel near the flames. Jagged interior edges indicate the body of the canvas was hastily cut free. Master Chee looks around the room at all the other paintings, either stacked or propped against a wall. He gathers a stack and heads out of the studio into the living room, where he abruptly drops the paintings, eyes locked on the closed door to a room he's never entered.

The door is unlocked, alleviating any search for keys to the deadbolts. He throws the door open to find the monkeys, who come screeching out of the room with Woofus Maximus barking after them. Zeus, Stevie Two Sharks, and Sir Alister Pickney charge through the cabin in search of their leader. Woof's nose leads him directly to the art studio, full of flames and smoke and the smell of his daddy's emotions.

Master Chee pursues the monkeys, attempting to usher them out of the house as they fly around the cabin searching for Littlethumb. Woof's barking draws the troop into the art studio. Woof is barking at the fire indignantly, protective doggie that he is, but the monkeys immediately recognize peril. Master Chee circles around in front of Woof to shoo the animals out of the room.

"Out," he commands, pointing at the door.

The monkeys don't need any more convincing. Zeus jumps atop Woof and tugs on the fur at the nape of the coydog's neck, riding him out of the room with his brothers in tow. Master Chee follows them out of the studio, watching as all four exit through the doggie door in the floor of the cabin's living room, then he regathers the stack of paintings he'd previously dropped.

Outside, the monkeys are attempting to untie Littlethumb as Master Chee brings stack after stack of paintings from the cabin. All that he can save. Then he goes after the computers, bringing all of the machines out, sans any unnecessaries like monitors or keyboards. There's no point in attempting to rescue the server from its impressive cage. If Master Chee managed to bust the cage's locks, he would still need a dolly to get the server out.

In the midst of all this, you may ask, does Master Chee have the time and skillset to hack into Littlethumb's computers to investigate the network's purpose and or download critical information about the Electric Medicine Men? I have no idea…

32

Routine living is a happy pursuit, when happy with your routine. Our friend Willy Peete thoroughly enjoys the consistency of his mornings. Wake up early and live the slippered-feet, coffee-handed, bathrobe-wearing life shown in movies, television shows, and a suburban neighborhood near you. Don't forget the newspaper. You've got to go get the paper off the front stoop, and you better do so before the sprinklers turn on, you pre-internet stereotype, you.

Fortunately for Willy, collecting the morning paper is as close to living any godawful Norman Rockwell nonsense as he gets, though his mornings are the most peaceful hours to each of his days. Not today, however. Today greets him with a surprise. This morning's front-page headline? What is Littlethumb Brooks doing asleep in his truck in the First Church of Good Deeds parking lot?

I won't go so far as to say Littlethumb is delirious. He is, however, mildly dehydrated from the chemical Redy used to subdue him and an extended period without food or water, and is also concussed from the explosion (whether from the blast itself or whacking his head against the floor when he was blown over, or a combination of both…). No, I won't say delirious, but I would go so far as severely loopy. Willy hunkers down and pulls Littlethumb directly from the cab of the truck onto his shoulder. The animals leap from the truck and follow as Willy carries Littlethumb inside.

A direct flight from Manhattan to Toronto takes just over an hour and a half. Short, though long enough for Sawyer Pettimore to nap or think or do a little of both. The call from Willy came early. With the amount of daily business travel between the two cities, Sawyer easily booked a same-day flight and was on his way by noon.

The drive from Toronto to The First Church of Good Deeds takes several hours. Or more. Or less. I've kept the town a secret thus far. No reason to expose the place this late in the game.

On the way, Sawyer reaches out to Daring Bird to alert him of the situation. Here's a sample conversation: "I've filled you in on what I currently know. You offer me assistance. I decline. No, no, I've got this. He seems fine. You have important work you need to remain focused on." This conversation doesn't happen because Daring Bird doesn't answer. Instead, Sawyer hangs up the phone and succumbs to the will of his memory, his past playing out before him as he stares down the highway.

A quick reference guide to Sawyer Pettimore: Extremely successful international art dealer worth millions of dollars. Littlethumb's grade school art teacher and mentor. Business Manager of Littlethumb's artwork. Husband to an amazing and aggressive philanthropist wife named Anna, doting father to Isabel, and current guardian of Hope Samanthoset Brooks.

In his early adulthood, Sawyer armored an open heart in childish bitterness and insecurity. I've often described him during this period as the type of person who typically does the right thing, but often with a lousy attitude. After the explosion at Littlethumb's exhibit, Sawyer navigated guilt, regret, and a penchant for negotiating the sale of famous art to extraordinary success. Daring Bird would say he has grit, but is kind of a puss until the grit activates. More recently, Sawyer's been living the benefits of forgiveness, from external sources and from within, while financing the Electric Medicine Men's exploits through the sale of Littlethumb's artwork. Littlethumb would say this is the man Sawyer Pettimore was always meant to be.

"It's been too many moons, my friend!" says Willy, looking up from behind his office desk.

"Yes, it has," replies Sawyer, standing in the doorway. "I'm sorry I haven't been back since the shelter opened. Hard to believe it's already been so long."

"Yes, it is. Life's tricky that way, isn't she?" Willy gets up and heads around his desk toward Sawyer.

"She sure is." Sawyer sticks his hand out to receive Willy's. "It's great to see you, Willy."

"You too."

"How's our boy?"

"He's fine. Out there making the rounds and saying goodbye to everyone."

"Goodbye?"

"Yep. After you and I spoke this morning, after he woke up, told me it's time to go."

Willy and Sawyer make their way to the common room. Standing outside, they can see Littlethumb through the windows in the doors. He's up on a table, smiling and laughing and doing silly magic tricks for his friends.

"Did you know this Sinclair fellow?" asks Sawyer.

"Nah, not well. No more than our boy in there."

"He explain what happened to you?"

"Not really."

Goodbyes suck. That's universal, right? We all agree, generally speaking, that goodbyes suck? Okay, cool.

The toughest is bidding farewell to Willy. Most of the guests at the shelter have lived such transient lives and are on such personal internal journeys, saying goodbye doesn't resonate with them for long. Willy and Littlethumb's farewell embrace is emotionally without end, and might as well have lasted forever. They'd built this place together, after all, this wonderful piece of humanity. And on the backbone of a chance encounter. Dang old chaos and fate…

Littlethumb promises to stay in touch daily, to return for a visit soon, and to bring a special guest when he does. Hell, he's been looking for a reason to get his pilot's license. Visiting friends is the perfect excuse, and flying would make for fast commutes.

Willy promises he and the fellas will get to work rebuilding the cabin. Littlethumb resists the offer, of course, but he doesn't have a choice. "Besides, what the hell else are these goofballs gonna do with themselves? And keep me updated on that pilot's license. Maybe we put in a landing strip."

After all the standing around "you're leaving but lingering" is finished, Sawyer follows Littlethumb out to the cabin to close up shop. The fire gutted the art studio, but apparently every faucet in the house was turned on by someone (presumably Redy), emptying the external reservoir and flooding areas of the house to combat the fire. An overnight rain finished the job. The frame survived, but the interior was ruined and the Electric Medicine Men's server was fried.

Other than pragmatic discourse on the results of the fire, Littlethumb and Sawyer don't converse much while surveying the damage. A few surviving items and some clothes are loaded into the truck next to the computers and artwork, then covered with a tarp for highway travel. Once the truck is loaded, Littlethumb takes a commemorative moment of silence for the cabin and the two men head for Toronto.

Sawyer drives Littlethumb's old truck down Interstate 90. Woofus Maximus rides in the middle between Sawyer and Littlethumb. The monkeys lounge on the dashboard.

After dropping off Sawyer's rental car in Toronto, Littlethumb tossed Sawyer the truck keys and promptly fell asleep on departure. Several hours later, east of Buffalo, Littlethumb yawns himself awake and stretches the confined stretch of waking up in a car on a long drive. Stretching reminds him of the gash in his chest.

"How long was I out?" he asks, poking around at the bandage.

"A few hours. Feel better?"

"I do. I didn't realize how tired I was."

"Yeah, I've heard being kidnapped and almost dying can be exhausting."

"Can you believe that shit?"

"Given the history of our lives, I'm gonna let that be a rhetorical question."

"Ha. Probably not a bad idea." Littlethumb raps at the truck's passenger side window with the knuckles of his right hand, watching the world fly by. "Where are we?"

"Outside Buffalo. I figure we drive a few more hours, then maybe find a place for some food and get a hotel room for the night. Unless you want to swap seats and drive on through?"

"Eh, either way suits me. Probably smarter to get a room."

"Sounds good to me." Sawyer steals a glance at his younger friend, then returns his eyes to the road and says, "So, you going to tell me what happened back there?"

"Nope."

"Seriously?"

A smart-assed grin is tossed in Sawyer's direction.

"I will wrap this truck around a tree." Both men take a moment for laughter, then Sawyer says, "Alright. Out with it."

The next thirty miles or so are spent recounting the episode with Redy and the unfortunate outcome for the dodeca. Hopefulness rules the day, in regards to the future of Redy Sinclair. If anyone besides Littlethumb or Daring Bird understands the inner-truths exposed in the subjects of Littlethumb's portraits, it's Sawyer Pettimore. An artist himself, after all, he may not be able to see exactly what Littlethumb or the subject of the painting sees, but Sawyer can see enough to understand the spiritual connection between Littlethumb's work and his subject. As described to him, Sawyer assures Littlethumb the portrait must have had a positive effect on Redy. After all, he did pull Littlethumb from the fire.

The conversation turns to the destruction of the dodeca. Both men lament the loss of a device capable of changing the course of humanity, or perhaps more accurately, *climate changing* the course of humanity. (Zing.)

Questions obviously remain. Who had they stolen the device from? Did Littlethumb and Daring Bird expose themselves by operating the device? Why did it explode? Was it a self-destruct mechanism? If so, was it activated simply because they stole the device, or had someone somehow been watching them? Unanswerable questions, leading to the only conclusion possible: Prepare for the worst and hope for the best. Head down, feet forward.

Later, in the midst of a comfortable silence, Littlethumb remembers Master Chee and blurts something out along the lines of, "Fuck. Master Chee! Fuck." This requires explaining to Sawyer who Master Chee is, which raises the question of whether or not it was actually Master Chee who rescued Littlethumb from the fire. The possibility of Chee having arrived at the cabin for a surprise attack and instead saving the day is legitimate. Littlethumb attempts to call Master Chee, but the number he has is no longer in service. Big sarcastic surprise.

"Shitty," he says. "I guess we'll never know."

Such is the way of the Chee.

Before the end of the day, their conversation turns to Daring Bird and any potential updates on the Electric Medicine Men's efforts to retrieve *The Marias*. Also, did Sawyer reach out to him about what happened with Redy?

"I tried this morning but didn't get through. No telling where he is."

"Oh, I have an idea."

Sawyer looks away from the road long enough to steal a glance at Littlethumb's facial expression. "Why'd you say it like that? You know exactly where he is, don't you? Did he hook up or something?"

"Apparently."

"Oh my. Anna's gonna love hearing this. You know anything about the lady?"

"Not much, but it sounds like he may have met his match."

"Awesome. Maybe he'll stop being such a grumpy bastard."

The next day, Sawyer and Littlethumb reach Manhattan in the early afternoon. Sawyer and Anna planned ahead to ensure that she and both the girls would be home for Littlethumb's arrival. Entering the apartment, Sawyer and Littlethumb find Isabel in the family room watching television.

"Uncle Littlethumb!" she shouts, launching off the couch and rushing to Littlethumb's side. Isabel is twelve and beginning a phase of expressing less outward affection toward her parents and other adult relatives, but Sawyer expected this reaction from her. After all, she hasn't seen her "uncle" in several years.

"How you doing, 'Bel?" says Littlethumb, before scooping her up for a bear hug.

Isabel wraps her legs around him to support her own weight, then pushes back and says, "Oh, pretty good. I'm so happy to see you!" Then she gives Littlethumb's neck a tight squeeze and lets her legs dangle, signifying she's ready to be put down.

During the exchange, Sawyer retrieves Anna and Hope. After setting Isabel down, Littlethumb looks up to see Sawyer with his arm around Anna, who's holding hands with Hope. Littlethumb Brooks hasn't seen his daughter in person since she was a newborn child. I'm at a loss for metaphor to explain the expression of joy on his face. Jokingly, I might say it's enough to make the average person uncomfortable.

Uncertain what to say or do, Littlethumb holds up a hand for a static wave hello and says, "Hi," then gains his bearings and says, "Anna, it's wonderful to see you," before Isabel grabs him by the wrist and drags him across the room.

"You too!" Anna reaches forward and Littlethumb steps into a one-armed hug, then she looks down and says, "Hope, do you know who this is?"

The child nods her head affirmatively, prompting confusion from Littlethumb.

"We took it upon ourselves to tell her," says Sawyer. "It didn't feel right to let her think we were her mom and dad."

"We hope you're not upset," says Anna.

"What?" Littlethumb beams. "No. Not at all. I just wasn't expecting…I'm surprised. And very happy. Thank you, both."

"Want to say hello to your dad?" asks Anna, looking back down at Hope again. Hope turns to look up at Littlethumb, who squats down to her level.

"Hello, little one," he says.

Letting go of Anna's hand, Hope takes a circle around her father, stopping to sniff at him from different angles, which sends Littlethumb's curious face in the direction of Anna and Sawyer.

"She smells things," says Sawyer, shrugging his shoulders to confirm the behavior is unexplainable. "Since before she could walk."

"Sweet," Littlethumb responds. "You know, the sense of smell is one of our strongest memory senses?"

"I did not," says Sawyer.

"I did," says Anna.

"You did?" asks Sawyer.

Hope has made her way back around in front of Littlethumb. Both smile brightly at one another, but Hope's expression maintains a level of stoicism not shared by her father, who's on the verge of spontaneous happiness combustion.

"She doesn't talk much," Sawyer says. "Waited a long time to do it, too. Probably would have freaked us out if not for, well, you know… Anyway. She knows a ton of words but does most of her talking without using them. Kinda like when I first met you."

"Apples and their trees, I suppose," replies Littlethumb.

"Doesn't she look exactly like Maria?" asks Isabel.

"She sure does," he says. Then he looks back at Hope. Hair so black it's almost blue. A dragon's emerald green eyes. "You do. You look just like your mommy."

At this, Hope takes a step forward and waves her father closer to her. He bends over and she leans in toward his ear. Cupping her hands, she whispers, "Where have you been?"

Littlethumb repositions Hope so they're eye to eye, then gently taps her chest, where even a child knows their heart is located, and with a lump in his throat, he says, "Right inside there. All this time, I was right there. Guess where you've been."

33

"So what are you guys thinking? Family. Kids. Begging your kids for grandbabies as soon as possible?" Jimmy the Tweaker and the rest of the team are giving Daring Bird all loving hell on a closed circuit video call after discovering Daring Bird's fling with Kumiko has hit phase two.

"Yes," agrees Bebiana. "How deep is your love?"

"I'm guessing three to four inches," says Silas.

"All of you may fuck right off," says Daring Bird.

"Hmm, I see," says Silas. "Counterpoint, does she know you aren't blind in your right eye?"

"Yes. Excellent question," agrees Garo. "Can it be true love if she doesn't know you have two good eyes?"

"The patch is a turn on," Daring Bird snarks. "And who said anything about love?"

"All jokes aside," says Jimmy, "can you trust her?"

"Yeah, I think I can."

"Then where is she?" asks Silas.

"Doing my laundry, or in the kitchen cooking, or something. I don't know."

"Whoa," says Jimmy.

"What? What did I say?" (Are there synonyms for the word incredulous?)

"Boss," says Silas, "maybe take a look at Bebi's face…"

"You guys started it. She's in the shower, and still on a need-to-know basis, so let's get on with this before she returns."

"How's Bodhi?" asks Silas.

"He's fine," says Daring Bird. "But he's out of commission for now. We'll be running this one without eyes overhead." A collective groan from the team and then, "Has anyone heard from Titus?" This elicits a round of no's and head shakes. "Dammit. Impossible fucker." Daring Bird takes a beat for the acceptance of reality, then says, "Hopefully he turns up before we activate. Silas, anything helpful on your end?"

"Yeah, sort of. The painting that fussy knucklehead in Prague was bitching about, I tracked down the location of her husband's hunting lodge. Had to follow him out there, and he took a group, so I didn't attempt recovery. I didn't want to create any sort of stir while we're still trying to find the rest of them. But it's legit. It's a *Maria*. Some of them have definitely already been moved. Not sure how many. I'm trying to trace this guy's payment. I figure if we can track the purchase, it may lead a trail to the rest of them."

"Copy that. Good work."

"Thanks. Sorry for the bad news."

"Eh. I should've known we wouldn't be lucky enough to find them all in one place. What did you guys find out at the fancy auction?"

"There was a fancy auction?" asks Garo. "I miss everything."

"Fancy? Bebiana, did you wear a dress?" Silas asks, overwrought look of astonishment firmly in place.

"Eat every one of my dicks," she says.

"You've got more than one?"

"Nine, like a cat," Bebi says, then she blows Silas a kiss.

Silas playfully does the math on his fingers, attempting to understand, while the rest of the team falls out laughing.

"Alright, alright," says Daring Bird. "Jesus."

"This is what happens when we're apart for too long," says Garo.

"I guess so," replies Daring Bird. "But we've gotta keep moving. I don't have long to talk."

"There's another auction next month being held on a boat in the Mediterranean," Jimmy says. "This appears to be the one. We confirmed the location with several invitees at the sale we infiltrated last week. My beautiful demon here lured them in with her siren's song, then I hypnotized the shit out of them." That beautiful demon comment will get Jimmy laid again much sooner than expected, and he won't have any idea why.

"The sale will be held in international waters, south of the Ionian," says Bebi, "at these coordinates." She holds a piece of paper to the screen denoting longitude and latitude.

"Man," says Daring Bird. "That gets really hairy. I don't like the idea of robbing a boat full of people. Too many witnesses. Likely too many security forces."

"I guarantee it," agrees Garo. "The auction house will be surrounded by the buyers' boats, and they will be filled with killers."

"We could try to take them en route," says Jimmy.

"That's the likely scenario," says Daring Bird. "But I would feel much better about finding them beforehand."

"Isn't figuring out the route they will take to the auction finding them beforehand?" asks Silas.

"Technically, yes," says Daring Bird. "But I would prefer they be sitting still. We need to limit the chances of the collection getting damaged. As much as we can, at least. Taking them in transit makes that more difficult."

"What about the docks, then?" continues Silas. "They'll be loaded onto the main boat before heading out to sea."

"That's the most likely scenario," says Daring Bird. "Though I suppose a separate cargo boat could meet the auction house at sea. Either way, we're looking at ports in Greece, Italy, Libya, Tunisia…all within range of those coordinates. Egypt, too. Whichever port they're launching from, they have to get the collection to the boat. The question is, from where? That's our focus."

"So, what's the plan?" asks Jimmy.

"First step, travel. Everyone head this direction. We've basically got a month to figure out where those paintings are being held. The good news is, I may have an ace up my sleeve."

"Less than a month with travel," reminds Garo. "And I'll need time for equipment requisition, once we know the assault parameters. Then we have to steal the collection before it is moved."

"Right," says Daring Bird. "So, we've got less than a month to figure out where those paintings are and steal them back. Let's go ahead and consolidate here, closer to the location of the sale. I'll see if Kumi can dig up anything further on top of the information you've gathered and if she can coordinate our equipment purchase locally."

The entire team is making coordinated facial expression hilarity over Daring Bird's use of a pet name for his new lady friend. Kissy faces. Goo goo eyes. Cheesy high-pitched repetition of the name Kumi. You name it.

"Fuck off," says Daring Bird with a smile. "And hurry up. We've got less than a month."

❀　❀　❀

Once time is lost, we never get it back, right? Or do we? Can lost time be recovered by the manner in which we utilize what remains? Is a higher efficiency of use equal to recovery? I damn well hope so, and so does Littlethumb Brooks. Fear cost him the earliest years of his daughter's life. An unchangeable reality he must remain mindful of for the rest of their lives together, however much time they have. Death, either hers or his, will call without care or concern for how this father and daughter have spent the hours, days, weeks, months, or years available to them.

How fortuitous, then, for Anna and Sawyer to have provided a jumpstart to Littlethumb's and Hope's relationship. The same two syllable word propelling Littlethumb into an artistic funk inspired their course of action. When Hope called Sawyer *daddy*, Sawyer was equally as upset by the idea as Littlethumb. Sawyer and Anna had purposefully never referred to themselves as mommy or daddy while they waited and hoped for Littlethumb to change his course of action. In hindsight, they realized that simply not using those words had been wishful thinking. Thus, after the *daddy* incident, Sawyer and Anna had immediately begun teaching Hope about her true father and mother.

To say Littlethumb and Hope take to one another like peanut butter and jelly is an understatement. Cut from the same cloth. Peas in a pod. Thicker than thieves. They go together "like rama lama lama ka dinga da dinga dong." Father and daughter are immediately inseparable, though they do make room for Isabel to squish in between them.

A new portrait hangs in the hallway of the Pettimore's apartment within a week of Littlethumb's arrival. The painting is small and depicts Littlethumb holding Hope on one knee and Isabel on the other. The depiction of the two girls is a consistent expression of Littlethumb's genius. His self-depiction is capped off by a bright yellow smiley face resting atop his neck. Having never painted himself, Littlethumb discovers that cartoonish expressionism is the only comfortable way for him to finish his own likeness. After he finishes, he creates a much larger and more traditionally beautiful portrait of the two girls. This one proudly hangs in the Pettimore family room.

Every waking moment is spent together. No, this won't last forever, but these first weeks of bonding feel eternal. Taking into account how we perceive time, the way it speeds up and slows down and our brains adjust for significance, these first few weeks together feel like the longest, greatest period of Littlethumb's life. Other than his marriage to Maria, that is, with Hope being the wonderful extension of his and Maria's union.

Imbued with newfound daddy strength, after many years incapable of the task, Littlethumb paints his first new portrait of Maria since her tragic death. This one is for Hope, and I promise you she can see in the painting the enchanting essence of everything her mother was. The wonder in Hope's eyes as she stares at her momma would be heartbreaking if not for, you know, being the exact amazing complete opposite of heartbreaking. How come we don't have a root-word opposite for heartbreaking? Heartwarming doesn't quite get the job done, you know? Lacks the oomph. Whatever. All I know is, watching his tiny daughter stare wondrously at a portrait of her mother makes my guy's heart blow apart in all the best ways.

Halfway around the world, our "wrap this nonsense up" plot thickens. Daring Bird has discovered the location of *The Marias* collection and the Electric Medicine Men are prepping for their assault. The team has gathered in the Marseille safe house, save for Titus, whose whereabouts remain unknown.

"We believe they're located in a bunker here, south of Sirte, in Libya," says Daring Bird, pointing to the location on a map.

"Where'd you get the intel?" asks Silas. "And no offense, but what's she doing here?" Silas gestures at Kumiko, then looks her direction and says, "Nothin' personal."

Kumiko simply raises an eyebrow.

"She's coming with us," says Daring Bird.

"Well that escalated fast," says Silas, teasing Daring Bird.

"We're already a man down. We need all the help we can get."

"And the intel?" asks Jimmy.

"I told you guys I had an ace up my sleeve."

"You said you might have an ace up your sleeve," says Garo.

"Well, yeah. Turns out I did. I had an ace up my sleeve. Everyone happy?" Daring Bird waits a beat for any response. Silas timidly raises a hand for approval to speak in a futile effort at comedy.

"Good," says Daring Bird, tossing a playfully pointed stare at Silas. "So, let's get down to business. Garo, you and Sal are on weapons detail. Kumiko has a local vendor who should have anything we need. She and I will secure transport. Jimmy and Bebi, you're on communications. Without L.T. watching our backs, I want a traveling relay. We can at least get one last overhead look from our rendezvous point before we engage."

"Rendezvous point?" asks Garo. "If we travel together, who do we rendezvous with?"

"Same ace, same sleeve," says Daring Bird.

"Are you going to tell us who this ace up your sleeve is?" asks Garo.

"No, I'm not. Just trust me. Besides, it's more exciting if it's a surprise. Now, let's get moving. We're going back to Africa."

"Ooh," says Silas. "Back to Africa. Like the movie with Robert Redford and Meryl Streep."

"Ha," says Jimmy. "That's *Out of Africa*, dummy."

"I thought it was *Back to Africa*," says Silas.

"No," says Jimmy.

"Oh. Then what movie am I thinking of?"

"Only God knows," says Bebi.

"What's the one with Dustin Hoffman and Warren Beatty where they go to Africa?" asks Silas.

"*Ishtar*," says Garo.

"Get moving," says Daring Bird. "We've got a ton of shit to do and we're out of here before sunrise."

"Yeah, that's not it," says Silas as the team exits Daring Bird's quarters.

"Yes, it is. Beatty and Hoffman were in *Ishtar*," says Garo. "A notoriously bad film."

"No, I mean *Ishtar*'s not the one I'm thinking of," says Silas.

"That's because the one you're thinking of does not exist," says Bebi. I'm sure the conversation continues, but Bebiana's words are the last bit Daring Bird and Kumiko hear.

"Are you sure about this?" Daring Bird asks, once he and Kumiko have finished snickering at his teammates.

"Yes," she says, "and it doesn't matter if I'm not. I've already contacted my superiors and requested a temporary replacement. This position is too valuable to let fall into the wrong hands."

"What about the network?"

"For now, the network thinks I'm bringing on a trustworthy assistant. By the time they discover I'm gone, it won't matter."

"I don't like putting your cover at risk."

"You aren't. I am."

At this, Daring Bird removes the empty space between he and Kumiko, wrapping his arms around her waist. He flips the eyepatch back and locks eyes, but before he leans in for a super passionate, still in the early phases of lust kiss, he says, "Shit."

"What?"

"What if your replacement is the mole? You said there was a mole inside your department."

"Yes, but the odds of that happening are extraordinary. And even if they were, there's nothing to be found here."

"Still. This puts you back on the department's grid. And possibly the mole's."

"Not for long. I'm never coming back here again, and you shouldn't either."

"Ah. The temporary reprieve is bullshit…"

"I never let them know where I'm going, or for how long. Once they realize I'm not coming back, they won't be able to find me. That's how I survive."

"You think they know?"

"Probably, but I prefer to keep them guessing. Sometimes I report, sometimes I don't."

"Who are you?" asks Daring Bird, with flirtatious suspicion. Kumiko's response is a seductive kiss. They've played this game before. Asking Kumiko "who are you" is basically the same as Daring Bird saying "kiss me like we're dying." When their lips finally part, Daring Bird says, "You know, I have to admit I'm a little disappointed. I really like this place."

Kumiko removes Daring Bird's arms from their embrace and lowers them back to his sides. Moving around him, purposefully brushing his body with hers, she gives his ass a firm squeeze and a pat, then heads for the exit. Halfway through the door, Kumiko looks over her shoulder and says, "So did I."

34

South of Sirte, Libya, the Electric Medicine Men are nestled behind a short dune. Half a mile or so from their target, about three miles west of Ghardabiya Airbase. The entrance to Xander's bunker faces south and is built into the side of a long ridge that runs from the southeast to northwest.

"No guards outside," says Garo, viewing the fortified double doors of the entrance through binoculars. "I suppose that means they don't need them."

"What's our move, boss?" asks Jimmy.

"We wait for our ace to arrive."

"If you don't mind my asking," says Garo, still looking through the binoculars, "how are we going to get in this place if we're planning on sneaking in and out? From here, the only way I see us getting in is to blow those damn doors open."

"I told you…" Daring Bird starts.

"Yeah, yeah," Silas cuts him off. "Ace up your sleeve. Can we call the hand and show the cards please?"

"Silas, that's a great fantastic metaphor," says Jimmy, playfully eyeballing Daring Bird.

"Thanks, but I can't take all the credit. D.B. started it."

"Is that a metaphor?" Daring Bird asks.

"I don't know," says Jimmy. "Didn't know what else to call it. You know what I meant."

"I know what I meant, too," says Silas to Daring Bird. "I got sand in my pants and in my crawl, and no idea what the hell is going on here or why you won't just tell us what the hell is going on here."

"Number one," Daring Bird says, "I haven't explained the full plan yet for basic security purposes, with no offense meant toward anyone present. Number two, and this one's real important, Sal, I like fucking with you."

"And I probably deserve that, but can you at least tell us how long we have to wait?"

"I think I see your answer," says Bebiana, looking toward the western sky.

Everyone follows her eyes as the distant rumbling of a single-prop airplane floats through the desert air to their ears. The plane is bobbing and weaving, tilting back and forth from wing to wing, making the approach for what projects to be a bumpy landing. I'm pretty sure the entire team mouths the words "What the…" all at once, choosing various endings to the sentence, all of which convey the exact same reaction.

The plane skadooshes into the desert about a hundred yards away. The Electric Medicine Men stand at the ready. The cockpit tosses open. One hand out. Another hand out.

A familiar face pulls itself up from the cockpit and waves one giant wave, then scrambles over the side of the cockpit and drops to the ground like a sack of clinically insane potatoes. Ladies and gentlemen, Titus the Nazarene has arrived.

The team explodes with laughter and varying expressions of disbelief. Something along the lines of, "Son-of-a-bitch you've got to be kidding me, I don't believe it, that crazy Greek bastard."

Jimmy looks at Daring Bird suspiciously, who shakes his head.

"Is he the ace up your sleeve?" asks Garo. "One crazy man?"

"No," replies Daring Bird. "He's a surprise." Then Daring Bird points northwest, where several heads have appeared in the distance. "That's our ace up my sleeve."

Six people ride into view atop camels as Titus hobbles his way to his compatriots. The Nazarene wears two walking boots. The plastic kind doctors make you wear to protect an injured foot. He's bobbing back and forth on them, stumble-running through the sand.

"My friends!"

"Where've you been?"

"What happened to your feet?"

"Are you drunk?"

"How the hell did you find us!?"

"I am Desposyni!" says Titus proudly, embracing his companions. "Titus was captured and tortured. They beat me. Break all of the toes. Torture my marbles! But I escape. I steal the plane, and I find Parthos, and he fix me with these stupid boots. And give me coordinates to the mission. And I am very drunk! I don't even know how to fly this plane!"

"I fucking love you," says Silas.

"You're a madman," says Garo.

"You really are an alien, aren't you?" asks Jimmy.

Bebiana simply nods her badass approval.

"Who's they? And how did Parthos know our location?" asks Daring Bird.

"I gave it to him, for emergency extraction purposes." That, dear friends, is the voice of Mr. Mortimer Cross. I know earlier in the story

I said Cross wouldn't have another cameo. You can either accept that this appearance is more significant than a cameo, or be happy knowing I lied. Either way, you're welcome.

An austere, tall, proper man in his late fifties to early sixties, I would not be surprised if a baby Mortimer Cross had demanded exit from the womb, dressed in a three-piece suit, wearing a bowler and gloves, and carrying a briefcase containing the appropriate paperwork. Presently, he sits atop a camel wearing a thawb and keffiyeh, looking as uncomfortable as a vegetarian in church. Regrettably for the ever-serious Cross, his discomfort is highlighted when the thawb gets caught on the camel's saddle as he attempts to dismount. The five agents with Cross do not crack a smile. The Electric Medicine Men, as is their privilege, laugh their asses off.

"Alright, that's enough," says Daring Bird as Cross gathers himself. "Mortimer." He sticks his hand out for a shake. "Good to see you, as always."

Cross shakes Daring Bird's hand and says, "Who's she?" motioning at Kumiko, who to this point has silently observed the adventurous tomfoolery of Daring Bird and his merry band of troublemakers.

"She's…" Silas starts.

"A new friend," Daring Bird finishes. "Loyal to the cause. We figured we would need all the help we could get."

"Most likely," says Cross.

"Never has a man so clearly uncomfortable in the clothes he's wearing looked so dignified," says Jimmy, stepping forward to greet Cross.

"And when falling off a camel," says Bebiana, who gives Cross a kiss on the cheek. Strictly platonic, of course, but you'd be correct to surmise the Brazilian Bitch may have a specific affinity for older men.

Mortimer smiles at Bebiana's remark and returns the kiss, then looks at Jimmy and says, "These are not the clothes of my people."

"Is that racist?" Silas steps up next to Mortimer, lays an arm across the tall man's shoulder, gives a friendly squeeze, and says, "I think that might be racist."

"It's not racism," says Cross, removing Silas' arm as if picking lint from his jacket. "It's respect. I should feel the same way dressed as a fireman or a geisha."

"Or a geisha fireman," says Garo, clapping Cross on the back.

"Now that I would like to see," says Silas.

"Alright, alright," says Daring Bird. "Tighten back up, everyone. We've got work to do."

"You gonna explain all of this?" asks Jimmy. "Or at least tell us how we're getting in that place?"

Mortimer checks his watch and says, "Our ride should be arriving in precisely two minutes." Of course, everyone is standing there wearing question marks on their faces. Oh, except Kumiko, who maintains her silence, including facial expressions.

"When I went to see Mortimer in Lyon," says Daring Bird, "he told me the team who stole the collection all had the same tattoo behind their ears. So, we had a couple of Mortimer's agents volunteer to get the mark and infiltrate the organization, whoever they are."

"God, I love this job," says Silas.

"Me too," says Garo.

"Wait until they shock your balls, my friends," says Titus. "You may change your minds."

"So, what do we know about the bad guys?" asks Jimmy.

"Not much," says Cross. "Whoever is in charge is exceptional at information control."

"But," says Daring Bird, "after you and Bebi found out about the location of the auction, I reached out to Mortimer. The schedule of the auction coincided with an incoming supply run and outgoing shipment our men on the inside were assigned to, at a location within our search parameters. That bunker right over there." Daring Bird stops and uses his binoculars. "And there's our ride." A cloth top military truck is moving in from the east. "Guess who's driving."

"You're a bad man, boss man," says Silas. "A bad man." Then he looks at Mortimer and says, "You too, Ichabod Khomeini."

"We got lucky," responds Daring Bird.

Cross responds with a "Hmph," then pulls off the keffiyeh and thawb and tosses both to the ground, revealing a formal combat suit designed by Parthos the Drunk and Horny Monk. Tailored, pocket squared, and dashingly cuff linked. The rest of Cross' team follows his lead and disrobes, though under their disguises they have on standard tactical wear.

"Gear up," says Daring Bird.

The team shoulders their packs and we watch them double-check all their buckles, straps, weaponry, and boot laces. You know the routine. The montage finishes with a closeup shot of Bebiana's black witch moth belt buckle snapping into place.

"Com check," says Daring Bird.

Everyone sounds off. Silas answers with, "My father always said, 'Men of consequence enter the darkness without fear of consequence, spelling doubt in their enemies, strength in their comrades, and silver in their boots'." The look of stoic poetic pride on Silas' face is short lived, as his fellows offer varying forms of insulting confusion and outright ballbusting.

"Silver in their boots?" asks Garo.

"Was your father a wizard?" asks Titus.

"I don't think you had a father," says Bebi.

"That's mean," says Silas.

"I liked it, Sal," says Jimmy.

"Thank you!"

"Maybe stop after the first part though, next time," Jimmy suggests. Silas offers a playful consideration face in response.

"Alright, eyes on me," says Daring Bird. "Remember. No one kills. That's what separates us from the bad guys. And no one dies. Got me? Not one of you." Daring Bird makes eye contact with each of his teammates for confirmation. "Masks up." Everyone, including the completely disinclined Mortimer Cross, dawns full head covering to avoid identification. "Alright, Let's go get my nephew's shit."

I'm not indulging in an elongated battle sequence here. The producers can have one in the film version if they want, but gratuitous violence isn't typically my style and even when I indulge, this isn't the time or place. However, I will tell you the basics because they're fun and no one gets hurt.

Oops, seriously hurt. No one is seriously hurt. Well, almost no one. Plenty of bad guys will wake up in pain from various bumps, bruises, breaks, tazings, and bonks to their noggins. Nothing too bad. Titus, on the other hand, gets shot eight or nine times. Three minor flesh wounds, four rounds that go straight through him, and one that stays inside him, which must ricochet internally and cause two bullets worth of damage. Otherwise, he takes nine gunshots and a bullet enters through one of the other bullet holes, leaving two bullets lodged somewhere in Titus' body. Needless to say, none of his injuries are terminal, and Titus hobbles out of the battle of his own accord. Goddamn alien.

While Titus is getting shot, the rest of the Electric Medicine Men recover the paintings, and Kumiko goes looking for information. No one knows the extent of what Kumiko finds but her, though she readily shares information regarding Littlethumb's collection with Daring Bird.

Cross and his team handle transport of the paintings. They liberate an armored truck from the bunker for passage through the desert to Tripoli, where they will catch a boat to Italy. The paintings' frames are left scattered in the desert, in case they were bugged or fixed with tracking devices. Once in Italy, the collection will be cleaned and each portrait tested for authenticity by art curating associates of Sawyer Pettimore before being crated and shipped back to Sawyer's warehouse in the States. Meanwhile, Sawyer will report to all the necessary law enforcement agencies that a privately contracted asset recovery group has successfully returned the paintings.

The unusual circumstances for this mission call for a break in standard protocol, sending the Electric Medicine Men their separate ways after the mission, rather than locking down together for thirty days. Everyone on the team agrees that mixing things up never hurts when trying to keep those who may be hunting them off their trail.

In this instance, whoever's bunker they just broke into will have a lot on their hands with the cancellation of a major underground auction, not to mention trying to determine if the thieves stole any important information during the raid, and figuring out how in the hell someone knew about their underground bunker in Libya. Any retaliation will most likely come down the road. Something for the Electric Medicine Men to look forward to.

So, Jimmy and Bebiana head for Portugal to hide by the beach. Silas takes off looking for a lady friend to hide inside, whereabouts unknown. Garo Kasabian goes home to his family to hide in plain sight, and Titus the Nazarene returns to Parthos' secret lair in Barcelona to lay low and recover from eight or nine gunshot wounds.

I wish I could tell you that Daring Bird and Kumiko ride off into the sunset together. I really do. Actually, in this specific moment, they do, but not for long. I'm not saying they aren't going to have a

cross-continental romance. I'm saying the affair is gonna be complicated and there won't be any settling down for litters of puppies and
grandpuppies. Kumiko will do a lot of disappearing and reappearing
by the light of the moon. For that matter, so will Daring Bird Jones.

They part ways in Egypt. Before they do, the lovers spend several
nights together. I know, I know, Daring Bird has business with Littlethumb, but he deserves the R&R. I'm confident Littlethumb
would approve. A brief sabbatical isn't going to change what Daring
Bird has to tell his nephew, but those two days and nights will forever
change the way Daring Bird and Kumiko remember Cairo.

35

Returning to New York is a guilt free pleasure for Daring Bird. The city tingles your toes from the moment your feet hit the ground. True, New York City can be exhausting, but the initial burst of "holy cow you can literally feel the energy coursing through your body" is invigorating.

Conversing peacefully with Littlethumb, Sawyer, and Anna for a few days is a welcome respite from international espionage. The Pettimores are both keenly interested in this new lady friend Daring Bird has acquired, while Daring Bird is more interested in discussing the turbulent finale to the conflict between Littlethumb and Redy Sinclair. Both topics receive plenty of attention, squeezed in between video game sessions with Isabel and invisible tea parties with Hope.

Speaking of his grandniece, as happy as Daring Bird is to return the bulk of *The Marias* collection to his nephew, witnessing the incredible bond formed so rapidly between Littlethumb and Hope brings Daring Bird a peace he hasn't felt in years. Not since before Maria died and Littlethumb ran off into hiding. Telling Littlethumb a bunch of the paintings are still missing winds up feeling relatively easy.

As it turns out, there are a dozen portraits of Maria still out there, illicitly entertaining the eyes of people who don't deserve to gaze upon her brilliance. Mostly dickhead men, though I'm sure there's a few Eva Braun-type bitches delighting in the glory of their wealth and sociopathy.

"Apparently," says Daring Bird, "whoever we're up against likes to keep records on the illegal transactions with their clients. Likely for blackmail purposes, assuming most of these people have above-ground lives."

"So, what have we got?" asks Littlethumb.

"Silas located one near Prague. For the rest, financial records and shipping information. Nothing that pinpoints the exact location of all the paintings, but enough to get started. I figure with Mortimer's and Kumiko's help, we should be able to track them all down. At least, whoever purchased them. From there it will be up to us to figure out exactly where the paintings are and steal them back."

"Not us, me. This one's mine."

"I'm not sure that's a good idea."

"Of course you aren't, and I understand, but I'm doing this."

"Look, kid. We just got you back into the real world. And with Hope. The last thing she needs is for you to disappear on her again."

"I'm not. I'm going after my paintings and coming right back."

"I don't know…"

"I do know. You've been telling me for years I can't live in fear, and you're right, but all this time, you've been living scared too."

"What are you talking about?"

"You've kept me hidden. Locked up. I've never once set foot in the field on a mission."

"That was practical. We need someone in your position, and your paintings pay for all this. I can't have you getting killed or injured." There it is, Daring Bird. There it is. Littlethumb doesn't have to say a damn word. You did all the work for him. The kid's right and you know it. What's the line again, about hypocritical physicians treating themselves? Daring Bird takes a big ol' dose of his own medicine right here and with a humble exhale says, "I'll put Mortimer and Kumiko to work."

Information comes in fast from Mortimer and Kumiko, as both have begun investigating the whereabouts of the final *Marias* before Daring Bird ever contacts them. Mortimer does so out of a sense of duty, having commanded the team that lost the paintings. Kumiko does so out of a sense of basic morality, and the extremely self-aware proposition of maintaining contact with Daring Bird.

One by one, Littlethumb tracks down the last of *The Marias*. Without delving too far into specific scenarios, I can tell you that all of his skills are put to the test. I mean, we're talking scuba-oriented aquatic cat burglary, building to building tightrope-walking high-rise cat burglary, and Spaghetti Western dude-ranch horseback-chase-across-the-plains cat burglary. At least one theft occurs involving his mime disguise, escape from an invisible box, and the use of a parachute. At least one theft involves Littlethumb painting his way through a crazed interactive art installation to the secret chamber of a rich jerk with a stolen art fetish.

After seven weeks bouncing around the world stealing back the paintings of his wife, there's one painting left to go. Number twelve. Number twelve is a combination kung fu and computer chess *Game of Death* cat-burglary on a French Polynesian warlord's compound in

French Polynesia, where Littlethumb fights his way through multiple henchmen on multiple floors of a building to discover the final villain is a Grand Master-level chess computer. Littlethumb's a wonderful chess player, but he's no Kasparov, Fischer, or Gabby Duvel. He is, however, an excellent hacker and computer builder. So, he outsmarts the computer with a bit of re-wiring and reprogramming before realizing none of it was necessary. Apparently, this warlord guy sells kill-for-thrill scenarios to other exorbitantly wealthy jerks, and the facility Littlethumb infiltrated was a display model. After learning of his mistake, he makes his way to the main building of the warlord's compound and finds the *Maria* on display for a simple middle-of-the-night grab and bag.

Upon his safe return to the United States, Littlethumb heads for Sawyer's warehouse in Jersey to drop off the final painting before heading home. The warehouse is full of Littlethumb's artwork. To maintain their value, Sawyer is very deliberate with the number of pieces he allows into the market, including long spells where nothing is available for sale. Thus, there is a backlog of Littlethumb's work to keep the Electric Medicine Men financially afloat for years.

Most of *The Marias* have been re-framed and are hung together in rows along a wall. The collection will eventually go back out on tour after putting new security protocols in place. However unlikely the scenario is for someone to attempt to steal them again, the hoopla will make the collection even more celebrated in a world obsessed with pop-culture nonsense.

Pieces recently saved by Littlethumb are resting on a large table protected by a hinged plexiglass casing, waiting to be cleaned and framed. Littlethumb pulls the final *Maria* from a protective tube and unrolls the canvas onto the table next to the others. With a satisfied deep breath and exhale of completion, he lowers the lid of the case and turns to the paintings on the wall, soaking in the vibrance of their desperately gorgeous subject. If I haven't been clear enough to this point, I'm not discussing Maria's physical beauty. Though she was an extraordinarily physically attractive woman, what glows from these paintings is her essence. The vital purity of a human being who was driven through life by a heart overflowing with love.

Very close to turning away and heading for home, something nags at Littlethumb. *What?* he thinks. *What's your problem?* A few seconds pass as he scans the rows of paintings and then, *It's not here.* He turns back toward the table and steps over for an energetic review of the contents. His heart rate accelerates.

The painting he's looking for is not on the table. *What the hell? It has to be here.* Littlethumb reviews the wall again, purposefully staring at each painting for a three-count to ensure he's fully present and not operating with a frazzled mind, then back to the table, and the one he's looking for still isn't there. Lungs empty in defeat, exhaling so completely his shoulders deflate, slumping in classic defeated fashion.

The reaction is cut short by determination. Our hero straightens his spine and puts his mind to work. There's a computer in Sawyer's office.

Littlethumb heads for the office, texting Daring Bird along the way: *Your shoes are untied.* This is code for Daring Bird to log into the Electric Medicine Men's secure network for a chat session. Waiting on a response from Daring Bird, Littlethumb logs into their network and discovers an unread message. The message is from an anonymous entity and somehow isn't timestamped.

Do you remember wondering about whether Master Chee had the necessary skills or time to hack into Littlethumb's computers before removing them from the cabin, during the fire? You do? Perfect.

We travel to a familiar location to unravel this last bit of mystery. A small estate with a historic brick home in Marseille, France. A historic brick home no longer inhabited by normal folk.

Charming exterior. Secret underground entrance inside a yard shed. Maintained by a covert operative concierge recently assigned by the Department of Agriculture. You know the one.

Inside, in what used to be Kumiko's office, DOA agent Ben Ford sits behind a computer at a large desk, typing with reckless abandon. We can't see Ben's face, but I will tell you we've met Ben previously, by another name. There's a book on the desk titled *Ubiquity Never Sleeps*. Next to the book is a plate smeared with the delicious gooey residue of donut glaze.

We're all on the same page here, right?

A text message from Daring Bird pops up on Littlethumb's phone: *Laces tied.* This signifies Daring Bird is logging into a computer, whereas *I need new strings* would mean he is indisposed indefinitely with a normal aspect of life and *I never learned how* would mean he's in some form of danger but still able to use his phone. The following dialogue is a dramatic representation of their electronic transmissions in a secure chatroom.

"*What's up?*" asks Daring Bird.

"*We've got a problem. Two problems.*"

"*Fantastic. What's the first one?*"

"*One of the paintings is still missing.*"

"*You didn't get the last one?*"

"No, I got it. It wasn't the last one."

"But it was the last one on the list."

"I know, but it wasn't the last one. One's missing."

"You're sure?"

"Yes, I'm positive. It's my favorite."

"Well shit. How'd that happen?"

"Got overlooked, I guess. Fell through the cracks between the pieces from the bunker and the list."

"Sorry, rhetorical question. Any thoughts on tracking it down?"

"That's the second problem. I think I know where it is."

"Sounds like a solution, not a problem. What's the catch?"

"Ask me how I know." Littlethumb hits send then quickly follows up with, "Never mind, waste of time." Send. "We've been hacked. That's the catch." Send. "Someone's watching. There was a message waiting when I logged in, addressed to everyone's accounts. No sender listed, no timestamp. Nothing but an address in Denmark. For what appears to be a freaking castle."

"Yeah, I see the message. Fuck. I don't like it."

"Me neither, but I'm certain the painting is there. I've got a feeling."

"I've got a feeling this is a trap."

"Of course. I assume it's a trap. Don't worry about that. You said Kumiko told you there were active forces who want us doing what we do. I think someone's trying to help."

"Maybe, but I don't like whoever it is hacking our communications. Or the possibility they've connected you to the Men."

"Maybe they haven't. My name's not on anything, but you're right about the hack. Our main concern is infiltrating our network. That was damn near impossible the way I had our systems set up. And it's odd they tipped their hand for this. They have to know we'll lock them back out."

"So, does someone give up their ability to monitor us to help us recover a stolen painting or to ferret us out for destruction?"

"I guess I'm going to find out."

"Let's not go off half-cocked here. We can meet in Barcelona to plan."

"No. I'm not waiting. I'm getting my painting back now."

"We should really plan this out. At least look for information on the castle."

Littlethumb ignores Daring Bird's final plea. *"Tell the team to destroy their machines immediately. Phones too. I will reset everything after I'm done storming Hamlet's summer home. I'll be back soon."*

"Copy that." Witnessing the return of such confidence in his nephew is great, but this is still the part where a devoted uncle wants to implore his nephew to be safe, or not to go on this dangerous mission, or to at least allow him to come along. Instead, Daring Bird bites his tongue and types, *"Have fun."*

This is it, gang. The big one. The final squall. Into the mouth of malevolence storms our champion creator. Our rascal philanthropist thief. Our genius sheep in a ninja-wolf's clothing, and goddammit, if I haven't made you appreciate him yet, I guess I never will.

The battlefield is a water castle in the South Funen Archipelago on one of the four hundred and forty-three islands populating Denmark's Kingdom. An architectural Frankenstein's monstrosity, Conrad Somvinslodkin's home is a seventeenth century slap in the face to that era's Baroque influences. Constructed in the half-timbered method, the different sections of the castle pay homage to visual styles of the Romanesque, Gothic, and Renaissance periods, leaving most discerning modern architects to wonder if the use of hallucinogens was popular in Denmark in the sixteen-hundreds.

Currently, Littlethumb Brooks is scaling the rotund exterior wall of an eastern tower, so chosen for climbing due to the lack of interior light escaping this end of the building. Security cameras are avoidable. Motion sensors on windows are trickier, but manageable, thanks to Parthos. The Drunk and Horny Monk holds the patent on a fantastic short-range handidoo built for motion sensor trickery.

Voilà, the lotion is in the basket. Inside the castle, all Littlethumb must do is quietly traverse and inspect a seven-thousand square foot, nineteen room building in the hopes of finding a stolen painting hanging on display. No sweat.

The security cameras and motion sensors are typical for a structure of this value. The interrogation chamber appears to be a purely decorative collection of antique torture devices. Odd, but ultimately acceptable as the type of thing in which a super wealthy person who has no moral qualms owning stolen art might indulge. Massive computer server room? Meh. Not crazy depending on the owner's line of work. Substantial armory? Okay, this guy (or gal…) may be a tad whackamole, but it's not until Littlethumb realizes this wing of the house is protected by substantial interior locking mechanisms that he decides whoever owns this place is probably up to nefarious shit. Also, he is going to have to find a new exit, because he discovers the locking mechanisms when the main door to this wing of the castle swings shut behind him and the locks activate.

Fast forward through the castle, we tiptoe in and out of rooms and up and down hallways at breakneck speed until we find Littlethumb finding the room he needs to find. Littlethumb stands in the shadows of a doorway, caught between the dim light of the hall and the thin strands of moonlight infiltrating the room. There she is. He can't see her clearly, but a large frame adorns the moonlit wall behind a large desk and he knows…

Slipping inside the room, Littlethumb eases the door shut and counts four paces to the edge of the desk. Once he finds the desk, he turns on a small lamp and rotates the light toward the painting, then pulls back his head covering.

Hello, my love.

This is the first portrait Littlethumb painted of Maria. The representation is of her on the first day they met, years ago on the Coney Island boardwalk. Maria was Isabel Pettimore's nanny, and the pair had wandered upon Littlethumb's caricature painting station. When he looked up to see Maria staring off to the ocean, hair gently flowing in the breeze, skin colored by the Mediterranean sun of her coastal Spanish childhood, he suffered the rapture of his heart and soul, called forth from his physical being and handed over, lock and key, to the living, breathing, embodiment of all that is holy in our world. The inspiration for his quest for manhood. An undeserved gift from the universe who compelled him to be the very best human being he could possibly be. This is what Littlethumb gazes upon as a hand reaches through the darkness for his shoulder.

Right before the hand grabs him, Littlethumb senses the presence. There's a slight change to the air around him, flaring his nostrils, raising the hair on his neck and arms, and sending him into action. Sliding his left foot and reaching over his shoulder in one movement, Littlethumb instinctively locks onto the wrist of the unknown assailant, pops his hips, and tosses the assailant over his shoulder and into a large set of shelves. Littlethumb turns the desk lamp in the direction of his attacker.

Ben Ford — or as Littlethumb knows him, Master Chee — sits up against the shelves and rubs the back of his neck. He offers Littlethumb an approving thumbs up for the successful defense of his attack, though I'm not certain an attack is what Master Chee had in mind, because he holds a finger to his lips, requesting silence, then signs, *Get the hell out of here, now.*

One beat of delay, as Littlethumb instantaneously debates asking Chee questions before swiftly moving to the portrait. In a flash, Littlethumb separates the painting from the frame and rolls the canvas into a protective tube. He locates the open window that served as Master Chee's entrance point. With one leg out the window, he looks back to Master Chee, offers him a two-fingered salute to the forehead followed by a peace sign, then makes his escape.

The crash from Master Chee hitting the bookshelves calls attention to Xander's office. The first to arrive is Xander himself, who opens the door cautiously, careful of a potential attack as he enters. Switching on the lights, pistol in hand, Xander scans the room to find Master Chee crumpled against the bookshelves. Xander knows Master Chee as the indispensable and absurdly codenamed deaf-mute ninja mercenary, Lo Mein.

"What are you doing here?" asks Xander.

In response, Master Chee points to the bare wall behind Xander's desk. Xander turns to see the painting is gone.

"Who did this? How did they escape?" He looks back to Lo Mein, but the mercenary has vanished.

"Goddammit." On the verge of rage, Xander tucks the pistol into the waistband of his housepants, takes his pulse to steady himself, and says aloud, "Calm down, Xander. Calm down. You know the price you pay for working with mercenaries."

Moving around behind the desk, Xander lifts the discarded picture frame and rests it on the floor against the wall, allowing himself a long, melodramatic sigh while two plus two works its irrevocable magic in his mind and dramatically adds up.

It was him! Suddenly, the villain isn't suppressing anger but is instead attempting to control an uncontrollable tidal wave of glee.

Count to ten, you fool. But he can't. He makes it to three, but three rhymes with glee and that glorious bastard is alive! *Littlethumb Brooks is alive! My arch nemesis, the world's greatest living artist!? The fathers would be so proud!* Xander reverently kisses the tooth chained around his neck, serving himself the pride he knows his ancestors would have bestowed on him.

I wonder if he knows who he just stole from? Xander asks himself, then immediately lets the notion go. *Doesn't matter, Xander. Doesn't matter. Either way, this is going to be fun. This is going to be an immeasurable amount of fun!*

36

Imagine, if you will, a vertical split-screen view, like in a film or television show. On the left, from behind, we see a man exiting the Paris Métro in the Montparnasse quarter. On the right, from behind, we see a man exiting the subway in New York City, holding the hand of a very young lady. The young lady holds the leash to a coydog atop whom three tiny monkeys ride bareback.

Our man on the left makes his way through the crowded sidewalks of Paris to the Cimetière du Montparnasse, one of Paris' numerous famous cemeteries wherein lie the bones and ash of many famous people. Our man on the right makes his way through the crowded sidewalks of New York, child and animals in tow, stopping along the way to treat the young lady to a cotton candy. One man stands at the entrance to the cemetery. The other stands at the entrance to a previously abandoned art studio on Coney Island. A freshly painted sign over the door labels the studio *The Maria Holguín Brooks House of Art and Love*.

Both men take a step forward as our view wipes left to right, replacing the split-screen with a solo picture of Redmond Sinclair entering the cemetery. This is no Flâneur on Flânerie, wandering without aim for the sake of doing so. No, slowly but surely, Redy deliberately makes his way to the final resting place of author and playwright Samuel Barclay Beckett.

Before moving on, please allow me to say I am loathe to witness or participate in stigmatizing any survivor of abuse or sufferer of mental illness. Especially Redy Sinclair. I love the guy, very much. His was a terribly unfortunate and very specific instance of response to trauma, and not something I've taken lightly in sharing. The good news is, the depth of pain and anguish he suffered for so many years is equaled in the strength and grace of his recovery.

After he escaped from the cabin fire, Redy made his way back to New York City to deal with his abuser. I stated before, there's no happy ending for you with regard to Uncle Carmine. There can't be, considering the scope of the damage done, but there is at least a sense of retribution. While Littlethumb is out stealing back the last of *The Marias* collection, Redy is sleuthing and gathering evidence on Carmine. And fighting the temptation to murder the old son-of-a-bitch himself, I won't lie. However, the ordeal with Littlethumb proved to Redy he does not want murder on his soul, so his pursuit of Carmine doesn't go down that way, but I'm not going to pretend the thought didn't cross his mind. A lot.

In the end, numerous media outlets received verifiable documentation of Carmine Strotham's atrocities, along with the New York Metro Police, the New York District Attorney, the U.S. Attorney for the Southern District of New York, and any other relevant criminal justice system authorities Redy could think of. The documentation included the addresses to multiple secret locations where physical evidence was discovered proving Carmine's heinous sickness and exposing his connection to a larger network of similarly disturbed and disgusting individuals. Evil human beings, representative of life's unequivocal demand for balance in all aspects of our cataclysmic yet propitious existence. Once more, my friends, chaos or fate? The choice is yours. Whichever you choose, I recommend implementing a structured daily routine for your life, and then breaking said routine on a regular basis in effort to keep yourself on your toes.

Let's return here to the present, with Redy in Paris. A working position is established from enough distance to maintain a view of the footpaths winding their way through the gravesites surrounding Samuel Beckett's modest tomb, so chosen for his parents' appreciation of Beckett's work. Years earlier, Redy had found antique copies of Beckett's plays among his parents' estate. Each play contains a love note written inside, from one of his parents to the other.

Facing Beckett's tomb, Redy unpacks a collapsible field stool, folding easel, and a tray of watercolors. Beckett's final place of resting isn't Redy's subject, rather, a backdrop for observing other humans observing other things. The weather is gorgeous, and the cemetery is bustling with tourists and fellow artists, Redy's true subjects.

Colors take over Redy's canvas, blending and blurring into a mess of human forms. Soulful creatures of energy and emotion wrapped in animal flesh, living and breathing their journeys, immortalized by Redy's brush. There's no inherent darkness in these works of art, only life, coursing through them as nature insists.

Before long, his mother and father take shape among them, observing Beckett's tomb. One of his father's arms rests around his mother's hips. The other is clasped in his mother's hands and pressed against a belly full of promise, three heartbeats forming one organism.

A young boy, standing nearby, pulls loose from his momma and quietly appears next to Redy, staring at the work in progress. Without any semblance of recognizing the boy's presence, in a few moments Redy has included the child in the foreground of the painting, staring blissfully at all the activity of the world around him. The boy hears his mother's call and yells back, "I'm coming!" then presents his mobile phone to Redy, wearing a "may I?" expression. Redy nods his head yes, and the boy takes a picture of Redy's watercolor for posterity. Then, much to his surprise, the boy gives Redy an approving thumbs up and a confident wink before happily trotting off into the wind, dissolving into the vibrant colors of the live world as Redy continues to paint.

You've witnessed our hero in a weakened state throughout most of this tale. I've come to realize parenthood may inherently provide a duality of strength and weakness. Strength in a parent's resolve to do whatever they must to protect their child, to better themselves in an effort to set the best example. Weakness in a parent's knees, the metaphorical buckling as when struck by romantic love, having given their heart over to another, incurring the possibility of succumbing to fear and worry.

Understandable then, I believe, that Littlethumb fell victim to self-indulgent fear and worry, considering the amount of loss he's been forced to accept in his life. Living in this merciless world provides a reasonable excuse for constant anger, or sorrow, or both. Though I would argue, and I believe Littlethumb would agree, the best way to fight this bully of an existence we've created for ourselves is to open our minds to joy. Laugh as you stand fast against the awfulness. Run toward the pain with fists full of punchlines. Armor yourself in heartfelt lunacy. Go crazy in the best way possible.

I guess what I'm really trying to say here is, it's okay to have a little sad cry every day, as long as you do it with a smile on your face? Who am I to know what I mean, honestly, when I'm still trying to learn these lessons for myself? What do I know?

I know this: Things are soon to get worse. I know it. You know it. Littlethumb knows it. Our world is on fire. People are dying in their own streets and their own goddamn homes and I can't tell if we're in the midst of the two steps forward or one step backward portion of progress. It's maddening. Hopefully, you can find a release, some peace in all this painful nonsense. I've found mine, though it escapes me from time to time, and Littlethumb's found his. He's holding her in his arms as he enters the Coney Island art studio that he and Maria built together.

The lobby of the art studio has a ticket booth and three doors. One door leads to a classroom, another an office, and another the studio theater where Littlethumb performed. After more than three years of sitting unoccupied, the building has been renewed. During Littlethumb's recent cat-burglaring sojourn, Daring Bird's vision became clear to him, so he traveled to Coney and prepared the studio for Littlethumb and Hope's arrival. A thorough cleaning and a fresh coat of paint provided the *Maria Holguín Brooks House of Art and Love* with new life.

Just a few blocks away is Littlethumb's former apartment, to which he still holds a lease. Hope will find her new bedroom there, meticulously painted in her favorite colors by her Grand Uncle Daring Bird. Of course, Daring Bird is no painter and Hope's favorite colors are "all of them," so Littlethumb has a fun, chaotic interior design gag waiting at home.

First things first, though. A note from Daring Bird is taped to the front of the ticket booth. The note reads, *I hope you like the paint…and the surprise!*

Hope points to the note and Littlethumb says, "It's a message from Uncle Daring Bird. He left us a surprise. Do you like surprises?"

Hope nods her head once, emphatically.

"I thought so," says Littlethumb. "Let's go find it!" Crossing the lobby, he opens the door to the classroom and flips on the lights. "This is where daddy will teach people about painting," he says, making his way to the lone window in the room and twisting the blinds, allowing the sun to shine through. "No surprises here. Let's try another room."

They make their way back through the lobby to the office. The monkeys hop off woof and stack onto each other's shoulders, Sir Alister on top, who cracks open the office door. Woof just wags his tail, pleasantly.

There's a hesitation before Littlethumb reaches forward and pushes the door. Maria had managed the business, and her presence dominated this room. Flipping on the lights, Littlethumb discovers the office exactly as she left it, though immaculately cleaned by Daring Bird. A wave of euphoria hits Littlethumb in the form of aroma-based memory. The recollection of his wife's familiar scent filling the room excites pleasant nostalgia, not pain, and he kisses his daughter on the forehead.

"No surprise in here either," he says. "There's only one place left. Are you ready to go find out what the surprise is?"

Hope claps her hands enthusiastically.

"You sure you don't want to wait? We can wait."

Whether she knows her father is teasing or not, Hope takes no chances and dramatically shakes her head no.

"Okay. Let's keep looking." Reaching for the light switch, Littlethumb changes his mind, leaving the lights on and the door open. They exit the room as Zeus, Sir Alister Pickney, and Stevie Two Sharks show Woof their favorite spots to lounge around the office. Naturally, all of them are completely off-limits to the coydog.

Next room up for Littlethumb and Hope, the theater. I mentioned earlier the studio being a theater in the round. This was Maria's idea. The painting area is a large round floor space encircled by a six-foot wall. Behind the wall are four rows of stadium seating and a small balcony section above. There is an entrance through the office and an entrance from the lobby.

"Are you ready," says Littlethumb, standing in front of the lobby entrance to the studio.

Hope nods brightly.

"You're about to see my favorite place in the whole world. Are you sure you're ready?"

Hope nods her head again, giggling.

"You're sure. You're absolutely, completely sure?"

Hope gleefully exaggerates one more dramatic head nod, bulging her eyes for effect. The eye bulge is a gift from Isabel, who most definitely taught the expression to Hope on purpose.

Entering through the lobby door, Daring Bird's surprise is immediately received. The circular wall of the theater is lined with paintings of Maria, equally spaced, with one spot in the middle remaining for a final painting to hang. Resting on the ground beneath the open space is a large rectangular package wrapped in brown paper.

Littlethumb turns to his left and centers himself in front of a painting. "Do you know who this is?" he asks, certain of the answer. "Isn't your mommy beautiful?" The little girl agrees bashfully, humbly receiving the compliment on behalf of her mother.

Hope reaches toward the painting, and Littlethumb leans in so she can place her hand on the glass over her mother's face. Then she pulls her hand away, as if lightly shocked, and looks at her father with a pleasantly surprised expression.

"I know," he says. "I know."

They move around the room, stopping to observe each painting. "You know, your mom and I built this place together so we could do good things for other people. Visitors would come and give us money to watch me paint, and we would use the money for other people who needed food, or a place to live. I would paint right there in the middle, and your mom would help me." They make their way to the empty spot on the wall. "Hang onto my neck," he says, swinging Hope around onto his back. She clasps her hand around his throat, resting a little too much weight against his Adam's apple, as children are known to do to their fathers.

Littlethumb bends over and picks up the package, pulling away the brown paper. Underneath is his favorite painting of Maria, newly framed. "Let's hang this together," he says. "Ready?" Hope smiles approval from over his shoulder as he steps forward and positions the painting on an anchor left in place by Daring Bird. "What do you think? Is she straight?" Hope answers with an affirmative nod. "Come-ere," he says, pulling her back around to his side, arm behind her back, her legs wrapped around his waist. "This painting is from the very first day I met your mom, did you know that?" Hope shakes her head. "You didn't? Well, it is. This is exactly what your momma looked like the first time I ever saw her. I looked up, and she was staring out at the ocean, and I gave my heart to her right then and there. Then, later that day, I went home and painted this picture because I couldn't stop thinking about her." There's a wistful pause here, until he looks at his daughter and says, "Have I ever told you the story about how me and your mom fell in love?"

The tale begins as they move on to the next painting. Littlethumb offers Hope a relatively condensed and age-appropriate version of his and Maria's affair, ending at their marriage and construction of the art studio. As he and Hope make their way to the final painting, he says, "And your mom would play music for me while I painted. Even though she couldn't hear. She said she could feel the music. And sometimes we would dance while I was painting." Littlethumb lifts Hope up and over the wall into the seating level, where she stands looking down at her father as he begins to dance around the room for her.

"Sometimes we would dance like this," he says, bending his knees and holding his arms above his head, shaking jazzy hands. "And sometimes we would dance like this," pointing to the ground, pumping his arms like pistons and intermittently lifting his legs. "And sometimes like this," he says, bending over at the waist and sticking his butt out, wiggling it back and forth with his fists balled out before him, elbows rocking. "And sometimes we would dance like this," he says in a robot voice, standing up straight and proudly working robot dance magic as Hope joyfully claps her hands, cheering her father on.

"But, most of the time," he says, "most of the time, we would dance like this." Littlethumb holds one arm out to his side, wraps his other arm around the air filling the space where Maria's waist would be, and begins to waltz around the room. Taking large strides as he box steps and slides, he closes his eyes to hear the music. Once the music arrives, Littlethumb opens his eyes to a vision of Maria, who smiles radiantly as they circle the room, bodies pressed together as tightly as possible. They dance, laughing and loving one another across all boundaries of existence, never breaking eye contact as they spin, while their daughter watches in mesmerized bliss and I smile through tears of joy as I type these words because I promise you, dear friend, Hope can see her momma too.

The end.

Post Credits Easter Egg

Interior, Ray Brook Correctional Facility. Through the bars of a cell, we see Tommy Toxic sitting on a cot. Tommy is holding a notebook and a bare, soft pencil lead in hand. Presumably working on lyrics to a new song, he softly hums a tune. He appears to write thoughtfully, pulling the pencil lead away from the paper, then reapplying it judiciously. The humming stops, briefly, as he adjusts a pattern to the rhythm, hitting a higher note and deciding he likes it better, then recording it in the notebook.

We pan the camera around the room as he hums, taking in the full spectrum of his living quarters. The walls are mostly decorated with posters of his favorite musicians and pictures of album covers, but there is one poster advertising the concert he and Littlethumb put on together, before he got in trouble. A few tiny figurines cut from soap are sitting on the cell's lone shelf and are organized to look like a band on stage. Next to the soap bar diorama are a few books stacked on their sides. Nothing of note, really.

Finishing the scan of the room, we turn back to Tommy as a moment of thoughtful inspiration hits him, and he writes with a feverish glint in his eyes. Our view adjusts up and over Tommy's shoulder to see the new music he's creating, but what we find is a page covered in manic scribbles for musical notes and disjointed phrases for lyrics. Words go unfinished, devolving into indecipherable shaky lines.

There are hash marks and slashes and dots with random color words like red and black in between. Geometric shapes represent what one must assume is a refrain, due to their pattern of repetition.

The camera pans back around to view Tommy's face as he diligently gets his thoughts out on paper, the tip of his tongue showing through his lips in a universal sign of childish artistic concentration. As the camera backs up and away from him, the whoop whoop whoop sound of a helicopter makes itself known through the walls of the prison cell. There's one window to the cell, and as we turn to look through the small portal, we hear machine guns fire rapidly and explosions sound, as the whooping of the helicopter grows closer. We're staring out through the window, nothing but blue sky in view, when two large steel hooks surprisingly clank onto the window's bars. With a scratchy groan of resistance from the steel bars and concrete, the window breaks free, pulling large portions of cinderblock loose as well. Sledgehammers bang against the hole, knocking more cinderblocks away and filling Tommy's cell with dust from the destruction.

As the dust settles, Xander Bowfly triumphantly steps through the hole and into Tommy's cell. Xander's wearing a dark red snakeskin jumpsuit trimmed in black and white and zipped all the way up the neck. On the lapel is a symbol, sewn directly into the jumpsuit. The image is a profile view of a large silver fang, with a sharp tip pointing downward and a riveted, steel-colored band around the top. I guess *The Iron Fang* it is?

Tommy looks up, confused, and Xander says, "Hello, Mr. Toxic. I hope you don't mind my stopping by."

"Who are you?" asks Tommy.

"Me?" Xander replies, innocently pointing to himself. "I'm your number one fan."

Truant D. Memphis is also the author of *Littlethumb Sneezed, Post Oh!pocalypto Poppycock, Daffodil,* and the novella *The Boy Who Fell from the Past.* He's written for the stage, performed in theater and on film, and curated multiple religious texts into one giant book of rules titled *Meditations With Monkeys.* When he isn't writing, he's painting or exercising or listening to music or watching screen content or reminiscing about the good ol' days or thinking about tomorrow or noodling with an instrument or ranting about the nature of existence. Or, walking with his best friend, a lil' doggie named Roscoe. You might find Truant and Roscoe roaming the streets of Louisville, KY, kicking rocks. You will know them by the smiles on their faces. Peace.

www.truantmemphis.com